MW01030207

William, by the Grace of God

The publisher dedicates this book to his son

Lodewyk Adolph Janssen

(born Dec. 9, 2005)

(named after two brothers of the first William of Orange)

and to his daughter

Hannah Charlotta

(born April 22, 2008)

(named after the prophetess Anna & Charlotte de Bourbon)

two instruments used by God
for the protection of the Faith in the sixteenth century

Index of illustrations and titles of main characters

Page

* William of Orange = William of Nassau = William the Silent

William, by the Grace of God

A Novel on William the Silent Prince of Orange Nassau Vol. 2

by Marjorie Bowen

author of *I Will Maintain*

"Guilielmus Dei Gratia Princeps Uraniae"
(William by the Grace of God Prince of Orange)
On a memorial coin of Orange 1568

INHERITANCE PUBLICATIONS
NEERLANDIA, ALBERTA, CANADA
PELLA, IOWA, U.S.A.

Library and Archives Canada Cataloguing in Publication
Canadian CIP data applied for but not available at time of printing

Library of Congress Cataloging-in-Publication Data
Bowen, Marjorie, 1888-1952.
 William, by the grace of God : a novel on William the Silent, Prince of
Orange Nassau, Vol. 2 / by Marjorie Bowen.
  p. cm.
 ISBN 978-0-921100-57-7 (pbk.)
 1. William I, Prince of Orange, 1533-1584—Fiction. 2. Princes—
Netherlands—Fiction. 3. Netherlands—History—Wars of Independence,
1556-1648—Fiction. I. Title.
PR6003.O676W56 2010
823'.912—dc22

                                                    2010002221

Cover picture *The Prince of Orange Crosses the Meuse River, 1568* by
J.H. Isings.

Published simultaneously in U.S.A. by Inheritance Publications
Box 366, Pella, Iowa 50219

Available in Australia from Inheritance Publications
Box 1122, Kelmscott, W.A. 6111 Tel. & Fax (089) 390 4940

Printed in Canada

Contents

William of Nassau (1533-1584)
Prince of Orange

PART I

OUT OF THE DEPTHS

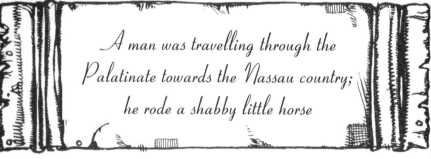

A man was travelling through the Palatinate towards the Nassau country; he rode a shabby little horse

CHAPTER I

MYNHEER CERTAIN

A MAN was travelling through the Palatinate towards the Nassau country; he rode a shabby little horse and his plain riding suit was both worn and mended, a cloak of dark blue Tabinet protected him from the March winds and a leaf hat without a buckle was pulled over his face.

He rode steadily until he came to an inn, the only house visible in all the long gray road, and there he dismounted, took his horse to the stable, passed into the parlour and, going straight to the fire, warmed his hands with an air of pleasure and good humour.

Two other men were there, travellers like himself; they looked at him keenly as men always looked at each other now, with suspicion, apprehension ready to change into open enmity.

One of these addressed the newcomer.

"Early in the year and late in the day to be on the road," he remarked.

"I come from France," was the answer, "business that will not wait forces me to overlook time and season." He removed his cloak and gloves and laid them carefully over a chair.

"My name is Certain," he added, "a merchant, a poor merchant, from the Netherlands."

He smiled straightly at them, uncovered, advanced to the table and seated himself there, looking at his companions still with that smiling intentness.

He had revealed himself as a man of middle height, hardly yet in his full maturity, but with no air of youthfulness, his figure and his bearing were both notably graceful, his hands extremely fine, his head was small, his complexion olive, his

9

eyes and cropped hair brown, his beard shaved close; a soiled muslin collar finished his ancient green suit; he wore no jewels nor ornaments; at his waist hung a short sword with a steel handle and a frayed leather wallet.

There was something remarkable in his appearance that caused the other two to gaze at him with undiminished curiosity.

Mynheer Certain, for his part, had soon summed them up and knew them very accurately for what they were, a French pastor of the Calvinist faith and a German clerk or shopkeeper of the poorer sort.

"You appear to doubt me," said the merchant pleasantly; he tapped on the table with his long fingers and when the drawer came ordered wine.

"I doubt the name you gave us," returned the Frenchman, "who in these times travels under his own name?"

"And I," said the other, "was wondering at your nationality — from the Netherlands you say! I did not know that Alva had left any Netherlanders alive."

"A few," Mynheer Certain still smiled. "A few."

The pastor, a sad man of insignificant aspect, shook his head dubiously.

"So few that we may consider it a country lost from the world, a nation consumed with the fires of its own homesteads, a people suffocated in their own blood," he said and he looked with a certain commiseration at the Netherlander.

"You think, then, there is no hope for my unhappy land?" asked that person.

"None," said the Calvinist. "The wrath of the Lord has unchained a devil upon them. Evil has strangled truth and piety over there — as in France — where indeed can the Reformed Faith claim a foothold save in this realm of the Elector Palatine! Are you of the Reformed Faith?"

"Of the Reformed Faith, yes."

The wine had been brought, and the merchant was drinking it slowly, with the relish of a tired man.

"Perhaps," said the German, "you have lost everything under Alva?"

10

Mynheer Certain gave his ready smile; his face, though lined with fatigue, was charming in contour and expression and his manner was one of exquisite courtesy.

"Everything," he answered. "My property, my houses — my son — my dignities, my revenues, my country. For I am an outlaw, an exile. Under the ban of King Philip."

"For your faith, Monsieur?" asked the Calvinist with sympathy.

"For that, yes."

"You must hate Alva," said the German childishly.

"Hate Alva?" repeated Mynheer Certain. "I do not know if I hate Alva — or King Philip."

"You have, then, no wish for revenge?" asked the pastor. "No wish to assist your wretched brethren, who, like you, have not only lost their all, but are under the hellish dominion of Spain?"

"Every wish," returned the merchant gently, "but no means."

"You are yourself a fugitive?" asked the pastor. "You fly, like all the persecuted, to the Court of the Elector Frederic?"

"No," said the Netherlander. "I am employed by a French house, trading in wool. I make my living."

The Calvinist regarded him with some contempt.

"You are too young to be so idle — there are men fighting for the Reformed Faith — fighting."

"Fighting in a hopeless cause," added the young German.

"So some say," said Mynheer Certain. He finished his wine and pushed back his chair. "Since Condé died at Jarnac —"

Neither of the others answered; the fatal name of Jarnac, where the Protestants had gone down to final defeat before the Roman Catholic legions of France, silenced them.

Only the Netherlander spoke, completing his sentence. "Who is there to take his place?"

"Coligny," said the pastor with a flash of hope.

"A great man — a helpless one," replied the merchant.

"The Prince of Nassau," said the clerk. He rose, brushing his hat with his coat sleeve.

"They are but as dust before the wind of Philip's wrath," returned the Calvinist. "And the Prince of Orange — he failed —"

"Failed so often," remarked Mynheer Certain, "failed so utterly."

"A great name once," said the German, "a great gentleman, too. I was in Leipzig when he was married to the Elector's niece."

The merchant looked at him sharply.

"You were there?"

"I, yes. I used to work for the Elector's alchemist. What an excitement that marriage was! — the Prince was Roman Catholic then and we all thought that it was a cruelty to the Princess," he laughed. "She has proved to be a madwoman and a wanton too they say, a disgrace to a proud family."

"Speak of what you know," reproved the merchant sternly, "the name of the Princess of Orange is not for vulgar handling."

"I speak of what all the world knows," returned the young man lightly. "A great wedding," he repeated, dwelling on the recollection. "I saw the Prince once, in the distance, there was so much gold in his ruff he could not turn his head. That seems a thousand years ago — now he is an outlaw like yourself, Mynheer Certain, probably without a white piece in his pocket.

"He failed; he failed!" cried the Calvinist impatiently. "Think no more of him, a landless, exiled man, a wanderer, an outcast — he failed!"

The merchant was again warming his hands over the blaze; he looked over his shoulder at the speaker and smiled.

"Who was he to withstand Philip?" demanded the German, clapping on his hat. "Though he had titles which would fill a parchment roll and the revenue of an Emperor — yet Philip! That is the greatest king in the world, what subject of his could dream rebellion against him?"

"He of whom you speak," said the merchant quietly, "is no subject of Philip, but a sovereign ruler — Prince of Orange, by the grace of God."

"By the grace of God," repeated the Calvinist. "Perhaps God will yet use him for our deliverance, but humanly speaking I have no hope of him."

"Nor I," added the clerk. "I am due at Heidelberg — so a good evening, sirs."

"A good evening," answered the merchant courteously. The Calvinist rose; a life of continual hiding, flight, secrecy, and persecution had given him a furtive look, a slow and subdued manner; the resignation taught by his stern faith lent some dignity to an appearance sad with the sadness of poverty, dull with the dullness of despair. He was an elderly man and all his life had known nothing but the disappointments of a losing cause, the bitterness of being one of a despised minority. "How long, O Lord, how long?" he murmured.

He drew his cloak precisely about him and left the room; when the door had closed his heavy tread could be heard mounting to the little room that was his temporary refuge in his wanderings.

The Netherlander stood motionless by the fire; at that moment the sense of the intense unreality of life came over him with terrible force.

He thought of the past and time ceased to exist. The days of his prosperity, the days of his exile, moments of anguish, moments of ease mingled together in one intricate pattern, all his life seemed without period or date, a confusion of events and emotion.

A thousand years ago seemed the marriage of the Prince of Orange, the young man had said — the Netherlander had also been in Leipzig for that ceremony — a thousand years ago — it seemed no less to him . . . he recalled his own past, easy days, pleasant days, of brightness, of sport, of jest — so lost, so utterly lost that no magic could recall them, days when the world had been normal, when all things had moved pleasantly in their accustomed grooves, days when he had not lacked respect nor companions, money nor leisure — smooth days, unmarred by dread, days such as might come into another's life, never again into his . . . half reluctantly his mind travelled the chaos that had followed the ending of those pleasant times, the exile, the poverty, the humiliation, the failure — the loss of all, the property he had forfeited, the country from which he was banished, the wife who had deserted him, the friends who had died or fallen away from his perilous cause.

No shadow disturbed the composure of his serene face, but the great sadness that was in his eyes, a sadness that only death would quench now, deepened, and tears filled them, dimming the lustre of his gaze, water and fire struggling for mastery.

With the restless movement of one in pain, he turned from the hearth to the window.

It was raining heavily; the pine trees opposite the inn seemed to intertwine their branches in the low loose clouds; these trees and clouds bounded the prospect; the Netherlander looked out steadily at this view of rain, wet trees and loose sky.

A word used by the stranger who had just spoken to him continually recurred to his mind — failed — failed — the Prince of Orange had failed.

At this moment the man looking out at the rain was acknowledging failure, accepting it, even a little marvelling at it, failure so complete, so persistent, failure of every project, every scheme, every endeavour until he stood stripped, barren, humiliated before his enemies, a landless exile, banned and proscribed.

Again his mind travelled back to the old days. He contemplated his downfall almost wistfully; he remembered that at one time he had counted on happiness as a right, expected it, taken it for granted — happiness and prosperity. Now that seemed to him extraordinary.

He returned to the table and took a very soiled little notebook from his pocket, looked through it and laid it down, then he brought out a handful of money, some silver pieces and one piece of gold; this was all he possessed. Counting the money carefully he made some calculations in the notebook, then returned both to his pocket, taking from his wallet a sheet of paper and a pencil.

He began writing a letter to his brother . . . .

"In the long coffer in my room is a suit of gray and a pair of hosen you may have mended for me — I am in sore need of these and shall thank you for your kind offices . . . could you find a cheap small horse? I need one for a good friend of mine who at present goes afoot, this is a very necessary thing if the means could be found."

He was penning this letter with a certain haste, as if eager to be rid of a disagreeable task, when the door of the little parlour opened. The traveller at once and swiftly put away his letter.

Voices sounded in the passage and a woman entered the room.

She wore a brown cloth riding suit and carried her wet skirts high, showing her muddied boots; the rain, so sudden and so heavy, had draggled the long black feather in her buff hat and the locks of reddish hair that had been blown across her wind-flushed face; she was handsome in an imposing, opulent fashion, but her expression was humble and sad.

Mynheer Certain had risen from his seat at her entry and was turning away, but the instant's glance he had of the woman caused him to pause and glance at her again.

She, entering, came face to face with him and stood arrested in all movement, her face flushing with a look of bewilderment and joy.

The innkeeper behind her began talking of her lame horse and when he might be able to procure her another.

She composed herself to answer him.

"If need be I can walk to the Castle," she said, "it is so near — and — I will rest a little while — the rain —"

She stopped and began pulling off her gloves with movements of great agitation.

The landlord left and the man and woman looked at each other again, she raising her amazed eyes from her gauntlets, he turning to glance at her over his shoulder.

"You remember me?" he said gently.

"I was your servant," she answered, "— but *you* remember *me*?"

"My lady's waiting woman, the heretic maid from Dresden — Rénèe le Meung. But perhaps you have changed that name?"

"No," she was looking at him breathlessly as if his personality, not his words, absorbed her so intensely.

"Why do you speak of *me*? What of yourself?"

All humility and reverence were in her words; her control suddenly failed her. She could not disguise the shock of this meeting; her knees trembled and her lips quivered.

"How I have *prayed* for Your Highness," she murmured. The tears sprang to her eyes. "All these years —"

He was moved at that; his sensitive nature was touched by the thought of her remembering and praying when he had forgotten her utterly until he had come face to face with her again.

"— All these years," repeated Rénèe le Meung.

"You were ever very loyal," he said kindly.

"Loyal?" she answered strangely.

"Loyal," he repeated. "I remember that I noticed that quality in you — from the first."

He recalled her now very clearly, her impassiveness and reserve, almost dullness, so at variance with her soft and worldly style of beauty, her endless patience before the caprices of an intolerable mistress, the steadfastness with which she had once or twice ventured to speak to him of her persecuted faith.

"I hope all is well with you," he said, and there was a certain tenderness mingled with the usual perfect courtesy of his manner; tenderness for the past and the part Rénèe le Meung had played in it.

She did not appear to hear what he was saying, so utterly absorbed was she by the wonder of meeting him, of seeing actually before her the man who had so long occupied her thoughts.

"We think of you so much at the Castle," she said "so much."

"You are at the Castle?"

"With the good Electress, yes. She shelters so many — Your Highness is coming to the Castle?"

"I had not thought to do so," he answered with a little smile for her breathless eagerness. "I have no news for the Elector Palatine. I travel as Mynheer Certain — to keep in touch with some agents of mine. My eventual goal is Dillenburg."

"But you will come to Heidelberg," she said, clasping her hands nervously. "You would not pass them by — they — I — we have waited so long for news of you — so patiently."

"I have no news," he said again and turned away his tired eyes.

"Your Highness must come," she pleaded. "Oh, Your Highness will come?"

She strangely tempted him — to be among friends, to snatch a few hours of ease, of comfort, perhaps of oblivion — why not, why not!

It had not been his intention to parade his failure, to ask the sympathy even of those whom he knew would offer it lovingly, but this resolve of his now faltered; something in the personality of the woman swayed him; he had long lacked the devotion of a woman in his life; lately he had met few, refined and comely as Rénèe le Meung; once such women had been as plentiful around him as the flowers in his costly parterres and as little noticed, now they were a rarity; he even felt grateful to this lady who looked at him in an amaze of pleasure and reverence.

"Why should I not come?" he said with his lovable smile. "It grows dark and you will need an escort to the Castle."

"You would ride with me?" she exclaimed.

He was almost startled at her tone.

"Why should I not ride with you?" he asked gently.

"I was your servant, one of the least of your servants," she said.

"I am a landless man now," he answered. "I have no servants, and but few friends — make these one more, Mademoiselle."

She moved a little away from him.

"To me," she said simply, "you are always William of Orange."

CHAPTER II

THE RIDE

SLOWLY they rode together through the pine forest; the rain fell steadily yet gently; there was a faint warmth in the air like the first beginning of the beautiful heat of summer; here and there fresh green tipped the winter darkness of the trees.

They rode with a certain leisure, as people who are at no haste to be at their journey's end. To the woman it was an episode of pure happiness in a life that had always been unhappy; to the man it was a pleasant interlude in a life of stress and turmoil unutterable; he rode his shabby hack and she the borrowed horse from the inn; their wet cloaks clung about them and the moisture dripped from their felt hats; the woman's heart glowed with a joy that made the gray afternoon as radiant to her as a midsummer noonday, her mind admitted nothing beyond the fact that they were riding alone together. It seemed incredible after all these years of patience, of abnegation, of dreams.

"You think often of the Netherlands?" asked the Prince.

His voice almost startled her by the stamp of reality it put on the wonder of his presence.

"Often," she said. "I have wondered if I am ever to return to my unfortunate country — believe me, I would go," she added, "if my going was of the least service, but I have always been one of the useless."

"We are all useless compared with our tasks," said the Prince gravely. "I feel myself a handful of dust before the wind, a straw before the tide."

"You are the guiding star of a whole nation," said Rénèe le Meung, "the hope of a Faith — the solace of a Cause."

He smiled, turning on her his sad and powerful eyes.

"You are good to think that of me — it is their own courage that guides and supports the Netherlanders, not I — I am a man who set himself against great odds and who has failed."

"But who is not defeated, Highness."

"No, not defeated," he assented quietly. "I have yet my brain, my two hands, the name — a name somewhat loved — nothing else."

She looked at him; under the broad brim of his hat his dark face showed pale; the exact fine features had changed since the day she had seen him first; the day when he had mounted the stairs of the Leipzig town hall to greet his bride, Anne of Saxony — the smooth olive cheek was hollowed, the brilliant eyes shadowed, in the thick close chestnut locks the white hairs were sprinkled; he looked infinitely tired, and there was great sadness in the resolute lines of his full lips.

Rénèe remembered — remembered golden days of pomp and magnificence and this man moving through them, courted, beloved, admired, powerful, and serene, a Prince, a Grandee of Spain, the greatest man in the Netherlands.

And the years between then and now were not so many, and yet she, his wife's waiting-woman, who had curtsied from his path with awe, had met him, a forlorn and penniless exile in a wayside inn, and they were riding together as equals.

Equals — her heart trembled at the word; she knew it was but another dream, that he would always remain a sovereign Prince and she a humble commoner, yet for the moment it was a dream with the semblance of reality; at least all outward sign of difference was done away with, they rode together as fellow exiles, as two of the same country and the same faith — as mere man and woman. And his wife was no longer between them; the worthless, faithless, wanton woman whom Rénèe had laboured so long and patiently to save, was repudiated at last, insane in the care of her own kinsfolk.

"If we could ride forever," thought Rénèe, "if the world would stop about us and we could ride on like this through all eternity."

The rain ceased and the trembling moist light of sunset showed in a faint blur through the straight dark stems of the trees, a pale saffron glow diffused itself through the wood, an indistinct gleam of sunshine quivered along the ground.

"Afterwards," said the Prince, looking at his companion, "when I am again lost in my obscure wanderings, I shall remember this ride very pleasantly."

She turned her glance to her gauntleted hands so slackly holding the reins.

"Is Count Lodewyk in good health?" she asked. "He is so much spoken of at Heidelberg."

A look of tenderness softened the Prince's face at the mention of his beloved younger brother.

"Lodewyk is well," he answered. "His bright spirits help us all to have confidence in our desperate cause."

Rénèe recalled her first meeting with Count Lodewyk — the idle young gallant lolling over the counter of the perfumery shop, fingering the boxes of cinquento with fine hands — she remembered too how she had despised him for his air of foppery — how he had shamed her judgment. She had also felt some contempt for the handsome gorgeous Prince of Orange and his political marriage, but that Rénèe had now forgotten utterly.

"You remember the days in Brussels?" smiled the Prince, "the feasts, the tourneys — poor wild Brederode — Hoogstraaten — Egmont, Horne — my brother Adolphus — Bergen, Floris Montmorency, all dead!"

Rénèe shuddered.

"How will Philip answer to God for all these lives, all those other lives, obscure, miserable as these were great?"

He glanced at her still with that wistful smile about his lips.

"Philip? He thinks he has pleased his god and knows no other."

Rénèe was puzzled.

"But there surely is Judgment for such a man?"

"There is!" said William calmly. "But Judgment is not in our hands, Mademoiselle. We perform our little task while we can and when our day is done — good night! So much to do, so little time to do it in!"

"Do you not hate Philip?" she asked as the Calvinist had asked.

"I have hated him. These last years I have gotten beyond hate — and beyond despair. Mademoiselle, I have been very much in the depths — I have seen grief and sorrow very close. I have been in those places where a man leaves his life or his passions. I lived. I think there was nothing left of what I used to be but a certain faith in God, a certain hope in the triumph of God's cause in this world — even against a Philip."

She was silent, overwhelmed that he should thus speak to her; the sunset breeze blew upon their faces and swirled the pine needles beneath their horses' hoofs.

"So I have hope, even for the Netherlands," continued the Prince. "So I have faith — even in the coming of that time when there shall be not one creed tyrannising over another creed. Even in that I have faith — but one can do so little — only all of us doing something may bring nearer the day of deliverance. So little!" he repeated softly, "to serve the truth as we see it — to serve God as we know Him — justice as it is revealed to us — so little!"

"This from Your Highness — who has done everything?"

"Lost everything. The two strangers I parted from just now spoke of my name and failure — coupled the words together — the Prince of Orange, he failed! failed!"

But as he spoke he smiled and his eyes were serene.

Rénèe thought of all he had endured — defeat, humiliation, contempt, the endless endeavour, the slow patience, the vast energy, the indomitable resource that had again and again been wasted in a fruitless task.

"You will achieve," she said in a low voice, "such as Your Highness always achieve."

"If I could do only a little," he answered quietly. "Lately I have been afraid they would kill me before I could do anything at all."

"Kill you?" she stammered.

"Philip thinks me of some importance still," he answered simply, with a little smile. "I am on the list of those he considers dangerous — the list on which he put Horne and Egmont."

"They — try to assassinate you?"

"Persistently. Philip has not forgotten that I escaped the net that caught the others."

Rénèe's face quivered, she looked away.

"God would not let you be killed," she said. "Too many need — too many love — Your Highness."

He did not answer this; he too had his faith. He believed that God had given him a special mission and could afford him any special protection. But he also realized that God did not need him and that he was as likely to be struck down as King Philip. He believed the truth of the Calvinist religion. It had not been an expedient thing for him to embrace, though it was congenial to him. Nevertheless, narrowness was hateful to him and the very essence of the cause for which he had given everything was liberty of conscience. He believed that God was also the owner of man's conscience!

They came out from the pine forest on to the high road; dusk was closing in and before them gleamed the lights in the windows of Heidelberg Castle.

As the Prince came out of the forest on to the high road and saw the black bulk of the Castle before him, his expression, even his pose, subtly changed; the moment of softness, when, in the half-obscurity of the forest he had spoken as a tired man speaks to a woman who understands, suddenly, intimately, passed; like a shadow the reserved look of the man of great affairs, of one engaged in perilous causes and burdened with heavy secrets, came over his face.

"Is the Elector at home?" he asked, and Rénèe saw that he had already put her from his thoughts and was considering how this unexpected visit he had been persuaded into might be turned into a political account.

"Yes, Monseigneur," she answered, instantly subduing herself to his service, "he will be most honoured at Your Highness's coming."

"It is a pity," observed William, with the astuteness of the trained politician, "that he is not so powerful as he is well meaning."

"He is very generous," said Rénèe, loyal to the man whose little Court had sheltered her and so many of her co-religionists, "He does not refuse his protection to the most destitute, the most insignificant. The Electress, too, is wide in charity."

"Mademoiselle de Montpensier is with her?" asked the Prince.

"Yes, Highness. I am her particular attendant. At some peril to themselves their Highnesses shelter this lady, who fled from France to them — Monseigneur knows the story?"

"Of Mademoiselle de Montpensier, the abbess of Joüarrs?" smiled William, then added with a sudden gravity, "I do not know why I smile, her action showed great courage in the lady."

"Such courage, Monseigneur, for one enclosed in a convent since she was a child of eleven!" said Rénèe eagerly, "but she is brave, the Princess, and strong."

"Such women are needed in these times," answered William. "Mademoiselle should marry and comfort some weary man."

Rénèe knew that there had been long and persistent talk of a union between William's brother, Lodewyk of Nassau, and Charlotte de Montpensier and she thought that it was to this that he alluded.

"The Electress is eager for such a marriage," she said, "but the Princess is dowerless; her father will give her nothing, and her sister, Madame de Bouillon, cannot."

"Many a man will marry without a dower now as many a woman without an establishment — your little princess will find her man — she looks a woman for a home."

Rénèe was startled.

"Your Highness has seen her?" she exclaimed.

"Once, when I was in France." He dismissed the subject with a certain abruptness. "We are almost at the Castle, Mademoiselle. I trust your good offices," he added with a very winning courtesy, "to assure my welcome."

"Your Highness humbles me," breathed Rénèe. She felt herself in an agitation almost beyond control; this meeting with the Prince had changed everything for her, so suddenly, so utterly that she was giddy with it.

In the courtyard he helped her to dismount; it was now so dark they could barely see each other's faces.

He held her gloved hand for a moment after she was standing beside him.

"I thank you for a pleasurable hour, Mademoiselle," he said, and his voice had a touching quality of gratitude as if he had not been lately used to such sympathy as she had offered him.

Rénèe laughed foolishly; she turned blindly towards the Castle entrance, stumbling in her heavy wet skirt.

The Prince, taking off his shabby hat and shaking the water from the brim, followed her.

An officer standing in the hall stared curiously at the slim shabby man behind Rénèe.

"The Elector?"she asked.

The officer noted curiously her shining eyes and flushed cheeks.

"His Highness —" he began.

As he spoke Frederic himself came down the wide stairs; beside his stern martial figure was the slender one of the young Count Christopher.

Rénèe turned to them.

"Messieurs, I bring you a very notable guest."

"In very notable attire," added William, and he laughed.

The Elector came swiftly down the stairs, his rather hard though noble face coloured with pleasure. He put his hands on the Prince's shoulders and kissed him on either cheek.

Rénèe sped past them, up the stairs and to the apartments of Mademoiselle de Montpensier.

She found the Princess seated at a little round table making lilies out of white velvet, an occupation she had learnt in the convent.

"Mademoiselle," said Rénèe very breathlessly, "he is here!"

"Who is here, my dear?" asked the Princess. "Your knight at last? I thought that you must have one, Rénèe."

Rénèe turned away; her lips trembled, her throat was dry and she could not speak.

Charlotte de Bourbon did not lift her eyes from her work; she continued wiring the white petals of the lily and fastening them to the centre stamen of yellow silk.

This Princess, daughter of the proud Duc de Montpensier, who had been forced by her parents into a cloister at the age of eleven, who had taken her vows under protest, and abandoned her position as abbess in one of the most princely and wealthy establishments in France, to fly into the Palatinate and embrace the Reformed Faith, was a slight fair girl of no great appearance of energy or force of character.

Her features were small and exact, her blonde hair soft and fine, the chin was a little heavy, the eyes dark blue and lively; her manner was one of gaiety and ardour, but above all of serenity. She wore a puce-coloured gown and a falling ruff of delicate muslin covered with needlework.

"Who is he?" she asked again without looking up.

"The Prince of Orange, Mademoiselle," answered Rénèe quickly.

Now Charlotte dropped her work. "The Prince of Orange?"

"Yes, Mademoiselle, he is now in the castle."

"Secretly — in disguise?"

"Yes, I left him with the Elector."

Charlotte looked thoughtful; Rénèe, who believed the common rumour that the Princess was interested in and would eventually marry Lodewyk of Nassau, remarked, timidly with a sincere desire to please —

"His Highness spoke of his brother — Count Lodewyk, who is safe and well."

Charlotte glanced at her calmly; the serenity that had enabled Mademoiselle de Montpensier to support with dignity so many years of conventual life was always apparent in her demeanour, but, Rénèe, at least, had never seen any of the impatience and spirit that had urged her to break her enforced vows and escape her convent, her country and her faith; there still seemed much of the abbess in Charlotte, the dignity of one trained to obey and to command, the poise of one who is remote from the world and impervious to worldly troubles.

"Do you think that I am so eager for news of Count Lodewyk?" she asked pleasantly.

"Yes," said Rénèe frankly; she was as intimate with the Princess as any woman, but Charlotte had a quality of elusive remoteness, difficult, and at the same time vexatious to the warm and impulsive nature of the Fleming, to whom reserve was a matter of habit, but also of distaste.

"You listen to gossip," smiled the Princess gently. "I shall be glad to meet the Prince. He has been wonderful. I believe he will do something yet, even against Alva."

"He has given all he has," answered Rénèe. "Everything — you cannot imagine how great and splendid he was, how magnificent — and now — like a beggar — lonely."

"You speak with great enthusiasm," said Charlotte, looking up. "You knew him very well?"

It was in Rénèe's heart and almost on her lips to disclose her long-kept secret — "I love him," but something in the utter gentle calm of the Princess checked her; she kept a stern rein over her agitation and answered quietly.

"When I was with his wife I saw much of His Highness."

"Where is his wife?" asked Charlotte; the disastrous ending of the Prince's marriage was a thing hushed and mysterious; these two had never spoken of it before.

"I believe she may be at Dillenburg in the custody of Count John," said Rénèe. "Count Lodewyk told me that the Prince had repudiated her and that the Elector of Saxony was to take her back. She is mad."

"Poor wretch!" murmured Charlotte.

Rénèe flushed.

"There is no need to pity her, Mademoiselle, she made the Prince's life a humiliation and a misery. I knew her as few others could and there was no good in her. And when the trouble came she deserted him — and — and stooped to another man."

"I know," said the Princess, "therefore I say, 'poor wretch!' Do you not pity such as these, Rénèe?"

Charlotte de Bourbon-Montpensier (1546-1582)

"No — at least for her I had no pity."

Charlotte was silent; she turned up the copper lamp that gave the light for her sewing.

"And now the Prince is free," added Rénèe.

"Free! He considers himself free?"

"He is now a Protestant, and Protestant Divines have freed him from a union the woman trampled on."

Charlotte said no more; she folded away her silks and velvets, wires and ribbons into a cedar-wood box set with silver intarsia.

The rain had begun again, heavy drops splashed down the wide chimney on to the log fire, a high wind shook the window behind the heavy curtain.

CHAPTER III

THE INTERRUPTION OF PRINCESS CHARLOTTE

THE Prince of Orange sat in the Elector's private cabinet and listened to his host speaking on the confusions and disorders that rent the nations; William listened with perfect attention; it was second nature in him to listen to all, to defer, to soothe, to flatter, to win with a smile and a compliment, to conduct intricate intrigue secretly and use people while they thought they used him; he was still the accomplished diplomat he had been in the days of his power when the redoubtable Cardinal Granvelle had described him as "the most dangerous man in the Netherlands," and he still masked his abilities with that show of perfect good humour, of tolerance and pleasantness that had always gained him so many adherents.

In his heart he was sick of many people; he himself saw so clearly, so straightly, both the great issues that he had at heart and the means to achievement of these same issues, that it was weariness of weariness to him having to wait always on the whims and crooked policies of others.

On every side these others baulked him; the Queen of England was a Protestant, but she would not help him, in despite of her half-promises, because it was not her policy to go to war with Spain; the Protestant Princes of Germany would not risk their all in an encounter with Alva; the French played fast and loose with Protestant and Romanist, Condé's little band with whom William and his brothers had thrown in their fortunes had been scattered like chaff; the Prince had no allies beyond his brothers, John, Lodewyk, and Henry, and no resources beyond his own capacity.

The Elector admired him and sympathised with both his cause and his situation, yet William would not even have troubled to visit Heidelberg had he not met Rénèe le Meung, so hopeless did he know it to be to ask Frederic for material.

So he listened to the good Elector's denunciation of Rome and Philip, Alva and the Inquisition, and in his heart was the great sadness and weariness of the man who has undertaken an almost impossible task and knows that he must shoulder it alone.

Frederic sat by the fireplace; the light of the flames turned to threads of scarlet the gold embroidery on his stout chest, his fine, rather heavy face was flushed and animated, his eyes shone under his gray hair and his mouth was firmly set between the gray moustaches and beard.

William, silent, shabby yet elegant, with his air of courteous attention, sat at the round table that occupied the centre of the room; he had his elbow on his knee and his chin in his palm, the yellow candle-light cast a glow on his dark face; his eyes were fixed intently on the Elector, yet when Frederic, ceasing his powerful yet vague reproaches against the supporters of the Christian faith, asked a sudden question it was with an effort that William recalled himself from his own straying thoughts to answer.

"Why do you rely on the French?" the Elector had demanded.

The Prince, utterly unable and with no wish to explain his intricate policies to even such a loyal friend as Frederic, answered smoothly. "I doubt if I could tell why I try for French support, save that a desperate man clutches at straws. I do not, however, rely on them."

"It would be wiser not to do so," remarked the Elector shrewdly. "Do you think that Catherine or her sons could play fair?"

"There is the Guise," replied William. "It is a country split with factions — one of their ambitious young Princes might be tempted."

"By what?"

"By the kingdom of the Netherlands," said the Prince calmly.

"Ah, you would offer that?"

"My ideal would be a Republic," answered the Prince, "but I think that unattainable in these times. Therefore I would create a kingdom and offer it to the Prince who would deliver us from Philip and the Inquisition."

"A bold plan," said the Elector with admiration and a little amazement. "Your Highness really thinks it possible to completely deliver the Netherlands?"

"Yes."

"Then it is Your Highness who should have the throne of this new kingdom."

William appeared neither startled nor flattered; the idea was not new to him.

"A more powerful Protector than myself is needed, Highness. I am a landless man. I can neither command one chest of money nor one regiment of foot. The Netherlands require one who can liberate before he can rule."

"If there is a man in Europe who can do that," declared the Elector, "it is you yourself."

William slightly flushed.

"I have tried and failed. More than once. I have gathered armies to see them scattered, I have spent all I had with no results. I have lost all I ever had in this cause, friends, rank, position — all but life," he added with a deepening of the colour in his olive cheek, "for what am I now but a derision to Philip and Alva and an object of pity to the world? I undertook what I could not do. I shall try again, but it cannot be done alone."

"Better alone than with treacherous help," said the Elector.

William did not answer; the vast schemes that he was meditating required the aid of nations, not only individuals; to attempt alone the task to which he had set his hand was to play a fool's part.

"Whom would you trust?" pursued Frederic. "France, Austria, or England?"

"I work," replied the Prince, "with all three, with all — with any. I cannot too carefully choose my means for these ends I have in view."

"These ends?" questioned the Elector.

"You know, Highness. The liberation of the Netherlands. And toleration for the Reformed Religion."

The Elector sighed; there was still that look of faint amazement in his face.

He could not forget that the man speaking to him with this quiet certainty, had, as he himself admitted, lost all and failed, not once but again and again.

To Frederic it seemed quite hopeless to defy Philip, and therefore he sighed, for he was sincere in his profession of the Reformed Faith and ardent in his championship of his co-religionists in the Netherlands.

For an instant the younger man's faith almost convinced him; he looked searchingly and wistfully at William's steadfast face.

Supposing these golden dreams did come true, supposing the humbled, defeated, derided Prince did snatch a nation from Philip's wrath and Alva's sword?

"Do you have great confidence in success, Highness?" he asked.

"I do not know," replied William slowly. "I cannot tell how long I have."

"You mean?"

"Life is so short," smiled the Prince, "and my life in particular uncertain."

"You think that Philip pursues you?" asked Frederic gloomily.

"I know it. I was on the same list as Horne and Floris, Egmont and Berghen. The King will not rest till I have joined them, Highness."

"Assassination! The Spanish hound!" cried the Elector.

"Death some way," said William. "They have tried several times. Once they will try and not fail."

"You think that?"

"Is it likely, Highness, that such a man as Philip would fail in such an aim?"

"This is a horrible thing for you to live with," muttered the Elector.

"I am used to it. I expect that some day Philip's steel or bullet or poison will end me as it ended them." His voice was tender as he mentioned his dead friends. "Unless a possible battle saves me. The question is," and his eyes suddenly brightened wonderfully, "how much I may by God's grace accomplish first."

Frederic had no good answer ready. Indeed, it seemed to him unlikely that Philip, who had set William under a ban, put a price on his head and resolved on his death by any means and at any cost, Philip with his spies and agents, priests and inquisitors, would allow the last and most illustrious of the Netherlanders who had defied his authority to escape.

The Prince's thoughts had travelled far from the subject; there was one question only he wished to put to the Elector. "How many men would you raise for me in the Palatinate?" Talk of other matters was but waste of time to William, despite his ready answers and courteous attention. He even began to consider his evening wasted if he could not obtain some promise of support from Frederic and almost wished himself on the road again, riding through the rainy dark towards Dillenburg.

He rose and crossed to the hearth with the intention of asking the Elector for a levy of men; he was reluctant to do this; the constant part of beggar and supplicant irked the man who was by birth, instinct, and temperament the great noble, the dispenser of benefits, not the receiver of them.

He would very willingly have been silent on this matter to the Elector; but his policy had been too long that of ceaseless endeavour in every direction for him to leave unused this possibility that had come his way.

He was about to speak when the door opened and two women entered the apartment.

The first was the Electress, she who had been the wife of the wild Beggar leader, Count Brederode, and her companion was Mademoiselle de Montpensier.

"Highness," said the Electress, addressing the Prince of Orange, "since you would not come to wait on us we are here to wait on you," she held out her hand frankly and smiled. "We used to know each other in Brussels, Monseigneur, will you ignore old friends?"

"I was in no trim to speak to ladies," answered William. "I go darkly, shadowed with misfortune, and would not offend gentle eyes nor sadden gentle hearts."

As he spoke he looked at her wistfully, for in truth she reminded him of those old Brussels days — the days of youth and pleasure.

"I knew they would bring you their homage, Prince," smiled the Elector. "Your name is ever on their tongues — this," he drew forward his young guest, "this is Mademoiselle Charlotte de Bourbon, the Duc de Montpensier's daughter, lately of that faith, Highness, for which you fight."

The Prince glanced at her quickly; the Elector had put his arm on the shoulder of the young girl and drawn her into the golden circle of the lamplight.

In that moment Charlotte looked beautiful, her face was flushed and soft above the fine gauze ruff, the fair hair loosened about the low placid brow and the blue eyes shining with an intense and eager light.

"We met before, twice," said William.

"Twice?"

"Once at the Louvre — you were a very little maid, you stood in an alcove and watched the Queen of Scotland dance. It was a little while before King Henry died."

She smiled radiantly.

"You saw me? A funny little child! Soon after that they made me a nun."

"And now you have taken your freedom. With great courage."

The Princess impulsively caught the Elector's hand, while her eyes turned affectionately towards his wife.

"These saved me. I am homeless but for them. My father disowns me, I am an exile as yourself, Highness; closed to me is France — but I am very happy here," she added instantly;

Frederick the Pious (1515-1576)

despite her dignity and her trained air there was a certain childishness about her as she spoke infinitely touching.

"She is not happy," said the Electress gently. "Who could be in such times as these! Who could be, cast from their home and their country? But we will find an establishment for her."

Frederic smiled kindly at the little refugee.

"She deserves good fortune, this fair heretic," he said.

Charlotte looked at the Prince, who was gazing at her very intently; he was recalling that morning, early in the year, soon after he had entered France, and how she had ridden by in robe and wimple, an abbess with her train of nuns and how she, even then, had wished him "God speed" on his perilous adventure.

Seeing his eyes on her she flushed, but her gaze was steady.

"What great talk have we interrupted with our foolish coming?" she asked seriously.

The Elector shook his head.

"The Prince has said nothing. You must use your persuasions to make him talk, Mademoiselle."

"Of what?" smiled William. "I have long since become rusty in subjects interesting to a lady's ears."

Charlotte looked at him gravely; he was impressed now, as he had been when he had seen her last, by a certain nobility in her small, fair, and infantile face.

"Your Highness must not dismiss us as trifles now," she said. "Women can be of use, even in these times. We have changed as the men have changed — is it not so, Madame?" she turned to the Electress.

"At least we understand," was the gentle answer.

"Your Highness would never realize how we have followed your exploits, waited for news, hoped, prayed — and blessed you, Prince, you and Count Lodewyk and Count John and all who fight.

William, looking at these two soft, earnest, and intelligent women, thought, with an ugly stab, of the wife who still bore his name, the woman who had insulted him and his cause, who had deserted him and his faith and stooped to a low intrigue with one scarce a gentleman.

The pain and shame of this thought caused him to turn away from the others abruptly — a proceeding unusual with him who was so masked and courteous to all — he walked to the wide hearth, then turned again, facing the three.

None of them could have guessed his secret disease, but all saw the sudden cloud on his face and a little silence fell.

It was Princess Charlotte who broke it; she did what was to William an unaccountable and amazing thing.

Coming round the table so that she stood between the Elector and the Prince, she turned quietly to Frederic.

"How many men can you raise for his Highness?" she said.

William started to hear on her soft, childish lips the question that had been so insistently in his own mind, started to hear her, the heretic fugitive, speak so to the man who sheltered her; ask so quietly the question he, a fellow Prince, had not cared to ask.

The Elector looked at her straightly, almost with a challenge.

"Who told you, Mademoiselle," he asked, "that I proposed to raise a levy for the Prince of Orange?"

She answered simply:

"I was sure you would help to your utmost, Highness." She smiled as she added, "The Duke Christopher is eager to go."

"How do you know, Mademoiselle?" asked Frederic sharply.

"He told me."

"Ah, he has no secrets from you, eh?" smiled the Elector.

"I do not know his secrets, Highness, only this, that he is eager to volunteer under the Prince of Orange."

The Calvinistic Prince looked at her seriously.

"Well, better that than to spend his life in sloth," he answered.

"And how many men can the Palatinate raise?" asked Charlotte.

Frederic looked from her to his wife and laughed.

"She has a courage," remarked the Electress with a smile.

"What courage?" asked Charlotte; she too was smiling. "Is it not true that the Elector is a Protestant Prince — and is it

36

not true," she turned shyly to William, "that His Highness requires men for his campaign against Alva in the Netherlands?"

William had been watching this little scene with an intent curiosity.

"It is very true," he answered at once. "How can I thank my gracious advocate?"

"Thank the Elector," said Charlotte, "when he has given you the levy — and now a good night, for I have had my say and hinder good converse. Before your going I shall see Your Highness."

She took the arm of the Electress and the two were gone as quickly and unceremoniously as they had entered.

Frederic turned to William.

"I will help you to the best of my power," he said, and held out his hand.

Charlotte left the Electress and ran up to her own chamber, where Rénèe le Meung was cutting out in white silk the petals of the roses and lilies the Princess mounted on the wire frames. The waiting-woman sat by the fire; she was thinking of the ride through the twilight woods and of her companion's last words to her as he had helped her from her horse.

"I have seen him," said Charlotte.

"The Prince?" Rénèe looked up.

"Yes."

"I thought that he was here secretly and would see no one but the Elector," said Rénèe slowly.

"But I needed to see him," answered Charlotte. "I have heard so much of him."

A slight sense of discomfiture touched Rénèe's heart; she looked searchingly into the face of the Princess that was now a strangely happy face.

"What did you think of the Prince?" she asked with reluctance.

Charlotte answered gravely.

"He is such as I should wish to marry, to serve, and be with always."

A chill fell on Rénèe's dreams; she rose without speaking and put away the white flowers.

CHAPTER IV

THE EXILES

THEY met again, the Prince and Charlotte de Bourbon; he, who was used to only a few hours' sleep, was up almost with the early spring dawn and made his opportunity to see her; the day was sunny and misty after yesterday's rain; she and Rénèe were walking in the garden when the Prince found them.

At sight of him the waiting-woman withdrew herself as she had withdrawn herself all her life, effacing herself before Charlotte de Bourbon as she had effaced herself before Anne of Saxony; her step was heavy and her shoulders drooped as she went.

The Princess made no effort to evade William. She greeted him with her simple serenity, which was partly an untaught childishness, and partly the schooling of the nun and the abbess, the Princess of the Church, trained to be composed and distant in graciousness.

"I wished to see you again, Mademoiselle," said William.

They fell into step side by side, walking slowly between the long flower beds where the snowdrops showed beneath the dark winter bushes.

"You leave soon?" asked Charlotte.

"In a few hours."

"Your Highness is not long in any one place," she smiled.

"No — an exile's life!"

"We are both exiles," said Charlotte, "and for the same cause."

He looked at her as he might have looked at an ardent child.

"Tell me," he asked with a certain tenderness, "how you came to this great resolution, Mademoiselle, to leave all?"

It did indeed seem strange to him that she, a mere girl, so sternly trained in superstitious ignorance, cloistered from all knowledge, all outside influence, should have dared to break her bonds, her vows, and return to the world from which she had been forever excluded and embrace the faith that was one with damnation to her people and her kin.

He was puzzled also because he did not see in her any great energy or force of character; she seemed rather simple and conformed.

Yet she had done this thing, uninfluenced and unaided.

"I never wished to be a nun," she answered. "When I took my vows I made a protest before the Novices. I was then eleven years old. I loathed the life — from the first."

"You did not wish to be a nun?" smiled William gently.

"No, Highness." She did not add her secret of secrets — that she had always longed to be a wife and mother — but hugged it close in her inmost heart.

"And you heard of what was taking place in the world?"

"A little. Something of this great new freedom that was coming — something of the great conflict in France — of what the Queen of Navarre and the Elector were doing, and my sister's lord, Monsieur de Bouillon. I thought it was the moment to free myself."

"And you left everything?"

She looked up at him as if she did not understand his meaning.

"I mean, you lost your inheritance, your country, your home?"

Still Charlotte did not answer, her face, very fair in colouring under the muslin coif and in the pale morning light, remained turned upward towards the Prince.

"Is this not so, Mademoiselle?" insisted William.

"Has not Your Highness lost as much, and more?" she replied.

"A higher position, greater wealth, more honour, a son?"

"Oh, I?" he smiled.

She continued looking at him, knitting her brows in the earnestness of her speech.

"And your life must have been pleasant, was it not pleasant?"

"Yes, I think it was, Mademoiselle."

"While mine was hateful to me — so mine was a very little sacrifice beside yours," said the Princess with a childish air of finality.

"And you," smiled William, "are a very little person beside me — and half my years."

He put out his hand as if to measure her height from the ground and she laughed.

"Not so short as that, Monsieur, but you think me very foolish."

"I wonder at you. I know what it was to break from all custom, old tradition — to renounce all that one had until now held sacred."

"But I," said Charlotte, "had never felt these things sacred."

"No?"

"No," repeated the Princess. "I thought we all have by God's grace the right to our own lives always — and freedom. I never believed in priests and I always thought one faith as good as another. And the Reformed Faith a deal more sincere. And I never could believe the plaster statues were the Mothers of God, or the little wax Christmas babies our Lord."

In these clumsy words, spoken with great earnestness, he saw now her strength, the calm force of her steadfast, honest unimaginative character, her common-sense view, unbiassed by sentiment, undazzled by tradition, unshaken alike by flattery and threat; the simplicity of her character pleased his mind, itself so tortured by a thousand intricacies of thought, and the boldness of her outlook a little amazed him, accustomed as he was to numberless sophistries, doubts, safer refinements of indecision and hesitations, both in his own innermost beliefs and those of the men whom he dealt with.

"And you have never repented your step, Mademoiselle?" he asked.

"Oh, no, truly not. I am happy here."

Yet he saw that there was an other longing besides the cause to which she had given such singular evidence of devotion.

"The religion was the excuse, was it not?"

"The excuse?"

"To leave the nun's life."

"Yes," said Charlotte slowly, "had I not been forced to be a nun I might have been content with the old faith. My whole sympathy, though, is with the Protestants and I shall ever be a true professor of the Reformed faith."

He believed her; there was great loyalty, he saw, in her character, as well as great frankness; she would be very sincere in all her dealings.

They came to a little stone seat beneath an ash tree just covered with the first black buds and seated themselves. Charlotte folded her hands in her lap; her attitude was very placid and peaceful; she looked childlike in her plain blue gown with the white ruffles; William found it pleasant to look at her; it was curious to think that she was an escaped nun, a personality regarded even by Protestants with a certain awe, almost with a certain horror.

And as he looked a sense of her sweetness, her softness touched him very deeply, he saw the gentle uses for which she was intended, the uses from which interest and bigotry had in vain tried to divert her; he imagined her as the centre of a home, as the mother of children, and the thought came to him — "If I had had such a woman these last years, how different my life would have been."

He spoke, prompted by these thoughts.

"Now you are in the world, Mademoiselle, will you do as the world does?"

She did not affect to misunderstand him.

"I wish to marry, Monsieur, when the time comes that one I can admire wishes for me, and to help in making life easy for one of your fighting men. But I am dowerless," she added with a smile.

"He who weds you will not look for a dowry," said William. "You have heard of my brother, Count Lodewyk, and his admiration of you?"

"I have seen him," she answered with great innocence. "He is not my suitor, Highness."

"Not openly as yet, he is afraid, because he has so little to offer."

She shook her head sadly. "Too much for me to accept."

"No, in worldly gear nothing," said William, "but in himself he is a knight for any maiden's dreams, Mademoiselle."

"I do believe it," she answered simply.

She looked around at him; he was gazing at her and as their glances met she faintly coloured but her eyes continued steadfast.

They were a strange contrast, she in her fresh untouched youth, fair and simple with her air of innocence and candour, in her spotless pale gown and her fragrant linen; he in his worn maturity, his shabby clothes, his dark face sad and thoughtful with many cares, his tired eyes, forever disillusioned, his reserved and practised manner, his trained courtesy; yet they had in common a certain ardour, a certain calm, for each had flung aside the shackles life had hung on them and now stood free.

And each nursed a dream; and though his was to free a nation, establish a religion and enthrone freedom so securely in Europe that no shock should shake her, and hers was but to have her own house and her man to tend and her baby in her arms, still each was equally sincere, equally deep rooted, equally passionate, and this gave them in common the steadfastness imparted by a burning desire and a deep resolve.

For even as William meant to accomplish his tremendous aims, so Charlotte meant to accomplish her trembling hidden hopes, but while he was active she was passive, while he strove she waited.

"If it should be Count Lodewyk," he said. "I should be glad."

"I thank you for that," she answered, "but you speak of what is not in the hearts of either of us, Monseigneur."

Again he was impressed and a little amazed by her calm, she seemed so untouched, so unmoved, yet so warmly of the world.

While he was silent she spoke again, as if she had completely dismissed Count Lodewyk from her thoughts.

"Your Highness leaves here today?"

His face became graver; he had allowed himself this rare interval of gentle distraction, this short repose, with a feeling of relief, and now he thought with distaste upon the resumption of his task. "If I had a home to go to, my own home," he thought strangely, "this work of mine would seem different to me."

The thoughts of the Princess were working on different lines.

"The Elector promised you the levies?" she asked with eagerness.

"He can do so little."

William smiled; he had heard that excuse, sometimes as now, touching, and sometimes insolent, so often.

"His good-will is much," he answered.

She leant forward a little, frowning, as was her habit when greatly interested.

"Your Highness has hopes from my country, from France?"

"France could do everything."

"Alas, that my people are Roman Catholic and on the side of Your Highness's enemies."

"At least you are not," he said.

He put out his hand and took hers.

"You are my friend, are you not? That is enough, Mademoiselle, good wishes such as yours do help as well as armies, that I do believe."

"But I would rather give you the armies," she smiled, again colouring a little and letting her small soft hand lie in his while she looked at him with her truthful eyes, so clear and earnest.

He kissed the fingers he held, then rose.

"I hope you will have good news of me," he said, "but you must expect bad, Mademoiselle. Meanwhile my pleasant hours pass, and I must leave Heidelberg."

She rose also and they looked at each other wistfully, as if they had more to say than words could at that moment express. Then they parted.

He returned to the Castle to take his leave and Charlotte remained in the garden.

The bright sunshine of the early day had now changed into a fitful light obscured by clouds, which, pale and colourless, formed a mist across the heavens, the air became chilly and the Princess drew closer across her bosom her little pelisse lined with fox fur.

Presently she began gathering the snowdrops and tying them up in tight posies.

Rénèe, who had not returned to the palace, now perceived she was alone and joined her; the chill spring light was not merciful to the waiting-woman; her florid beauty looked over-blown beside the youthful Princess in her neat freshness.

"The Prince has gone?" she asked.

"He has left to take his leave of the Elector," replied Charlotte.

She showed Rénèe her flowers, cold, fresh, virginal like herself; the other woman disliked these precise posies; she looked at the Princess.

"What a life is this!" she exclaimed.

Charlotte gave her a glance of surprise.

"Are you tired of Heidelberg?"

"Tired of life."

"Why?"

"Your Highness would not understand."

"I do not know," replied Charlotte gravely. "I understand what it is to be dull and unhappy; you forget how many years I was a nun."

Rénèe laughed bitterly.

"For longer years I have been a waiting-woman, exiled, dependent on charity."

"It is a weary life — it must be," said the Princess gently.

Rénèe was surprised, but not softened by her sympathy. "I think I will end it," she said with a great sigh.

"How can you?"

"Some way — any way — I could return to the Netherlands — even on foot, and die as others are dying, every day."

"You serve better by waiting — the tide will turn — perhaps soon."

"I am tired of waiting," said Rénèe passionately.

"I know — I know how tired I was, of the eventless life, the even days."

"But Your Highness," said Rénèe, still with some bitterness, "had the fortune to gain release."

"I had to make my own fortune."

"But you were a Princess, with powerful relatives, with champions, with friends. I have no one. I am so obscure no one cares if I live or die; why should they, since neither my living nor dying can make any difference to anyone."

She turned away abruptly, but not before the Princess had seen the tears in her eyes.

Charlotte, despite her simplicity, was trained to deal with others, to command and to comfort.

She put her hand on the elder woman's sleeve, and spoke, without attempting to look into her averted face.

"I do not know your special grief," she said gently, "but if it is mere loneliness — I know indeed what you suffer — believe me."

She paused a moment, then added sadly —

"Do you suppose that I am happy? Am I not also dependent on charity? Are these kind people my people? Or even of my nation? I also am homeless, penniless, cast out."

Rénèe was silent.

"If ever," continued the Princess simply, "I should have the happiness to have a home, you shall share it."

Rénèe turned and looked at her wildly.

"Truly Your Highness does not understand," she said in a low voice.

She turned very pale and clasped her hands tightly, struggling hard for control; how could anyone understand her wretched heart, her miserable secret? She sickened at herself and was sorry for her outspokenness with the intense regret of the long and deeply reserved.

"Your Highness must forgive me — I am not well today. These winds give me pains in my head — I speak more than I mean and of things I do not understand how to express."

She moved away; Charlotte, looking after, shook her head.

More than once this barrier had come between them. Friendly as they had been during their short acquaintance, Charlotte did not know, though Rénèe did, that it was the difference in their natures that came between them, Charlotte was incapable of feeling passion or even of understanding passion and Rénèe was capable of assuming, but not of feeling, the calm serenity that maintained the Princess through all her misfortunes.

Charlotte returned to the Castle and arranged her posies in her bare bed-chamber, then went to join the Electress in the still-room.

She did not even know exactly the hour when the Prince left the Castle, but Rénèe was at an upper window watching for his departure.

She saw him ride away, wrapped in the shabby cloak, on the shabby horse, and her gaze followed him until the walls of Heidelberg hid him from her view.

And her heart ached after him with a great and intolerable yearning.

If she could have ridden behind him — as his foot-boy — as his slave, if she could be with him, to soften ever so little his troubles and discomforts —

But she was useless — as ever useless.

And now he had gone and she must live on rumours again, such scraps of news as she could gather from people who never considered that she had any special interest in, or right to know of, the doings of William of Orange.

Long she remained looking from the window, her elbows on the sill, her face in her hands, her eyes gazing at the dull gray clouds that now filled the sky.

She recalled other times when she had watched him ride forth from his house in Brussels — his gold attire, his bright face, the gentlemen who had crowded around him; as she recalled these companions one by one, she counted men who had all fallen victims to the wrath and the guile of Philip.

Magnificent Egmont and stately Horne, who had died by public execution in the market-place; Berghen and Floris Montmorency, inveigled to Spain and strangled or poisoned

Egmont, left & Horne, right

in Spanish jails; Hoogstraaten and Adolphus of Nassau dead in battle; poor brave Brederode dead of a broken heart. Who now was left of all those gallant nobles who had defied the tyrant king and the bigot priest? None save these two ruined men, William and Lodewyk of Nassau.

"And how long have they?" thought Rénèe, "for they also are under the ban of Spain."

She trembled for the lonely rider she had just seen depart and the difficult tears washed the tired eyes that had so often wept for the Netherlands and William of Orange.

CHAPTER V

BROTHERS-IN-ARMS

WILLIAM, acting on a change of humour prompted by his visit to Heidelberg, decided not to go to Dillenburg.

The sight of those dear to him, his motherless children, the wrecks of his once princely establishment, always disturbed him — now he felt he could not face them — and with empty news, as always, news of fruitless effort, of achievement baulked, of plans come to nothing — to talk of further need of money, of fresh schemes raising it, to demand new sacrifices from those who had already sacrificed almost everything — to be reminded, most painfully, of his mad wife and his son a prisoner in the hands of Philip.

This time he would avoid these things.

He turned aside instead to a little village on the edge of the Nassau lands and went to the house of a certain miller who was one of his agents; with great labour William had constructed an elaborate system of spies and agents in Germany, France, and even in the Netherlands and Spain. He had been trained by Charles V and was no novice in ways of guile; despised and penniless as he was he yet had his emissary in the very cabinet of Philip.

It was to pay for these things that he wore a threadbare suit and rode a worn hack.

One of his posts or messengers was waiting at the mill for news. On meeting the Prince in person, he handed him a packet in cipher that had come slowly from Spain, having been slipped secretly from one faithful hand to another.

William finished the letter to his brother that had been interrupted by the entrance of Rénèe le Meung and added a postscript telling of his whereabouts and asking Count John to come there and see him — "as for the moment I have no courage for Dillenburg."

He sent this on by the messenger who had brought him the news from Spain and took up his lodging in the mill-house.

The place was curiously peaceful with that sense of utter detachment from the world found in some rustic spots that are unvisited by change or trouble. The mill-stream ran past the wooden house and the wooden mill, clear brown water running over clean brown stones and edged with rows of broken reeds and water flags.

Behind, the hill rose to a little forest of chestnut and hedges where the first wild roses showed; a little vineyard and a little vegetable garden were attached to the house, both, at present, bare, with the fresh earth newly turned and shadowed by the linen gowns of the miller's wife and daughter drying on high poles in the keen spring wind.

The mill-wheel, dark and dripping with weeds and slime stood on the other side of the house where the stream rushed past the rock on which the building stood.

Here the Prince must pass the empty hours, looking up at the high line of the bare chestnut trees against the cold blue sky, or down at the racing water and the dark banks lined with green, or further below where the girl knelt at the edge of the stream and beat the clothes on the large smooth stones.

Here, seated on a fallen log, he read the letter from Spain.

It told him little or nothing that he had not known or guessed before.

Spain was full of unrest, of dissatisfaction, of faction, the King was desperately in want of money, the people were bent beneath the load of taxation, the Court favourites absorbed all, Philip was driven by the monks — "like a blinded mule."

Yet, as William bitterly knew, the King had his secret obstinate principles and ideas from which not even monks could have moved him.

If the Pope himself had preached tolerance and mercy Philip would have given no heed; if an angel had appeared advising

Here, seated on a fallen log, he read the letter from Spain.

gentleness to the heretics, Philip would have quoted the Council of Trent as the yardstick by which to measure Christians and have gone his way.

His was the terrible strength of bigotry, of ignorance, of a nature unbalanced by unlimited power; his was the unswerving purpose of a nature corrupt and cruel to the inmost fibre, the diseased, half-insane product of a degenerate race.

William had never deceived himself into thinking of Philip as a puppet in the hands of men like Granvelle and Alva or women like the Princess of Eboli — Philip in himself was terrible, awful, and greatly to be feared.

His personal, ceaseless industry had woven the nets that had caught the grandees of the Netherlands; his personal flattery had lured the Roman Catholic Egmont to the block and the stout Berghen to his secret death; his personal wish had forced the Inquisition on the Netherlands and imposed those edicts which had made a hideous ruin of a prosperous country and condemned to deaths of a horror unspeakable thousands of those innocent of all save the desire of liberty of conscience.

He had had willing, greedy, and unscrupulous tools; but the mainspring of all their actions had been his own inexorable will, his unfaltering command, his pitiless intrigue, his insatiable cruelty.

Behind Alva, as behind Granvelle, was Philip, always Philip.

William knew that he had to struggle with Philip, Philip of Spain, that thin precise figure with the white face and reddish hair and beard, the bright blue eyes, and the underhanging jaw that he had known in the old days when he was friend and favourite of Charles V.

What use the corruption, the faction, the intrigue, the financial embarrassments of Spain while Philip continued to be her unquestioned ruler — his narrow policies might involve in ruin his own empire as well as the countries subject to him, but they would never yield.

No peace, no concord, no stable agreement could ever come to with Philip, who "would rather lose all his dominions than see them peopled with heretics," and who would never spare even his own in pursuance of his inflexible resolves, as he had not spared his miserable son. William had long ago faced this; he was fighting a foe who would never bend, who would spare no means to crush him, one who had stripped him of everything and was using infinite pains to deprive him of life itself. To fight Philip was like fighting wind and tide in a rudderless, sailless boat.

Yet the Prince of Orange never faltered in his belief that it could be done.

He slowly read the last part of the letter which contained details of the recent death of Horne's brother, Montigny.

He had died in prison, of an illness, it was said, but William had never believed this, and now his spy confirmed his suspicions.

The gallant young Netherlander, after long enduring the torture of a Spanish jail, had been secretly executed on the eve of Philip's third wife's entry into Spain.

The king knew that the dowager Countess of Horne had besought this bride, the Austrian Princess, to ask her son's life as a first favour from her husband and Philip had forestalled her petition.

Montigny had been strangled and so another struck off the list of those who waited his vengeance.

William folded up the paper and stared down into the swirling mill-stream.

A slow colour mounted into his face; Montigny had been his friend — well he recalled him, young, honourable, impetuous — a man who loved life. A man a few months married to one who loved him.

A brilliant life, a worthy life, full of fair hopes and promise — and because he had defied Philip it had ended in that gray prison scene, the fair young man in the hand of his enemies, the executioner putting the cord around his proud neck.

William mused bitterly; he wondered, if ever he should even partially succeed, whether any of his friends would be there to rejoice with him.

Even now there were so few . . . he felt curiously lonely; yet if only they left him Lodewyk, his beloved brother Lodewyk, and Henry, the boy who had so eagerly followed the fortunes of his older brothers, and John, the faithful loyal —

Could these but remain there might yet be happiness snatched from bereavement.

He wished Lodewyk would marry, and, thinking this, he thought of Charlotte de Bourbon.

She would make a man happy in his home; she was formed for that; his mind dwelt on her with great tenderness.

He had no passion, no romantic adorations to give any woman now — but he might need a wife. At this reflection he smiled to himself — she a renegade, a runaway nun, he a homeless exile — that would be a match to make Philip smile and Granvelle laugh.

And his wife lived, disgraced, mad, repudiated, she yet lived.

He thought of her with no pity; that loveless marriage of convenience had burnt itself out into bitter ashes indeed and he could rake no spark of sympathy nor kindness from them; but he thought of her son Maurice with affection — his only son, since that poor prisoner in Spain was out of reach of him and the Netherlanders.

But Maurice "who may live to complete what I can scarcely begin" — William dwelt on him with pride — a fine boy, though little more than a mere infant in years; and again he thought, he and the others would be better for a home and a gentle woman over them.

Count John came to the mill as fast as his horse could carry him, but the time of waiting in that placid place had seemed long to William, who almost regretted that he had not pushed on to Dillenburg.

They met outside the mill-house, on the rocky banks of the stream.

John of Nassau was the most ordinary member of his house, he had neither the genius of his older brother nor the force and fire of his younger brothers, but he was dearly loved by all, and his character, stalwart, loyal, industrious, sensible, and courageous, was felt by them to be something always stable

John of Nassau (1536-1606)

and unchanging in the midst of their shifting and desperate fortunes.

They could always turn to John, keeping up the home at Dillenburg, offering asylum and protection to the weaker members of the family, supplying what assistance he could.

He was not, perhaps, the man to have done what William and Lodewyk had done, but rather one to go peacefully with the tide, but this made his self-sacrifice the finer, for he had practically ruined himself for the cause which his brothers had embraced and staked all, without a complaint, in a quarrel that was none of his seeking.

The Prince often thought, with a gratitude that was not unlike remorse, of what the quiet John had done for him without a thought of recompense or return and in his heavy moments it seemed to him as if he had dragged the whole of his family into an undeserved ruin.

Today John was cheerful; his good-looking, blunt-featured face expressed elation and almost triumph and pleasure.

The brothers embraced and sat down on the short dry grass.

"It is so dark in those small rooms," said William, "and I have grown enamoured of the open air."

He asked after all at Dillenburg, and John answered with an eagerness that was almost impatience; it was plain that he had great news to impart.

"You have something to tell me?" asked the Prince keenly.

"Something that you should have known before," replied the other with a certain reproach, "but you keep us so short of news — we know not of your whereabouts from one week to another."

"It is not so easy to send messengers," said William, "wandering as I do in disguise from place to place through unfriendly countries. Now give me your news and hearten me."

His worn face slightly flushed in response to the obvious excitement of his brother's.

"Guess," said John, "from where comes this good news."

"From England?"

"No, their game is too cautious — they play but for their own profit — it is no great nation, but your Sea Beggars who have brought you success."

"The Sea Beggars?" said William and the light died from his eyes.

He had no faith in these pirates who sailed his flag and held his charter and had long since dismissed them from his mind as of no profit and some disgrace to his cause.

Under his right as a sovereign Prince he had some years ago issued "letters of mark" to a number of Netherland nobles, with the idea that the ships they commanded would form the nucleus of a navy to annoy Philip and defend the Low Countries.

But his mandates had been disobeyed and his authority defied, and the Sea Beggars, as they called themselves, in reference to the old party name of Granvelle's day, had degenerated into pirates, whose excesses had dishonoured their flag and whose plunder went no further than their own pockets.

In vain William had protested and had twice changed their commander and furnished them with a code of conduct, yet they remained the terror of the seas and carried the standard of Nassau into many an act of robbery and violence.

The last that William had heard of them was that Elizabeth of England, in deference either to the continued protests of Philip, or because of the behaviour of the pirates themselves had closed her ports to them and that they were, from then on without harbours or any refuge, and compelled to remain on the High Seas, without a base, and depending on coast raids. Yet now his brother told him that these ruffians, lately reduced to desperation, had brought him success.

"I had not looked to hear good news from De la Marck," smiled William.

John laid his capable hand on his brother's shabby sleeve.

"He has descended on Brill — captured the Spanish garrison, received the keys in your name and hoisted your flag."

William coloured swiftly.

"De la Marck has done this?" he exclaimed, and he thought of the despair and contempt with which he had until now regarded

The Taking of Brill in 1572

his Admiral — as a useless instrument he had always considered him.

"Yes. We now have a base in the Netherlands, a town we can call our own. It is a great thing — the turning of the tide."

For one sweet moment William shared his brother's enthusiasm; he saw this success as the beginning of a real change of fortune — himself taking up, by will of the people, the former stadtholderships he had held, Holland, Zeeland, and Utrecht — then his native prudence, strengthened by so many disappointments and such great misfortunes, cast down his spirits.

"Can one trust De la Marck or his Beggars?" he asked sadly. "The thing is hasty, I will not build on it. I have better hopes in this tax of Alva, which he is resolved to enforce and which greatly rouses the Netherlands."

"That also works in our favour," agreed John. "There has not been so much dissatisfaction since Alva began to rule."

"That I count on — not on De la Marck!"

"But you are wrong," said John earnestly. "Have you heard Lodewyk's news?"

"He is still at La Rochelle?"

"No — but descending into the Netherlands on Mons — he too, they say, called the Beggars hasty, but he is endeavouring to follow up their success. I believe he has affected some agreement with the French Huguenots, but his letters are brief."

"I have not heard from him for so long that his letters must have missed me. What are his men?"

"I do not know; the news was brought to me by Godfrey. You remember him? He knew so little."

William sat thoughtful, staring into the stream that flowed beneath him.

"Lodewyk was ever sanguine," he said with a slow tenderness, "and so he would fall on Mons, eh?"

"And you?" asked John.

"You would ask what I have done? I rely on Coligny, John — he is a great man, a great power, and may bring a quarter of France to our aid, the Protestant faction is strong there."

"And the King — the Queen-Mother?"

"I believe that they may think it wise to conclude a Protestant alliance — the marriage between the King's sister and the King of Navarre seems likely to be accomplished."

"You trust them?"

"No, — but I believe that expediency will force them to act in our interests — and on Coligny I do rely."

"Lodewyk writes the same. I think this time we hold a charter to hope."

William smiled and said nothing; he was already revolving in his mind how he might turn to account the capture of Brill and the advance of Lodewyk; neither of them was an action which he would have advised, but desperation had made him an opportunist.

"What will you do?" asked John.

"I must consider a little while," replied the Prince; he rose and gave his brother his hand, "let us go into the house and taste their dinner."

As they turned towards the mill he spoke again and abruptly.

"What of the Princess — Anne, my wife?"

"She is at Beilstein still, under restraint — partially."

"She should be wholly so — we maintain her?"

"Yes — it is a heavy drain, William, her mad fancies cost dearly."

"She shall," replied the Prince with a most unusual force, "be returned to her people. And Jan Rubens?"

"Is still in prison."

"Let him go — to punish him would be to make the affair public, and, poor fool, we know whose fault it was."

"She did confess as much when writing to me to intercede for her."

"I will never," said William, "see her again — from all my being she is blotted out. Yet I would have her honour kept very secret, for the sake of the name — and of Maurice."

"It is not breathed abroad, I have been careful as to that."

The Prince warmly pressed his brother's hand, and the two stooping their comely heads entered the low door of the mill-house.

CHAPTER VI

THE TURNING TIDE

THAT spring of 1572 was a time of great hope and even joyousness for the until then apparently lost cause of the Protestants and their leaders, the Nassau Princes and Admiral Coligny.

The bold capture of Brill, though accompanied by outrages and cruelties on the part of De la Marck and his seamen, which disgraced their success, still had undoubtedly been a turning-point in the long struggle between Philip and his Dutch subjects.

The rebels now possessed a town, had proclaimed their leader Stadtholder of three provinces and held a stronghold in the Netherlands, as the Huguenots held La Rochelle in France. Never had the country been more favourably inclined to throw off the dominion of Philip, never had Alva been so unpopular, nor his agents so hated.

The tax of the tenth penny, proclaimed some time ago, but not so far enforced, had done more to rouse the people even than persecution and cruelty, injustice and the Inquisition; even the weak and worldly, those who were prepared to abjure their faith and their convictions, those who had stood aside from their brothers through fear, were not prepared to submit to a tax that struck at the roots of their livelihood, and the menace of revolt, once silenced with blood and tears, was again heard threatening Philip from Zeeland to Brabant. But Alva was desperate as well as pitiless; he could get no money from Spain and did not hesitate in the ruthless, but to him agreeable, expedient of wringing the last drops of blood from the country crushed by the force of his tyranny.

The tax was enforced with great vigour, men now suffered for their property as they had formerly suffered for their religion,

Fernando Alvarez de Toledo (1508-1582) the Duke of Alva

tradesmen who had proved obdurate were hanged outside their shops, merchants who protested were denounced to the Inquisition and hurried away to a secret death.

None the less the money came in slowly and the mutterings of revolt grew louder, and Alva, though he sincerely believed the Netherlanders crushed and the Prince of Orange broken, was angry enough to increase his cruelties and thereby the hatred felt against him, his master, and his servants.

The capture of the Brill had been a rude blow to Spanish pride and now Lodewyk of Nassau was advancing on Mons with an army of French Huguenots, and a high tide of enthusiasm was rising for the Protestant cause and the Prince of Orange.

St. Aldegonde's song "William of Nassau" was spreading through the provinces, and not all the efforts of Alva's agents could extinguish the brave and hopeful strains of what speedily became the hymn of a people in bondage and straining at their chains.

William of Nassau, scion
Sprung of an ancient line,
I dedicate undying
Faith to this land of mine.
A prince I am, undaunted,
Of Orange, ever free.
The king of Spain I've granted
My lifelong loyalty.

I've ever tried to live in
The fear of God's command,
And therefore I've been driven
From people, home, and land.
But God, I trust, will rate me
His willing instrument
And one day reinstate me
Into my government.

Let no despair betray you,
My subjects true and good.
The Lord will surely stay you
Though now you are pursued.
He who would live devoutly
Must pray God day and night
To throw His power about me
As champion of your right.

William himself was not idle; he did not wholly approve of the capture of the Brill, nor at all of the men who had done it, nor was his brother's impetuous march into Flanders entirely to his mind, but though himself cautious and prudent to a fault, he knew how to take advantage of the reckless actions of other men. His pamphlets, inciting citizens to protest and towns to revolt, were distributed, despite Alva's precautions, in the length and breadth of the Netherlands, and many a bold lampoon and pointed pasquinade found its way into the palace at Brussels and into the Viceroy's own hand, as formerly they had found their way into Cardinal Granvelle's cabinet, and proved that the spirits of the Netherlanders were not yet wholly crushed nor their printing presses wholly silenced.

Abroad also, politics now favoured the Reformed Faith. Elizabeth of England, despite the recent closing of her ports to the Sea Beggars, was not on friendly terms with Philip, whose dismissal of her ambassador to Madrid she chose to regard as an affront, and she held out more than one tentative and secret hope that she might help the Netherlanders when they had a little further helped themselves. William did not place much reliance on these half-promises, knowing that the haughty Queen of England cared for neither rebels nor Calvinists and was certainly not ever likely to espouse a losing cause. At the same time she had good reason to both hate and fear Philip and might easily ally herself with any rising power which should threaten his dominion; the daughter of the Englishwoman who had displaced a Spanish Princess, the Protestant who was regarded by Roman Catholics as illegitimate could not have anything but expediency in common with Philip of Spain, who had burnt alive and tortured to death many a less ardent Protestant than was Elizabeth of England herself.

But the Prince of Orange's greatest hopes were fixed on France.

It seemed that finally the shifting, dubious policies of the Italian Queen-Mother had decided on a pacific course with regard to the powerful party of the Protestants within her kingdom.

The marriage of her daughter Margaret, with Henry, son of Antony de Bourbon and the heroic Jeanne D'Albret, Queen of Navarre, was finally arranged and to take place that autumn; Coligny and his faction were more or less in favour and William's representations on behalf of the provinces listened to at least graciously.

It appeared not to be ungrateful to the Queen-Mother to put forward one of her younger sons as competitor for the sovereignty of the Netherlands when they should be wrested from Spain, nor was she at all averse to dealing underhand mischief to Philip. William of Orange cared for none of these intrigues, despised all these motives, but he believed that he could not free the Province without powerful foreign aid, and to obtain this he was prepared to make many a sacrifice. He was willing to himself step into the background and offer the crown of the Netherlands to any Prince who would take them under his protection; he knew, in his heart, that while he lived, any such King would be only a puppet, and he had long since taken the measure of the degenerate half-insane princes of the House of Valois, yet he was prepared to use any of these who might come forward, prepared to flatter them, to outwardly defer to them, to invest them with all show of authority as long as he could obtain the alliance of France to set against the might of Spain.

Not all his advisers agreed with him in this, but William did not see how he could succeed alone in the task he had undertaken. If at first, when he threw down the gage to Philip, he had ever cherished such dreams — which is not likely — he would now have long dismissed them with other illusions of his youth. If he had ever thought of himself as wresting the Netherlanders from Philip and making himself their ruler as well as their liberator, that idea had been long ago abandoned.

Too clearly did he see the difficulties, too well did he measure the obstacles, his temperament was too calm, his outlook too wide for him to be dazzled by such dreams.

Yet he was not sluggish or half-hearted in the cause in which he had staked and lost all — he knew he was fighting the Lord's battles.

The spring had not blossomed into summer before he had once more taken the field and was marching towards Mons to effect a juncture with Lodewyk, who had now forced Mondvagon, the commander of the garrison, to surrender, and himself occupied the town.

William's troops were partly German mercenaries and partly levies supplied by the rebellious provinces of Holland and Zeeland, who had accepted him again as their stadtholder, ignoring Philip's nominee, Count van Bossu.

Money began to come in, some provided by the State, some offered by private individuals, and even William was encouraged.

He was still, by a ludicrous adhesion to formula, acting as Philip's lieutenant, as such he had been received by the estates "without prejudice to any of the customs and rights of the land," so, bound by judicial convention and the laws of the states he was defending, William defied Philip in Philip's name and carried on a revolution in the outward symbol of the power he was rebelling against.

Delay followed delay, as was usual and indeed inevitable in these dealings in local politics, before sufficient supplies were guaranteed to enable William to proceed in his campaign.

Lodewyk was beleaguered in Mons, and as yet his brother was not strong enough to attempt to relieve him.

When at last the supplies came William crossed the Meuse and occupied Diest, Tirlemont, Louvain, and Mechlin, which last town opened its gates and accepted his authority.

William had now every hope of being able to raise the siege of Mons, join his brother and march through the Netherlands, delivering the towns and calling the people to his standard as he proceeded.

He sat in his little tent this still August night and read letters from Admiral Coligny, promising him three thousand foot and twelve thousand arquebusiers which he was levying to help Lodewyk in Mons.

William could not restrain a leap of the heart as he read the news, he allowed his fortitude to relax and his hopes to paint a glorious future; at last — at last . . .

"Why not?" he asked himself. Men's affairs did turn, it was possible that after all he was born to achieve and succeed.

He and Coligny, the two of them together, could they not do something?

He had always believed in Coligny.

The letter hung slackly in his hand, his eyes became absent as he stared at the canvas of the lamp-lit tent, imagining what might yet be — the terms he might wring from Alva and force from Philip.

Freedom — liberty of conscience, the end of persecution, of bloodshed, the return of prosperity, thriving cities with their busy market towns, a flourishing country-side, a new kingdom founded in freedom, inviolate in that freedom, growing, becoming powerful, respected, while such tyrannies as those of Philip decayed from their own inward rottenness and sank into contempt and then into oblivion.

A mad dream, a wild impossible dream — yet such things had been. "Will not God use my wretched efforts to lay the foundation of such a kingdom as I dream of? Will not He use my puny blows to sound the knell of Spain?"

So he mused; for all his astuteness and caution there was a quiet confidence that responded to the unseen forces about him; tonight he felt them strongly — angels seemed to fill the close tent and whisper auguries of success. This sense of being in God's protection was strong when suddenly he heard some noise. The tent flap was raised and a strange face was looking in on him, a face illumined by the lamp and outlined against the darkness of the moonless summer night, a face yellow, haggard and lit by a melancholy smile and surrounded by lank wisps of hair.

"The Prince of Orange dreams?" said this stranger and advanced into the tent.

William regarded him steadily; the newcomer was a tall man whose ragged attire was partially concealed by a large shabby black cloak.

"His Princely Grace is ill-guarded," he continued in a tone between insolence and fawning.

William put his hand on his dagger; he thought this was one of Philip's assassins; with his senses all alert he waited.

The stranger spread out his arms, which had been folded in his mantle, and thus showed that he was weaponless.

"I am harmless," he said.

He was indeed such a poor thin and miserable creature that William's curiosity was mingled with pity.

"What strange errand have you come upon?" he asked.

The other folded his arms again and gazed at him searchingly.

"You do not remember me?"

"No."

"Yet we have many memories in common," replied the stranger. "I am a wise man, an astrologer."

William looked at him with interest.

"Now I recall you — the alchemist's assistant — Duprès."

"Indeed."

The Prince was interested in this fellow who had appeared in some scenes of his life. He had been present at his fatal marriage in Leipzig and at the fatal battle of Heiligerlee when the first Nassau sacrifice had been made. He thought of the fourth stanza of St. Aldegonde's song:

> *Life and my all for others*
> *I sacrificed, for you!*
> *And my illustrious brothers*
> *Proved their devotion too.*
> *Count Adolph, more's the pity,*
> *Fell in the Frisian fray,*
> *And in the eternal city*
> *Awaits the judgment day.*

"Sit down and talk to me," he said.

William was seated on a folding camp chair of leather; behind him was a little desk covered with papers. He had put aside his mantle, for the night was oppressively hot, and his slight figure was clad in the brown cloth suit worn beneath armour, spurs were on his high dusty soft boots and a crumpled collar of white lawn showed above the tight lacing of the high coat. His face, tanned above pallor, was thin, almost hollow, the dark powerful eyes were marred and shadowed, the rich dark hair was mingled with gray on the temples, he bore his forty years heavily and seemed a man whose youth was utterly gone. There was little trace now of the splendid young Prince who had come to Leipzig to marry Anne of Saxony, nor of the magnificent Grandee who had held his court in Brussels during the rule of Margaret of Parma.

"We have come to much the same level, Prince," said Duprès.

"You are a strange fellow," answered William. "Why are you in my camp?"

"I am like a dog, I follow where there is meat and drink."

"That is more the jackal's part."

"I am your jackal then."

William laughed.

"What did you come to tell me?"

"Your future if you will."

"God takes care of my future."

"Yet you cannot foresee tomorrow."

"No, I can't."

"Your Highness has much courage," said the astrologer. "Do you foresee your future before you?"

"I believe," replied William, "that I shall no more escape Philip than my friends have escaped him, whom you have seen fall one by one."

"And Count Lodewyk?"

"Lodewyk and Henry and John," said the Prince. "I think the whole House of Nassau is dedicated to sacrifice, as God sees fit."

Duprès did not answer and William too was silent, staring at the strange figure of the man who had come so suddenly upon his path. No prophecies could frighten the Prince. He trusted his God, as Aldegonde had also captured so beautifully:

Steadfast my heart remaineth
In my adversity.
My princely courage straineth
All nerves to live and be.
I've prayed the Lord my Master
With fervid heart and tense
To save me from disaster
And prove my innocence.

Alas, my flock! To sever
Is hard on us. Farewell.
Your Shepherd wakes, wherever
Dispersed you may dwell.
Pray God that He may ease you;
His Gospel be your cure.
Walk in the steps of Jesu.
This life will not endure.

William was confident that he might accomplish much yet. He also cherished a secret hope that the young Lodewyk and the boyish Henry would be spared and see the triumphs of a freed country.

Duprès looked at him —

"And Coligny?" he said. "What does Your Highness expect of Coligny?"

William was startled.

"I have much confidence in him," he answered quickly.

"You hope much from France?"

"That is common knowledge."

Duprès looked at him long and earnestly as he replied —

"It would be wise for Your Highness to rely on none but yourself — so you will best escape disappointment."

"No! I have learned to rely more on God. In His time He will make all things well."

Duprès bowed and left the tent as silently as he had entered.

The Prince turned again to the Admiral's letter; his mood was one of elation — he seemed to hear drum beats and the cries of victory and all the ill-lit gloom of his tent was filled with the joyous light of the dawn of another and triumphant day.

CHAPTER VII

AUGUST, 1572

A GREAT heat fell over the land; the moon seemed to burn with as great a radiance as the sun, for the nights were as stifling as the days.

The army of William of Orange moved forward under the blazing skies, always towards Mons.

As yet Alva had made no sign; they were unopposed, and at first everywhere the peasants rose to welcome them, believing that justice would follow in the wake of the banner of the Prince of Orange.

But William's advance began soon to be attended with the difficulties and perils inseparable from his enterprise and the humiliations always attendant on a leader of mercenaries.

Excess, pillage, murder, and ruin began to mark the track of his army and he was as powerless to control the men he led as he had been powerless to control the wild pirates of De la Marck.

The villagers began to flee at their approach, the towns to shut their gates, preferring the tenth penny tax to the mercy of the German mercenaries. But William refused to be disheartened, even when Philip Marnix, Lord of St. Aldegonde, was discouraged and fell into a melancholy.

St. Aldegonde was, after the Nassau brothers, the Prince's truest friend and most trusted councillor. His eloquent pen was always at William's service and the song of his writing had proved of material service in furthering the cause of the rebels in the Netherlands.

To his sensitive and gentle nature the conduct of the Prince's troops was a bitter grief.

He even ventured to remonstrate with the Prince for taking things too easily.

The little invading army had pressed on within two leagues of Mons; between them and the city was the army of Alva, under the command of Don Frederic de Toledo, his son.

Scouts had reported that their headquarters were at the little village of St. Florin, near one of the town gates.

William was cautiously making for this point; when the reinforcements arrived from France he intended to fall on the Spaniards and force his way into his brother in Mons.

He had already managed to send a letter to Lodewyk in which he conjured him to hold out until the arrival of Coligny and the Huguenots, and Lodewyk had replied cheerfully; his faith was also placed on the French.

The Prince's lodging was in a deserted farmhouse of yellowish brick with white paintings and green shutters that stood amid low lush pastures and short poplar trees.

The rambling out-buildings were occupied by troops and horses; none of the farm creatures were left save only the great flock of white pigeons that flew in and out of their half-ruined houses and fluttered to and fro in the big brick-paved courtyard.

It was on to this courtyard that the Prince's chamber looked — a low pleasant chamber with whitewashed walls and wooden floor, the bed and furniture covered with coarse blue and white cotton.

In the centre of one wall stood the large white china stove, opposite a big black linen press with drawers full of fine napery; on the deep window-sill stood jars of blue pottery full of herbs and dried flowers.

The Prince's residence had little changed the room; he had touched nothing; his mantle over the bed, his pistols on the bureau, his dog asleep in the square of sunlight on the floor, and a wallet full of papers on the linen press were the only signs of his occupation.

He had been several hours in the saddle, inspecting his army, and was tired.

He sat at the window, reclining in one of the deep old wand-bottomed chairs with arms; the rough white curtain shielded him from the sun that blazed against the thick diamond panes.

When St. Aldegonde entered he hardly turned his head; he was interested in watching the innocent play of the pigeons below as they chased each other across the warm bricks, ruffling their breasts and spreading their tails.

St. Aldegonde saw his Prince's fatigue, but was too full of his subject to refrain from speaking.

"Your Highness is pleased with your men?" he asked with some abruptness.

William slightly lifted his shoulders and did not answer.

"You are too easy," said Philip Marnix.

William smiled; he was still looking at the pigeons.

"I mean that, Highness," added his friend, slightly vexed.

William looked at him with sudden keenness; it occurred to him, with a touch of bitter humour, that he had always been too easy — to all, from his wife to his dog, it was proof of it that Philip Marnix was so talking to him now.

"Go on with the indictment," he said, and again looked from the window.

St. Aldegonde was in earnest; he spoke of what had long rankled in his heart and disturbed his conscience.

"It were better for you to be as formerly," he said, "without a sword to answer your call, than to lead these cut-throats."

William did not answer.

"Your soldiers," continued St. Aldegonde, "commit the very wrongs they come to redress."

"It is one of the ironies of life," replied the Prince, "that evil must be fought with evil."

The idealist would not listen.

"You cover yourself with discredit — you make your approach dreaded as much as the approach of Alva," he said.

"What would you have me do?" asked William. "Dismiss these mercenaries and wait to be captured by the Spanish — abandon Lodewyk and fly back to Dillenburg?"

"There should be control, discipline, punishment," said Philip Marnix.

The Prince looked at him sternly, and spoke, contrary to his custom, with force and some passion.

"Have you not seen for yourself that I have tried these! If I were a great and sovereign Prince I might hang every man who touched the property of the poorest kind — I might make myself obeyed and feared. But I am a poor adventurer, St. Aldegonde, whose pay is miserable and whose authority is dubious. I am a rebel defying a great king — a man outlawed and exiled, shall I then get any but the desperate and the undisciplined to fight for me?"

"You have the greatest cause in the world!" cried Philip Marnix —"the cause of liberty."

"Find me saints and angels to sustain me," replied the Prince, "and we will keep this cause unsullied, but while I have to buy human assistance I shall have such an army as this I lead now. Do you not see it, Philip?"

"I see, Highness, nothing but confusion," replied his friend bitterly.

"You take too near a view — look ahead and see the thing in the broad."

Philip Marnix walked up and down the polished floor,

"De la Marck — do you approve of him?"

The Prince raised his eyebrows but answered gravely, "The capture of the Brill has proved a turning-point for us."

"And a shame also. How many martyrs may the Roman Catholics make from De la Marck's victims? Did he not behead four Spanish captains?"

"Two for Egmont and two for Horne," said William with a smile. "And what of it? Do you think that this issue will be decided with kind words and by gentle deeds? Do you think that all the fiends of hate and vengeance and jealousy and madness that Philip and Philip's men have roused in these wretched countries, can be easily silenced, easily chained? This was a peaceful people — if monks are murdered, blame the Inquisition which made the name of monk an infamy; if churches are sacked, blame the hideous deeds that were committed in the name of God; if the poor and helpless are wronged and slain, blame that tyranny which showed how little value the humble had in the eyes of Princes and of Governments."

He spoke quietly but with force and his words brought the colour into his thin face.

"You will then take any means to your end?" asked St. Aldegonde.

"I must take the only means or stand aside with folded hands."

"Is this the only means? You are Stadtholder again of three provinces, do you need men like De la Marck — troops like these German mercenaries?"

The Prince smiled at his friend's earnestness, which had something childish and pathetic in it.

"I do indeed," he answered. "Do you think that I am yet on stable ground?"

Philip Marnix looked away with a clouded face.

"At least Coligny is a clean ally," he said.

"Coligny, yes!" answered William, "and his soldiers are men who fight not for money but for our faith — but they are not enough."

He rose, stretched himself and looked out of the window; he was ever in the hopes of seeing a messenger from the Admiral telling of his near approach; William had expected the arrival of the Huguenots before this, in as much as it had been agreed that the attack on the Spanish was to wait until French help was available and Lodewyk would not be able to hold Mons much longer.

In the courtyard sat Duprès, the so-called astrologer, who had attached himself to the camp, where he was tolerated because of the rather terrible amusement to be derived from his dark profession, which he was always willing to exercise in exchange for food, clothes, or a handful of white money.

William left the impudent melancholy man, whom he earlier had sheltered so long in his palace. That Duprès had repaid this protection by allowing the Princess of Orange to use his laboratory as a place of rendezvous with the young lawyer,

Gaspard de Coligny (1519-1572)

Jan Rubens, William did not know. So indifferent was he to the doings of little people that he would probably have cared nothing had he been aware of the charlatan's intrigues.

He now called St. Aldegonde and pointed out the tall thin figure of the strange man, seated huddled on the base of the wall that ran around the courtyard.

"Behold a fool, a jester, and an astrologer," he smiled.

"Your Highness is too easy," Philip Marnix repeated.

"While we live in the world we must use some things of the world," said William.

Philip Marnix of
St Aldegonde
(1540-1598)

"You are in a good mood," replied St. Aldegonde, still unwon.

"Oh, Philip, I do feel within me the portents of success. Shall we not all be happy when Coligny comes?"

He took his friend's arm with a loving pressure and St. Aldegonde smiled.

William's personality was stronger than his cause in winning men.

That evening arrived the stupendous news that on the eve of St. Bartholomew's and the wedding day of Margaret de Valois and Henry of Navarre all the Huguenots in Paris had been massacred by order of the Queen-Mother and that Admiral Coligny, after having been butchered in his own home, had been flung from the window amid the insults of his assassins and then dragged to the public gallows.

CHAPTER VIII

THE FUGITIVES

FOR the first time in his career William was stunned by the extent of his misfortune; he remained, as did all the Protestants of Europe, bewildered and amazed.

The thing was so incredible, so unparalleled, so sudden, had been prepared with such cunning secrecy, that it silenced like a blow delivered in the dark. Catherine de Medici had completely deceived the Protestants, who were rejoicing at her alliance and at the marriage of her daughter with the Huguenot King of Navarre at the very moment when she was planning their utter destruction.

And utter destruction it had been; the defenceless victims gathered in Paris for the marriage festivities had no chance of resistance nor of escape; in the streets, houses, shops, in the palace itself they were butchered where they stood and the lunatic king himself sat at his window and fired on the wretched fugitives in the courtyard.

The Admiral and his son-in-law had died a hideous and ignominious death and with them ended the party of the Huguenots in France.

William saw that very clearly. What had been a compact powerful movement led by a man of enthusiasm and genius had now ceased to exist, nor was there any hope that it might be re-created — at least not for many years.

The flame of the Reformed Faith that had burnt so bravely and steadily in France was now quenched in blood; the Netherlands must look elsewhere for help.

At one blow William's strongest hopes had been swept away.

He could almost hear Philip's laughter and Granvelle's words of triumph; no reinforcements would come from France, no encouragement from Coligny. He stood alone, isolated with his little mercenary army, more or less in Alva's power.

And Lodewyk too had been counting on French help, and Lodewyk had loved Coligny; William's heart ached for his brother facing this in the beleaguered city. The morning after he had received the news he sent again for the messenger that he might hear the incredible, horrible thing in full detail.

This messenger was an agent or spy of his own whose post was on the French frontier; he had heard the awful story from some half-insane survivors who had fled from Paris and had at once travelled into the low Countries to inform the Prince, whose ordinary agencies would not be able to get the news through for some time yet; he had brought with him some of these fugitives, who were lodging now at the village of Hermigny, near the camp.

William received this man, Joost van Rengers, who had been long in his employ, in his room in the farmhouse.

The shock of the news had told on the Prince; he was pale and swollen-lidded from a sleepless night and moved heavily with his chin a little sunk on his breast.

Van Rengers could tell him no more, he knew nothing beyond the bare facts; he stood, a depressed little elderly man, sadly eyeing his master over the edge of his stiff white collar.

"And Coligny, you do not know how Coligny died?"

"Only that he was murdered, Highness; they told different tales. But he was killed and thrown from the window and afterwards hung on the gallows."

William could still hardly believe it; hardly credit that he had been so utterly deceived in his estimate of the French Court and what they would do. If this was Philip's doing, if he had engineered this to prevent the Huguenots bringing help to the Netherlanders, then, William admitted, this time he had been outwitted by the cunning of the Escurial; the blood rushed to his face with this thought and he stared with angry eyes at Van Rengers.

"So they killed him — butchered him like a rat in a corner. Poor, brave Coligny! He has gone after the others. As I likely will go."

"God forbid!" cried Van Rengers.

"Ah," — said the Prince in a strange voice. "Why should God save me in preference to the others?"

The old Netherlander was not at a loss.

"Because Your Highness is the very staff and support of a whole nation. What matter if the tree be lopped of its branches if the trunk remain?"

William did not answer; he shaded his tired eyes with his hand and looked down at the floor. He was recalling a certain day in the woods of Vincennes when he had ridden with the King of France and Henry had spoken in rash confidence of a scheme undertaken in conjunction with Spain for secretly planning a massacre of "these pestilent Huguenots."

William, shocked and startled, had held his peace, but from then on he had felt that interest in, and sympathy for, the persecuted Protestants to whom he was now the guiding star.

Yet he had allowed himself to be fooled, to be taken unawares and unprepared; he had never trusted France any more than he had trusted Spain . . . yet he had been fooled.

Not an inkling of Catherine de Medici's purpose had leaked out, nor from the cabinets of the Escurial had a single word of warning issued.

His spies had been at fault, his costly and elaborate system of secret service had failed.

And Lodewyk was trapped in Mons and he was trapped outside, and Alva had but to move to crush them both.

William, in the bitterness of his grief and disappointment, felt himself a useless fool.

"I am no general and no statesman," he thought passionately, "and I had better give up this hopeless task."

Van Rengers, looking at him wistfully, waited for his further word.

The Prince roused himself to speak.

"You know nothing more, no details — nothing of what happened in the palace?"

"I only know the stories they tell, Your Grace."

"The King of Navarre escaped?"

"Through good fortune and no lack of pains on the part of the Roman Catholics. Most of his companions were slain."

"And the King was cognisant of this?"

"With his own hand he shot his subjects down," said the old man solemnly. "Many saw him, leaning from a window of the Louvre with a smoking carbine in his hand and shouting, 'Kill! Kill!' "

"He is insane," said William.

"Yes," replied the Netherlander sadly, "but he is King of France."

The Prince looked sharply at him.

"You are right," he said, "these madmen must be dealt with."

He sighed and glanced out of the window, where the bright sun sucked up the morning mists and dissolved them in golden vapour.

The meagreness of Van Rengers' account disappointed him; he longed to know every detail of St. Bartholomew, to satisfy himself that this horror had really befallen, that Coligny was really dead.

"You can tell me no more?" he asked. Van Rengers saw his dissatisfaction.

"I have those under my protection who could tell Your Highness everything."

"The fugitives?"

"Yes."

"Why did you bring them here?" asked William sadly, "we can do nothing for any."

"Highness, these are two women —"

"Women!"

"Indeed, women of gentle nature. They had no escort but myself and I was engaged to find Your Highness. So they accompanied me, but I think their thought was Switzerland where one has friends."

"It was from Paris they fled?"

"Yes, Highness."

"Who are they? I may know their names."

"I have sworn," said Van Rengers humbly, "not to give their names, but if Your Highness will visit them I believe that they will tell you everything."

"Where are they?"

"At Hermigny."

"We push on there tonight and make that our headquarters, since I alone must attempt to relieve Lodewyk."

"Will Your Grace see them?"

"If they will allow me. Go ahead and acquaint them of my coming, Van Rengers."

That evening when the camp was struck and the little army moving nearer Mons, William rode to the tiny village of Hermigny and stopped at the humble cottage where the fugitives from Paris sheltered. Van Rengers, who had conducted him, ushered him into the kitchen and left.

A peasant woman was setting yellow bowls and wooden spoons on the round wooden table; she hastened shyly through a side door as William entered.

The place was very poor and made the Prince's lodging seem luxurious by contrast; a dim oil lamp of rough pottery gave the only light, the plaster walls were filled by rude shelves of crockery; in the wide open fireplace burnt a few boughs and sticks, over which hung an iron pot on a tripod.

So bad was the light that for a moment William did not see a girl who sat on a bench inside the ingle-nook and who was intently regarding him. When he observed her she moved and came forward into the room.

She was no more than seventeen, very delicate, fair with the ashen fairness of some French women, her features were firmly marked, her eyes large and pale blue, her lips full.

Her gown was of a coarse dark woollen stuff, too large and fastened by a leather girdle; her hair was carelessly held by a few pins and strands of it fell on to her shoulders.

Her face was strained and sunken like the countenance of one disfigured by a severe illness; she looked at William without smiling.

Her desolate and pathetic appearance touched his heart; looking into her tragic eyes he could guess what St. Bartholomew had been. "Mademoiselle" —

She interrupted.

"I am a widow, Monseigneur. Your brother was at my wedding."

"My brother?"

"Count Lodewyk — you are the Prince of Orange, are you not?"

"Yes."

"Your brother, then. A few months ago he was at my wedding."

William looked at her; she had flushed a little now and stood near enough to the yellow glow of the lamp for him to see that her features were swollen and her eyes bloodshot with weeping.

"Why did Your Highness come?" she asked, without either smile or resentment, but dully, like one who has ceased to feel much.

"I hold myself the friend of all who suffer for Coligny," he said.

At that name she winced.

"I am Louise de Coligny," she said.

"The Admiral's daughter?"

"His daughter and Charles de Teligny's widow. Both are dead, Monseigneur, both murdered."

For a moment he was too moved for speech; he raised her slack damp hand and pressed it closely between his and gazed into her face; in the delicate features of the daughter he could trace a touching resemblance to the father's noble countenance.

The girl's tears overflowed again and ran slowly down her marred cheeks.

"I loved your father," said William.

"I know. He spoke of you so often."

"I thought to meet him before Mons."

"To the last that was his intention — He was most hopeful of this enterprise."

Louise de Coligny (1555-1620)

She withdrew her hand from his and seated herself at the table, supporting her chin in her palm.

"And now he is gone — is dead," she said, "he and Charles — Your Highness has heard of my husband?"

"Monsieur de Teligny — he whom the Queen of Navarre sent to Joüarrs to help in the escape of the Princess de Bourbon?"

"That was he. And now he is dead."

"What can I say?" answered the Prince gently. "He died a martyr."

"He died as they all died, in terror and silence. All day the slaughter was — all day — in the morning the bells rang the signal and in the evening the work was not complete. They did not spare the women nor the little children — it was all blood, from the Louvre to the walls."

She rose, staring at the Prince as if her own thoughts amazed her.

"God let it be — though I saw it I can scarcely believe it."

"And I," said William in a tone of great sadness, "am helpless to avenge them."

"Vengeance will come from God," replied Louise de Coligny sternly.

William saw that she held the same strong faith as her father had cherished. The intensity of conviction in the truth of the Reformed faith as confessed by John Calvin: a sincere belief in the protection and justice of God.

"Your messenger told me you would want to hear how my father died," continued the girl in a softer tone.

"Not from your lips, Madame."

"It does not hurt me to speak of it. Will Your Highness be seated?"

He took the chair opposite to her; they had between them the table with the coarse yellow bowls and wooden spoons and the earthenware lamp which cast a thick yellow light over his dark face and her pale features and turned to gold the masses of her blonde hair.

"He was wounded, Monseigneur. When he left the Louvre on the King of Navarre's wedding day one shot at him from the window of a house belonging to a creature of the Guise."

"It was the Guise — I knew!"

"He and his mother. The shot missed his heart but shattered his arm and his fingers."

She paused, steadying herself, then went on in a lower voice.

"I came to help my stepmother, Jacqueline, to nurse him — my husband was with me. There began to be many rumours and many fears in Paris. That day — St. Bartholomew — the bells began to ring, very early — all over Paris.

"There were so many people in the streets I went to watch at the window to see what was afoot and so I saw the Guise coming — with all his men behind him — all villains with the white bandage on their arm — Monseigneur, they broke into the house, only the Duke remained below.

"My husband ran out on to the stairs — they killed him and flung him into the hall.

"Jacqueline and I stood in front of my father. There was no one else, but they pulled us apart and sent a pike through his bare breast.

"He said no word and they dragged him from the bedclothes and to the window, and I, following, saw the Guise laugh and put his foot on him and his soldiers hacking at the naked corpse."

She was silent a moment, staring at the lamp, and William could not speak.

"I do not know what happened then — they overlooked us, I suppose. When night came on we fled blindly and passed, somehow, the city gates — and so to your agent, of whom I had heard Charles speak, and he brought us here."

"Madame de Coligny is with you?"

"Yes. She is ill and quite broken in spirit, she cannot leave her bed."

"But you have a high heart."

"I am his daughter, Monseigneur. I know he would not have wished me to despair."

"I do not think you will despair," answered William. "You are very young, you will yet live to see the golden age," and he smiled.

"I wonder," said Madame de Teligny and the light of the enthusiast shone in her swollen eyes, "perhaps when I am very old I shall know peace and think of this as of a dream."

"And I, who am not so young, shall never see peace, I think."

"It is Your Highness," said Coligny's daughter simply, "on whom we all rely."

Her words were obviously sincere and he wondered why people should still have confidence in him when he had achieved nothing and failed so often and so completely.

"Your Highness was my father's great hope," continued the girl earnestly. "I know that he thought of you — with such satisfaction — to the last."

So she, who had seen her men killed at her feet, did not despair — as he had despaired, a few hours ago — despaired even as he had come into her presence.

He thought of Charlotte de Bourbon and compared the Princess of the Royal House of France with the daughter of the Huguenot leader, they were very different and showed a different training, yet they both held this unconquerable faith; their minds seemed not to measure but to overbridge difficulties. He smiled half wistfully at this childish earnestness; surely neither of these women who believed in him guessed at the truth of his position, nor at what he had to face.

Yet it did encourage and hearten him to see these soft yet strong creatures who had lost all, themselves looking towards him with such trustfulness for the salvation of their common cause.

"Do you know Mademoiselle de Bourbon?" he asked upon an impulse.

"No Highness, my husband saw her when she was Abbess of Joüarrs."

She seemed glad to speak of the young man to whom she had been such a few months wedded; William noticed the pathetic pride with which she mentioned him, as if she would not have him forgotten.

He smiled from that sense of tenderness these quiet loyal women roused in his heart; and this one was so young — he thought of her as a child.

"Mademoiselle de Bourbon is at Heidelberg since this spring — you and Madame de Coligny would find a home there."

She shook her head.

"We would live quite hidden. We saved some of our jewels and we have friends in Switzerland. Van Rengers was my father's close confidant, he will escort us, if Your Highness permits."

She spoke exactly as one who talks of a long matured plan, so soon had she put in order her shattered life and arranged the long prologue of her tragedy. He did not attempt to argue with her.

"I will see Van Rengers takes you away before there is an engagement," he said.

And she answered, "Thank Your Grace and commend me to Count Lodewyk."

And so they parted.

CHAPTER IX

BEFORE MONS

WILLIAM could get no message through to Lodewyk and no word came to him from Mons.

But he knew that Lodewyk must be aware that his brother was still pressing to his aid, despite the terrible disappointment of the French tragedy, and the thought of the Count and the little French garrison relying on him strengthened him into a firm resolve not to give up his task, despite the daily discouragements he received and the disheartened and even mutinous behaviour of the troops.

Meanwhile no news came from the Spanish camp; no scouts nor spies could bring any information as to the likely movements of Don Frederic, who remained at St. Florin, guarding the principal entrance into Mons.

The Prince fell into a resigned sadness, the reaction from his late brief period of hope; there seemed to him nothing substantial that he could catch hold of in the chaos of his affairs, nothing that he could do, his actions seemed to have become futile, even foolish, like beating at iron doors with straws; the clamour of the restless mercenaries, the advices of the deputies of the states who had newly recognised him as Stadtholder, the earnest and agitated talk of his friends, like St. Aldegonde, the daily coil and toil by which he was surrounded, alike appeared frivolous and useless.

He had no grip on the life of camps, no love for the things of war, he could not control with sufficient authority to ensure success the various elements that went to form his armies.

His heart was not in this work; his place was in the cabinet or in the Court; he himself knew his own strength; as a statesman he had no equal in Europe, as a general he was inferior to his brother Lodewyk, and as an adventuring captain of mercenaries he was entirely unsuccessful.

He viewed his task with distaste, and all the hardships of his wanderings seemed preferable to this position of mock authority — in his heart he felt himself and his followers to be indeed no better than the "men of butter"Alva had once haughtily declared them to be.

On the night of the eleventh of September a council was held in his tent.

To the Prince's present mood it seemed half ludicrous, like children gravely consulting on a game, but he presided with his usual urbane manner and pleasant attentiveness.

As he leant back in the deep chair that was his seat of state he looked at those gathered about him.

His scrutiny had the calm interest of the man who sees too much and too clearly; these men, honest, well meaning, faithful, yet seemed to him so infinitely small compared to his requirements as to be hardly of any account.

The dead friends of the past, Egmont, Montigny, Horne, Hoogstraaten, even Brederode, with all their faults, seemed gigantic in comparison with these with whom he now had to deal, and among whom he felt himself somewhat of an alien.

There were none left of his peers, save his brothers and Aldegonde.

Coligny had been his mental equal and now Coligny was gone.

He clasped his long fingers under his chin and glanced from one to another of the little captains and petty burghers who comprised his council.

All were talking together, eager with advice and suggestion.

Only Philip Marnix was silent; his gentle poet's face was downcast and he pulled at the brown tags that finished the laces of his doublet.

William was not listening; his thoughts were with the men themselves, not with what they said.

"If I would ever accomplish anything it is with such as these I must work. Kings and Princes fail — these little folk remain; they mean well, they are honest."

Yet he knew that nothing they could say would alter his intentions or in the least sway his mind. He intended to make an attack on the Spanish early the next morning.

The deputies of the three States were devoted in their expressions towards him, yet they preserved the fiction that Philip was still their king and master and that in his name they were fighting his generals.

This did not irritate William nor even cause him to smile, it was a sophistry agreeing with his own line of thought.

He would sooner fight Philip under forms of laws than openly avow himself a rebel, because, deep in his heart, there yet lingered the hope that he might force Philip to accept his terms and still remain Protector of the Netherlands. Some such thought animated the burghers, they were in revolt against Alva and the Inquisition and not against that far-away and vague figure, Philip of Spain.

One stated that no more trust was to be put in France, and a murmur of assent went up from the others.

"Not after St. Bartholomew," said a little deputy from Holland.

His face was red and shining above his white ruff, and he looked appealingly at the Prince as if he expected to be applauded.

William spoke, almost for the first time since the meeting had assembled.

"Messieurs, we may have to use France, even after St. Bartholomew."

They all looked at him, and he in turn looked around the circle of firm lined faces on which the lamplight shone steadily, bringing them into relief against the dark background of the tent.

The Prince explained himself.

"What else have we to play against Spain?" he asked.

They accepted his bluntness, not reminding him of the fiction of their loyalty.

Only one said,

"Better to be under one's natural tyrant than a foreign one."

William smiled.

"I said France might be used — not submitted to."

"Ah, but can it be used?" asked Philip Marnix swiftly.

General voices echoed his distrust.

"The King is mad —"

"The Queen a sly Italian —"

"They have murdered all the honest men."

"Better trust England."

"Better," said William, "trust no one. Messieurs, I said 'used' — use France!"

He placed his hands on the table, leaning forward and looking at them; a little flame of enthusiasm crept into his eyes, until now so indifferent.

"England is as crafty as France," he continued, "and both as crafty as Spain. Do you think there is any pity, any admiration, any charity for us in the heart of Elizabeth? She works her own policies for her own benefit and if she gives us reluctant promises or still more reluctant aid it is because she sees her interest in so doing. Yet which of you would refuse her help?"

St. Aldegonde replied —

"At least she is Protestant and has disfigured herself with no great treachery."

"Such deeds as this of Bartholomew are not in the nature of the Northerners. The English will work in other ways."

"Let Your Highness, then," said the Deputy from Utrecht, "deal with England, not with France."

But William would not relinquish the long cherished idea of the French alliance.

"I must deal where I can, Monsieur," he replied. "Do you not see that the position is a desperate one?"

But there was not a man there who could bring himself to the least faith in France, or hope of assistance from her Princes.

Their trust had been in Coligny and Coligny's following and now these were no more and their enemies triumphed they looked upon France as but a second Spain.

A captain of the German mercenaries ventured to remonstrate with the Prince.

"Highness, who is left in France? Is not the Queen of Navarre suddenly dead at the French Court and her son forced to adjure his faith? Coligny and his friends murdered?"

"Truly," replied the Prince. "I rely neither on the King of Navarre nor on the party of the Huguenots. These are no more to be considered, nor do I think that they will ever come to power again."

"Why then," asked St. Aldegonde, "does Your Grace speak of using France?"

"I would use the Valois themselves."

"In what way?"

"By tempting their greed, their ambition, and their vanity," said William calmly.

There was silence; no one agreed with him, and he smiled a little, perceiving this.

"It is soon to talk of this," he added pleasantly. "The next move is certainly in our own hands, Messieurs. It depends on us and on us alone whether or not we relieve Mons."

He rose, dismissing them; his easy courtliness and his long experience made him completely master in any such gathering; they accepted his opinion without further demur and left the tent.

In the leave-taking he was particularly courteous to the deputies.

The three States that now called him Stadtholder had already granted him larger powers than had ever been given before; he enjoyed a firmer foothold there than in any town in the southern provinces which had submitted to his authority.

Philip Marnix lingered.

The secretaries had left and William had now no personal attendants, so strict was the one-time opulent Prince with his expenses.

St. Aldegonde pushed back the table at which the council had sat, put away the ink dishes and pens and taking off the Indian cover returned it to the Prince's long low iron couch which stood in the farthest corner of the tent.

William went to the entrance and looked out on to the night. There was a moon, but a thick white mist obscured her light and made every object dim and shadowy; the air was chilly and on the canvas of the tent hung beads of moisture; the forms of the sentries moving to and fro were vague and unsubstantial in the haze; a few poplar trees in the centre of the camp stood up, wavering lines of darkness that were lost in the shrouded heavens.

Yet the moonlight rendered all this dimness luminous like a lamp shining behind a veil.

William's thoughts travelled far: back into the past, the glad days in Brussels — the early days of the struggle when he had been the greatest man in the Netherlands and had met Philip almost as equal to equal.

He did not regret his lost power and splendour, but he would never become content with helplessness and poverty; he meant to regain what he had lost or in the attempt find his grave.

His resolve dominated his soul even in the moment of his despondency.

For the cloud had not lifted from his heart and sadness tinged all his thoughts.

"St. Aldegonde," he said, returning to the tent, "I grow old."

"Old, Highness?" smiled Philip Marnix.

William was in his forty-first year, yet he spoke seriously when he spoke of age.

Life seemed unbearably long and the passage of time intolerably slow.

He seated himself on the couch his friend had prepared.

"Old unto death," he said.

"Yet Your Highness is well —"

"In my spirit I am not well," returned the Prince.

St. Aldegonde recognized the cry of the man who has lost everything, home, children, wife, a place in the world, and who has cared for these things and misses them bitterly.

"Your Highness was not made for this rough life," he answered sorrowfully.

"You think that I hunger after the flesh-pots?" smiled the Prince. "Not that — but I am sometimes very lonely."

As his smile faded he frowned and stooped to caress the spaniel that slept by his couch.

St. Aldegonde's quick sympathy knew that he was thinking of that secret shame, that cankering grief, his wretched wife, whose miserable existence drained his purse as it dishonoured his name.

Whether he considered himself free or not St. Aldegonde did not know, so closely had the Nassau family concealed from even their friends the disgrace of the Princess of Orange and the particulars of her repudiation by her husband.

It was only known that he never saw her nor spoke of her and that she lived at Beilstein under the guardianship of Count John, but never came to Dillenburg.

"Do you think Count Lodewyk will marry?" asked William suddenly.

"If he can find an heiress," said St. Aldegonde frankly.

The young Count, an easy lover and a favourite with women, had never disguised his intention of following the custom of his house and marrying a fortune. But to hear this tonight did not please William.

"Heiresses do not wed with knight-errants," he replied. "I wish Lodewyk would marry with Mademoiselle de Bourbon."

"It has been suggested — but would be, Highness, unpopular."

"Why?" asked the Prince keenly.

"Because she is penniless — a renegade —"

"That should endear her to the Protestants," smiled the Prince.

He unlaced his boots and cast them off.

Philip Marnix smiled also; whatever sympathy Charlotte de Bourbon might enjoy among her co-religionists it would not counterbalance the fact that she was disowned and dowerless and a runaway nun — which last inspired even many Protestants with horror.

"Well, well," said William, "I think she is a woman to make a man happy, even if she comes without a white piece in her poke. And now good night," he added, "we talk of nothing — like two old women."

As soon as he was alone he laid himself down to sleep, dressed as he was, having only removed his boots and his collar.

These lay on the great chair, ready, with his cuirass, mantle, sword and pistols, for the morrow's enterprise.

Before William had put out the light he had looked to these weapons.

When he was lying down he thought of them again, and rising went and fetched one of the pistols and placed it on the stool by his side.

He knew that he was well guarded, but he knew also that Philip's emissaries did not ever relax their efforts to destroy him, and with the dark came the thought of his constant danger and dread of the hideous death of assassination.

The fate of Coligny had brought this danger more clearly to his mind.

The Admiral had been murdered in full day, in his own home, shortly after a friendly visit from the King . . . if he had thus fallen, what chance had the rebel, the exile, the adventurer?

William knew that his life hung by the slenderest thread of "chance," and with each of his colleagues who fell he felt his own fate closing in upon him more relentlessly.

He pulled his mantle over him as well as the bed covering, for the tent was chilly, and tried to sleep; yet could not, but lay staring into the darkness watching the pictures his own thoughts painted on the depths of the night.

He saw the figure of Charlotte de Bourbon on the Castle terrace at Heidelberg, in the blue gown with the snowdrops growing out of the brown ground behind her — he saw Louise de Coligny in the coarse lamplight of the peasant's kitchen, but what he saw more vividly and persistently than any other, was the mangled form of the Admiral suspended from the common gallows.

He wondered if his own dishonoured remains would one day hang upon such a tree — and all the instincts of the aristocrat and all the pride of the Nassau revolted against his fate.

And while he wondered this his senses drowsed and he fell asleep.

He was partially roused by something wet and warm on his face; he moved his head and sighed, being still in the thick torpor of dreams.

Then a shrill barking penetrated his dulled ear; he felt a weight on his chest.

All at once he realized that his dog was standing on his chest and feverishly licking his face in the intervals of barking.

He sat up at once, putting out his hand to the creature, who whined in joyful excitement out of the darkness.

"Danger, eh, Friend?" whispered the Prince, now collected and alert.

He could hear faint groans and little clashes and jars outside.

Hastily he fumbled his way to the chair and pulled on his boots, picked up his weapons, threw on his cloak, and left the tent, the spaniel at his heels.

It was still completely dark; the mist had been blown away by a high wind that now strained the tents at their pegs and poles, but the moon had set.

The Prince could not see what had happened; no sentries challenged him; the distant sounds of confusion grew louder.

He found his way to the tent of St. Aldegonde, which was but the third from his own.

As he reached it some one gripped his arm. "Who is it?" William recognized the voice of Philip Marnix.

"I — the Prince —"

"God be praised — they have surprised the camp, all are slain — I have two horses ready —"

"A night surprise! — the Spaniards! And I slept?" He said nothing else; the sounds of the carnage grew louder about them — the army was being butchered as it slept.

A few officers joined St. Aldegonde; one had a torch; they helped William to a horse; then he spoke again. "Give me the dog."

The little spaniel was lifted to his saddle; the others mounted; they could hear the Spanish musketry close behind them, almost feel the hot air on their necks. They fled through the little village street and into the merciful darkness of the wet meadows.

CHAPTER X

OUT OF THE DEPTHS

A SMALL party of soldiers were proceeding through the Low Countries towards the German frontier; four of their number carried a litter; the curtains of this were drawn back and a young man looked out with sad eyes on the passing landscape.

His head, which he seemed scarcely to have the strength to turn from one side to the other, was raised on a pile of cushions, his features were sunken, his eyes dim, the fingers with which he steadied the curtain the breeze flapped in his face were pale and wasted. The remains of one-time comeliness showed in the elegant shape of his small head and the fallen contours of his countenance, in his bright waving hair and fine hand.

But disease and disappointment had marred his youth.

Melancholy dulled the face that had once been so bright and fearless, as the fever of agitation and hope deferred had prostrated the restless young body.

Such was Count Lodewyk of Nassau, the darling of his party, as he was carried from Mons to his home in Dillenburg.

The news of St. Bartholomew had overthrown health already feeble from sickness, the autumn fever of the Low Countries, and the swift following disaster whereby William's troops had been cut to pieces in a night surprise had completed the work; Count Lodewyk was ill of chagrin, grief, and the shock of the tragedy that had befallen his dear friends in France.

Lodewyk had loved Coligny almost as a father and had himself been the star of the Huguenot party now destroyed.

Unable to any longer hold Mons, he had surrendered the town to Don Frederic, having obtained good terms and being allowed to march out with the honours of war.

His army, however, was disbanded, and he remained, like his brother, a defeated man, accompanied by only a small escort.

Late in the afternoon the little procession halted at a humble village and the Count was carried to the best room in the poor inn.

His brother had promised to meet him here; he sent anxiously to ascertain if the Prince had arrived. By his particular wish his couch had been drawn near the window and he lay on his side and looked out at the brilliant autumn afternoon.

Near by were shorn wheat-fields with the great thatched stacks of yellow straw and dull grain standing in the corner, beyond, the vineyard and the chestnut woods withering to hues of golden scarlet and blazing against a bright blue sky.

Close to the white walls of the inn was an apple orchard, where the fruit shone crimson and jade colour between the sea-green leaves which close curled around the twisted boughs.

Under these trees sheep pastured on the thick bright grass and a child in a blue dress was stitching a length of yellow cloth.

Here was no trace of war nor of desolation; the prospect was soothing to the sick soldier, yet filled him with a sense of regret for his own inactivity, that he lay silly as the sheep and weak as the child below, part of this useless scene of peace.

The door was opened softly and the Prince of Orange entered, stooping his head to avoid the great entrance beam. Lodewyk looked at him.

There was silence; neither knew of any word to say in this moment.

Lodewyk put out his hand; the Prince came up to him and sat on the edge of the low bed.

And he also looked out of the window at the child and the sheep in the orchard and the fair prospect of harvest field and wood.

Their right hands held each other; the younger brother was the first to speak.

"We have nothing but bitterness to discuss," he said.

And William answered —

"I am sorry that you are so ill."

"The news of St. Bartholomew took my strength from me."

"And I was unable to help you."

"So Mons has gone."

"My brother," said the Prince, "more is lost than the city of Mons."

"I think that the cause is lost."

William looked at him intently.

"And you were always so hopeful!" he said very gently.

The sick man closed his eyes.

"That was while Coligny lived."

"You have, then, no more hope of France?"

"None."

"The King is mad it seems," said William evasively; he did not care to disturb his brother's direct judgments with his own subtleties.

"I think," said Lodewyk, "my heart broke when I heard of St. Bartholomew."

William did not reply.

With great tenderness he looked at his brother and pressed the feeble hand that lay in his.

"I go to Dillenburg," added the Count, "but when I can stand on my feet I will return."

He raised his head a little on the cushions.

"Something may yet be done," he concluded.

The westering sun was over the two faces, both so alike, both so grave and worn.

"Something may yet be done," repeated the Prince.

"Your news?" asked Lodewyk.

"My news?"

"I have heard nothing since I left Mons," replied the Count.

"Lodewyk, what is there to say?"

"At least tell me what your position is."

The Prince put his free hand to his breast and fingered the gilt buttons on his shabby doublet.

"I have failed completely," he said and there was a slight tremor in his voice.

98

The Count lay silent.

"I have," continued the Prince, "accomplished nothing from the moment I crossed the Meuse four years ago. Nothing."

He looked thoughtfully at the sun-flushed sky as if he was wondering a little at this adversity of his, this persistent misfortune.

"I thought recently," he continued, "that the tide had turned — the capture of the Brill and your success encouraged me. I met much enthusiasm and help in the Netherlands —"

"So much I heard and saw — whole cities were in revolt owing to the tenth penny tax — was it not so?"

"But now all are discouraged."

"So soon!" exclaimed the Count bitterly.

"Our brief campaign is ended, our armies disbanded, our cause seems hopeless."

"And all are discouraged?"

"More than that — they are terrified," replied the Prince quietly.

"Terrified?"

"Of Alva — of Philip."

"This Philip?" muttered Lodewyk.

"On all sides cities lose heart and fall away. One place after another has ceased to resist the Spaniards, one after another."

"And we have no foothold left?"

"None."

A groan of impatience and despair left the Count's pale lips.

"I left a garrison in Roermond, but no sooner was I gone than they abandoned the town," said the Prince.

"Is there no one left who has any affection for the cause?" exclaimed Lodewyk.

"As I said, they are frightened, they see us powerless to protect them and they know what Alva — and what his master is."

But Lodewyk could not so easily accept William's attitude of resignation.

"Only a short while ago all was so hopeful!" he said.

"But now there is a great change — even our warmest sympathisers are discouraged. Coligny is no more."

"And it seems that we," returned Lodewyk bitterly, "might as well have ceased to exist." William rose without speaking.

"Do you see any hope?" persisted the Count, raising himself on one elbow.

"Unless God performs a miracle —"

"A miracle — the cause is good enough," returned the young man eagerly.

"One place after another has ceased resisting the Spanish —"

"Haarlem and Alkmaar hold out?"

"Those two, yes."

"But you have no hopes of relieving either?"

"None," replied the Prince laconically.

"Some endeavour must be made," said Lodewyk feverishly. "These people cannot be allowed to miserably perish."

"With the few Netherland troops that I have I will endeavour to do something — I might get further assistance from Germany or even from England, but, as I said, I have no hopes."

Lodewyk sighed — the sound was like a sob.

"I fear that in the end I shall find myself alone, abandoned by everyone," continued the Prince, "death takes the stout-hearted and the faint-hearted fall back."

Lodewyk made a passionate movement that dragged him up on his pillows, he clasped his hands and turned his distracted young face heavenwards with a look of despair and supplication.

"Out of the depths have I cried unto Thee!" he said, "out of the depths, oh Lord!"

William heard in the exclamation the note of faith he had perceived in so many others, particularly in the two women who had lately crossed his path, Charlotte de Bourbon and Admiral de Coligny's daughter. His brother, blithe and easy by nature, also had the strength of his Calvinistic faith; William, who, though he had ceased to be a Roman Catholic, had not so far proclaimed himself as belonging to any of the Protestant groups, again was assured that he also had to join the faithful Church of the Lord Jesus Christ. And the strength and comfort of the Reformed faith appealed to William in this moment of his utter discomfiture and overthrow.

"Do you think the Lord will help us, Lodewyk?" he asked tenderly and with a certain wistfulness.

The younger brother replied firmly —

"I do believe it — though I have my moments of despair, I do believe it."

"Only not in the southern provinces," said William with a certain sadness.

Lodewyk was silent, but an indomitable light gleamed in his eyes.

"Here everything is lost," added the Prince.

"Where then would you plant your flag?"

"In the States of Holland."

"They remain staunch?"

"They and they alone."

"You will go there?"

" So I have determined — and you?"

"I have decided nothing. I have been, indeed, too weary."

"Poor Lodewyk, you must stay awhile and help John at Dillenburg — there is much business there which you can do and he cannot."

"For a while, for a little while, but I shall join you very soon."

William returned to his side.

"Lodewyk," he said, smiling, "will you not marry soon?"

"If Your Grace will find me a good fortune," replied the Count.

"I did not think of that."

"Then let it be. I need money, not a wife, William."

"I thought of Mademoiselle de Bourbon."

"The nun?"

"She was. But now she is as free as yourself."

Lodewyk smiled.

"Are my fortunes in good trim for a penniless marriage do you think?"

William lifted his shoulders.

"How can I keep a wife," continued the Count, "when I have not two suits to my back?"

"Mademoiselle de Bourbon does not think of worldly things."

"But I must."

"Which means that you will not think of her?" smiled William.

"In the way of marriage, no."

"I am sorry."

"Who am I," said Lodewyk with a rare bitterness, "to think of marriage! Sooner should I find my grave than my wife."

"Our graves are near to our hands, I well believe," replied the Prince quietly, "but I did not speak of an ordinary woman but of one well prepared to face misfortune."

"I think that of her also," said Lodewyk, "but she is not for me, speak no more of it."

The Prince said again, and with a certain wistfulness:

"I am sorry."

Lodewyk looked at him in silence a little while; the shadow had touched them both, the last sunlight lingered only in a pool of heavy gold on the floor behind them.

The foolish words came to Lodewyk's lips as he stared at his brother, he wanted to say — "How gray you have grown!" For in the cold light the Prince's hair seemed ash-coloured at the temples, but he checked himself.

They sat motionless till the sun had sunk behind the rim of the flat landscape and all colour faded from field and tree, meadow and orchard, leaving it gray and murky.

Thin wreaths of vapour were now discoverable in the fields; in the distance they showed a cold white, like winding rivers, nearer as drifting veils; the child took up her work and went into the house, the sheep were lost to sight under the shade of the apple trees.

The poplars shaken by a perpetual motion, even in the still air, showed dark against a pale and lifeless sky.

There was no longer any light in the chamber where the brothers sat, encroaching dusk invaded them and blotted their likeness from each other. To Lodewyk they seemed as remote from the world as if they lay in the chapel at Dillenburg. Yet

The Dillenburg

his mind was full of great actions and deep resolves, though the quietude of his surroundings and the helplessness of his body made these seem as dreams, unsubstantial as the mists lying on the meadows.

So, he thought, the dead might dream in marble tombs, the gross details of the world forgot and only pale visions of glories and endeavours left to paint with dim gold the blank sleep of eternity.

William rose, his movement sent a jar through the quiet room.

"What will you do?" asked Lodewyk, yearning after him.

"I shall go to Holland," replied the Prince, "and there maintain my cause, or there find my sepulchre."

THE NETHERLANDS

AT THE TIME
OF WILLIAM THE SILENT

Boundary shown thus ·······

NORTH

SEA

EMDEN

JEMMINGEN

DELFZIJL.

OMMELANDEN
GRONINGEN
HEILIGERLEE

LINGEN

LEEUWARDEN

GRONINGEN

OLDENZAAL

FRIESLAND

OVERYSSEL

DEVENTER

R.Yssel

ENCKHUYSEN

ZUYDER

ZEE

EDAM

AMSTERDAM

NAARDEN

ZUTPHEN

ZUTPHEN

UTRECHT

GELDERLAND

ALKMAAR

UTRECHT

VIANEN

MOOK HEIDE

CLEVES

BREDERODE
HAARLEM

LEYDEN

OUDEWATER

R.Ysel

R.Waal

NYMEGEN

R.Maas

R. Lippe

HAGUE

DELFT

SCHIEDAM

ROTTERDAM

DORDRECHT

GORCUM

GERTRUIDENBERG

BRILL

ZEVENBERGEN

BREDA

SCHOUWEN

DUIVELAND

ZEE

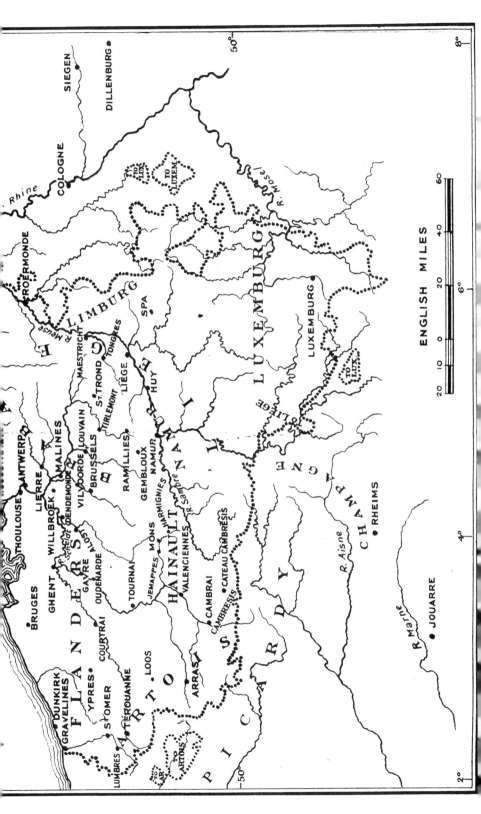

ENGLISH MILES

50°

SIEGEN
DILLENBURG
COLOGNE
Rhine
ROERMONDE
LIMBURG
R. Meuse
MAESTRICHT
SPA
TONGRES
ST. TROND
LIÉGE
TIRLEMONT
HUY
LOUVAIN
VILVOORDE
BRUSSELS
RAMILLIES
GEMBLOUX
NAMUR
HARMIGNIES
MONS
JEMAPPES
VALENCIENNES
R. Sambre
CAMBRAI
CATEAU CAMBRÉSIS
CAMBRÉSIS

ANTWERP
LIERRE
MALINES
WILLBROEK
DENDEMONDE
GHENT
GAVRE
ALOST
OUDENARDE
TOURNAI
BRUGES
COURTRAI
YPRES
DUNKIRK
GRAVELINES
ST. OMER
TÉROUANNE
LUMBRES
ARTOIS
ARRAS
LOOS
THOULOUSE

FLANDERS
A R T O I S
P I C A R D Y
HAINAULT
NAMUR
LIÈGE
LUXEMBURG
CHAMPAGNE

TO LUX
TO LUXEM
TO LUX

R. Moselle
LUXEMBURG
TO LUX

RHEIMS
R. Aisne
R. Marne
JOUARRE

50°

2°   4°   6°   8°

ENGLISH MILES
20 10   0   20   40   60

JE MAINTIENDRAY.

William the Silent (1533-1584)
Prince of Orange

PART II

THE NEW REPUBLIC

"Lapis rejectus caput anguli."
(The Stone which was rejected has become the Corner Stone)

Orange Medal, 1574

PhilipII of Spain (1527-1598)

CHAPTER I

THE KING

A MAN sat before a great pile of papers neatly arranged on a black wood desk.

The little cabinet about him was sombre and lit only by one high arched window, from which issued a pale light that fell coldly on the worker at the desk.

He had an air of being depressed and overwhelmed by his task, from which he never lifted his eyes. With neat patient fingers he sorted and docketed the papers, read, selected and arranged the letters, now and then writing comments on the margins or putting a query to some sentence (and there were many such) that he did not understand.

He was a man of middle age, slight and of a remarkable appearance.

The pallor of his thin face was emphasised by his scanty red-gold hair and beard, his blue eyes were strained and slightly bloodshot and had a blank but steady expression, his mouth was large, his jaw underhung; his jaw and broken teeth added to his appearance of ill-health. He wore an almost mourning suit of dull black taffeta, buttoned tight with gold buttons across his narrow chest, and a stiff little collar of pleated lawn high under his ears.

There was no ornament or object of beauty in the room and no view from the window, which was set too high to show anything but the sky.

Above the large, much worn desk hung an ebony crucifix on the white wall, on the other side of the window was a dark picture of an emaciated saint, bleeding from many wounds, praying in the midst of a stormy landscape.

The whole closet had the air of a monk's cell, cheerless, austere, and melancholy.

Such was the person and the occupation and the surrounding of Philip, King of Spain, ruler of the largest, mightiest, and wealthiest nation in the world.

Presently he came upon a letter that interested him more than any he had so far perused.

It was from the private secretary of the Duke of Alva, Viceroy in the Netherlands, to the King's chief secretary, and had been placed there for Philip's special attention. This passage was underlined:

"The man who brought Coligny's head has offered to strike off the head of another who has injured Christianity as much as that scamp now in Hell."

Philip reflected.

Then he neatly wrote his commentary on the side margin of the parchment.

"I do not understand this, because I do not know where Coligny's head was taken, or whose this other head is, although it seems to be that of Orange. Certainly they had shown little pluck in not killing him, for that would be the best remedy."

As he finished writing the door was opened and closed; the King looked up to see Cardinal Granvelle before him.

Philip glanced at the little brass clock on the desk; he did not wish to be interrupted, but on seeing that the Cardinal was exact to the time he had appointed for him, he said nothing, but sprinkled sand over his newly written note and put it away.

The Cardinal came forward with familiar ease; he appeared more worldly than the King, as he certainly was more graceful and urbane in appearance and manner.

Philip eyed him gloomily, then sighed, resting his elbows on the desk and the tips of his long fingers together.

The Cardinal seated himself; his rich ecclesiastical dress, his jewels and his handsome smiling face lightened the gloom of the cabinet.

"Your Majesty wished to speak of the Netherlands?" he asked.

Philip had always relied on the Cardinal's knowledge and judgment of the rebellious heretic provinces, which he had ruled over the shoulder of Margaret of Parma in the early days.

"I have to let you know," said the King, speaking in a voice weak from long silence, "that I have decided to recall Alva."

The Cardinal bent his head.

He was not surprised at the decision, but rather that it had come so soon and without his knowledge; in it

Antoine Perrenot de Granvelle (1517-1586)

he traced the influence of Antonio Perez, the King's secretary, and the Princess of Eboli, Ruz de Gonez's widow, who were fast becoming more powerful than himself or any other adviser, open or secret.

"Alva has failed," added Philip with the ghastly calm with which he announced any news, good or bad.

"Not through lack of zeal," said Granvelle.

"He has failed," repeated the King as if the statement admitted of no qualification.

"Who will succeed?" asked Granvelle with slight bitterness; he was thinking that he also had failed in the task of ruling the Netherlands.

"Alva's letters," said Philip with the same calm which was not tinged by any disappointment or displeasure, "have for some time past spoken of nothing but failure."

He looked at Granvelle out of his implacable tired blue eyes.

"The tenth penny tax has failed — force has failed to raise money — the siege of Alkmaar has been raised, they have not yet taken Leyden."

"And Orange lives."

"And Orange lives," repeated the King impassively. "And while he lives the rebels will never be subdued."

"He and his brother," said Granvelle, "should be treated like Turks."

"Like Coligny," replied Philip.

"Where is the man to do it? There lacks the Guise here."

Philip drew a paper from one of the pigeon-holes of his desk and unfolded it.

It contained a list of all the nobles of the Low Countries who had incurred, either by protest or rebellion, the King's displeasure.

At the top was the name of William of Orange, beneath it that of his brother Lodewyk.

These were the only two names unmarked.

The others had a cross in red ink at the side; the King handed the paper to Granvelle.

"Only two left," he remarked.

The Cardinal smiled; he knew that the red crosses meant that the dangerous enemy had in each case been disposed of, all, from Egmont to Montigny, by Philip's means.

"But the most dangerous remains," said the Cardinal.

"Yes — but it cannot be for long," replied Philip. "God will not for long permit such a monstrous rebel and heretic to live."

He meant what he said; he could not believe that his prayers, his penances, his self-inflicted sufferings, his austere, labourious life, the tremendous efforts that he had made to repress heresy in his dominions would go for nothing in the eyes of Heaven, or that such a lost soul as the Prince of Orange would long escape the judgment of God.

In one just day of vengeance Coligny and his Huguenots had been swept away like a nest of hornets cast to the flames.

Philip waited for such another day to dawn over the Netherlands — for such another act of vengeance to take place.

He had ceased to expect Alva to accomplish this.

112

The ceaseless cruelties, the rigorous legal enactments, the iron rule and the military successes of Alva were not sufficient in the eyes of his master. He had not crushed the heretics — he had not slain the Prince of Orange.

On the contrary the great Rebel had established himself in Holland and Zeeland, held his Court at Delft and conducted a rival government to that of Brussels.

Lodewyk of Nassau had reopened negotiations with the French and English and was reported to be leading a new army to the support of his brother. Meanwhile the Regent was completely at the end of his resources, unable to raise money, burdened by private debts and overwhelmed by public hatred. And Philip, poisoned against him by Antonio Perez and Aña de Mendoza, took a hard view of his failure.

"I had hoped better from the Duke of Alva," he said; this, from his reserve, was a notable expression of opinion.

Granvelle saw that the Viceroy would return in disgrace; the priest was not the man to put in a word for the fallen and he had never loved the haughty Alva.

He knew also the impossibility of altering any idea Philip might hold, and therefore was silent though he thought in his heart that Alva had done all that could be done with an impossible task.

"Who takes his place, Sire?" he asked and he added the name that had been most discussed in this connection. "Medina Cœli?"

"No," said Philip slowly. "I think — the Grand Commander of Castile."

He looked thoughtfully down at his papers and traced a pattern on his desk with the dry point of his quill.

"The Netherlands must be subdued," he added, "and soon. This plague spot in my Empire must be healed or cut away — cut away, eh?"

He sighed again; the thought of this great taint of heresy among his subjects was with him day and night, poisoning his repose.

He had used every weapon in his power and the rebels were still defiant.

From the midst of their blood and tears, from the ashes of their towns and the ruins of their country-side, they faced him undauntedly; he had sacrificed in vain one of the richest portions of his realm; in vain he had stamped out industry, commerce, trade, and prosperity in his effort to stamp out heresy.

The provinces that had brought in a princely income to his father were now an immense drain on his almost bankrupt resources; but Philip did not care for this — gave no thought to it, any more than he had given any thought to the ruin he had inflicted on a large and flourishing portion of his kingdom by his recent expulsion of the Moriscos from Andalusia.

What burnt into his head was that heresy still flourished in a land under his rule, and that he, God's appointed Regent upon earth, was powerless to check the abomination.

But he submitted humbly and patiently, immersing himself in the minute daily toil by which he strove to rule his vast dominions from this cabinet in the Escurial.

Now his mind was on the Prince of Orange, whom he hated with an exceedingly deep hate.

"Your Eminence knew of a man suitable to the purpose?" he asked.

At last, in his slow, roundabout way, he had come to the object of the interview which he had commanded from Granvelle.

"The purpose, Sire?" asked the Cardinal. Even he, adept as he was in Philip's ways, could not always sound the meaning of the King's cautious sentences.

"Of dealing with Orange as Coligny was dealt with."

Granvelle understood.

"It is certainly needful that this William be removed soon," he said.

"It is necessary," said Philip.

"The man I had in mind was one Gaspar D'Anastro, a Spaniard living in Antwerp," said Granvelle. "I believe for a reward he would find an instrument."

"Give him," said Philip, "whatever he should ask, Eminence."

114

"But since I spoke to Your Majesty I have heard reports that have made my faith in the fellow slacken. It seems that he is more inspired by love of money than love of God."

"That is no matter," remarked the King, "as long as the deed be done."

"It shall be done, Sire."

"I believe it — yet the man seems to me to bear a life charmed by evil arts."

"It is indeed difficult to come to him — several good Roman Catholics have met their death before ever they could put foot in Delft."

"God will reward them," said Philip.

He took back his list from Granvelle and carefully returned it to the pigeon-hole and a slight gleam came into his passive eyes as he dwelt once more on the names of these, the flower of the Flemish nobility, who had fallen victims to the past wrath of God and Philip.

And the Prince of Orange would fall too, even the Devil could not always protect such a man, the King thought.

He rose stiffly; it was the hour for his relaxation and his devotions.

Today these would be long, for his news had been bad.

The English had plundered several more of his silver ships, some money he had hoped to raise from the nobles of Castile had failed, several peculations on the part of his American Viceroys had come to light, the young Valois princes were again tampering with the accursed rebels.

And everywhere was a demand for money and a lack of money.

His brother, Don Juan of Austria, wrote frantic letters from Messina, entreating for means to follow up the victory of Lepanto, the laurels of which were beginning to wither and threatening the loss of Tunis and La Goleta.

Philip maintained a patient silence towards these appeals; he had no money to send; besides Don Juan also had his enemies who whispered that he tried to found an Empire for himself in the East.

Granvelle arose and followed the King, who went into a little gallery which overlooked the garden.

This was hung one side by tapestry of a dark green colour and on the other was open on the garden by a series of delicate arches.

An autumn grayness was abroad, the sunless air was heavy; in the garden below was the darkness of ilex trees, in the sky the darkness of rain clouds.

In a stiff chair of leather with her feet on a gold cushion, sat the Queen, Philip's fourth wife, Anne of Austria, daughter of the Emperor.

She was pretty in a bright vivacious style and gowned in austere splendour of red and lustred gold velvet; despite her smile and her quick movements she looked ill and unhappy.

By her side stood a child of a bright and noticeable beauty who was winding a ball of white yarn from an ebony frame.

Behind were the ladies in attitudes of repressed dullness, and here, as everywhere in the Escurial, were priests.

Two walked soft-footed up and down the gallery, the Queen's confessor sat with the waiting-women.

The whole group had a sad and formal air; they seemed people who had reduced life to an empty ceremony.

Philip looked kindly at his wife, but with far deeper affection at the child.

She was his favourite daughter and bore a likeness to her mother, the late French Queen, the beloved and lovely Isabelle de Valois.

Looking at her he sighed, thinking of her mother, whose death had been the deepest grief of his life, but he did not speak either to her or to the Queen and they remained dutifully silent.

Instead he turned to the priests, those eyes, ears, and tongues of the Escurial, and keepers of his conscience. These were all about him instantly and he walked up and down the gallery with them, the Cardinal at his side.

The Queen's dark glance travelled after him; the child continued carding the yarn; she already had the austere manner of the Spanish Court.

The duennas yawned behind their stiff tortoise-shell fans.

It seemed as if nothing had ever happened or would ever happen to break the monotony of this exactly ordered life.

The Queen took her gaze from the meagre figure of her husband and glanced at the gray clouds, then down into the formal garden.

A clock struck.

Anne rose and, giving a little signal to her ladies, left the gallery.

It was the hour for prayers, which here were as regular as in any convent.

The Queen's confessor followed her, the other priests came behind with the King.

Among them was the one who had put Granvelle in touch with Gaspar D'Anastro, the Spanish merchant in Antwerp who had offered to find a man to assassinate the Prince of Orange.

"But I have since discovered a fellow better adapted to your Majesty's purpose," said this priest. "A young captain from Arragon, full of a devout spirit and much loyalty."

"Is he willing to undertake the business?" asked Philip.

"Very eager, Sire."

"He knows the difficulties?"

"I believe him well aware of them — and also that he would shrink from nothing in the service of your Majesty."

The King did not appear wholly convinced of the usefulness of this new instrument.

"Is he familiar with Flemish?" he asked, for he remembered that another emissary sent to murder William had failed to obtain an entry into Delft on account of his scant knowledge of the Flemish language and the strong Spanish accent which had betrayed him.

"I believe he is proficient in it," put in Granvelle. "He was in the service of the Council when I was in Brussels."

"He may try then," said the King, who stood to lose nothing by the sentence the emissary would have to pay in case of failure, and Philip would not put his hand in his pocket unless success was assured.

"Is he one of these penniless fellows?" he added, as they entered the palace.

"I believe he can pay his own expenses," replied the priest who had spoken for him. "But it would be worth your Majesty's while to give him a few ducats to further bind him to your service."

But Philip, always hampered by poverty, was chary of his ducats.

"I will promise him the cross of Santiago if he succeed," he answered. "And you, Father, shall confess and absolve him before he starts. This is sufficient favour."

They reached the door of the dark and sombre chapel, where the Queen was already on her knees.

"Afterwards I myself will see this man," said Philip, on a prudent reflection that he had better judge of this creature of Granvelle's for himself.

He was unsparing in his attention to these petty details.

Dismissing all mundane business from his mind he humbly entered the chapel and prostrated himself in abject adoration and supplication.

In a passion of self-abasement he prayed for the subjection of the heretics and the peaceful reign of the true faith, and declared to God, in a fervour of self-sacrifice, that if he had not done yet sufficient penances, if he had not yet been sufficiently punished by the loss of his dear wife and the tragic end of the insane son on whom so many high hopes had been placed, he was willing to meekly endure any misfortune that might be laid on him as long as he might be permitted to be the means of rooting out the heretics.

When the stately gloomy service was over, Philip rose from his devotions and went to interview the man who had undertaken to murder William of Orange.

CHAPTER II

THE CARDINAL MUSES

CARDINAL GRANVELLE had apartments in the Escurial, the only chambers in the huge gloomy unfinished building furnished with taste and luxury, for even the Queen's rooms were dull and sombre.

But the Burgundian priest had surrounded himself with something of French elegance, something of the florid Flemish magnificence to which he had become used during his residence in the gorgeous capital of Brabant.

Stamped leather and tapestry shot with gold thread adorned the walls, the furniture was rich and costly, the clocks and lamps of gold and silver, the books choice and numerous, though nothing could soften the stiffness of the narrow window which admitted a cold east light that no internal splendour could counteract.

Granvelle, a man of a soft and easy habit and of voluptuous tastes, did not like the Escurial, sometimes he confessed to himself that he did not like Spain.

Today after he had left the King and Queen in the gallery he retired to his cabinet in a spirit of profound dissatisfaction.

That morning his old and beloved dog had died and this fact, trivial in itself but important to the Cardinal, for the creature had roused the only affection of his life, served to set him thinking, with some bitterness, on what he considered the extraordinary inner failure of his life.

For though he might have been supposed to have achieved a vast ambition he had all the lurking disappointment of the self-made man who, never quite equal to the position he has gained, is continually disgusted by the limit his own consciousness imposes upon himself.

Cardinal Granvelle was not a great man; his keen intelligence was continually irritated by this fact; he was not of noble birth and this pricked his sharp pride; he was clever enough to see how far short his success fell of his ambitions and this recognition of his own limit galled him unbearably. He was, after all, nothing but one of the many tools of Philip, and this position which entirely satisfied such as Antonio Perez or Alva was irksome to the proud Cardinal. He did not see how he could ever be other than what he was; his nearest approach to separate greatness had been when, as adviser to Margaret of Parma, he had been virtually Governor of the Netherlands.

That chance he had lost through the persistent opposition of the great Flemish nobles who had finally obtained his recall.

The Cardinal retained the bitterest hatred towards these men.

Most of them were dead; Philip had fully avenged himself on the opponents of his favoured Minister — Egmont and Horne on the block, Adolphus of Nassau and Hoogstraaten on the battlefield — Berghen and Floris de Montmorency in a Spanish prison — Brederode of a broken heart — it might seem as if the Cardinal could be satisfied.

But the Netherlands were not subdued — and William of Orange lived.

And this Prince the Cardinal regarded with an intensity of hatred that nothing but death could satisfy.

The Prince was ruined, discredited, humiliated, he had fallen from the position of one of the greatest grandees in the world to that of a penniless exile, a mere adventurer — but the Cardinal's hatred was not appeased nor his fear of his opponent at rest.

He had long ago called William the most dangerous man in the Netherlands and his opinion had not altered — even though the revolted Provinces were now crushed under the rule of Alva and the Nassau family had ruined themselves in vain for the cause which they had espoused. It was an exceeding grievance with the Cardinal that William was still alive; there seemed to him something miraculous in the rebel's constant escape from peril, the manner in which he perpetually evaded the meshes of Philip's net of intrigue and secret plot, as there was something miraculous in the way he was, in face of his constant misfortunes, able to maintain his influence

120

among the Netherlanders, to lead parties in France and England, to raise armies and collect money, to now even hold a court in Delft.

The Cardinal, bitter today because of the death of his dog, thought of William of Orange with murderous rage — a plague spot, a twice damned heretic and rebel — a cunning unscrupulous devil he called him in his angry thoughts — but great, by Heaven, great, as Philip was not and never could be — Philip — the Cardinal's fierce thoughts rested on his master whom he both envied, despised, and stood in awe of — not because he was Philip — but because he was ruler of half the world.

It seemed to the Cardinal that if Philip could not destroy William, William would destroy Philip —

"— like a rat gnawing at the foundations of a house," he said to himself.

This thought, apart from his personal animosity to the man, affected him with a nobler grief — the Spanish Empire represented all that he believed in and admired and he was sincere in his passionate abhorrence of the heretic and the rebel.

"If I were a younger man," his thoughts continued, "I would take my musket and track down the cursed Prince myself."

He rose impulsively and looked about him as if suddenly aware and impatient of the confinement of the room.

Though the apartment was both luxurious and peaceful he was conscious of neither luxury nor peace.

An atmosphere of trouble and tumult, change and fury pervaded his soul and coloured his surroundings; he saw himself as a mere detail in a vortex of events utterly beyond his control, he saw destiny weaving her shuttle and the designs of her texture was not to his liking.

His mind turned again to his dog; the death of his favourite seemed an outrage on his pride and power — there was only one thing he had cared for, and that he could not keep.

His rage and irritation became so acute that he cast about for someone on whom to vent his mood.

The King was both the nearest and most satisfactory object on which to turn his venom; the Cardinal left his rich apartments for the dark and narrow chambers of Philip. As he passed up a steep cold staircase, he saw the Queen and her ladies cross the landing beneath him.

They were on their way from the chapel and carried their books of prayer.

Granvelle, he knew not why, leant over the thin stairrail and looked at them.

He noticed, as he had never noticed before, the expressionlessness and the utter sadness of these women's faces.

They also seemed discontented, though cherished and housed in a palace and protected by the greatest King in the world.

Philip was kind and affectionate towards his wife, but the look on the young Austrian's face was that of cowed and sullen endurance; and Granvelle remembered the look on the frail features of the last Queen, a look of dumb terror — and the look on the face of Don Carlos, the King's only son — a look of fear and cunning — the stare and grin of insanity.

There was no happiness in the Escurial — what then was the good of any of it, since all of them were discontented — so thought the Cardinal with a certain fierce impatience, for he was one who wished for material joy and pleasure as proof and sign of power and place.

He was at once admitted to the presence of Philip; the King seldom refused him admission to his cabinet; his slow and suspicious mind liked the support and enlightenment afforded by the Cardinal's keen intellect, when he was engaged in the labourious details of what he considered statecraft.

Philip was as usual at his desk, writing one of his long and dull despatches which were all penned by his own hand and compiled with the minutest care.

The King worked harder than any clerk in his employment and with the persistent application of the dull-witted.

Granvelle despised him for this, yet he could not dissociate the man from the King and he always looked with a certain awe at this bent thin figure in the gray dull room — the man who could devote a nation to destruction by signing his name.

"I write to England," Philip said in that tone of respect he always used when speaking to a churchman, even when it was one whom he secretly hated; as he liked Granvelle his manner was friendly as well as courteous.

He put down his pen and leant back in his stiff black chair; his pale prominent eyes fixed Granvelle with a thoughtful look; he wore a high tight white cap and a close white ruff; his heavy lower lip was loose and flaccid, showing his broken teeth; the sagging skin showed the bony structure of his face.

Cardinal Granvelle considered him; this was not his ideal of King or master; he recalled that graceful yet robust figure, both magnificent and charming, comely and at ease — William of Orange.

Had they met in private life William would not have considered Philip of sufficient capacity to be his humblest clerk; Granvelle knew this — he saw Philip as he was, mean of soul as of intelligence, but he was King of Spain; all that was servile in the Cardinal bent to that.

And Granvelle saw in Philip another thing besides the sheer fact of kingship; the adamant obstinacy of bigotry and prejudice; the Cardinal respected this because it was entirely beyond his management and had again and again defeated his purpose and his wish.

His one satisfaction was that this quality in the King had also defeated the genius of the Prince of Orange.

Philip pushed back his papers and his lids drooped.

"England meddles in the Netherlands," he said as if he stated a secret.

"And France," answered the Cardinal gravely.

"The party of the rebels is very powerful in France," returned Philip with an air of utter gloom. "I think they will set up the Duc D'Anjou as a pretender in my provinces."

Granvelle did not wish to indulge the King in a minute discussion of events that were already argued threadbare; he knew to a nicety the exact position of the rebel Netherlanders in the politics of Europe.

He came delicately and with precision to the point which was always uppermost in his own mind.

"It is the Prince of Orange, Sire, who does you active mischief, both in England and France, and in the Empire."

Philip seemed to have forgotten his recent idea to remove the Prince, now, struck through the maze of detail with which he was occupied by the clean logic of the fact, he blinked like a man pushed from darkness into light.

"The Prince of Orange, yes," he muttered.

"He and no other, Sire. Remove him and you go at ease in Europe. As you know and have decided, Sire."

The King went off the main subject again.

"There are others — I hear Lodewyk of Nassau would marry the Abbess of Joüarrs. God protect us," he shivered and crossed himself.

"There are no others," said the Cardinal firmly. "If the Prince were dead the rebellion would be dead and no more would be heard of these enemies of your Majesty in foreign states."

"But Lodewyk — John —"

Granvelle calmly interrupted, keeping the King to the point with infinite care and strength of purpose.

"None of those men matter — Count Lodewyk is an adventurer, Count John a ruined, broken man, the rest are but the desperate knaves and fools that gather around any great villain."

"The Prince of Orange is also ruined," said the King slowly. "He has nothing left of all his possessions, he is disgraced through his wife. I am assured that he has neither credit nor abiding place anywhere save in that pestilent town of Delft."

"That is all true, Sire, but for all that your Majesty has no other enemy to reckon with save this one. I would not have you forget that, nor slacken in your endeavour to remove this ruffian."

Philip frowned as he grasped the importance of what Granvelle was saying; it irritated him to be convinced of what his minister told him; it was hard for his dull pride to realize that one whom he regarded as his rebel subject could be so dangerous, that he still remained alive.

"What power has this man?" he asked sullenly.

The answer — "the quality of greatness," was on Granvelle's lips, but he checked the words and replied, "The devil supports a thrice perjured heretic."

This satisfied Philip; he was used to fighting the devil; his watery eyes gleamed with a sombre enthusiasm.

"He must die, this William," he said; with his misshapen chin propped on his fine hand he considered the destruction of his enemy.

124

"He must die, this
William," he said.

"The heretic escapes all efforts of your Majesty's wrath," the Cardinal reminded him. "We have heard no more of D'Anastro's man."

"I would he could have come to Spain," said Philip slowly. "As Egmont did. And Berghen. And Floris Montmorency."

"He was always cunning."

"If he had come to Madrid," continued the King, "he would have died quietly — years ago — your Eminence knows that I distrusted him, even before the rebellion."

As Philip was staring at his desk, Granvelle allowed himself an impatient frown at this childishness.

"But the Prince did not come to Madrid and is still at large, Sire," he remarked.

"But the others," said Philip more cheerfully. "I have crushed the others. They pay their debt in Hell now."

The Cardinal tapped his velvet-shod foot on the dark floor.

"None of them mattered as the Prince matters, Sire. And he escapes — always escapes."

"He too will go," returned the King with more energy than he had yet shown. "Do you doubt that? Do you think, Eminence, that the Almighty God will long tolerate such a foul heretic?"

Granvelle very slightly lifted his shoulders.

"Your Majesty should not rest day or night while this man lives."

Philip fired at that.

"Do I rest? Do I not labour, labour incessantly? What have I not sacrificed in the cause of my God and my Realm? My eyes fail and my hand shakes and my head is weary but I do not cease to labour."

There was something of grandeur in his words, but as he spoke his face had a sudden resemblance to his murdered son and the Cardinal lowered his glance, almost imperceptibly blenching from what gazed at him from the eyes of Philip.

"Is it for some sin of mine," continued the King, "that this man lives? I have done great penance for my sins. Have I not been punished? Did I not sacrifice my son?"

He looked around the room as if searching for a third presence. "In His good time God will permit me to destroy this William." "It should be done swiftly," urged the Cardinal.

"Have I not tried?" asked the King. His head fell forward a little, his black clothes blended with the fast increasing shadows; his voice sounded hoarse and mournful.

"The instruments were wrong and it is hard to trace one who wanders in disguise — he also has spies and friends everywhere, even in the cabinet of your Majesty — yet the deed can be done — especially now he is often in Delft."

Philip groaned.

"They all play me false, all of them — but I am not deceived."

Granvelle knew that he was, and by those most in his confidence, such as Antonio Perez and the Princess of Eboli, yet the Cardinal winced, for Philip, believing in none, might at the slightest cause strike at all or any.

"I at least have been a very faithful servant," he said quietly; and it was the truth.

Philip was silent; either out of disbelief or because his thoughts had wandered.

The Cardinal held his peace, there was a certain weariness upon his spirit; to be with Philip made him melancholy.

"Alva," said the King suddenly out of the dusk. "I wonder if Alva is loyal?"

Granvelle was utterly amazed; even though he knew Alva was under recall he would not have believed that even Philip's untiring suspicions would fall on Alva, that brilliant and merciless instrument of Spanish power and Romanist wrath.

"The Duke of Alva," he ejaculated.

"Why did he put on the tenth penny tax?" demanded the King. "It has greatly inflamed the Netherlanders."

Granvelle could have laughed; he knew that the burden of the Viceroy's letters was one desperate demand for money which Philip never sent.

"The Duke could not govern without gold," he said. "Money is necessary — Resquesens will be the same.

Philip broke in fiercely.

"Money, money. I have no money!" he cried, confessing with these words that all the boasted wealth of Spain was becoming exhausted in the effort to crush heresy in the Netherlands.

"But you have power, Sire," said the Cardinal.

Philip's energy waned as quickly as it had flamed, he drooped in his chair like a sick man; his right hand reached out to the desk and grasped the quill with feeble haste.

"Candles," he said harshly, "candles. I must finish my dispatch."

CHAPTER III

NEWS FROM THE REBELS

BUT Philip did not write long even after the candles had been brought; for once his mind turned from the petty detail to the large issue; Granvelle's words rankled in his mind; he could not but admit that the news from the Netherlands was far from good and that the Prince of Orange was still a perpetual goad in his side.

True, Haarlem had been reduced after a desperate resistance and laid in ashes, but Alkmaar had resisted successfully, Middelburg had fallen into the hands of the rebels, leaving them masters of the islands of Zeeland and Walcheren and of the sea coast; on the sea itself they from the first had been, and still were, victorious.

The Prince of Orange had established himself in Delft and had surrounded himself with the nucleus of an independent state; he was known to be in close communication with the great rivals, France and England, and to be skilfully playing one against the other; how far he had succeeded in obtaining help from either, Philip did not know, but he was informed by his spies that the Duc d'Alençon had promised countenance and help to Lodewyk of Nassau, who was in France endeavouring to raise troops with which to relieve Leyden, a city which stood for the Prince and had been long hardly pressed by the Spaniards.

Philip sighed.

He almost regretted Alva; Resquesens, the new Governor, was as poor a statesman and not so good a general, and his policy, less ferocious and bloodthirsty than that of his predecessor, had not proved any more successful in subduing the rebel heretics; how could the King forgive him the defeat of his Armada at

Romerswael, which had left the rebels with the supremacy of the sea?

If Alva had failed and Resquesens had failed, who was to succeed?

Philip bit his quill and blinked at the candle flame.

The door opened gently and a woman entered with a light yet decided step.

She wore a dark green gown and a black lace mantilla of a close pattern; her hair was dark and arranged in heavy masses either side her sallow face, which was pale in complexion and aquiline in feature and not beautiful save in the large dusky and intelligent eyes, black lashed and browed.

Large pearls of fine lustre and colour hung in her small ears; her only other ornament was a large tortoise-shell comb, set with coral carved in the shape of large roses — these being the sole colour in her attire.

She looked at Philip with something of the same expression with which Granvelle had looked at him — a mingling of disdain for the man and awe for the King.

She was Aña D'Eboli, widow of his Minister, for a long while his adviser and his lover, but in neither respect faithful to him, for Antonio Perez held what she had of heart and loyalty; no one deceived Philip more bitterly than these two to whom he extended that confidence of which he was usually so niggardly; the Princess D'Eboli believed that he trusted her completely, and so was, perhaps, over-confident in her bearing towards the King, but so far her domination and her fascination held him; she was absolutely the most brilliant person, the most alert, the finest in wit and judgment, of any who had come in contact with him.

"Cardinal Granvelle has been with you," she said; she seated herself opposite the King; her presence filled the meagre chamber with a certain magnificence, even softness, her voice and her eyes were caressing; she was beguiling but superb; the disdain of the clever woman for the dull man was never wholly hidden.

"Granvelle worries me," said Philip; before Aña D'Eboli he permitted himself a little show of irritation; though long habit had made his impassive manner hardly capable of displaying any emotion.

"I believe that I have come to worry you also, Sire," said the Princess.

"You have news?" The King knew that she had her own secret channels of information and that her spies were often quicker than his own; what he did not know was her long intrigue with Antonio Perez and that the gain and advancement of this man was the thread that held together all her actions; at present she intended to ruin the Governor of the Netherlands, who was the political enemy of Perez.

"I have news that Lodewyk of Nassau is marching on Maestricht," she answered, gently waving to and fro her tortoise-shell fan.

Philip sighed as was his habit to do when other men would have cursed; that he was profoundly agitated showed from his shaking hands as he clutched the arms of his chair.

"Which means raising the siege of Leyden," added Aña D'Eboli gently.

"God will protect us, God will deliver us," muttered the King.

"Not while Resquesens is your Majesty's Governor in the Netherlands."

The King shook his head dismally.

"There is no one else," he said.

But Aña D'Eboli had her own schemes; not only did she wish to disgrace Resquesens by a recall, but she wished to ruin another man by sending him to undertake the impossible and heart-breaking task of governing the Netherlands.

"Don John has been so successful with the Turks, surely he can crush the heretics," she replied.

The King stroked his chin.

"Don John," he said thoughtfully; he did not love his half-brother, whose glorious achievements had cast so much splendour on his reign, for it was not in him to love youth and beauty and gaiety in a man; certainly he had raised Don John up but he was equally prepared to cast him down and there was an ingenuity about the suggestion of the Princess that pleased him; Resquesens was obviously incapable, Don John was clamouring for employment and possibly his brilliant gifts might avail where even Alva had failed.

"Do you think," he added cautiously, "that Don John is a match for the Prince of Orange?"

"No man is a match for that devil," answered the Princess decisively.

"But some day," said the King patiently, "God will permit that a knife or a bullet reach his heart."

"What of Gaspar D'Anastro's man?"

"I have heard nothing more."

"It is a strange thing," said Aña D'Eboli with some contempt, "that so many try and none can succeed."

The King turned his mind from this disagreeable subject.

"What troops has Lodewyk of Nassau?" he asked.

"He has engaged the escort that was taking the Duc D'Anjou to Poland — other troops raised in France and German mercenaries."

"How will he pay these troops?" asked Philip bitterly.

Aña D'Eboli shrugged her delicate shoulders.

"How have the Nassau family paid so far?"

"How indeed?" groaned the King.

"They are ruined men — and yet they can always raise money — men —"

"This should be the last time."

The King looked at her and a feeble light blazed in his dull eyes.

"Whether or no it be the last time, rest assured that they will not succeed in their rebellion, even if I have to raze to the ground every town in the Netherlands."

"Your Majesty must be careful that the rebels do not raze the towns themselves — Count Lodewyk, as I said, advances on Maestricht."

A light foam gathered on the King's lips and his hand quivered as he wiped it away with his laced handkerchief; he stared fixedly in front of him past the yellow halo cast by the candles into the darkness beyond.

His enemy seemed to loom monstrous before him, casting a dark shadow over his might and his power; menacing even the existence of his Empire; he saw William of Orange as evil incarnate before whom every weapon was powerless, and the rebellion of which he was the life and soul as a plague spot, which, spreading, would in time ruin all his kingdoms.

It seemed as if the rebels had nothing and he had everything; yet in truth he was cruelly hampered: embarrassed for money, surrounded by a corrupt Court and governing vast dominions by means of a network of minute and tortuous intrigue, watched with jealousy and suspicion by both England and France, each of whom were ready and eager to foment trouble in his realms. Philip of Spain was by no means entirely powerful and completely master of his vast means.

Still the odds were greatly on his side, and it remained a wonder to his pride and a marvel to even his dull intelligence that the rebels could so long hold aloft the flag of their independence.

Aña D'Eboli was quick to see this feeling in him and to play upon it for her own secret purpose.

"Your Majesty's credit is sufficiently shaken already in the Netherlands," she said, "by the manner in which the Prince of Orange has been able to establish himself in Holland and Zeeland — this expedition of Count Lodewyk must be crushed."

"It shall be."

"Your Majesty must see to it — under pain of your displeasure Resquesens must crush Count Lodewyk — on him are staked the hopes of all the rebels."

"Not on him, but on William of Orange," said Philip with a rare flash of insight.

"But William now depends on Lodewyk."

"Resquesens must do his utmost," returned the King sullenly. "Can I do more than command him to do that?"

Aña D'Eboli saw that she had sufficiently pressed her point and deftly changed the subject; she knew by long experience, just how far she could make the King dance to her piping.

She smiled — a flash of perfect teeth against her dusky skin.

"The ultimate end is not in doubt," she said.

"Nor the ultimate punishment," said the King grimly.

Aña D'Eboli rose.

Even to her there was an oppression in the air of the King's cabinet; a terrible sense of dullness and gloom in the presence of the King; even to Aña D'Eboli the Escurial was a dreary place.

She looked out of the narrow pointed window on to the unfinished gardens, cold in the still light of the February afternoon.

Like Granvelle had thought — so she thought — what is the use of all of it since none of us are happy?

She leant her sick head against the mullions and the chilly gleam of the hidden sun was full on her sallow face.

At that moment the Princess D'Eboli felt as hungry and forlorn for happiness as had ever Rénèe le Meung or any poor Netherland exile. Yet why?

She asked herself the question with disdain — she had security, power, and even love, yet somehow her crooked life was not pleasing even to herself; the smell of the blood poured daily at the foot of Philip's throne stank in her nostrils and the close air of the Escurial seemed crowded with the presence of murdered men.

Aña D'Eboli had had no pity for any of them; yet the thought of them oppressed her; she could not, either, soon forget those two who had died so near together — Isabelle de Valois and Don Carlos; to the first she had been indifferent, the second she had disliked — yet she did not care to reflect upon the sudden end of either Queen or Prince — Isabelle's fallen loveliness was as unpleasant to recall as the mad hideousness of the Prince.

She glanced, half furtively, at Philip.

He sat with his chin resting on his chest and his hands spread out on the dark arms of the black chair in which he sat, like thin white claws, so closely did the blanched skin cling to the bones.

His jaw had dropped a little and his eyes were half closed.

He looked both like his father, the great Emperor, in those last days of insane penitence, and his imbecile son whom he had been forced to destroy.

Aña D'Eboli did not care to look at him; she unfurled her fan before her face and crept from the room.

In the first chamber through which she had to pass, the Queen and several of her women were gathered before a fire of pine logs which filled the musty chamber with a pleasant odour.

Anne of Austria was seated in a deep chair of red and yellow tapestry, fringed with heavy gold; her attire of black and silver, though splendid in itself, was loose and disordered, her ruff open around her full throat, threads of tumbled fair hair caught in this ruff of crooked cambric and waved across a candid brow.

She had something of an air of nobility, and seemed as if she might have been, under some circumstances, happy and blithe.

Aña D'Eboli came up behind her chair; the dark head was bent near the fair one; the powerful favourite was familiar and even haughty with the foreign Queen; yet Philip loved Anne of Austria, though not to the extent with which he had loved Isabelle de Valois.

The Queen looked up with a clear glance from her gray-blue eyes.

She knew perfectly well the position and power of Aña D'Eboli and was not afraid of either; she had the nerve and spirit that her predecessor had lacked and she was the Emperor's daughter; besides being of the same blood as Philip and having something of his craft.

"With what gaieties shall we pass the time?" she asked.

She laughed and her laugh was hard.

"No one speaks of anything but this rebellion in the Netherlands," she added with malice, for she knew perfectly well that Aña D'Eboli had been with the King and conferring with him on this subject.

"It is something to talk of," said the Princess calmly. "Lodewyk of Nassau has raised a large mercenary army."

Anne asked what her husband had asked.

"How does he pay for them?"

"Count John finds the money."

The Queen made a little grimace.

"It is astonishing how Count John continues to find money," she remarked.

"His pocket is deep but it has a bottom," returned the Princess.

Anne of Austria smiled slowly.

"You may say the same of the coffers of Spain," she said.

"No," answered the Princess. "I do not think you can say that there is a limit to the resources of Spain, Madam."

And her dark eyes rested steadily on the fair face of the foreigner.

"Perhaps," said the Queen easily. "Count Lodewyk is a gallant knight," she added.

The Spanish ladies glanced at each other; the bold speaking of their mistress filled them with mingled delight and awe; some crossed themselves when they heard her speak of the heretic rebel.

John, Lodewyk, Adolphus, & Henry of Nassau

"A gallant knight your Majesty thinks?" asked the Princess with great bitterness and meaning in her tone.

Anne of Austria looked at her with complete composure and contempt scarcely concealed.

"I think," she said, "a gallant knight — such as one might admire — and love."

Again a little movement went through the waiting-women.

"And love?" echoed the Princess.

"Why not?" smiled the Queen. "Young, beautiful — audacious, leader of a desperate cause — such have always evoked love, Madam."

"Among the light and frivolous, yes," returned the Princess. "They say that this Nassau is beloved by the renegade Abbess of Joüarrs — your Majesty has heard that?"

"She will marry some one — why not Lodewyk of Nassau?" said the Queen.

"Certainly — a fitting match, the heretic and the nun," answered the Princess drily.

Anne of Austria slightly lifted her shoulders.

"I hear she also is beautiful — and young," she said, "therefore no doubt it is a fitting match."

"It is your Majesty's pleasure to be tolerant," remarked Aña D'Eboli sarcastically.

The Queen's shapely hand further loosened the stiff cambric from her throat and bosom and toyed with a little ornament of rubies that hung there.

"I was not trained in harshness," she replied quietly. "I can admire even these rebel heretics when they are brave."

She looked into the fiery logs and her sad face softened.

"And they *are* brave," she added. "I have heard tales —" she paused and smiled, as if at inner thoughts, "and the Nassau Princes — are they not fearless as lions?"

"The Devil doubtless gives them confidence," said Aña D'Eboli.

"Ah — the Devil —" repeated the Queen in a curious tone, still gazing into the fire.

"Your Majesty perhaps approves of the Devil?" asked the Princess.

Anne of Austria laughed with a superb indifference.

"Sometimes," she answered.

The Princess's dark face flushed, for there was a certain insolence in the reply that seemed levelled at her, and the waiting-women shuddered at the royal blasphemy.

But the Queen remained unconcerned; fair and voluptuous she looked in the dull yellow glow of the pine fire.

Anne of Austria (1549-1580)

The creaking of a board caused the two women to look around.

From behind the tall screen of stamped gold and ruddy leather came the thin figure of the King.

In a moment the waiting-women were at attention, erect and as if lifeless in their stiff attitudes of respect.

The Queen retained her indifferent position and looked at her husband with sad and weary eyes; Aña D'Eboli withdrew into the vast shadows that filled the tall chamber; she had seen that Philip's first glance had turned to his wife and she could afford to sometimes remain in the background; besides she cared so little for Philip that it cost her no pang of jealousy to see his attention drawn to another woman.

"What do you muse about, Madam?" asked Philip.

He put out his cold hand and half timidly touched her rich sleeve.

"On the glory of your Empire, Sire, and the folly of those who rise in rebellion against you," said the Queen quietly.

CHAPTER IV

DELFT

THE same day that Philip and Aña D'Eboli were discussing the expedition of Lodewyk of Nassau, the brother of that daring general was writing him from Delft a letter full of encouragement and hope.

To William of Orange this invasion of the Netherlands was of signal importance.

He hoped with those troops the now independent states of Holland and Zeeland could supply him, to effect a juncture with Count Lodewyk that would effectually cut off and check the Royalist troops and draw them away from the siege of Leyden — he felt justified in contemplating a success more signal in its effects and more important in its results than even the capture of Brill.

As usual he had but little ground for these hopes, which depended entirely on himself and his family, and, also as usual, the difficulties were immense, and to any but a Nassau would have appeared stupendous. Lodewyk's troops were all mercenaries whose services depended on their pay, and that pay depended on the personal efforts of William and his brothers; a rising in the Provinces still under Resquesens was hardly to be expected, as these were still too firmly held in bondage by the Spanish, and the tiny Republic which William had founded was straining her utmost to maintain herself.

Still the Prince had found his foothold — he could call Delft his home and Holland his Kingdom — "Here I stay to conquer or to find my grave," he had said.

He was surrounded by men who were faithful to him, who trusted him, who were eager to carry out his commands, yet his soul was lonely for he had not a single confidant, no one, save his brothers, who either fully understood his aims or the means by which he hoped to achieve them, no one on whose capacity and judgment he could rely.

Even St. Aldegonde had weakened through the rigours of a Spanish prison and wrote sometimes despairing, sometimes almost craven, counsels tinged by the gloom of his confinement.

Even he, once the firmest of friends and most enthusiastic of supporters, seemed to think William's task hopeless; Philip could not be defied with impunity; would it not be better to submit and trust to the King's mercy?

There remained only John and Lodewyk. John, full of patience and trust, if not of faith and hope, and Lodewyk, as energetic and unflinching as the Prince himself and again full of the enthusiastic confidence and blithe self-reliance belonging to his more buoyant and less far-seeing nature.

These two were the Prince's great reliance — but there were two others equally eager and single-hearted in his cause, the youngest brother, Henry, a youth like that Adolphus who had fallen so early in the struggle, and Duke Christopher, the son of the Elector Palatine. Both these were now with Count Lodewyk.

William recalled them with great tenderness as he sealed his letter to his brother.

And thinking of them he remembered his marriage day in Leipzig. His mind dwelt on that wedding day — no prophecy of that marriage's ending could have been wilder than the truth.

With what splendour, what pomp had that marriage, barren in all save misery, been solemnized!

What would bride or bridegroom have said to one who could have shown them a mirror of the future? Ruin, exile, peril, hatred, disgrace, for him the life of an exiled wanderer, for her dishonour, imprisonment, insanity.

William bent his head as he thought of that marriage and the useless ambition that had dictated it; as an act of policy the union had been fruitless and in itself had been productive of great misery and humiliation.

The desertion of his wife, her repudiation of him and her faithlessness had been the last stab to the hunted and homeless Prince.

Even now, when the sore was somewhat healed, and the shame was hidden from the eyes of men, William recalled her behaviour with bitter pain and disgust.

His present loneliness — a loneliness now of long duration, was to be traced to that mistaken marriage.

He could not but feel homeless in this new home of his, for he had never been one to love solitude and a life alone.

His children were with his brother, Count John, for he had nothing to offer them and he passed his life in the company of soldiers and servants; he often thought of his first wife, Anne of Egmont, and how pleasant she had made his days — he greatly lacked some gentle ministrations to his wants, the sweet companionship of love and sympathy.

Restlessly he wandered up and down the room, which was that of a middle-class burgher.

The floor, neatly tiled in black and red, the black panelled walls, the dark furniture, the blue and white check curtains, the candle-sticks and bowls of polished brass, the white china vessels on the plain bureau all bespoke the simple prosperous merchant or shopkeeper.

There could not well be a greater contrast than between this and the Prince's palace in Brussels, yet, compared with what his surroundings had been since his exile, it was luxury.

The Prince noticed neither the comfort nor the plainness; he had long ceased to take heed of what was about him, as, though once the most magnificent grandee in the Netherlands, he had long ceased to take heed of what he wore.

His clothes now were dark gray and of coarse cloth, his falling band of plain linen, his little sword of the simplest workmanship, his shoes of rough leather; yet the innate grace of his figure and bearing was in no way affected by these things.

Presently he tired of his pacing and seated himself at his table by the window, the upper part of his figure, his head supported in his hand, was reflected in a large mirror of a greenish hue of glass framed in ebony which hung on the wall beside him.

The fine profile was worn and haggard, the dark waves of hair yet further dusted with gray, the hand had lost its smoothness and showed both nerves and veins, his complexion was darkened by exposure, and all savour of youthfulness had gone though the Prince was no more than in the prime of life.

All that was left of the bright cavalier and brilliant grandee who had been the greatest man in the Netherlands were the poise and manner of one equally at home with King and peasant, the gracious composure and the ready smile of the accomplished noble and the self-possessed diplomat.

Such was the man the old glass reflected as he sat before his humble desk, musing, even as, so far away, Philip of Spain sat and brooded over him, and Aña D'Eboli and the Queen discussed the rebel family of Nassau.

William was not thinking of Philip; the loneliness of his own life which somehow today had been brought home to him by the solitariness of those hours not occupied in business had taken his thoughts to those of his friends who had fallen earlier in the struggle.

Especially he thought of Hoogstraaten, the little lion-like soldier whose life had been taken so wantonly it seemed and in the early dawn of that day of prolonged battle which had not yet drawn to a close.

Almost did the Prince of Orange wish that such a fate could have been his; at times he longed for the repose even of death, to escape, even that way, from the overhanging clouds of war and tumult, from the cries and lamentations of despair, from the sights of suffering, misery, and violence that surrounded him — the continual sacrifice of numberless victims to a cause that was perhaps, after all, hopeless.

His clear judgment told him that never again could he hope to see the world serene about him — a prosperous country enjoying peace — a nation given to the arts and comforts of leisure, never expect to see himself living a life of security and ease.

If the miracle was achieved — if a free country, an independent and powerful state should arise from the blood and tears now being shed — it would not be during his life; his son or his grandson might see that day — he, never.

For him it would be storm and violence, battle and intrigue, suspense and anxiety, heartache and pain until the very end.

And that end — he could not hope that it would be peaceful either.

He knew that he was surrounded by continual danger, open and secret, that Philip's spies and Philip's assassins were continually on his track and that it could only be a question of time before his name was added to that of Egmont and Horne and those others on that list in the Escurial who had already satisfied the wrath of Spain. He could only hope that first a little time might be allowed him in which to do some of the work which he had before him and to forward the cause on which he had set his very heart.

This work was slow and at times distasteful; his present intrigues with the French Court were not pleasant to him; it could not be agreeable to the great champion of the Reformed Faith to deal with the king who had sanctioned Saint Bartholomew.

But William knew that if he would try to use only clean tools he would never accomplish anything, and one of his favourite schemes was to pit France against Spain and secure, for the struggling little states he had rescued from Philip, the powerful protection of one of the Princes of the House of Valois.

So far he, and Lodewyk as his agent, had succeeded not only in obtaining constant expressions of repentance for the infamous massacre from the Court of France, but also its formal assurances that henceforth it would not molest those of the Reformed Religion in its dominion and would aid to the utmost the cause of the United Provinces.

To such concessions was France driven by internal disorders, hatred of Spain, and desire of the friendship of England and the hand of England's Queen for François de Valois.

Lodewyk had raised soldiers there, had spoken and written fearlessly and boldly to King and Dowager, had a large party

on his side which his confidence and ability made daily larger
— but William was not one to be lulled by this appearance of
success. His position was by no means brilliant; even Zeeland
and Holland were not completely his; though Middelburg had
fallen, Zeeland was divided by the loss of Haarlem and the
siege of Leyden; the Estates were difficult and often irritating
on the question of supplies, and though the patriots held the
sea successfully, the land forces were mostly mercenary and
therefore not to be depended on if the money raised now with
such difficulty should entirely fail.

So it was that William's hopes rested mostly on France;
the Duke d'Alençon and the King of Poland had sworn assistance;
the Prince knew both to be puppets of circumstance, but he
believed he might pull their strings to his own purpose.

Putting his letter to Lodewyk in his pocket he left the room
and the house and stepped out on to the brick pathway that
ran beside the canal; this was planted with lime trees whose
leafless boughs cast a pleasant tracing of shade on the cheap
bricks, and were reflected in the quiet waters of the canal.

A small boat was moored in front of the steps that led from
the causeway to the water in front of the Prince's house, and
in this boat were seated two boys who were busily engaged in
mending a bright kite; the long tail tied with bright bits of rag
fell over the white painted side of the boat and into the canal.

The door of the house opposite stood open and near the
step sat a woman knitting; by her knee stood a child engaged
in unravelling her ball of bright blue wool.

At an upper window an old, old man looked down into the
street.

The red tiled roofs were covered with pigeons that circled
high and low and ran after each other with gleaming, drooping
wings.

Over all was the clear cold sky of early spring and the light
of pale unstained sunshine.

Standing here, as the Prince was standing, by the quiet canal,
watching the children at their play and the woman at her work

and the old man at his rest, it might almost seem as if it was a time of peace.

To William it appeared as a prophecy of what might yet be in the years to come — when all the land would be always as this spot was now; he thought of the time when men would go to and fro and not wonder at seeing peace about them, but accept it naturally and look upon war and violence as some dreadful dream — a thing to be imagined and read of, not to be experienced.

Not for him those days — yet it was pleasant to think that by his means and the means of those whom he inspired they might be at some distant date achieved.

Pleasant indeed to think that the children of their children might come to remember and bless the name of William of Orange as that of one who had secured to them the priceless gift of liberty.

The Prince turned towards the fortifications of the city.

He walked quickly, for the air was sharp and the sun without strength and there was a certain insidious chill abroad that penetrated to his very blood.

He passed over low bridges, under the gleaming windows of straight houses and before Gothic churches now spoiled of their original splendours and changed from their original uses; here and there an early tree was faintly veiled in green, here and there a hyacinth of blue or pink showed in a garden patch, or a few snowdrops pushed up through the dark earth.

There were very few people abroad and those few, harmless folk, women, children, old men; all the strong manhood was at the war.

William came to the bridge that separated the great canal leading to Rotterdam from the smaller canal running through the city.

Here he paused and leaning on the low brick parapet gazed on the flat prospect of land and water already beginning to be blended by the thin mists of evening.

The paleness of the sky, reflected in the water, became silver, and on this gloomy surface of the canal rested the dark shape of boats, and by the low straight banks grew the straight dark spikes of reeds and grass.

Along the horizon, partially rising from the mist and partially encroaching on the sweep of pellucid sky, dark clouds gathered, gaining every instant in size and intensity, above, in the dazzling clear space of sky swung the sparkling evening star.

A low strong wind blew abroad over the land, the Prince felt it on his face like the touch of a cold hand.

As he gazed across the land which the inhabitants had rescued with such desperate courage from the sea and from the oppressor, the spread of cloud grew larger and rapidly enveloped the sweep of open sky, and the current of the wind rose higher like the swell of water rising against the land.

Still the Prince stood motionless on the bridge, a solitary figure fast being absorbed into the encroaching darkness which was hiding from his gaze the land that he loved, for it was the land on which he had planted his final standard, the spot of ground where he would maintain himself or die.

While he was deep in reverie a messenger from his house came hurrying through the gloomy streets. He brought dispatches from Lodewyk.

William read them by the light of the lantern his valet carried.

They were but a few lines that told that Lodewyk was already marching into the heart of the enemy and hoped soon to effect a juncture with William between Delft and Rotterdam.

CHAPTER V

COUNT LODEWYK

THE winds blew with bitter force around the Castle of Fauquemont, howled through the ruined portion and shook the doors and windows and lifted the tapestry in those rooms that were still habitable.

In one of these, which once had been a magnificent apartment, but had been despoiled when the castle had been ruined in one of the obscure frays of this rapacious war, the younger brothers of William of Orange sat at Council with the few dependable officers of their little mercenary force which had advanced thus far into the enemy's country and was now encamped on the Meuse, in the Duchy of Limburg a few miles from Maestricht, the first objective of the expedition, the second and principal being the junction with William and the forces of the Estates at Bommel in Holland.

The Council chamber was dreary and cold; all articles of furniture had long since been removed from the castle save those of an unwieldy heaviness, the principal of which was a great bed of carved black wood from which the blue velvet curtains had been torn so hastily that portions of them hung still from the ebony rings.

Here sat Count Lodewyk and on the bed steps the two other young leaders of the expedition, the youngest Nassau and the son of the Elector Palatine.

The other officers, French and Dutch, sat on such heavy chairs of state as the pillagers had left; on a great bare and black table stood candles thrust into the necks of bottles and a stable lamp, for none of these Princes travelled with camp furniture.

A hasty fire of such logs as could be found near by burnt in the wide grate and gave a fugitive heat to a portion of the great cold chamber, and cast a flickering and sombre light on the three young men seated by the black bed.

Of these Count Lodewyk was by far the most remarkable, though all had in common a singular air of serene ardour, of bright youth and enthusiasm.

The Nassau brothers were alike in their slight gracefulness, in the elegance of their appearance, in their alert manner, but Lodewyk had an added charm of face and deportment, a gaiety, a vivacity, an air of dignity and command that made him well fitted to be the leader of a noble and romantic cause.

He was now in the prime of life and, though not tall, full of grace and strength; his countenance, no longer so soft as it had been in the days of his extravagant youth, was eminently pleasing, his steady eyes were full of light and fire, and the full curls of his pale brown locks fell on either side of a brow still smooth.

He wore his armour, black damascened with gold, over which was knotted a scarf of orange silk, a high collar of white linen was buttoned under his chin; he was leaning slightly forward, his left hand on his hip.

His brother, Henry, was darker and taller; he had the Nassau gaiety and had already proved himself to have the Nassau boldness and discretion; he wore a leathern coat and breeches marked by the pressure of his armour.

The Elector's son was a youth of a melancholy deportment but of steadfast eyes and mouth; he spoke little and seemed to greatly lean on the words and even the presence of Count Lodewyk; he was large, fair, and comely and was partially armed in heavy plate.

Lodewyk held a little parchment on which was roughly drawn a map of the Meuse and the fortifications of the enemy who was encamped on the opposite bank of the river.

He was explaining this to the assembled officers, who listened to him in a silence that was somewhat gloomy.

Disaster had already marked the progress of the little army; they had been unable to cross the Meuse owing to the ice, which, insufficient to bear the passage of troops, had yet been sufficient

Lodewyk of Nassau (1538-1574)

to prevent the use of boats, more than a thousand of the mercenaries had deserted at the first hint of failure and Mendoza had inflicted on them a night surprise which had cost them seven hundred men.

In view of these facts the general opinion was that it was now necessary to abandon the project of taking Maestricht, which had been reinforced by the arrival of Braccamonte and Mondrogan with several companies of foot and horse.

"But we must," said Lodewyk with great earnestness and firmness, "cross the Meuse and effect a juncture with the Prince in Holland else this expedition from which so much is hoped will prove fruitless indeed."

149

They did not contradict him; the whole project had been at best but a desperate enterprise and they were all soldiers of fortune.

"Besides," continued the young General, "the men become impatient, without some action one cannot hold them long satisfied."

It was not his policy to admit his financial position, even to his officers, but the truth was that his troops were on the verge of mutiny for lack of pay and he had nothing but promises to give them.

"Therefore," said Duke Christopher with a little smile, "since we cannot go backwards, we must go forward."

And he looked at the company with calm if tired eyes.

"Therefore," answered the Count, "I propose to move down the river to this point," he indicated it on the map, "and there to cross and give battle to the Spaniards. Mark me, gentlemen, if we are successful we shall go far to drive these devils out of the country."

To those listening to him there seemed nothing wild in these words, for they were men who lived on hope in the midst of desperate circumstances; and they knew that Count Lodewyk had already accomplished much out of nothing and had re-arisen again and again from defeat to further endeavour.

As for the Count, he believed what he said; even William had declared that a decisive victory now and a successful juncture with his own troops would suffice to drive the Spaniards from Holland and Zeeland.

And in his heart Lodewyk still had the hope of taking Maestricht, despite Mondrogan and Braccamonte and their foot and horse.

Rising he went to the table and by the light of the guttering candles pointed out, on his rude map, the course he proposed to follow, along the right bank of the Meuse, between that river and the Rhine, towards Nymegen.

"There," he said, "we can cross the river and give battle to the forces of D'Avila."

His bright eyes flashed from one face to another.

"If we can achieve a victory now," he added, "half the Provinces will rise against Resquesens."

"If we turn back?" suggested one of the captains quietly.

"We leave the Hollanders to despair," replied Lodewyk briefly.

"But we shall not turn back," said Count Henry, looking at his brother.

"No," said Lodewyk.

There was a little silence.

Each man was thinking of what was likely to be the result of this venture, already attended by misfortune and becoming daily more doubtful in character.

It was no ordinary combat in which they proposed to engage but a battle in which they must conquer or most certainly fall victims to the wrath of the victors.

In these fierce struggles of mutual hate there was never any pity for the vanquished; and the little force of Lodewyk, was advancing into the enemy country with all means of escape closed behind it — and the enemy was skilful, powerful, and ruthless.

The Count, the gold lines in his dark armour gleaming out of the shadows of the background, his bright face and hair full in the candle beams, looked from one to another of his captains and, smiling, dismissed them.

Count Henry and Duke Christopher alone remained; neither had moved from the steps of the great black bed.

As the door closed on the last of the officers, another figure, until now concealed in the heavy shadows at the end of the room, crept forward into the ruddy gloom of the now dying fire.

A miserable figure, bent and shabby, with an unsteady gait and a cowering air, crept to the embers and spread out shivering hands.

Count Lodewyk, standing at the table, sunk in reverie, the open map in his hand, did not observe this figure, but the other two noticed him with a little movement of distaste.

It was Duprès, fallen on the extreme of evil fortune. Lately, having met Count Lodewyk in Paris, he had presumed on his acquaintance with the Nassau family to attach himself to his person. And Lodewyk had shown himself no other than kind to this wretch who was now reduced to the lowest means of making a miserable livelihood.

He remembered him at his brother's wedding in Leipzig and as belonging to his brother's establishment in Brussels, but most clearly and most kindly in association with the battle of Heiligerlee and the death of his brother Adolphus.

The other two princes also remembered the fellow and it did not please them to see him in attendance on Count Lodewyk.

He now stood in the great wide space of the fire rubbing his hands together and shuddering. Lodewyk, turning suddenly, saw him.

"Ah, you — forever at my heels," he said, good humouredly. "Like my dog —"

"Say rather a bird of prey or evil omen," remarked Duke Christopher gloomily.

Count Henry laughed; Lodewyk, still gazing at the charlatan, smiled.

"See, these gentlemen are afraid of you, Duprès," he said.

The Frenchman wheeled around; his tall, thin, and bent figure was clearly outlined against the steady glow of the fire.

"Afraid of me?"

"Yes," answered the Elector's son.

The charlatan glanced towards the window. "It is near the hour of the dawn," he said.

"So late?" exclaimed Count Lodewyk.

"Why, I would sleep a little before we march," said his brother and slipped his arm through that of the Elector's son.

Count Lodewyk went to the window and lifting the iron bar that held the shutters in place flung them open.

The chamber faced east; the whole sky opposite was pale and luminous with light; but about the horizon lay banks of black clouds and the land lay dark and lifeless.

Count Lodewyk stood with his hands resting on the sill and the pure cold air of early morning blew on his face, the powerful wind lifting the hair from his brow and shoulders.

With the opening of the window the remaining candles sank out and Duprès shivered in his mean garments.

The two young soldiers looked at each other and each saw his companion's face as ghastly in the colourless light of dawn.

Lodewyk stood motionless and his thoughts flew wide, he thought of the brother waiting for him in tense anxiety and breathless hope, of the people of Holland expecting his coming with such joy and impatience, of how much hung on this battle that he must undertake despite all his own strange foreboding, and despite all the misfortunes that must attend a defeat.

He could still have saved himself by a retreat, but he had never been of that temper to give way to doubt, to turn back before any obstacle.

His judgment told him that he must abandon Maestricht, but he resolved to endeavour with his last strength to effect the junction with his brother on which so much depended.

As he gazed at the east the black clouds hurried aside, swept by the headlong wind, and rose obscuring the clear space of sky and then leaving it unstained and brightened by the rays of the yet unseen sun.

No thing so moves my pity
As seeing through these lands
Field, village, town, and city
Pillaged by roving bands.
O that the Spaniards rape thee,
My Netherlands so sweet —
The thought of that does grip me,
Causing my heart to bleed.

A stride on steed of mettle
I've waited with my host
The tyrant's call to battle,
Who durst not do his boast.
For, near Maestricht,[1] in hiding,
He feared the force I wield:
My horsemen were seen riding
Bravely across the field.

---

[1] The reference to Maestricht in this stanza of the *Wilhelmus* is not to the present time (1574) with Count Lodewyk, but to William of Orange's failed attempt to invade the Southern Netherlands in 1568.

CHAPTER VI

MOOKERHEYDE

BY the middle of April Lodewyk of Nassau was encamped at the village of Mook, on the Meuse, near Cleves.

Don Sancho D'Avila, the Spanish General, had outmarched him and now was facing him on the same side of the river which he had crossed by means of a bridge of boats.

The position of Lodewyk was not favourable; behind he was hemmed in by a chain of hills, so that his superiority in cavalry was greatly discounted by the limited space in which he could move; he had with difficulty quelled a mutiny which had broken out on the eve of a battle among the mercenaries, who had demanded their pay as was their custom to do at the moment when they considered their services most valuable; and he had received the news that De Hierges and Valdez were on their way with reinforcements for the Spaniards to the number of five or six thousand. More desperate than ever seemed his chances of success as that success became more needful and more precious in his sight.

Passionately did he long to effect the promised meeting with the Prince; it seemed to him that could he but clasp his brother's hand in his all would be well.

But before that could be accomplished he had to fight his way through the flower of the Spanish forces.

He had not wished for this battle, least of all under these circumstances, and he was acutely conscious that misfortune had followed his expedition from the first, but it was now obviously impossible to make the passage of the river without giving battle to the enemy, and there was nothing in the heart or mind of Lodewyk of Nassau that bade him flinch from the inevitable conflict. Nor was he outwardly downcast or discouraged.

His cheerful and gallant demeanour had even persuaded the mercenaries to fight without further ado; Lodewyk had pledged his honour for their pay, and neither he nor his brother had ever failed in that — those who fought for them had always been paid to the full extent of their engagement, even if Lodewyk went without camp furniture and William had not the wherewithal to make a present to one who had done him a service; moreover, something, in even the lowest of the French and German adventurers, had responded to the figure of fortitude and honour represented by the young Count.

The day of battle dawned dull and stormy; low black clouds filled the sky and were reflected in the dark waters of the Meuse; the few alders and poplars that grew about the banks and edged the fields that, this year, there had been no one to till or sow, shivered in a light, cold wind.

The spring was late this year and in the minds of all men the winter seemed interminable and the summer very far away.

Count Lodewyk armed in the bedroom of the farmhouse that he had made his headquarters. A lantern hung on the whitewashed walls and through the small unshuttered window filtered the pallid glow of the yet unrisen sun.

Between these two lights stood the young commander; his squire had just left him and he was himself knotting the scarf of orange silk across his breast.

On the rush chair near the low bed where he had spent a few hours of rest, but not of sleep, were his casque with black plumes, his baton and his sword attached to the baldrick of embroidered leather given him by some French ladies.

Lodewyk recalled the gentle donors when he came to fasten on his weapon; but there was no particular woman in his mind.

He was sorry for that; he had been victorious and fortunate in his loves; but he had never attached himself to the one woman who would have been alone in his thoughts at such a moment as this.

Though rumour had persistently coupled his name with that of the Abbess of Joüarrs, she was nothing to him but a gracious figure among many gracious figures of women; his mind dwelt on her a little, then his thoughts wandered away again among all the fair faces which had ever smiled on him.

Smiled, yes, smiles were easy but were there any who would weep should they know of his defeat and overthrow; anyone who would stain her beauty with tears for the sake of his memory should he fall as Adolphus had fallen?

No, there was no one who would do more than heave a sigh — he had no lover.

With a little laugh he shrugged his shoulders — why should he think of these things now? He turned to the window and gazed at the black and gray land and river and wide pale sky, every moment brightening.

The nearer prospect was filled by his troops of foot and horse, now beginning to move into the pre-arranged order of battle, some of the cavalry reaching as far as the hills that formed the horizon. As the Count looked his brother came behind him and touched his arm.

"The day is cold — a late spring," Lodewyk said.

"The merrier when it comes," answered Henry with a certain wistful gaiety.

"I think it will come too late for you and me," returned the brother. "The flowers of this year will not be for our gathering."

"I have never known you gloomy," said Count Henry. "What presentiment is this?"

"No presentiment — the conviction of my heart. Our task finishes today. What we have done, good or ill, stands to our names and we have no more time to efface it. Look well upon this sun — I think we shall not see another earthly dawn."

"God's Will be done," said Count Henry.

"I would first have taken the Prince's hand again — but he will understand."

"That we did our utmost," added Henry simply. He leant slightly from the window and gazed to where lay the gathering forces of Spain. "But why should you talk of defeat — we had such high hopes."

"My hopes have failed me," answered Lodewyk — "for me this battle ends all."

Taking his baton of command in his hand he left the humble room and stepped through the adjoining kitchen into the open air.

Henry followed him; the two mounted their great Flemish steeds and turned towards the centre of the patriot troops.

They had scarcely started before they were joined by Duke Christopher, who rode a white horse of remarkable size and beauty trapped with fine scarlet leather and golden bosses.

The young knight was not so sternly melancholy as usual, and wore in his casque, beneath the white plumes, a bunch of spring flowers, cuckoo pint and primroses, fading against the polished steel.

"Will they give battle before the reinforcements arrive?" he asked, gazing in the direction of the enemy.

"Remembering Heiligerlee they may wait, yet I do not think so," returned Lodewyk. "D'Avila is both bold and prudent and will not risk our slipping past him."

The sun rose above the hills, casting long rays of light on armour and lances, harness and cannon, muskets and pikes, and the tiled roofs of the little village of Mook.

Duke Christopher looked towards this rising light which fell full on his grave and comely face and raised his hand as if in salute.

"You also?" said Count Lodewyk. "Do you say farewell?"

The Elector's son smiled at him.

"My auguries are even as yours — of gloomy speech — this day we are not destined to conquer, Count."

"Then it is foolish to do battle," said Count Henry lightly.

"But it is too late to turn back," answered Lodewyk quietly. "Too late! The sun has already risen — the armies are ready — our fate hangs upon the next few hours."

"When this sun sets this battle must be lost or won," said Duke Christopher.

"When this sun sets I at least shall be beyond the darkness," smiled Count Lodewyk.

The three embraced and separated, each to take command of his own division.

The Spaniards still showed no sign of advancing and Lodewyk began to be impatient for the battle to commence.

He rode from one part of the field to the other visiting his forces, which were now drawn up in full battle array; ten companies of infantry arranged between the river and brook — the bulk of the infantry massed together in the centre and four squadrons of cavalry reaching as far as the low hills which circumscribed the field.

The forces of the enemy could be plainly discerned; the pikemen and musketeers to the right, the cavalry and sharpshooters to the left with the carbineers in front and the Spanish lancers behind.

At the first hour of light the Spaniards had made an attack on the deep trench with which Count Lodewyk had surrounded himself, and an intermittent skirmishing was taking place at this point without bringing on a general engagement.

The Spaniards, who had already received reinforcements to the number of a thousand men, were, in truth, debating the expediency of deferring the combat until the arrival of Valdez with about five thousand more troops which might be looked for by the following morning; at present the royalists were outnumbered by about three thousand men.

While the Spaniards were holding a hurried council of war, Lodewyk was forcing them to a combat; his trumpets sounded a defiance and his army stood ready.

This challenge was soon answered by the shrill notes of the Spanish bugles, for D'Avila decided not to wait for the reinforcements, lest, during the oncoming night Lodewyk should contrive to effect the passage of the river and join his brother.

Therefore another assault was ordered on the trench; which was slowly carried, the royalists charging on the village, from which, however, they were soon expelled by the patriots, Lodewyk having sent a large number of men to strengthen this point.

In a short time (it was now not much past ten of the clock), the battle involved almost the whole of the troops either side, the army of Lodewyk and the army of D'Avila swaying to and fro in serried masses either side the disputed trench and village. Lodewyk sat motionless at the head of his cavalry, watching the struggle.

The sun had been soon obscured by light rising clouds and had disappeared behind their watery vapour to be seen no more that day; the first brightness of the morning had passed and the weather was dull and gray, cold too, with a fine thin wind blowing above the river and the wet marshes.

The clouds seemed to press low and heavily on the heads of the gathered armies, and lances and armour, swords and muskets, helmets and carbines gleamed here and there with a sinister brightness amid the dark confusion of the battle.

Count Lodewyk glanced once up into the higher spaces of the clouds that were yet undefiled by flame and smoke, then, raising his baton, gave the order to charge.

His keen and practised eye had discerned that his infantry was beginning to break, and indeed almost before his cavalry was in motion, they had given way and were flying from their posts, completely routed, leaving the enemy in possession of the trench and the village.

Lodewyk set his teeth as he saw his men going down like cornstalks before the tempest and hurled himself with fury upon the ranks of the Spanish horse.

The men who followed him in that desperate charge were not German mercenaries or any soldiers who fought for hire, but noble gentlemen of the Netherlands, stern patriots of Holland and Brabant and French Huguenots who had served under Coligny.

The hired cavalry was behind them, but these, pressing close behind their leader, bore the brunt of the battle as befitted the flower of the army.

With the first fury of their charge they bore down before them the carbineers who formed the vanguard of the royalist cavalry and who broke at once and fled in panic towards the river.

Rising in his stirrups and waving to his men Count Lodewyk followed in pursuit; in the marshes and on the river bank the royalists went down, horse and man; the patriots only paused in their pursuit when the sullen waters of the river lapped at their horses' feet and they saw the fugitives either sinking beneath the sullied ripples or desperately swimming to the opposite bank; then Lodewyk turned to see the issue of the general battle.

A confused action was now taking place on all parts of the field; the Spanish lances and the German Black Horse, who had withstood Lodewyk's onslaught, had fallen on the remainder of his cavalry when they had retired to reload their weapons and a fierce and desperate conflict ensued.

Spaniard and Netherlander, German and Frenchman struggled together amid the report of musketry, the smoke, the spurting flame, the flash of uplifted weapon; nodding plumes were struck to the ground, men fell from their horses to be trodden into the mud by frenzied hoofs, foot and cavalry were intermingled in one maddened mass; shouts and oaths of men rose with the cries of wounded animals and pierced with rage and terror the hoarse clamour of the encounter.

While Lodewyk gazed he saw that the fight was going against him — even as his heart had predicted.

Galloping to the head of those who had followed him in his pursuit to the river bank, he dashed back to the centre of the conflict where his forces, horse and foot, were being borne down before the Spanish spears and the German lances.

Lodewyk, galloping from one part of the field to another in the effort to rally his remaining men, saw that the day was lost before well begun.

Black clouds were rising from the horizon and closing over the gray vault of heaven; a low thunder rolled in the west and heavy drops of rain began to fall.

A Spanish captain, recognizing the Nassau chieftain by his orange scarf, rode at him full tilt; Lodewyk drew his sword and struck the enemy down, then, controlling his plunging horse, turned to where the last nucleus of his cavalry were drawn together by the entrance to the village of Mook; at the head of them was Count Henry, taut as a bow in his saddle, keen as a hawk in his eager glance, waiting to see how best he could fall on the enemy and meet his own inevitable fate. Lodewyk rode to his side.

"The day is lost," he said, pointing to the black and bloody field above which the storm clouds hung low, "the fight is over, it is now but a carnage and a massacre."

The youngest Nassau looked towards the battle where so many fair and high hopes were being forever shattered.

They were joined by the Elector's son; his surtout hung in tatters over his dirtied armour and he held a broken sword in his hand.

"It is over, it is over!" he said, breathing heavily, "it is over and I have said farewell to life."

Lodewyk of Nassau took the casque from his head and threw it away; his fair face and bright hair showed radiant above his soiled armour; the little body of cavalry gathered about him; the thunder rolled louder; in the pause were the groans and shrieks of the dying and the fierce Spanish shouts of murderous revenge and triumph.

The three young princes clasped hands; their figures were illumined by the glare from some farm-houses near by which the Spaniards had fired; the rain fell on their uncovered heads.

Gathering their men about them with words of encouragement, they charged with the fury of despair into the midst of the dark and hideous fight.

Thus the two Nassau princes, and Duke Christopher, the Elector's son, went down together on that day of woe and terror and never, alive or dead, did any again behold them.

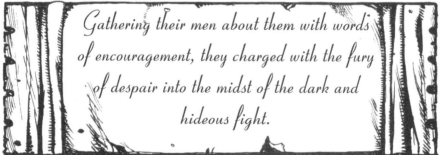

Gathering their men about them with words of encouragement, they charged with the fury of despair into the midst of the dark and hideous fight.

CHAPTER VII

RÉNÈE

THE fields around Heidelberg were full of flowers; the first days of May soft with sunshine lingered pleasantly over woods flushing into leaf, and banks of violets, of narcissus, primroses, and the young fronds of fern all fragrant in the damp richness of the forest.

Among these flowers, towards the fall of the day, Charlotte de Bourbon walked with Rénèe le Meung.

A silence that seemed to hold the promise of mysterious sweet sound encompassed them, they wandered aimlessly between the slender trunks of the young aspen and the round polished and massive trunks of the ancient beech trees.

The Princess carried a flat rush basket and now and then plucked and placed therein long-stalked flowers; but Rénèe did not pick the blossoms though she moved so as not to tread them under foot.

A gentle light was diffused through the high branches so delicately covered with the budding green, and pale shadows fell over the slowly moving figures of the two women.

Charlotte de Bourbon wore a gown of violet cloth with a white cloak and hood; her blonde hair was slightly disordered by the soft spring winds which had also brought a colour to her usually pale face.

Rénèe's attire was plain and careless and ill accorded with the scene; her beauty was under its habitual eclipse of indifference and apathy; lines of weariness were beginning to disfigure her smooth contours and sadness to dim the light of her eyes; for life still passed her by and she had no longer the hopeful charms of youth to support her loneliness, no loner any service to perform with which to occupy her time; she missed even the exacting days of labour passed under the rule of Anne of Saxony, for then at least she was performing a self-imposed task and satisfying her own ideal — rendering the only service in her power to the only human being for whom she had ever cared.

But now — what was she but a useless dependent on charity, a creature devoted to little tasks any serving-maid could have performed as well.

Her most constant companion was the Princess Charlotte, but the two had not come close together; this was not the fault of the Frenchwoman, Rénèe had no love, no confidence, no friendship to give to anyone, all was concentrated in that one feeling that ran deep and secret as life itself.

Rénèe thought of the Prince and nothing but the Prince, it was the devotion of the soldier for his captain, of the patriot for his leader, of the oppressed for his saviour — and the love of a woman for a man, all strengthened and idealized by time and distance until the passion had become an obsession, the devotion a creed, from which she had no distraction, no relief, nor would she find or accept any.

Charlotte de Bourbon, with the tact of one trained to observe and command, had always respected her reserve; the Princess herself had a self-contained nature that required no confidant, a firmness of purpose that required no support from others.

In their wandering they reached a bank where the primroses grew thick in clusters between the damp mosses and dead leaves of last year and there Charlotte seated herself, on the fallen bough of a beech tree which had sunk half into the earth.

With steady, delicate fingers she picked the flowers to the right and left of her and laid them in her basket.

"Do you think," she asked, lifting her candid eyes to Rénèe, "that Lodewyk of Nassau is dead?"

Rénèe was a little startled at this calm in Charlotte, for she had always believed, in common with many others, that Count Lodewyk was the chosen husband of the Princess.

"I know what you know, Madam," she returned, "that only a few survived the fight of Mookerheyde."

"Duke Christopher, too," said Charlotte thoughtfully, "and Count Henry — all gone together — it does not seem possible."

"The Elector will not believe it yet, so why should we?"

"In his heart the Elector believes it, though he will not hear mourning."

"He believes it?"

"I think so," returned the Princess quietly. "He told me this morning that he had received a dispatch from the Prince — His Highness has written and written to his brother and received no answer, and no news whatever of the Princes has come to him."

"It is too terrible," said Rénèe, "such a disaster! Why has God turned away His face! All our hopes went down at Mookerheyde."

"No," answered Charlotte. "William of Orange lives."

The waiting-woman looked at her swiftly.

"But His Highness cannot do everything," she murmured.

"Why, I think he can — do everything," said the Princess.

She had picked all the primroses within reach and now sat with her hands in her lap.

"Even if these two other branches be lopped from the House of Nassau," she continued, "the cause is not lost — not while the Prince lives."

"Why — she never cared for the Count — never cared," thought Rénèe; she leant against the mossy trunk of the great beech tree that threw a soft shade over the Princess; she was in a darker shadow herself.

"You do not weep for Count Lodewyk, Madam?" she asked.

"Why should I weep?" returned the Princess. "He died young and splendid. What did the Elector say of his son! — 'Better die thus than live in sloth or evil.' "

"Hard words for love to say, Madam."

"Brave words," returned the Princess.

Rénèe was looking at her curiously.

"I could not take so calmly the loss of one beloved."

Charlotte looked thoughtfully at her flowers.

"No," she said slowly. "Perhaps I could not — it is easy when one is heart free!"

"Heart free?" echoed Rénèe. "Then Count Lodewyk was nothing to you?"

Charlotte flushed at the abruptness of the question and Rénèe coloured also when she realized what she had said. But the Princess answered gravely —

"He was no suitor of mine, if that is your meaning, though I know that our names have been coupled."

"Why, Madam, what right have I to speak?" interrupted Rénèe with a certain recklessness. "I have never been in the confidence of Your Highness."

In some way, strange even to herself, she was troubled that Charlotte had not given her heart to Lodewyk of Nassau.

"I have no confidences to give," replied the Princess serenely. "Believe me, none."

Rénèe did not reply; her heart was weary and the spring woods hateful; she was thinking of another forest, dull in its winter barrenness, through which she had ridden one magic day, with the hero of her secret dreams.

Charlotte rose.

"Let us return," she said. "See how low the sun shines through the trees."

Rénèe followed her in silence.

"I am thinking," continued Charlotte, "of the Prince of Orange."

Rénèe looked at her intently.

"Is it not a sad life now and a lonely one?" added the Princess. "He had so many hopes on this enterprise — think now, the suspense, the waiting, the anxiety, and gradually the sure knowledge of disaster — again disaster."

"You think more of him then, than of those who have fallen?"

"They are beyond my pity," answered Charlotte gravely. "No, pity I would not say, for who am I to pity such as the Prince — but they are beyond my tenderness — they suffer no more. They are with God." Her voice faltered a little on the last words.

"Do you think that the Prince suffers?" asked Rénèe slowly. "He must suffer — one who has undertaken such a task — against such odds?" replied Charlotte, showing an emotion that she seldom showed. "And alone — he tells the Elector that there is no one in whom he can trust."

"He was always alone," said Rénèe, "even in Brussels — he is better now than when he had his wife."

"Do not call her his wife, she is that no longer — the theologians have declared his divorce valid."

Rénèe had not heard this news; it startled her to think that the Prince was free, her thoughts went to the wretched woman whom she had so long served.

"And Anne of Saxony?" she asked.

"She has been returned to her people," said Charlotte. "She is mad."

"Well for her when death releases her," replied Rénèe, "her life has been but suffering and she brought pleasure to none. I was much with her and I know the truth. The Prince was very patient and magnanimous, Madam, and of a great kindness."

"He married for ambition," replied the Princess, "and therefore paid."

They had now reached the end of the wood and were passing through the last scattered trees.

The spring fields lay sweet about them; the faint azure of the sky was stained by the rosy gold of sunset; pale clouds were piled about the western horizon and a low wind was abroad which gently shook the budding boughs and bent the frail early flowers and caused the two women to shiver a little within their cloaks.

Rénèe, shading her eyes from the level rays of the sun, that she might see the pathway home, discerned a man coming towards them.

He was a ragged fellow and leant upon a stout stick.

Mendicants who were, or claimed to be, wounded soldiers from the theatre of war, or fugitives from the persecutions in the Netherlands were common enough; but this one, despite his attire, seemed to be of the better sort.

"A soldier," said Rénèe.

Charlotte turned and the man approached them, took off his ragged hat and very civilly asked the way to the Castle.

"You are a Fleming?" asked Rénèe, speaking in her own tongue.

"Yes," he answered with pleasure.

"Your speech shows it," answered Rénèe; she looked keenly at his ragged leathern clothes, his emaciated figure and haggard face.

"You want the Castle?" asked Charlotte.

"Strange that must seem to you, Madam," he answered with a smile and an air of breeding, "but I wish to see the Elector himself."

"You have news?" exclaimed the Princess, "we are from the Castle and you may speak fully to us, Sir."

"I was one of Count Lodewyk's officers, Madam, and have escaped from the fight of Mookerheyde," he answered.

"Then indeed the Elector will welcome you," said Charlotte. "Have you news of his son, Duke Christopher?"

"I last saw him in the fight, Madam — he and Count Lodewyk and Count Henry — and no man has seen them since, I think. All went down together in the battle."

"And none know how they died?" asked the Princess.

"How should one know in such a fight, Madam?" he answered. "And after the fight there was great slaughter. And many were trampled into the marshes or burnt in the flames of the villages and the farm-houses which the Spaniards fired — who can tell which way these three princes died?"

Charlotte shuddered.

"Does the Prince of Orange know this news?" asked Rénèe.

"I have not been to Holland, Madam, and know nothing. One hears rumours, reports — little is certain. Probably the Prince is at Bommel or Delft, by now he would know. This everyone says — that Leyden is again beleaguered."

"This defeat has been indeed a disaster!" exclaimed Rénèe.

"Yet not of great advantage to the Spaniards," replied the officer, "for there was a meeting among their troops after the battle and they marched on Brussels and occupied the city with much disorder. Nor is there the money to pay them or any means of quieting them."

Charlotte roused herself from her thoughts.

"You must tell these things to the Elector, we detain you, Sir. Whether this victory be fruitful or barren to the enemy there is no one who can replace the loss of Count Lodewyk."

The soldier responded with great animation and earnestness.

"He was loved by all of us, Madam — the soul of the army — the guiding hand."

"A charming gentleman," said Charlotte, and the tears were in her eyes.

"Sweet and brave, Madam, and of a great cheerfulness even in adversity."

"The Prince —" began Rénèe.

"The Prince will weep for him, Madam, even till the day of his own death."

"The Prince has but one brother left," said Charlotte as they turned towards the castle, "three princes lost from the House of Nassau since this bitter fight began."

"Do you think any will be left?" asked the soldier mournfully. "Ah, Madam, it is not the House of Nassau only that has been stripped of its sons — many a noble family is desolate — when will the good times come that will repay for this time of tears?"

"If the Prince is spared," said the Princess swiftly, "we shall see these good times."

"The Prince?" replied the Netherlander, "Do you think that the Prince will be spared? His life is not worth a white piece — Philip's assassins are forever on his track — it is but a question of time."

Charlotte caught hold of Rénèe's arm; she laughed and her step was unsteady.

The waiting-woman stared down at her; her impulse was to shake her off; to speak to her with anger, demanding — "What is it to you that danger threatens the Prince of Orange?" But the Princess, all unconscious, clung to her as one woman will cling to another in a moment of agitation or trouble.

"The Prince must go — go," she said. "All our hopes are on the Prince."

Rénèe read the truth in her flushed face and startled eyes. She drew away so sharply that the Princess almost stumbled in her walk.

"When so many have gone is it likely that the Prince of Orange will be spared?" she demanded, harshly. "As certainly as Philip punished those others who offended him will he punish the Prince."

Charlotte gazed at her in amazement. "You speak so strangely," she said.

"Do I?" smiled Rénèe. "I have strange thoughts in my heart."

They had now reached the Castle gate and Rénèe abruptly left her two companions and went to her own small chamber in one of the turrets; there she flung herself on her knees beside her humble bed and rested her beautiful head on the pillow; from the narrow pointed window a little ray of the last light penetrated the shadows of the room and fell over her bowed figure.

She had surmised the secret of Charlotte de Bourbon which was the same as her own; the Princess also had made a hero of William of Orange — probably loved him.

And he was free — and she was of the same rank — the same faith.

Rénèe understood now; it was not Lodewyk but William who would be the husband of the exiled Princess.

And she — she was to play her old part — to be the confidante before marriage, the serving-maid afterwards — a convenient figure in the background. It would be different, yes, as Charlotte de Bourbon was different from Anne of Saxony.

But Rénèe knew that the kindness of the new mistress would be as hard to bear as the harshness of the old.

And her days for patient self-sacrifice had gone by; she could not do again what she had once done.

She could not serve Charlotte's happiness as she had served Anne's misery; she could not again be a dependent in the house of the Prince.

170

"I need to go," she said, pressing her face to the cold pillow. "I need to go — I have never been of any use and now I should go."

Presently, and before the hour of the supper when her absence would be noticed, she rose from her kneeling posture and taking nothing with her but what little money she possessed, left the room and the Castle.

The keen evening air and the light of the pale May moon pleased her; she turned her back on the Castle of Heidelberg and took the road by which the Netherlander had come.

CHAPTER VIII

LEYDEN

ATTENDED by a small mounted escort William of Orange rode from Delft to Polderwaert, a fortress between that city and Rotterdam.

A summer sun was overhead and the fields reclaimed from the sea were green with the first lush green of grain and grass. High banked clouds, rising like battlements into the upper arch of the heavens, were reflected clearly in the motionless waters of the canal along the side of which the Prince rode.

His demeanour was melancholy, and, for the first time in this struggle of seven years, he appeared both ill and tired.

Mookerheyde had gone as far to break his spirit as anything could; even his superb health had been shaken under the continued strain of waiting for news, the long anxiety, the final realization that Lodewyk and Henry were both lost forever — that his right hand, his own confidant, his beloved friend and ever faithful follower, had gone down in that dark battle where so many fair hopes had been trampled into the marshes by the Meuse.

Politically the defeat of the patriots had had but little effect upon the fortunes of war, quickly followed as it had been by the mutiny of the Spanish troops and the success of Admiral Boisot, who after the victory of Bergen had sailed up the Scheldt and at Antwerp destroyed the fleet, which had escaped him on a former occasion, thus securing the supremacy of the Netherlanders on the sea, and Resquesens himself admitted that as long as they held that it would be impossible to bring them into complete subjection.

Of almost equal importance in the eyes of the Prince was the fact that the amnesty recently issued by Resquesens had entirely failed in its effect.

This document, by which Philip humbled himself so far as to offer a complete pardon to all of his rebel subjects who would return to the Roman Church, had been accepted by none.

The Reformed religion had acquired too firm a hold among the Netherlanders and there was not one of them who was not prepared to combat to the last, both for the land of his birth and the religion of his adoption.

William, who for a moment had feared the effect of a general pardon coming so soon after the disheartening failure of Lodewyk's expedition, had been exceedingly encouraged by the disdain with which it had been received.

But there was one consequence of Mookerheyde which now almost entirely occupied his thoughts.

The beautiful city of Leyden, one of the fairest in the Netherlands, was now strictly beleaguered again, no less than eight thousand troops closely surrounding it; while the town itself was ungarrisoned and unprovisioned.

And they were depending on the Prince, who had entreated them to endure a siege of at least three months, earnestly promising them, as did the Estates of Holland, that relief was at hand, and that, sooner than Leyden should perish as had perished Haarlem and other fair cities, taken by the Spaniards, the whole country would contend to the last man.

And the Prince felt that indeed the whole issue of the struggle was bound up in the fate of Leyden. If that city fell there was but little hope for the struggling Provinces.

Day and night he toiled, devising schemes for the rescue of the people whose sole trust, beside God, was in him and who were passing long hours of anguished suspense waiting for the succour that had not yet come, which he had assured them of, and which they, with confidence, yet agony, waited for.

Land relief was, since Mookerheyde, out of the question. There remained the sea.

Since the first the sea had been in William's mind as the means by which he could save his city.

Leyden was not on the sea — but the sea might come to Leyden.

Although the Spaniards held the coast from The Hague to Vlaardingen, the Prince held the dykes along the Meuse and Yssel.

The Estates were yet to be finally convinced of the absolute necessity of this bold and desperate plan, but the Prince was resolved that they should give their consent.

As he rode now he looked from right to left at the flat rich country, at the fair plenteous fields, the numerous windmills, the villages, orchards, and country houses which he was prepared to give to the ocean to save Leyden.

A curious love for this country that was not his by birth, filled his heart with a deep tenderness; the tenderness felt towards the thing for which he had forfeited everything, on which he had staked his all, and to which, he never doubted his life would be finally sacrificed.

"— Or here to find my grave," he had said of Holland; and he knew that somewhere among the low fields, in one of these old churches that rose massive above the low line of the land his body would rest — this was his home now and would be his tomb.

Might that tomb be among a free people and perhaps looked on with a little love by unborn generations — this was now his sole ambition. Under God's blessing: liberty for the future, a prosperous country flourishing in freedom.

> *I, nobly born, descended*
> *From an imperial stock,*
> *An Empire's prince, defended*
> *(Braving the battle's shock*
> *Heroically and fearless*
> *As pious Christians ought)*
> *With my life's blood the peerless*
> *Gospel of God our Lord.*

A shield and my reliance,
O God, Thou ever wert,
I'll trust unto Thy guidance.
O leave me not ungirt,
That I may stay a pious
Servant of Thine for aye,
And drive the plagues that try us
And tyranny away.

He raised his eyes to the clouds and something in their distant loftiness touched his spirit with a sense of loneliness.

"Ride, ride," he said to the men behind him, "for the rain comes."

He wrapped his black cloak about him and shivered, despite the sun, for the fever was upon him.

For several days he had been ill but the energy of his spirit had forced the weariness of his body, and to none had he admitted his state, which was betrayed by his pallid cheeks and languid eyes and the feebleness of his movements usually so full of life and force.

When the little cavalcade rode into the courtyard of the Castle of Polderwaert the Prince nearly dropped from the saddle; he had been exercising great effort of will to maintain himself upright so long.

"I can do no more today," he said with a smiling look, taking hold of the arm of one of his companions, Cornelius van Mierop, the Receiver-General of Rotterdam, who, seeing him stagger, had hastened to his assistance, "never have I felt so weak," he added, "and never have I needed strength more."

They helped him upstairs to the little chamber furnished for his use and he sank with a sigh into the great rush-bottomed chair by the window.

He had scarcely flung off his hat and cloak before the commandant of the castle was in his presence and had presented him with a letter arrived that morning by carrier pigeon from Leyden.

With fingers that had lost their usual steadiness William tore open the missive.

As he read the feverish colour deepened in his worn face.

The letter was an appeal for help, a reminder of his promise — a statement of the fact that provisions were running out — that Leyden had endured almost as much as it was possible to endure.

The Prince crushed up the letter in his hot hand.

"The dykes must be cut," he exclaimed, "the sluices must be opened!"

"Your Highness must then persuade the Estates," said Van Mierop.

The Prince leant back in his chair, taken by a sudden giddy weakness.

He stared out of the window and fields, clouds and water swam before his eyes.

The appeal of the starving city struck to his heart and brain like a tongue of flame.

"Leyden must be saved," he said passionately. "If she sinks the country sinks with her!"

"But tonight let Your Highness repose," said his secretary, looking anxiously at his haggard face.

"No," replied William, "I have to write to the Estates and with my own hand."

Collecting his strength he rose with an effort and went to the little black desk in the corner of the chamber.

He called for candles, for the light was beginning to leave the room, but when they came he winced, for the flame hurt his feverish eyes.

Refusing the services of his secretary he took up the quill.

"What is it Your Highness must write with your own hand?" inquired Van Mierop, humbly standing before him.

"Mynheer," answered the Prince, looking at him with eyes unnaturally bright, "they starve in Leyden."

"Then let Your Highness remember," returned Van Mierop earnestly, "that the hopes of this city are on Your Highness."

"Do you think that I shall fail them?" asked the Prince quickly.

"I think," replied the Receiver-General, "that your health may fail Your Highness."

But William shook his head with the confidence of a man who had never been sick nor feeble, nor had to give a thought to his body.

"My strength will last me for my work, Mynheer," he said.

He drew the paper towards him and began writing with eager haste.

With lucidity and force, eloquence and passion, he described the city of Leyden's plight and urged the one means of her relief — the cutting of the dykes.

As he sealed this epistle which was quickly written, he turned to the Receiver-General who was seated near him, on the other side of the candle glow.

"Mynheer, the sluices must be opened," he said, narrowing his eyes to watch the other's face.

Cornelius van Mierop bent his head; he was thinking of his own fair villa and farm, achieved by a lifetime of labour, which he had hoped to leave to his children and which would be among the first to be swallowed by the waves once the sea was let in over Holland.

"How exactly does Your Highness mean to relieve Leyden?" he asked.

William read the thoughts of the man before him and was pitiful towards them.

"Mynheer," he said gently, "I would open the sluices at Schiedam and Rotterdam and cut the dykes along the Yssel. Then I would gather together the fleet at Rotterdam and Delfshaven and let them float to Leyden on the rising waters."

"But the Landscheiding, they can never pass that," answered Van Mierop.

He referred to a difficulty that had been in the Prince's mind from the first.

The Landscheiding was a great dyke within five miles of Leyden which city it shielded from the sea, and even if the ocean should rise high enough to permit vessels to float over this, there were beyond it several mighty bulwarks built to defend the town against the water which it would be necessary to break through.

To add to the difficulty all this portion of reclaimed land, which contained rich pastures and several villages, was in the hands of the Spaniards, who also held the Landscheiding.

"It is difficult," admitted the Prince, "but it must be done. The Landscheiding must be stormed and pierced for the fleet to sail through."

"And if the wind is contrary?" asked Van Mierop, "and blows the fleet back or keeps it motionless, Highness?"

"They must wait till it sets fair."

"There are a thousand obstacles."

"What is our life," returned the Prince, "but the overcoming of obstacles?"

"If the thing is humanly possible Your Highness can accomplish it," said Van Mierop.

William lifted his dark eyes now so sunken and shadowed.

"It is strange to think that any have faith in me," he answered, "I feel myself so weak and impotent."

He raised his hand and let it fall on the desk; his breath was coming quickly and the flush of fever darkened his brow.

"I must go to Rotterdam today," he said.

"Today! It is already late, Highness."

"My work cannot stop for time nor season, Mynheer van Mierop."

"What urges Your Highness to Rotterdam?"

The Prince rose, steadying himself by holding on to the arms of the rush chair.

"I wish to press this question of the opening of the dykes — there is no time to be lost — none — none."

"Your Highness takes much to heart the fate of Leyden."

"Because with the fate of Leyden is bound the fate of Holland," said William, and handed his letter to the Estates, bidding it be dispatched immediately.

"And with the fate of Holland," he added, after a little, "is bound the fate of a new nation and many generations yet to come."

He picked up his cloak and slowly put it round his shoulders.

"Ah, Mynheer," he said, "we do not struggle for a little thing nor contend for a mean advantage but for what will be precious in the future."

But Van Mierop was thinking of his pleasant villa and fertile pastures that must be sacrificed to save Leyden and his face was gloomy; he was growing an old man and the struggle which was to strip him of everything seemed very long and the bright future it was to purchase very far away.

The Prince laid his hand gently on the Receiver-General's sleeve.

"Courage, Friend, courage," he said quietly, "God will grant the good time to come — for all."

Van Mierop turned his face away quickly with the shamed tears in his eyes, for he saw that the Prince had read his thoughts, and there came quickly to his mind all that William had sacrificed in the cause of a country and a religion not by birth his own; sacrifices compared to which the poor little quota of such as he was indeed as nothing.

The Prince picked up his hat and left the chamber followed by his secretary and Van Mierop.

When they again took horse for Rotterdam the west was blazing red about a lake of molten gold where the sun was sinking below the watery horizon, and the wide waters that traversed the pastures were also shot with gold, and with gold was flushed the ripening harvest fields and the leafy orchards, gold gleamed in the ribs of the long sails of the windmills and blazed like fires in the windows of the scattered farm-houses where the white and black cattle were returning to their red tiled sheds.

There was a silence in which the bells of the slow-moving cows and the surge of the water around the pole of a barge painfully proceeding up the canal were the only sounds.

William rode a little ahead of his companions; it did not seem to him that he was alone.

His thoughts turned, as they ever did when he was at a little leisure, to Count Lodewyk, and it seemed to him he was accompanied by that young and martial figure that smiled at him with eyes of unquenchable hope and a look of tenderest love and confidence.

CHAPTER IX

NEWS FROM HEIDELBERG

THE Prince lay ill at Rotterdam; a humble house near the harbour was his lodging and there he lay during the long days and close nights of a burning summer in a fever that now rose to delirium and now left him prostrate with utter weakness. The physicians could do nothing for him — it was, they said, an illness of the mind and unless he might have repose of brain and spirit they feared for his life.

But none could give him this repose while Leyden was unrelieved.

Leyden was the burden of his thoughts as he lay helpless and sick, Leyden and the country involved in the fate of Leyden.

He had obtained the consent of the Estates to the cutting of the dykes and the opening of the sluices and the work was in progress, but it proceeded slowly, the more slowly, he felt, for the lack of his presence.

In the intervals of his sickness he dictated letters of encouragement to the beleaguered city, of exhortation to the states and the relieving fleet, which, ready provisioned, lay waiting under the command of Admiral Boisot at Delfshaven.

Beyond that he could, for the moment, do nothing, and the oppressing sense of his own inaction heightened his vexation and therefore his illness.

Too long had he borne the burden of a whole people, a nation struggling into freedom, on his shoulders; even his perfect health had broken beneath the continued strain of mind and body.

His new feeling of helplessness added to the agitation of his spirit; it was long since he had known what it was to be even slightly ill — never before had he known what it was to have his body fail him and to lie helpless at the moment when he most needed his force and energy.

One afternoon he lay thus, weak from an access of fever and waking from a long heavy sleep he looked about his room regarding it as if it was a strange place.

For unfamiliar seemed his surroundings and tainted with the feverish horror of his sickness.

He turned himself on his side and stared around the chamber.

The windows were open wide on the sunshine; on the sill was a blue and white pot of coarse earthenware holding a plant of scarlet geranium which showed vivid in its red and green amid the encircling light.

This light entered and filled the chamber with a sense of freshness, of fragrance, and of the open air.

The short curtains of coarse white linen very slightly waved in the delicate breeze.

The walls, half light panelled wood and half whitewash, were full of shelves and open cupboards which held articles of brass and copper, china and earthenware in shining hues of blues and reds.

The chairs were dark, as was the bed of the Prince.

He noticed this and the texture of the curtains of blue silk drawn away from his pillow.

The linen about him and the coverlet of fine lemon-coloured wool was of an exquisite sweetness; on a table near him were the utensils of the sick-room and a crystal jar of white scentless roses. Beyond was a desk.

The Prince looked at the shining front of this with its drooping fuchsia-shaped brass handles and his mind flashed vividly back to the last letter placed therein.

An appeal from Leyden reminding him of his promise to relieve them.

"We have endured the three months to which we pledged ourselves; we have held out two months with bread and a month without."

The sentence rang in his excited brain, he tried to move himself but fell back, for a fierce pain shot through his limbs.

He lay there helpless, his head sideways as it had fallen, and again his tired eyes travelled around the chamber.

This time, and with a sense of shock, they encountered the figure of a woman sitting, almost motionless, in the corner of the room farthest from the bed.

She wore a plain dress of dark gray and a ruff of fine muslin, she had her back to the Prince, so that he could not see her face, only the piled-up locks of her red-gold hair which circled one into the other to form a crown on her head.

Her only movement was in her hands, which passed quickly to and fro over a length of fine embroidery.

The Prince watched her with the suspended interest of a sick man.

He liked to see her there in her grace and calm, her delicate fingers working so steadily, her whole presence suggestive of repose and comfort. It was long since he had seen such a woman in any house or apartment of his; as this thought of his loneliness came to him he sighed.

Instantly the lady turned her head and looked at him.

Her face was perfectly familiar, but he could not give her a name nor tell where and when he had known her before.

He lay still, in a curious world of his own bred of fever and weakness, he thought the old life in Brussels was about him, the ease, the luxury, the pomp, and yet he thought he was lying out on a wet field shivering in a thin cloak.

"Your Highness wishes for something?" asked the woman, laying down her work.

Her voice broke through the Prince's dreams; with an effort he recalled himself to the present,

"No," he answered, "only to know your name, which surely I knew once."

She smiled very faintly.

"Yes, Your Highness knew it once."

She was beautiful with a chaste beauty of sorrow and reserve; it seemed as if she had never fully bloomed — and that, if she had, she would have been gorgeous.

Her red-brown eyes were slightly shadowed, her lovely mouth slightly strained, and her look was both grave and inscrutable.

"I knew it once," repeated William slowly; languor held him motionless; his thought would go no further than the familiar stranger before him.

"In Brussels."

"Ah, in Brussels," muttered the Prince.

"You remember, Highness?"

He slightly shook his head on the pillow.

"And once since Brussels," repeated the woman quietly.

"Where?"

"At Heidelberg," she said; her clear cheeks delicately flushed; she began, very slowly and exactly, folding up her embroidery.

"Heidelberg," William repeated, "Heidelberg;" he closed his eyes and thought.

The word brought before his mind a fair and gentle woman who had spoken in his cause and with whom he had talked in the Castle gardens — a fugitive vision of great sweetness.

It was not the first time that this memory had come to him; it was indeed, one on which he loved to dwell.

"You were at Heidelberg?" his mind worked slowly.

"Yes, Highness," she hesitated a moment and then added: "We rode there together you and I, Prince, one March day."

He opened wide his eyes.

"One March day — a wet day. I remember — you are Rénèe le Meung."

"Who was in your service once."

"In Brussels — yes. In my — the service of the Princess."

He lay silent awhile, looking at her. Nor did she speak. He recalled her now very clearly and the interest and curiosity her repressed loveliness and patient service had provoked — an interest but fleeting and a curiosity soon forgotten — yet both revived now finding her here in these circumstances and these feelings were deepened because he looked upon her as a link with that pleasant and cherished memory of another woman.

"You come from Heidelberg?" he asked.

"Some weeks ago I left the Castle, Highness," she replied.

"Why?"

"I was weary of my exile."

"Exile?"

"I am a Fleming, Highness."

"Ah, yes!" He closed his eyes again and once more was silent for a little while.

"How goes life at Heidelberg?" he added presently.

"Highness, they are all sad for the fight at Mookerheyde."

"The Elector would feel that, yes," answered William slowly. He opened his eyes full as he spoke and looked at Rénèe.

She was gazing at him steadily, her hands folded in her lap; slowly the Prince began to realize her personality — so far she had been but a memory, a name, someone from the Castle at Heidelberg.

"How have you come again into my service?" he asked with a faint smile.

She answered calmly —

"Through taking service I have gathered my little money. I came to Rotterdam when I heard that Your Highness was here, sick — your steward is one who was with you formerly and so knows me. And so I obtained permission to wait on Your Highness, seeing that you had no women in your household beyond a rough serving-maid."

"My household has long lacked women," replied William. "You, more than any other, know my long loneliness."

"As much as a man can be lonely you have been, Highness, I know."

"Why do you say that?"

"Because a woman can be lonely as no man ever is, Prince."

"A woman?" again his thoughts went to the Castle at Heidelberg and the young exile there.

"A woman can have no great occupation to distract her loneliness."

"Mothers and wives have much to do if they are earnest of soul and good of heart."

"Mothers and wives are not lonely," returned Rénèe with a sudden flash in her large eyes. "I speak of women who are neither — or who have been and are now bereaved."

And still William thought of Charlotte de Bourbon among strangers, a dependent, and estranged from all her relatives — surely her loneliness was greater than his.

184

He moved his head impatiently, turning his eyes from Rénèe and looking at the blue silk curtains in which the sunlight lay in gold patches in the folds.

"Where are all the others?" he asked in a feeble voice.

"Does not Your Highness remember that but a few hours ago you sent them away on various errands — soon after you received the dispatch from Leyden?"

"Leyden," muttered the Prince, turning to look at her again. "Ah, Leyden —"

"Leyden holds out, Highness."

"But how long can she hold out?" With a great effort he raised himself on his elbow. "Will the dykes never be cut — will Boisot never sail?"

"Your Highness must get well — for all depends on you."

"On me!" he laughed weakly. "And I am so little and useless.

"There is need," he added, "of another, stronger than I and of greater influence. Therefore I have thought of France. Or England."

"No Prince from France or England could be as beloved as is Your Highness in the Netherlands," said Rénèe.

"But I have not the power to repay this love," answered William.

Rénèe arose, still looking at him with earnest eager eyes.

"Trust God that you will accomplish that to which you have put your hand, Prince," she replied.

He gazed at her as steadily as she gazed at him; he seemed to recognize something strong and loyal and steadfast in this woman; something on which one might depend and lean.

And this sense of her strength and faithfulness touched him as with a great comfort in the feebleness of his sickness and moved him to open his heart on a subject on which it had hitherto remained closed.

"You were the companion of Mademoiselle de Bourbon?" he asked.

Rénèe very slightly drew her brows together as one may who feels a sudden sharp touch of pain.

"Yes," she said quietly.

"You loved her, perhaps?"

"No," answered Rénèe, "why should I love her, Prince?" she added with a certain swift fierceness.

"She seemed to me one who might —" he paused, and in his turn frowned a little.

"— inspire love?" finished Rénèe calmly.

"One at least gentle and unfortunate — and courageous," said William.

"Yes," Rénèe assented, "she has those qualities and she is, I suppose, unfortunate."

"Was there no talk of her espousals?"

"With Count Lodewyk?"

"With any — my brother, no."

"No name was ever mentioned but his — a dowerless Princess does not so easily find a husband," replied Rénèe dully.

"There is a sweet wife there," said the Prince wistfully.

A faint pallor overspread the face of the woman who listened; her heart seemed to close over a depth of memory, close and shrink and shrivel as under an icy touch.

She put out her hand and rested it on the low mantelshelf where stood the shining brass pots and candlesticks.

Then, speaking slowly, she answered William's thoughts more than his words.

"Does Your Highness mean to ask for the hand of Mademoiselle?"

A flush, that seemed of pleasure, rose to the Prince's thin face.

"You, at least, would not think me mad if I had that intention?" he answered.

Closer, closer closed the heart of Rénèe; she watched with what eagerness he welcomed the boldness with which she had put into words what he perhaps had been shy to even think; she saw his distant look and knew that he had forgotten her save as someone who knew Charlotte de Bourbon.

"I am worn out," he added in a tired voice, "old before my time — penniless also and encumbered with obligations and debts."

"The Princess holds no better fortune," returned Rénèe dully.

He glanced at her gratefully.

"You know her," he began, then paused.

She divined what he would say but she could not speak the words for him; she stood there silent, one hand over her trembling heart.

"Has she ever spoken of me?" added William at length.

"Yes." Rénèe forced herself to the truth, she was looking down that she might not see the eager interest with which he awaited her answer.

"And in a kindly fashion?"

"With admiration, Prince."

William noticed the constraint of her tone but did not remotely guess the cause.

He raised himself in bed and spoke with animation.

"I would not force your confidence, I have no right to ask — but this thing has been much in my mind of late — and now surely we may consider each other as a friend," he smiled, looking at her with great charm and sweetness, "and you can do me a service."

Rénèe was silent; she did not raise her eyes nor move.

"Tell me," insisted the Prince, "if you believe, from your knowledge of Mademoiselle, that she would listen to my addresses?"

Rénèe was still silent; his humility stung her; why should he be humble before Charlotte de Bourbon, the meek little renegade nun with her calm air of authority and serenity?

"Will you not answer me?" added William

Rénèe looked at him; it was in her power to make him believe any lie she liked, for he would never suspect her of any motive for telling an untruth, she might assure him that the affections of the Princess were engaged, or that she was indifferent towards marriage.

But as she looked at him, eager, wistful, waiting for her answer, the truth rushed to her lips. She moved towards him with a sudden tenderness — almost a maternal tenderness.

"Rest assured," she said, "that Mademoiselle de Bourbon loves you."

CHAPTER X

THE CHILD OF THE REFUGEE

SOON after, the Prince's secretary returned and with him Cornelius van Mierop.

William left thoughts of women and raising himself up in bed began discussing the prospects for the relief of Leyden and his answer to the appeal of that city. Rénèe moved from the room, nor was her going noticed.

As she stood at the door she lingered a moment and looked back at the dark thin face of the Prince, propped up by the white bed pillows and cast in shadow by the blue bed curtains — looked at him intently as if to impress those features on her mind; yet she knew every lineament by heart.

Without cloak or kerchief she went out into the sunny street.

The shallow double steps of the simple house led to the wide flagged causeway that edged a deep canal; short full-leaved elm trees shaded both water and stone, where the sun penetrated the deep leafage it shone in vivid fakes in the ripples of the canal and in patches of pure gold on the worn stones and smooth trodden bricks.

The air was very warm and full of a distant murmur of noise, footsteps, voices, and all the interwoven sounds of a city.

But here there was peace.

Through the open window of the house opposite Rénèe could see the serving-maid polishing a brass dish, which, like a globe of gold, gleamed in the dark interior of the room.

The only person in sight along the vista of the canal-way was a boy who floated a kite of white and purple which fluttered feebly in the slight summer breeze.

Rénèe stood silent in the stillness, the warmth and the peace.

She leant against one of the elm trees and looked up at the pots of geranium which marked the window of the Prince's room.

Strange that he should have chosen her as his confidante and from his own lips have confirmed what she had already guessed: the unspoken understanding between himself and Charlotte de Bourbon. So he would marry again, and had already chosen his wife — a woman who, as Rénèe knew, would not hesitate to accept him.

And she, the little escaped nun, the meek exile, who had seen him but on two occasions and knew him only by hearsay, would be his companion, his confidante constantly with him, the sharer of his difficulties, his troubles and of that ultimate triumph of which Rénèe never doubted.

It was natural that this should be so — natural that he should choose this wife, a woman of his own faith, who had suffered for that faith in much the same way as he had suffered, it was natural that her loneliness and exile, her unprotected state and the courage with which she had maintained her conviction and her liberty in front of the opposition of all her kin, should appeal to him, as it was natural that she should make a hero of the man who was the champion of the cause and the religion she had embraced.

Yet the confirmation of what she had guessed ever since her last interview with Charlotte de Bourbon, came with a certain shock to Rénèe.

Some things cannot be discounted; Rénèe could no more have spared herself the pang she had that day received than she could have spared herself the pang of the Prince's death by knowing beforehand that he was doomed. Yet no hopes had been dashed to the ground, no prospects blighted — the Prince could never have been more to her than he was whether or no he had met Mademoiselle de Bourbon.

The gulf between them would be no wider than it was now, they could not be further removed than they had ever been.

Yet the sting, the grief, and the bitterness remained and could not be argued away.

And in her heart she knew that Charlotte de Bourbon, as woman compared to woman, was of no finer quality than herself — and she doubted if she could bring him as much devotion, as much admiration — as much love.

But she was the woman on whom his eye had fallen, the wife of his choice — while Rénèe had always been the waiting-woman — a part of the background.

And circumstances had again combined to cast her into his service, to bring her into his presence as a dependent; she had not meant this to be so, when she had left Heidelberg it had been with no idea of seeing the Prince again, till knowing him ill and even lonely she had thought again of nothing but his service.

And with this result — that she had been forced to tell him that he had nothing to fear from Charlotte de Bourbon.

She would never forget his look of amazement and shame at having, as he thought, forced her confidence, the way the blood had rushed to his face, his quick attempt to turn aside her words, to make a jest of the whole matter — and yet, all the while, as Rénèe well knew, he fixed in his heart a hope and a resolve — firmly and forever.

"He will ask her hand on the first occasion that offers," thought Rénèe, "and I may hear her marriage bells and see her arrive joyously to meet him."

She turned slowly along the causeway to where the child was floating his white and purple kite.

She tried to soothe the dull sickness of her spirit by thinking of all the sorrow and misfortune abroad in the world in this time of horror.

Of the starving women in Leyden who had to watch their children die at the breast, of the maidens who had to see their lovers go forth, never to return, of the women whose husbands were taken from them by disease, by torture, by prison, by the sword or the bullet, of the homeless and broken, the exiled and defeated, the crying unconscious children, the weeping women, the despairing silence of strength, the laments of age and feebleness in this time of war.

It seemed to Rénèe as if never again would the world be bright and gorgeous, never again would youth go gaily forth to greet the spring, never again would love flourish uninterruptedly, and those dear to each other remain united in happy homes.

As her thoughts ran thus she looked at the boy with the kite, and like a gleam of light at the end of a tunnel the idea came to her that perhaps this child would live to see the peace she imagined forever lost.

And this peace — once achieved, would last and blossom in a golden age in which all the present unhappiness of which she was part would be forgotten.

"What avail will that be to me?" thought Rénèe. "I shall not have helped — I am no use to any — I and my incompleteness will pass away, the children of the future will play over my dust. I was born to uselessness."

She walked slowly along the causeway, thinking of her own story interwoven with the great events among which she moved, yet touching them not; of the Prince, whose life had come so near to her life yet from whom she was for ever separated, of the nation coming, with throes and agonies, into being about her, of whom she was part, yet in which somehow she seemed to have no interest.

Her enthusiasm was dead, her patriotism did not warm her; she had been exiled too long to any longer feel pleasure in her native land, she had been homeless too long to any longer feel the sense of home.

Her faith had become vague; the convictions for which her parents had died no longer seemed near and powerful, but far away and feeble.

Was it possible that some hope still lurked deep in her heart amid all her hopelessness — that there was still some use for her in the world?

She was still young — strange as it seemed to her to think it, life might yet hold something for her — some work, some duty, perhaps even some pleasure. In this flutter of hope, youth and health asserted itself.

The warm air was about her, the sun overhead and the green leaves, even to her dulled spirit these things brought some comfort.

No passer-by would have thought the beautiful gracious woman walking with leisured step in the sunshine, was so near despair, for the calm of long habit appeared the calm of serenity.

She reached the end of the canal and turned into another street of a poorer sort.

As she glanced down this a poor funeral met her eye; the coffin, covered by a simple black cloth which looked faded in the sunlight, was born aloft on the shoulders of four men.

There were no followers and no flowers; only in the doorway of the house from which the coffin had been carried stood an old woman with a bundle in her arms.

The desire for some distraction from her thoughts, for some action in the midst of her inaction, moved Rénèe to go up to this woman and ask whose body it was the four old men were carrying away.

The withered creature looked at her with the patient friendliness of the unfortunate.

"A woman," she answered.

"Young?"

"Eighteen years."

Rénèe gazed after the slender coffin.

"Why did she die?"

"Who knows? He was with Count Lodewyk's army and she never heard of him since Mookerheyde," was the answer.

"But Mookerheyde — that is already some time ago," said Rénèe.

"Ah, there was the baby coming, she lived for that, kept herself strong and well too. It is a beautiful baby. Then when it was born she lost her strength all at once — and went out. Like a lamp without oil."

"And the baby?" faltered Rénèe.

"A fortnight old, today. We could not find a foster-mother, but it does well with a spoon."

"A boy or a girl?"

"A girl."

The funeral had now passed out of sight; Rénèe looked down at the bundle in the old woman's shrunken arms which showed, brown and dry, from her short blue sleeves.

"Is this the baby?" she asked with a certain curious sense of awe.

The old woman raised with pride the striped red and white shawl.

Rénèe looked in.

Wrapped in an inner covering of white wool and linen lay a little baby asleep.

She wore a close cap of Flemish lace, the deep border of which fell over and shaded her minute face, which was of a marvellous delicacy and beauty. Her complexion was of a pearly fairness, the exquisitely faint lashes and brows traced in dark gold, a tiny hand, with the fingers outspread, lay on the edge of the shawl.

As Rénèe gazed she felt as if her heart had been suddenly broken to pieces within her; her limbs trembled and the tears rushed to her eyes. The heartrending serenity of the baby seemed to her unendurable.

"May I hold her in my arms?" she asked; for she felt an aching in her bosom that only the presence of that little body could still.

"Come into the house," returned the old woman, "I am alone and there is much to do. Sickness makes work."

Rénèe followed her into the dark room, where the green lattices were drawn over the windows, excluding the sun, which only filtered here and there, in fine pencils of gold into the dusky atmosphere.

A door stood open into an inner room; set in the wall of this was the smooth white bed still pressed by the form of the dead woman; here too the shutters were closed and the chamber was filled with a golden darkness.

Rénèe looked about her; the white porcelain stove was lit, despite the heat, and before it were arranged the child's swaddling bands and clothes, newly washed.

A fine steam rose from them and overhung the stove.

At the other end of the room was a wicker cradle filled with nice soft cushions.

"You are the grandmother?" asked Rénèe.

"No. I am a stranger. They fled from Haarlem before the siege. Then he went to fight and she took lodgings with me. They had saved a little money."

"All gone now?"

"Some time since," replied the old woman quietly.

Rénèe looked at the heartrending little garments by the stove.

"And the baby?" she asked.

"I do what I can. But I am poor. My son is at the war and does not come back. The other works at an armourer's, but the pay is not good now."

The old woman spoke with a certain wistful eagerness as if she ventured to hope that this stranger who belonged obviously to the better sort might be interested in her miserable fortunes, until now too obscure and too ordinary to attract the attention of any.

"And the baby?" repeated Rénèe.

"My son wants to send her to the hospital — I would keep her if I could. The pastor says he may find someone to take her. He paid for the funeral, but he too is poor."

And she suddenly smiled as if there was something diverting in this almost universal poverty and misery.

Rénèe seated herself in a chair by the cradle.

"Keep her for the time; I will think of something," she said.

The old woman crossed the room and placed the baby, warm from the pressure of her shrunken heart, in Rénèe's arms.

"You will take her perhaps?" she asked.

"I am not rich."

"Married with little ones of your own?"

Rénèe shook her head almost as if she was ashamed.

"I come from Heidelberg," she answered. "I was one of the Electress's women. Now I am in employment in the house where the Prince lodges."

She spoke rapidly to disguise the extraordinary awe and rapture she felt in the close contact with the baby.

"Ah, the Prince?" the old woman was turning the wet clothes. "Do you think him a great man, now?"

"Yes."

"Ah, you do? My son thinks Count Lodewyk was the one."

"No, he was but the Prince's Lieutenant."

"So some say. But my son maintains he would have saved us all if he had lived. Yes, that was a black day at Mookerheyde!"

"The Prince will save us all," returned Rénèe earnestly.

"Only God knows," said the old woman; she went into the inner room and began to rearrange the bed.

Now that she was alone Rénèe timidly and eagerly raised the baby and laid its face against her own.

With a hand that trembled she touched the tiny head, the clenched hand, the soft cheeks.

The baby moved and with a little cry awoke, opening dark eyes.

The old woman came hurrying.

"You do not know how to hold her," she said indulgently.

"No, I will not hurt her," pleaded Rénèe.

The baby closed her eyes again and moved her head to and fro.

"She is hungry," said Rénèe, with quick instinct interpreting the searching movement; and in her own heart she felt an intolerable ache, as she also was hungry — for what could never be.

"I would have lived if the child had been mine," she added almost fiercely.

"Ah, she thought of her husband, that girl, and so she died."

"But it is not certain that he is dead!"

"Who survived from Mookerheyde?"

As she spoke the old woman took the child from Rénèe's reluctant arms.

"She must have her food and go to sleep," she added, "before my son comes in."

Rénèe rose.

"I will come in tomorrow and talk to you of the child," she said. "What is the name?"

"Van Posen, they called themselves. She was a goldsmith's daughter, she said."

"And the name of the baby?"

"She was baptized as Wilhelmina, because, the pastor said, of the Prince."

"I will come tomorrow," repeated Rénèe. She left the house and returned with a quick step to the Prince's house.

On the dark stairway she met William's secretary. He looked at her keenly.

"You seem as if you had had good news," he said, smiling.

Rénèe smiled too.

"What of Leyden?" she counter-questioned.

"Boisot makes progress — if only the city can hold out!"

CHAPTER XI

AT DELFT

THE days of a hot summer passed into the days of a stormy autumn and still Leyden was not relieved.

The ocean had now overflowed the pierced dykes and was coming slowly to the relief of the beleaguered city.

But too slowly for the starving thousands in Leyden, who daily climbed the ramparts and the ancient tower of Hengist to gaze across the waste of waters for a sight of the sails of the fleet of Admiral Boisot. But the winds were contrary: Boisot was stranded at North Aa, in a depth of water not sufficient to float his smallest vessel, and the powerful forts which guarded Leyden, such as Soeterwoude and Lammen, still remained in the possession of the Spaniards.

And though the patriots had made great advances, such as seizing the Landscheiding, there still remained in their way great obstacles, such as the lake by the city, the redoubts manned by the enemy and the ridges bristling with cannon which protected the approach to Leyden.

And the sea hung back and only slow and reluctant waves lapped the ruined crops, the abandoned houses, the desolate farmsteads, which seemed as if they had been sacrificed for nothing, while the fleet of Holland remained idle and impotent within sight of the starving town.

The Prince dragged himself from his bed to come on board Admiral Boisot's ship and inspect the gallant and desperate means being taken to relieve the despairing city.

He saw that all that human endeavour could do had been done and nothing could help now but the ocean, and he returned to Delft sad but not despairing.

He saw that all that human endeavour could do had been done . . .

St. Aldegonde, released from prison on parole, was with him and lodged with him in the quiet house at Delft which was now William's home.

The Prince loved his friend and trusted his affection, but no longer could he put faith in his fortitude and courage.

The continued misfortunes of the patriot cause, the seeming hopelessness of the task William had undertaken, the loss of all those stout hearts who had lent such a glory to the opening of the conflict, and his own personal experience of imprisonment at the hands of the Spaniards had combined to turn St. Aldegonde, once so ardent and confident, into a waverer and a doubter; only the Prince's personal influence over him prevented him from retiring in despair from an active part in the conflict.

He returned now from the visit to the fleet profoundly depressed.

The Prince, with that sense of humour no misfortune could destroy, laughed at his gloomy and melancholy face.

"You are not in Leyden," he said as they sat at supper; "there is no need to starve."

St. Aldegonde sighed.

"You have ever too light a temper, Highness," he rejoined gloomily.

"Had my disposition been heavy it would have sunk beneath my misfortunes," returned the Prince. "Let me smile while I can, Aldegonde."

He leant back in the dark carved chair, and with a little movement of weariness, his head sunk against the black leathern cushions.

He was still pale and haggard from his recent illness, from which indeed he had hardly recovered, the comely face was thin, the eyes lacked something of their wonted fire and as suddenly as the first snow of autumn the white hairs had appeared thickly among the chestnut locks.

His dress was that of a burgher, gray cloth and riding boots and a little ruffed collar of native needlework.

St. Aldegonde looked at him and was not greatly encouraged.

He thought of the magnificent cavalier, a grandee, a power, rich, young, who had set out with his noble companions to

198

break the power of Spain and in the quiet tired figure before him he could see nothing but the signs of failure.

William still smiled, looking at him as if he divined his thoughts.

"We shall conquer yet," he said.

St. Aldegonde played with his glass.

"Your Highness is indomitable."

"The country is indomitable."

The other was silent.

"You saw those Zeelanders today," continued the Prince, "you noticed the spirit of those men! They would sooner all perish, man by man, than abandon Leyden."

"They will not relieve Leyden."

"With God's help they will," said William.

"Does Your Highness think that the city can hold out till the wind changes?"

"I do."

St. Aldegonde shook his head.

"Have they not already captured fort after fort and driven the enemy from the great dyke?"

"There are other forts — and the men."

"Yes," responded the Prince, "there are always difficulties in every enterprise, always. But we," he looked steadily into his friend's face, "are not here to enumerate them."

"God grant that your fortitude and hopefulness will be rewarded," returned St. Aldegonde in a moved voice.

"I have never," replied William quietly, "doubted the ultimate victory. But if we are doomed to perish, God's will be done!"

> My God, I pray Thee, save me
> For all who do pursue
> And threaten to enslave me,
> Thy trusted servant true.
> O Father, do not sanction
> Their wicked, foul design;
> Let them not wash their hands in
> This guiltless blood of mine.

Once David searched for shelter
From King Saul's tyranny.
E'en so I fled this welter
And many a lord with me.
But God the Lord did save him
From exile and its hell
And, in His mercy, gave him
A realm in Israel.

Fear not, 't will rain sans [= without] ceasing;
The clouds are bound to part.
I bide the sight so pleasing
Unto my princely heart:
That when I death encounter
I honour find therein
And as a faithful warrior
The eternal realm may win.

William turned his head and looked out of the window at the quiet street where the last sunlight lay peacefully on brickwork and canal.

"At least," he added, "we shall have the honour to have done what no nation ever did before us — for we have defended and maintained ourselves in a small country against the tremendous efforts of a powerful enemy. And as long as the poor inhabitants here, even if they be deserted by all the world, hold firm, it will cost the Spaniards half of Spain, in men and money, before they can make an end of us."

St. Aldegonde was, if only for the moment, and against his own private judgment, convinced. When the Prince spoke, even the waverers were silenced, even the most timid was reassured.

William looked again towards his friend.

"Why are you so sad? Do you think it nothing to have been born in these honourable times?"

"I would," replied St. Aldegonde, "have been born a hundred years since, before these troubles began."

"Or a hundred years hence," smiled William, "when they are all forgotten — or, perhaps worse, are abroad for our grandchildren to battle with. But you are strong, St. Aldegonde.

Humanity has no greater privilege than this — to help in the establishment of liberty and truth."

"And I echo the Apostle — 'what is truth' — and add 'what is liberty?' Philip believes that we are rebels and traitors, swine fit only for the shambles. And that liberty consists in his liberty to do as he wishes — we would curtail him as he would curtail us."

"Liberty and truth," replied William, "are understood by the poorest and humblest, they know what is real liberty and what is genuine truth and for these things are prepared to die. These and not the standards of the Escurial are right."

"I think the King would die for his belief as cheerfully as any Calvinist."

"Aye," replied William. "Tyranny has its courage, and wrong its fortitude. But leave these matters, where we confuse ourselves with terms. I will talk to you on another theme."

"Another theme?"

"Do you think there is no other?"

St. Aldegonde smiled.

"Truly," he answered, "I thought there could be no other in your mind now, Highness."

"Then you are mistaken."

As he spoke the Prince bent his steady eyes on his Friend.

"There is," he continued, "a matter which I have had much in mind of late."

He paused thoughtfully.

"And now the time has come to speak of it," he added.

"Highness, you arouse my curiosity," said St. Aldegonde, leaning forward a little across the supper table.

"I shall surprise you," answered William; he suddenly laughed.

"It is a happy matter, then, Highness?"

"It is this — I have a mind to marry."

St. Aldegonde was more than surprised, he was startled, almost shocked.

"Your Highness thinks of marriage?"

St. Aldegonde evolved a thousand aspects of the case in his mind — William's previous marriage, the fact that the wretched Anne of Saxony still lived and was by many still considered as the Prince's wife — the facts of her behaviour having been kept obscure, and her return to her family having been made under the excuse of her health — the dissension and bitterness the marriage of the Prince was likely to cause among Anne's German relations whom it was most essential to keep in a good humour and the general comment, not to say scandal, that was likely to be everywhere aroused.

On the other hand, as St. Aldegonde was quick to see, if the Prince married politically and wisely, his cause might be benefited, his influence extended, his coffers filled.

"You disapprove?" smiled the Prince.

"No — I wonder."

"At one of my age and fortunes seeking a wife?"

St. Aldegonde warmed to the defence of his friend and Prince.

"Your Highness is yet young and your fortunes are such as any would be proud to share."

"My forty-two years weigh heavily upon me," replied William, "and I can give no marriage portion, no, I am burdened with debts and settlements."

"A good dowry would repair these."

"This lady has no dowry."

"The bride is chosen then?" exclaimed St. Aldegonde in amazement.

"Yes," replied William. "I do not speak of any marriage, but of a particular marriage."

"Politics —" began St. Aldegonde.

"For once," interrupted the Prince, "you must leave politics out of the question."

"Out of the question of your marriage?" exclaimed St. Aldegonde.

"Yes."

"Then why," asked the other in unfeigned astonishment, "should Your Highness marry at all?"

The Prince slightly flushed.

"For affection, Aldegonde."

"Affection?"

"You think I am too old, too soured, too broken, eh?"

"Really," said his friend warmly, "I think you are not the man."

"Instead I need this companionship, this affection, this home — I need all that this marriage can bring me — will bring me if it is accomplished, need it as the thirsting man needs water, as the runner needs repose."

St. Aldegonde was silent.

"Has it never occurred to you," added the Prince almost wistfully, "that I am very lonely?"

St. Aldegonde hung his head.

"And have been so," continued William, "for many years?"

His friend had no answer; certainly he had given little thought to William's inner life; he had always considered him as the leader, the man of affairs, the soldier, the politician, he had never given a thought to the other side of the man, who, warm-hearted, must do without affection, who, fond of home, must be homeless, who, kindly and sociable in disposition, must spend many long hours, many sad hours alone; he had never thought what it must mean to William to reflect on the misery of his last marriage, the outrage inflicted on him by his half-insane wife, the pain and humiliation of her desertion.

But now that the Prince spoke so, St. Aldegonde reflected on the matter — and considered — why should not this man be as other men?

"You marvel at me," said William, who had been watching him keenly.

"No, I was endeavouring to understand."

"My motives?"

"Yes."

"I love the lady," said William simply.

His life of late years had brought him so little into contact with any woman and not at all with those of his own rank, that St. Aldegonde was completely puzzled.

"When has Your Highness found time for courtship?" he asked with a little smile.

"There has been no courtship," answered the Prince gently.

"But you know this lady well?"

"By report, yes."

"Only by report?"

"I have seen her."

"And spoken?"

"No."

"But Your Highness seems sure of her consent," said St. Aldegonde.

Again William slightly flushed.

"She is of the same temper as myself — the same faith — her circumstances are even the same — an exile."

"Her rank?"

"As mine."

Still St. Aldegonde could not think who this lady might be.

"Why does Your Highness give me this incomplete confidence?" he demanded bluntly.

"I will tell you all," returned William, "for I wish you to be my emissary to ask the hand of this gentlewoman."

"A poor proxy," smiled St. Aldegonde ruefully. "I have forgotten Court ways."

"She also, I think."

"Her name, Highness?"

St. Aldegonde still had hopes that this astonishing move on the part of the Prince might be redeemed by some desirable quality such as rank or money on the part of the lady.

William slightly hesitated; the name of Charlotte de Bourbon had been so long treasured in the silent depths of his heart as something sacred that he disliked to divulge it even to the man whom he had chosen to be his ambassador to his beloved.

"It is Mademoiselle de Bourbon," he said at length.

If St. Aldegonde was amazed before he was now completely stupefied.

He stared at William as if the Prince had spoken the words of madness, so utterly impossible, from every point of view, seemed the match that he proposed; St. Aldegonde was a Calvinist, but even to him Charlotte de Bourbon was a renegade nun who had broken her vows — then, her name had been persistently associated with Lodewyk of Nassau, then, again, she was friendless as well as penniless and could bring no friends, while she would certainly make, by her marriage with William, a host of enemies. She was estranged from her father and the Court of France and living on the charity of the Elector — in brief, the marriage was as impolitic and rash as any could well be.

William was prepared for this astonishment — he looked into St. Aldegonde's amazed face and laughed.

"I know your arguments," he said good-naturedly, "so spare them!"

"Your Highness has considered —"

"Everything."

"And the advantages of this match?"

"For once," returned William, "I would consult my own inclinations."

St. Aldegonde was silent.

"I sold myself once for wealth — once for political advantage," continued William sternly, "well for me that I am blessed in my son. You know something of what I have suffered from this Saxony marriage. But not all. Now I want peace — at least in my heart and in my home."

"And this lady will give it to you?"

"I do believe it, Aldegonde."

"Yet you have only seen her twice."

William rose.

"But I know that I am not mistaken in her worth," he replied.

He pulled the bell cord and when the serving-maid came asked for lights; he wished indeed to cut short the protests and arguments he knew that his friend was burning to make.

"You will — as soon as may be — undertake this mission to Heidelberg," he added.

St. Aldegonde made a gesture of despair.

"You know what will be said!"

"I can guess."

"No one will support you!"

"I am prepared for it."

"Even Count John will disapprove."

"St. Aldegonde — I have told you, this time, with God's grace, I do what I believe is right."

He spoke seriously and with a touch of authority, and his friend could say no more.

CHAPTER XII

FORTUNE TURNS

RÉNÈE LE MEUNG had a room in the top story of a house in the Cathedral square at Delft.

The tower of the great church cast this room into shadow, and when the bells rang they filled it with sound.

It was the house of the verger, and he was old and his wife bedridden, so Rénèe helped them in the house and in the church.

And in her leisure she worked the fine lace that she had learnt to do in Brussels and for which there was still a sale and a good price when it could be sent to the markets in England and France.

So Rénèe made her poor living; her life had been always so circumscribed, her tastes so modest that she did not notice her present restriction.

Her poverty did not gall her, for she had all that she wanted.

And, after the long dissatisfaction of her life she seemed at last to have found peace. She was not alone.

The wide room with the smooth sloping floor and latticed window was shared by the refugee's baby.

Rénèe, when she left the service of the Prince in Rotterdam had taken the child with her; the old woman had been glad to be rid of the embarrassment, and there had been an outbreak of the plague in the city rendering the air infected and unsafe for the little creature.

So Rénèe had brought the baby to Delft, leaving her name with the armourer's mother in case anyone should come to claim the child.

But this was unlikely indeed; little Wilhelmina seemed as certainly without friends or relatives as was Rénèe herself.

An unbounded tenderness for the baby filled Rénèe's heart and this tenderness illumined all her life as the sun will illumine a landscape.

She took an interest in things that before she had not even noticed; in dresses, and laces and ribbons, because the baby must wear them, in children, little girls able to walk and bigger girls able to knit and sew, because presently the baby would be as these; in the humble work of the house, the polishing of brass and silver, the sweeping and cleaning, because everything must be kept sweet about the baby, in the fine work of her own fingers, the money for which would be needed soon when the baby grew bigger and needed, ah, so many things.

She even began to take some interest in her own appearance, for she was pitifully anxious that the baby should love her and she had heard that children turned from plain and dowdy people.

A girl was hired to take the baby out, but never further than the square, so that Rénèe, seated at the window at her lace-making, might see them every time she raised her eyes.

It was wonderful how the old couple who had lost their all, relations, children, money, in the war, noticed and soon loved this tiny stranger, it was wonderful how soon she became the centre of interest in the quiet old house, the one flower in so many desolate lives, the one pleasure for so many sad hearts. Rénèe liked her life.

It pleased her to go in the morning into the great church and help this old, old man clean and sweep and stack the huge stoves with wood ready for lighting a little before the service, for though it was yet early in the autumn the church was cold, especially in the evenings.

The church, stripped of all Popish decorations, the walls once rich with gilt and painting whitewashed from vaulted roof to floor, the windows with plain glass instead of coloured, was very wonderful to Rénèe.

This despoiled, purified, altered temple of the old faith converted to the uses of the new faith, represented a triumph which Rénèe could well appreciate the value of.

Her people had been among those whose blood had gone to pay for this liberty, for the freedom now enjoyed by the city of Delft and the worshippers who daily gathered in the cathedral of Saint Ursula.

The whitewashed interior, the unshaded windows, which filled every corner with a cold clear light like that reflected from snow, the hard benches and pulpit of plain dark wood all were to Rénèe beautiful, for they seemed to her part of her inheritance — and one for which she had dearly paid.

And gradually she withdrew herself from her long isolation of mind and spirit and came more in touch with her fellow-creatures, sharing their anxieties and hopes.

She would mingle with the other women after the service and listen to their talk until she drew a certain comfort from these other lives passing so near her own and filled with cares and sorrows so much the same.

Often she saw the Prince, for he was much in Delft these days, occupied mostly for the relief of Leyden, which was yet beleaguered by the Spaniards, despite all the efforts of Admiral Boisot.

But William never saw her; she had disappeared from his house in Rotterdam before he had recovered from the sickness and they had not spoken since he had asked her about Charlotte de Bourbon.

When he attended church Rénèe watched his passing from her window and when he was in his place hastened down to take hers, near the door, where she, concealed by one of the thick white pillars, could watch him throughout the short and ardent service; and before he rose to go she would slip away and from her window mark his return.

Sometimes, in the evening, when the baby was asleep she would carry her down in her wicker cradle and put her beside the verger's wife, who lay patient under her white linen and blue coverlet, her starched muslin cap surrounding her fallen and sad face, the Bible ready to her hand, and leaving these two together she would go softly from the house, cross the dark square, pass a few houses, the bridge over the canal, and stand beneath the dwelling of the Prince.

Sometimes she would see him at a window, or returning late, nearly always she saw a light in his room.

If it happened that he had left Delft and she did not know it, and coming there she found the house in darkness she experienced a curious sense of disappointment like one who has missed a secret joy greatly counted on.

Yet it might seem a strange joy indeed to come here, in the wind and cold very often, or beaten upon by the rain, to stand in the dark and watch for that little light in an upper window.

She knew that he was contemplating a marriage with Mademoiselle de Bourbon.

The matter was almost common knowledge and she had had it direct from the mouth of the Prince's secretary whom she had met by chance.

But it would not be yet, he had added, till Leyden was relieved the Prince would think of nothing else, and he wished to see his cause on a sure way to success before he thought of taking a wife — but next year — if things were happier —

Rénèe was no longer disturbed by the thought of Charlotte de Bourbon.

But she was glad that she had definitely severed her life from her own.

She felt her present existence happiness compared with that she had led at Heidelberg, though there she had been one of a Court and now she was little better than a maidservant.

The last days of September were cold and stormy and Rénèe had to go into the church before the services to light the stoves and draw the heavy green curtains across those portions of the church not used, so as to make a little protection against the draughts that filled the church when the cold winds blew.

There was one curtain across the space where there had once stood the altar and the lady chapel; this was large enough for a church in itself and beneath were burial vaults.

The verger remembered when it had all been canopied in gold tapestry and the altar had been dressed in purple and scarlet with candlesticks in Florentine copper, the height of a man, and the Host in a white shrine curtained with dove-coloured silk. And there had been seats for the monks in carved wood, and velvet carpets and lamps that burnt day and night with a red flame.

And incense burnt perpetually, so that the air was full of a faint blue smoke, and there were glass-like jewels in all the windows, making the whole church dim.

But all these things had been destroyed by the people in righteous wrath.

And the church was now bare and cold and white.

"It is well," said Rénèe.

It was the second day and first Sunday in October. The sullen stillness following a great storm had fallen over the land.

Huge masses of dark clouds lay piled on the horizon and towered up into the higher spaces of the heavens, a chill wind blew across the flat country and ruffled the waters of the canals that traversed the city of Delft.

The limes and elms were stripped of their last leaves by this steady bitter wind, gold and brown leaves that swept in little eddies against the house fronts and the whitewashed steps and brick doorways.

Rénèe, standing at the door of the church, watched these leaves hurrying across the great bare square.

She shuddered in her gray cloth cloak; though it was yet early in the autumn the summer seemed very far away and a long heavy leaden winter seemed to stretch ahead in an endless succession of short dull days and long stormy nights.

Rénèe had rejoiced in the storm, because she knew that the strong easterly wind was driving the sea across the broken dykes and sending the ships of Admiral Boisot on the bosom of the tumbling waves to the very gates of Leyden.

But these hopes, which she shared in common with the entire population, had been destroyed by a letter a carrier pigeon had brought from Boisot to the Prince and which told him of new difficulties, and announced, almost with despair, that the

210

storm had lulled before he had been able to pass the great lake and the almost impregnable forts which guarded the entrance to the city and unless another tempest should arise he would be obliged to make a long detour around Leyden, which would take more time than he believed the city could endure.

Rénèe wondered if this wind that was blowing now was sufficient to float the patriot fleet; the vane on the spire of the old church and that above the town hall told her the easterly direction, which meant that the sea was again blowing across the land.

She shared the firm belief of the Prince that the fate of Leyden was representative of the fate of the little states which were just struggling into independent existence.

If that beautiful city fell there was little to hope for the rest of Holland; if the inhabitants of Leyden shared the fate of those of Alkmaar and Haarlem a shock would run through the infant states which would probably deprive them of life.

If, on the other hand, Leyden should triumphantly resist, if Admiral Boisot should succeed in breaking the leaguer and driving off the besiegers, then the arms of the Netherlanders would have secured a victory such as had not fallen to their lot since the capture of Brill, and one that would be as instantaneous in its effects, material and moral, as had been that action of the Sea Beggars, which had meant the turn of the tide for the cause of the Netherlands.

The old verger joined Rénèe in the doorway of the church.

He also looked at the clouds and the weather-vanes.

He put out his hand to feel the wind rushing by and shivered under his darned woollen shawl.

"The Prince will be anxious today," he said and pulled down the lapels of his cap over his ears.

"The Prince is always anxious," answered Rénèe.

"Yes, I do not think he sleeps much at night," muttered the old man. "He walks with a spring under his feet and a sword over his head. I dreamt last night he was dead, drowned in the waters that come to relieve Leyden."

He shambled back into the church and crouched near the stove by the door warming his gnarled red fingers half encased in woollen mittens, in the hot air which faintly penetrated the vast coldness of the church.

Rénèe instead remained at the door; she looked at the house where the old woman and the baby and the little hired maid waited alone.

They held their own service; the girl read the Bible to the old woman, and then they would pray together for the Prince, for Holland, and for the relief of Leyden. And between them, beside the great clean bed, in her small cradle, lay little Wilhelmina in a rose-coloured cap and under a rose-coloured coverlet.

A little smile curved Rénèe's lips at the thought of the baby.

She seemed to hold a happy secret safe in her heart, something that consoled her, warmed her, and even gave her a certain protection against sorrow.

Differently from her usual custom she did not return home to await till the service commenced but retreated into the shadow of the double doors.

The church was full that morning; young and old, rich and poor had come to offer up a prayer for Leyden.

Rénèe saw the Prince coming across the square; she drew her hood closer across her face and moved further into the cold shadow.

William had his secretary and St. Aldegonde with him; he walked a little apart from these and absently returned the salutations of the people, most of whom passed him on the way to the church, for his step was slow this morning.

As he passed Rénèe in the porch she marked how pale and haggard he looked, and how grave, for him a thing most unusual.

She knew that he was thinking of the letter from Admiral Boisot.

As he entered the church she followed and took her place near the door.

Her eyes filled with unreasonable tears as she looked across at the figure of the Prince, seated erect, like a soldier on duty, opposite the place for the preacher and other clergy, where stood the great Bibles with their long green markers.

As she gazed at that slender figure in the coarse brown frieze, at that grave face so thoughtful and sad, at the locks so scattered with white her heart ached with intolerable longing for the old days — for the young cavalier in gold and brocade with the smiling lips and the chestnut curls who had come and gone from the splendid mansion in Brussels.

She wondered if William ever thought of those times, if he ever recalled and contrasted with these bare walls and cold-lit spaces the luxurious church of St. Gudule, where he had worshipped amid the pomp of the Romanist faith.

She would not have had him other than he was; his very homeliness was proof of his self-sacrifice and heroism — he had given everything, even his youth; she would not have had him different — but being a woman her heart contracted with pain to think that the days of his gorgeous careless magnificence were gone for ever, that never more would he go hawking with his famous white falcons and hounds, never more would he laugh at a banquet or step the figures of a dance — such foolishness, thought Rénèe, yet the tears overbrimmed and ran down her cheeks.

She speculated eagerly as to what the Prince's thoughts were at this moment — did he recall the past or think of Charlotte de Bourbon — or was he thinking of nothing but Leyden?

None of these things were in the mind of William of Orange.

He had even for the moment forgotten what had been in his mind for months — the peril of Leyden.

Instead he dwelt with that uncontrollable stab of anguish that accompanies the sudden unsought recollection of a great sorrow, on the death of Count Lodewyk; even now he could hardly realize that he would never see him again, never receive a letter from him — never bear news of him — he was dead, dead, the young, the ardent, the faithful — his body trampled into the marshes of Mookerheyde.

William listened to the sermon; it was with a start he turned to see one of his servants beside him who gave him a letter and hastened away to the back of the church.

A letter from Admiral Boisot.

The Prince broke the seal, glanced at the contents, and then sat still, his hand over his face.

A few moments later, at the termination of the service he sent the letter up to the pulpit with the request for the pastor to read it aloud.

Leiden was relieved!.

Relief of Leyden

CHAPTER XIII

THE PRINCE'S WIFE

ON the eleventh day of the June following the relief of Leyden William of Orange was married to Charlotte de Bourbon, despite rage of the German Princes and the disapproval of his own party even including his brother John, until now so docile to all the schemes and projects of the Prince.

The modest wedding festivities were held at Dort, and soon after William brought his wife to the quiet house in Delft which was the sole marriage gift he was able to make, for, though he was on the eve of accepting the Government of Holland and Zeeland with sovereign powers and the name of Stadtholder, this meant little betterment in his private fortunes, which were encumbered by debts and settlements.

But the dowerless bride made no complaint at the modest maintenance offered her; secured by the declarations of the Protestant clergy in the legality of her position she accepted with grace and dignity the role of Princess of Orange and wife of the chief magistrate of the freed Provinces.

Rénèe, living her quiet monotonous life, of which every day was a copy of the last, heard on every side a good report of the new Princess.

And somehow, within herself, she smiled; she had always known that Charlotte de Bourbon would not fail in anything she undertook.

That summer, soon after the solemn ceremony by which the Prince had accepted the government Rénèe resolved to wait upon Charlotte de Bourbon.

She was calm in her desire to speak again with the woman who was now William's wife, for some while she had been strangely and coldly curious to see his present home; she did not doubt he was happy and she did not want to see his happiness, but she did want to see Charlotte de Bourbon.

She chose a day when the Prince was absent at Rotterdam, put on her best gown and went to the house opposite the old church.

There was no more pomp than there had been in the old days; a maidservant showed Rénèe directly into the presence of her mistress.

Charlotte was seated in the window space, sewing, her lavender-blue gown and lawn ruffles, her bright hair and lace cap were all of exquisite freshness and neatness, her serene sweet face bloomed with gentle contentment.

Rénèe saw at a glance that she was softened, slightly humbled and no longer so absolutely mistress of herself. She rose with surprise, almost confusion.

"I did not know you were in Delft — I have so often thought of you."

Rénèe came forward to kiss her hand, but Charlotte with sincere modesty, prevented this and instead embraced her and led her to the seat near her own.

A silence and an embarrassment quelled the spirit of Rénèe; her calm and her curiosity both left her; she sat mute, wishing she had not come.

The Princess noted her worn dress, so bare of ornament, her hands spoilt and roughened with work, her person which had lost something of softness and roundness, and her face which was a little hollowed, a little blurred in line and faded in tint, but still lovely beneath the plaits of red-brown hair.

Charlotte, secure in her own destiny now, was acutely aware of something strange, closed, and secret about the Fleming, something she had always been aware of, but had been too self-absorbed to dwell upon.

"You live here?" she asked gently. Something prevented her from questioning Rénèe as to the motive of her sudden leaving of Heidelberg or in any way forcing her confidence.

Rénèe was prepared for this question.

"No," she said quickly. "I happen to be in Delft. I have no home."

The lie came readily to her lips; she had a desire that was almost passionate to disguise from Charlotte and from the Prince the life she had evolved for herself in Delft.

This and the existence of little Wilhelmina were secrets she would never divulge.

It was in Charlotte's heart and almost on her lips to ask her to enter her service; but again something, perhaps the sense of the aloof, the strange, the hidden, in Rénèe, prevented her.

"I am glad that you came to see me," she said instead. "I am much alone."

Rénèe looked at her sharply.

"Alone?"

Charlotte's smile was not without sadness as she replied —

"You would not believe how absorbed His Highness is in affairs and how little I see of him."

"Yes," said Rénèe, "he would have much to do now."

"So much — he works day and night. For the rest I have few friends. I am still the foreigner — the newcomer."

Rénèe's great eyes remained fixed steadily on the fair face of the Princess.

"Does it seem strange to Your Highness," she asked, "to sit here as the wife of William of Orange?"

The bride of a few months coloured, but she was moved to frankness and kindness; she had as yet few acquaintances in her adopted country and she had known Rénèe longer and with greater intimacy than she had known anyone else at present about her person.

"Sometimes it seems very strange," she answered simply. "You remember, at Heidelberg, how we used to talk of him?"

"And of Count Lodewyk."

"Count Lodewyk — yes."

"I always thought you would many Count Lodewyk."

"I know."

The two women were silent for a moment and continued to look at each other.

"You think that I am very happy?" asked Charlotte at last, under her breath.

Rénèe gave a little shudder but did not answer or move.

"I have made many enemies by my marriage," continued the Princess, "and, I fear, plunged my lord into much dispute and imbroglio. Sometimes I think I did wrong."

"His Highness pleased himself," answered Rénèe in a constrained tone.

"I brought him nothing," said Charlotte with the same simple frankness. "I can make a home for him and his children, that is all."

"Any woman could do that," thought Rénèe; she averted her eyes and said aloud:

"It is curious you should speak as if you justified your marriage — to me, Madam!"

"I know you have been a faithful friend to the Prince. You may have thought, as other friends of his have thought, that this marriage was wrong — a mistake."

Her eyes filled with tears as she spoke; as she continued her voice shook.

"Believe me — my great desire was to serve him — believe me — I suffer."

"Suffer?" Rénèe was startled. Charlotte took her hand earnestly.

"I live with him in the midst of death — he never leaves me but I say farewell thinking it may be farewell indeed — every day some new peril arises — *do you think that Philip will suffer him to live?*"

Rénèe looking at her, saw that lines of care already marked the brow that had been so smooth, that the serene eyes were tired by secret weeping, saw that Charlotte, whom she had judged hard, cold, precise, mistress of herself, a little proud, a little confident, was after all a wretched woman like herself, full of anguishes that must be suppressed and fears that must be hidden, saw that she, the self-contained, the calm, was shaken and trembling and afraid.

"You could not think," continued the Princess, and her voice was quite broken now, "the letters he receives — the warnings, the threats, the scurrilous attacks — there is only he left now — three Nassau Princes dead. And Philip on the watch, always. Philip and his spies."

She clutched Rénèe's hand desperately.

"Some day it will happen," she said, "and I may have to stand by."

Rénèe's heart seemed suddenly unlocked; she turned her head sharply aside and burst into hot tears.

"I have thought of this — have I not thought of this day and night?" she cried.

"It will happen," said Charlotte. "God help us — God help us."

With a mutual instinct the women turned to each other and clasped hands.

Charlotte was the first to thrust her sorrows back into her heart.

"Such fools we are, we die a thousand deaths," she said with a trembling smile.

"But you — you," stammered Rénèe, "why are you so afraid! His Highness grows greater every day — a nation surrounds him now."

"The more reason Philip should seek to destroy him. Ah, I am afraid of Philip!"

"No," replied Rénèe in great agitation. "Your Highness must not think of these things —"

"But you," said Charlotte, "did you not say you had thought of this — day and night?"

The ashamed blood beat in Rénèe's tear-stained cheeks.

"Your Highness unnerved me," she murmured. "I — yes, I have had — fears — about the Prince," she paused, then added with an effort, clutching her hands tightly under Charlotte's soft fingers. "The Prince," she repeated, "the life of His Highness means so much to us Netherlanders."

"I know," replied the Princess, "take this comfort — he has already done a work that not all the might of Philip can undo. He has established in Holland that which no earthly power can destroy. And if God gives him a few more years, you will see a great nation established in these states."

The pride of wife and comrade sounded in her voice and Rénèe bent her head.

She felt that she had been mistaken in Charlotte de Bourbon in judging her cold, incapable of great emotion and noble feeling.

The woman who spoke now was the real woman, the woman who had had the courage to fling off a vocation into which she had been forced, the spirit to renounce a creed that was hateful to her and to defy a family that was forgetful of her, the woman who had had the courage to choose her own life and pursue her own course with unfaltering steps.

Under the precise manner of one trained since childhood to restraint, and, since early girlhood, to command, was the lofty spirit and serene soul of a good and sweet woman.

Rénèe saw this; as she also saw that Charlotte suffered, that her marriage had brought her the burden of pain as well as the garland of joy, and that her life was one of anxiety and foreboding, and might at any moment be changed into the darkness of bitter anguish.

She loosened her hands from the gentle clasp of the Princess and turned away.

She no longer felt hard or cold or bitter but humbled and abashed.

Charlotte looked at her with puzzled eyes; she had not the key to the heart of Rénèe le Meung.

"You were very intimate — in the Prince's house in Brussels?" she asked; Rénèe had never given her any confidence as to this part of her life.

"Yes — with the Princess."

Charlotte steadied her voice with a palpable effort.

"Tell me — about her."

"About her! Madam, it seems another life."

"Yes — but I must think of her sometimes. You understand that."

Rénèe had thought of her too; she knew the fate of Anne of Saxony.

Returned at length to her outraged and indignant relatives, divorced from the husband she had reviled and abandoned, separated from the children she had never cared for, and from the lover for whose ignoble sake she had cast the last remnants of her honour and dignity aside, the wretched Princess, whose mind was now completely gone, was now kept as a hopeless prisoner, the windows of her chamber being walled up and food passed through an aperture in the door where a clergyman who exhorted her to repentance was constantly stationed.

This punishment of the last Princess of Orange for a life that had indeed been full of fault and folly was no secret.

Rénèe believed that Charlotte must know of it; but it was something that she could not speak of to the woman who occupied Anne's place.

"The Princess was mad," she said, "and His Highness ever magnanimous."

"He never — cared for her?"

"A marriage of convenience. But he was ever gentle and considerate. She might have been a happy woman."

"It was that I wished to know — you, so continually with her, must be aware of the truth."

"That is the truth, Madam. She was mad — even before her marriage."

Charlotte was silent awhile looking out over the sunny courtyard.

Then she spoke, suddenly.

"I asked you because I have her children with me."

"Yes!"

"And try to make a home for them. Maurice is a beautiful boy."

Rénèe remembered him but vaguely; she had been continually with Anne and therefore had seen but little of the children, who had always lived apart from their mother.

"He has the spirit of his father," said Charlotte wistfully, and as she spoke Rénèe divined another of her sorrows — that she was not the mother of the Prince's heir.

"The Princess's father was the great Elector Maurice," answered Rénèe; "perhaps the young Count favours him."

"Would you like to see him?" she asked, and without waiting for an answer she pulled the bell-rope near to her hand.

"What am I to him?" answered Rénèe; it seemed to her a curious fancy of Charlotte to speak of William's son.

In a few minutes he came, easily and frankly into the presence of the two ladies.

The Prince's eldest son, Count Philip William, remained, lost to his family and his country, a prisoner in Spain, and Maurice was his only other son, and, in the eyes of all, his heir.

He stood before the two women, a well-grown boy of eight years; he held a green and blue parrot on his wrist.

He was like neither of his parents; he showed promise of a heavier make than the Prince, and the thick hair that fell around his comely child's face was light brown, almost blonde.

His eyes, large and clear gray, were full of intelligence and fire and he had already a very notable carriage, graceful and bold.

He glanced at the stranger with little interest; but Rénèe noted that for the Princess he had a smile of affection.

Charlotte asked him some trivial questions about the parrot and sent him away.

He ran off laughing, the gaudy bird on his shoulder.

"You are fond of him, Highness?" asked Rénèe.

The Princess looked at her straightly.

"I try to train him to take his father's place when the time comes," she answered gravely. "Perhaps, after all, the famous Saxon marriage will not have been in vain."

She smiled at Rénèe, who was silent, bewildered by this new point of view.

"You see I try to do my duty," added the Princess bravely. "And to help in the work of His Highness."

PART III

THE BAN

*"God in His Mercy will maintain my innocence and my honour
during my life and in future ages. As to my fortune and my life, I
have dedicated both, long since, to His service."*
— William of Orange

Father William

CHAPTER I

SPANISH COUNCILS

THE Burgundian priest sat by the bedside of his sovereign. A low fever kept Philip in his room, but now the weakness of his illness was passing and he had summoned Granvelle to discuss with him the eternal business that forever occupied his mind.

For the moment, however, he slept, and the Cardinal waited at his ease in the great chair of stamped leather with gilt arms that stood by the King's bed curtains. Philip disliked light as he disliked noise; the chamber was dark, silent, overheated, the air heavy with the sickly perfume of drugs and herbs and the unchanged air of a sick-room.

It was yet early afternoon, but the shutters were closed and the glow of an oil lamp mingled with the red glimmer of the fire.

The black furniture threw heavy shadows on the walls hung with tawny leather; the only colour in the semi-obscurity was the scarlet, gold and blue of the King's bed trappings, which gleamed fitfully out of the gloom, a coverlet that reached the ground, wide and heavy curtains that concealed the occupant of the bed, all shot with silk and metal woven into the design of the armorial bearings of Spain.

On the wall opposite to the foot of the bed hung an ebony crucifix of massive size, beneath it, veiled with a green cloth, was a beautiful wanton Italian picture recently purchased by the King and brought here for his inspection.

At the side of the room an open door showed the antechamber, there waited the chamberlain, the doctor, and the apothecary.

They were all seated at a round table, and as Granvelle looked at their figures they seemed to him to be asleep.

The Cardinal himself yawned, but he was far from slumber. His active brain was alert; he sat motionless, withdrawn into the shadows, but his pose was full of energy, his eyes watchful.

With a bitter philosophy his acute judgment reviewed the recent events in the struggle in which he had taken so personal an interest, the scenes and actors of the world amid which he moved.

Eight years had passed since he had first suggested to Philip the wisdom of removing William of Orange by assassination, and that Prince still lived and by sheer skill of statecraft had guided the destinies of the rebel Provinces until by the Pacification of Ghent he had secured the adhesion of seven states to the Union which defied Philip.

The Cardinal, never one to blink facts, did not deny to himself that William was so far the victor in the long and terrible conflict which he always considered to have begun that day the young Prince, then regarded as a mere brilliant Grandee, of the quality of Egmont, had come to defy him in his luxurious house outside Brussels.

The sudden death of the Governor, Resquesens, the subsequent confusion of the country left without a Viceroy and the hideous mutiny of the Spanish soldiery, culminating in the ghastly sack of Antwerp — these events had been turned to good account by William of Orange.

And the new Governor, the famous, the adored, the beautiful brother of the King, Don John of Austria, the dupe of Philip, the victim of the hate and jealousy of Aña D'Eboli and Antonio Perez, what had he been but William's puppet?

The most brilliant hero in Christendom, the most charming of gentlemen had exerted his fascination in vain against the influence of the Prince of Orange, whom he could neither buy nor win, cajole nor subdue.

In despair at his impossible task, overwhelmed by the steady power of the man who opposed him, all his gorgeous schemes laid in the dust, abandoned by the cold distrust of Philip in whose service he had obtained such deathless renown, the brilliant adventurer had died heartbroken on the muddy floor of a pigeon-house in the fields outside Namur.

And William of Orange pursued his way.

Granvelle hoped more from Don John's successor than he had ever hoped from that peerless knight himself, Alexander of Parma, nephew of the King and son of the late Regent, the Duchess Margaret, now held the reins of government, and Granvelle had greater faith in the cold crafty Italian, cruel, energetic, and masterful, than he ever had hoped from Don John, generous, impulsive, ambitious, worthless as a statesman and inferior to Parma as a soldier.

But even the qualities of Alexander Farnese had not as yet proved equal to the qualities of the Prince of Orange.

He also had had his puppets, from behind whose back he had governed the states he had wrested from Philip.

First the Archduke Mathias, who had served his turn, and now a more formidable figure-head to flout and irritate Spain, namely Francis Hercules, Duke of Anjou, brother of the King of France and in the favour of the Queen of England, even, as rumour still said, her future husband. This personage had William secured as his mask and protection, and the twisted policies of the Duke's mother, the Medicean Queen, were thus supporting the heretics against the King who had most rejoiced in the massacre of Saint Bartholomew.

It was a great thing for William to have thus obtained the open support of France, and the tacit support of England, and Granvelle could well imagine the satisfaction with which he allowed the French Prince to assume the trappings of Duke of Brabant and all the symbols of authority, while he, as ever sleeplessly watchful, patient and wary, continued to steer the ship of state through the perilous depths of wars and diplomacy.

What was Anjou?

No more than Mathias in power or prestige, and of the base, half-mad Valois blood.

Already he was tampering with Parma; Spain could always buy him if the price was high enough, he was but another royal adventurer, a mere counter in the game who might at any moment be swept from the board as Don John and Mathias and many another had already been swept.

But the Prince — he, now as always, was the man with whom Spain had to reckon. For years Granvelle had been constant to this one hope and aim — the accomplishment of the death of the Prince of Orange.

So far all private attempts on his life had failed. He had escaped these perils as he had survived the dangers and fatigues to which he was constantly exposed. His body seemed as sound and perfect as his mind, since it successfully resisted disease, sickness, weariness, and almost superhuman labour.

Lodewyk of Nassau had gone now, gone was the younger brother who might have taken his place, gone the young heir of the Elector — who indeed was left of those who had set out to defy Philip? Only this one man.

"But all the others might have lived," said Granvelle in his heart, "could this great man but have been taken."

A feeling of despair overcame him as if William were protected by some supernatural power; it seemed little less than miraculous, even to the cynical mind of the Cardinal, so little disposed to believe in miracles, that William had so long escaped every danger and peril, every trap and snare when so many less illustrious and dangerous persons had fallen victim to the wrath of Philip.

It might have seemed as if every weapon had been tried in the armoury of violence and craft, but the acute brain of Granvelle had evolved yet another means with which to strike at the heart of William of Orange.

As he sat there, silent in the shadows by Philip's bed, he held a roll of parchment in his elegant hands which was the most powerful instrument yet directed against the life of the rebel heretic.

The Cardinal had designed, and Philip had approved and signed, a Ban against the Prince as direct and wide embracing in its effects as any Bull of Excommunication issued by any Pope.

This document, after an elaborate preamble setting forth the crimes and treasons of the Prince from his first ingratitude to Philip till the Union of Utrecht, declared him "traitor and miscreant, enemy of ourselves and of the country. As such we banish him perpetually from our realms, forbidding all our subjects of whatever degree to communicate with him openly or privately, to administer to him victuals, drink, fire, or other necessaries. We allow all to injure him in property or life. We expose the said William of Nassau as an enemy of the human race — giving his property to all who may seize it. And if any one of our subjects or any stranger should be found sufficiently generous of heart to rid us of this pest, delivering him to us, alive or dead, or taking his life, we will cause to be furnished to him immediately after the deed shall have been done, the sum of twenty-five thousand crowns in gold. If he have committed any crime, however heinous, we promise to pardon him, and if he be not already noble, we will ennoble him for his valour."

Cardinal Granvelle knew these words, which were of his own dictating, by heart.

This time the net of Spain had been thrown wide — it was intended to catch all the villains of the world and turn them to the King's uses. All the swarming mercenaries, the refuse of years of war, all the wandering homeless ruffians, the scum of Europe, all the professional assassins of Italy and Spain, all the fanatics who had viewed the rise of heresy with frantic horror were now tempted and exhorted to remove this man.

They were promised the protection of Spain, admission to the ranks of the proudest nobility in the world, forgiveness of any crime they might have committed, and a sum of money that represented a fortune.

Granvelle could not believe that among all those who would assuredly try for these prizes, there was not one who would eventually be successful.

And there was the moral effect of the Ban; the Cardinal greatly reckoned on that.

William's courage had been tried in many ways but he had not yet been tried by the supreme test of all the certainty of assassination, the knowledge that all the villainy, cupidity, and fanaticism of Europe was being urged and bribed to remove him — that poison might lurk in every dish he tasted, a dagger in the hand of every stranger who approached him.

"Let us see now," said the Cardinal to himself, "if this rogue is able to pursue his business unperturbed."

Alva, Resquesens, Don John, Parma, and Granvelle himself, had failed to bribe, cajole, or move this man, he had proved impervious to all attempts to win him and escaped all efforts to dispose of his life or his liberty; now the wrath of Spain was unmasked, her full venom and deadly sting were exposed — perhaps by the hand of some obscure ruffian she could accomplish what she had failed to do by means of her greatest captains, Princes, and statesmen.

Philip stirred in the great bed and the Cardinal moved the heavy curtains and looked at his master.

So slight and thin was Philip that his meagre figure hardly showed beneath the massive coverlet, his head resting low on the huge pillow looked like an earthen mask placed there, so closely did the skin, dry and hot with fever, cling to his bones, so lifeless were the eyes, sunken and half closed.

A white cap of puckered lawn covered the King's head and from under it hung his limp reddish locks.

The years had not softened nor ennobled Philip of Spain nor deepened Granvelle's love for him.

The Cardinal looked with little affection on the dried insignificant face, worn with years and disease, of the man whom he called his sovereign.

Neither had the Burgundian grown softer with the passing of time which had left his ambitions unsatisfied and his position stationary.

As he looked at Philip his lip curled.

"The dupe of Aña D'Eboli and Antonio Perez?" he thought, "the puppet of a wanton and a rogue."

These two still ruled the Court of Spain; they had been able to bring to the dust Don John and to remove by murder his secretary Excordo, and still Philip suspected nothing of an intrigue of which he alone in Spain seemed ignorant.

Granvelle stared closer at the miserable wasted face of the King and the contempt deepened in his own countenance.

Philip suddenly opened his eyes and seeing Granvelle bending over him moved back his head a little and gazed at the Cardinal.

The contempt froze on Granvelle's face; he drew back with a cautious swiftness; the movement of one who has suddenly found himself too near something poisonous and fierce.

The King's pallid eyes fixed him with a steady stare; his straight gaze was terrible and Granvelle saw now no longer the sickly dupe, the prey of such as Perez and his lover, but the man who was ruler of half the world.

"I wished to read to Your Majesty the finished version of the Ban," he said, smoothly.

"The Ban," repeated the King in a voice utterly monotonous and weak. "I remember very well the contents. Twenty-five thousand crowns is too high."

"Your Majesty yourself wrote to the Prince of Parma that thirty thousand crowns would be well spent in this affair."

"But you," replied Philip, still staring at him with unblinking eyes, "dictated that letter. I always thought the sum too much."

He raised himself in bed and looked around to see if there was any food ready on the table by his side.

There was none and he stretched out a trembling yellow hand and struck the bell of cut silver near him.

"No sum would be too high to pay for the removal of the Prince of Orange," said Granvelle, controlling his exasperation at Philip's parsimony, which was to him a continual source of irritation.

"But if we can get the work done for ten why offer twenty-five?"asked Philip, and he reached out for a fur tippet which he drew closely around his lean shoulders.

"The higher the reward the greater number it will attract," answered Granvelle.

"There are many," insisted Philip, "who would do the business not for money but for the love of our Lord."

"Those who demand no pay need not receive any," said the Cardinal, "but there are very many neither good Roman Catholics nor honest men who would do this thing for money."

"I regret the amount," said Philip; his chamberlain entered and the King ordered food.

"Sire," returned Granvelle, "it is not likely that the man who kills William of Orange will live to claim a reward."

"True," said Philip, brightening.

"He will almost certainly be captured and put to death by the Estates."

"But there will be his family," objected the King, depressed again.

"Your Majesty can satisfy the family out of the property forfeited by the Prince of Orange."

Philip considered this suggestion so brilliant that he smiled, showing his broken teeth above the ragged line of a red beard.

The idea of rewarding William's murderer out of William's own pocket gave him great pleasure; his eyes brightened and he continued to smile at Granvelle.

"The twenty-five thousand crowns can remain on the Ban," continued the Cardinal, "and Your Majesty can make up the amount in lands — those in Franché-Comte, for instance."

The King nodded; his *valet de chambre* was entering with a tray of food and this for the moment engaged his whole attention.

Granvelle folded up the copy of the Ban; he saw that it was useless to try and read it to the King while the latter was engaged in reviewing the young fowl cooked in wine, the mushrooms stuffed with snow, the spiced meats, the tarts, sweets, and forced fruits that had been placed before him.

This rich food was always ready when the King called for it, as, even in sickness, he preserved an enormous appetite.

The Cardinal was somewhat disgusted by this sight of Philip so intent on his meal; he himself was fond of luxurious living, but not to the exclusion of higher interests.

"Your Majesty is then satisfied with the wording of the Ban?"

"Surely," said Philip, testing the tenderness of the fowl with a silver knife, "we can say no more. When I hear the Prince has been taken off it will be a happier day for me than that of Saint Bartholomew," this reminding him of French affairs, he added mournfully, "I wish we could put a price on the head of the Duke of Anjou."

"He is a son of France," replied the Cardinal, "and for the moment we had better not meddle with him."

"Parma may buy him yet," answered the King. "Parma is the best man I have had in the Netherlands."

Granvelle did not endorse this statement; to hear another praised in the conduct of the Netherlands, reminded him of the ever galling subject of his own ill success there.

Seeing the King absorbed in the meal, he took his leave; he was glad to be away from the close unhealthy air of the sick-chamber and smelt at a little gilt pomander of herbs he kept at his girdle with his rosary.

When he reached the corridor he opened the nearest window and leant out into the cold March air.

With a little smile he held up the Ban as if he traced the form of the man he hated in the loose flying gray clouds.

"A good many years since you defied me, William of Nassau, but perhaps now, at last —"

CHAPTER II

THE FIRST FRUITS
OF THE BAN

THE June of that year the Ban was published in the Netherlands. If Philip had thrown aside the mask, so now did William of Nassau.

His answer to the Ban was the "Apology," in which he defied the thundered wrath of Spain, point by point defended his conduct, and arraigned Philip for his crimes against liberty and honour as fearlessly and emphatically as Philip and Granvelle had arraigned him.

There was no longer any subtleties, any juggling of words between these two. Philip no longer flattered, William was no longer deferential; their long enmity had taken on another phase, it was now open, ruthless without disguise or hope of reconciliation, war to the death.

Philip gave William's life to the assassin, his property to the thief, his substance to the four winds of heaven. William in his reply gave Philip's actions to the judgment of all mankind.

Wherever the Ban was circulated the Apology went also, and before all noble minds William was vindicated.

And the months passed without producing either any outward sign of the effect of the Ban upon minds that were not noble but low, fanatic, and mercenary.

William seemed too encircled by love and devotion, respect and gratitude for any murderer's arm to reach him.

Neither was he, as Granvelle had hoped, in the least intimidated by Philip's awful threats.

Unmoved as ever by the machinations of his enemies and the extraordinary internal difficulties of a country that was yet divided, unsure of itself, struggling into separate being out of confusion and terrors manifold, he proceeded to consolidate the position of the Provinces by act after act in which they asserted their freedom and threw off the Spanish yoke.

In the midsummer of 1581, the United Provinces solemnly and forever renounced their allegiance to Philip; the sovereignty of Holland and Zeeland was vested in William, the other Provinces agreed to accept Francis of Anjou as the successor to Philip, the Prince from many motives having declined to accept the entire government and having only received that of the Northern States with extreme reluctance.

It had never been his desire to advance himself by the troubles of these times, and he was resolute not to incur the imputation of having contended for his own private fortunes instead of for the freedom of the Netherlands.

Besides, he believed that the struggling states would be safer under the protection of the brother of the King of France and the friend of England than trusting solely to him, a landless man, plunged deeply in danger and difficulty. For this reason he endeavoured, though without avail, to induce Holland and Zeeland to join the other Provinces in electing as their sovereign the Duke of Anjou — the union of all under one chief being his great desire.

That the French King's brother was the ideal person to fill this position the Prince did not pretend, but there was no one else offering; if assistance did not come from France there was nowhere it could come from. Anjou was an unknown quantity, but St. Aldegonde had spoken well of him; he was young — he might serve.

So, while William persuaded the States and persuaded himself, and it was generally considered probable that Anjou would marry the Queen of England, and thus a double protection be secured for the States, in the early spring of 1582, the Duke crossed from England, where he had been fêted and flattered by Elizabeth, and landed at Flushing accompanied by an English escort.

A few days later he took the oaths at Kiel and entered Antwerp as Duke of Brabant.

His inauguration was made with a display of wealth, pomp, and magnificence which astonished and vexed the French.

The Duke subscribed the constitutional pact of twenty-seven articles and was accepted, after much exchange of flowery courtesies, as Duke of Brabant. The Prince who had placed him in this position had circumscribed his power, so that he was no more than a chief magistrate of a republic; the Frenchman made no protest, he swore the oaths glibly, he replied to the compliments bestowed on him with amiable courtesy, but in his heart the unscrupulous adventurer was by no means pleased by the limitations imposed on an authority which he had hoped and expected would be absolute; he wanted not only Philip's place, but Philip's power,

For the moment the festivities offered by Antwerp, which pleased his idle and luxurious nature, wholly occupied his mind, but while preparing for the great banquet which he was giving on his birthday, a few weeks after his arrival, he suddenly expressed himself as tired of the position in which the Prince of Orange had placed him.

"I am not," he said, glancing around the little court of young nobles who surrounded him, "this Dutchman's doll."

His favourites heartily endorsed this statement; but His Highness was not in the mood for further speech and waved them haughtily into silence.

He sat in a great gilt chair in the gorgeous bedroom of the palace of Saint Michael, and a long mirror placed opposite him that he might view himself in his festival garment, reflected his entire figure.

The man whom Fate had chosen as the last rival to Philip on the troubled scene of the Netherlands, was now twenty-eight years old and of a singularly unprepossessing appearance.

When William had met him on the quay at Flushing he had glanced from him to the beautiful face and stately figure of the English nobleman who had accompanied him; the French Prince appeared grotesque by the side of Robert Dudley, Earl of Leicester, and William, looking from Elizabeth's favourite to Elizabeth's suitor, had but little hopes for the pretensions of Francis of Anjou.

Like his brothers, puny and undersized, he was plainer of feature than either Henry or Charles.

His originally insignificant face was seamed and puckered by the scars of smallpox, which disease had so swollen and disfigured his nose that it appeared to be double.

His small light eyes sparkled with cunning and malice, his mouth was loose and ugly, a quantity of smooth fair hair was turned back from his narrow forehead and his stoop was so pronounced as to be almost a hump.

This miserable figure was clad in the utmost pomp and magnificence, perfumed, curled, and adorned.

His doublet of white satin, stuffed to render more imposing his meagre proportions, was braided with gold and seed pearls, an enormous triple ruff of the finest needlework surrounded his face and from his shoulders hung a mantle of rich blue velvet lined with yellow satin.

Hose of fine white silk, garters of pearl and turquoise, gilt shoes completed his attire.

On his left arm he carried a muff of white fur, on his breast sparkled several jewelled chains, and in one ear was a long brilliant drop, attached to which was a plait of auburn hair, believed to be that of the Queen of England.

The demeanour of the Duke was in keeping with this elaborate attire; he was by no means depressed by his physical disabilities, but carried himself with the air of a handsome cavalier.

His little group of "mignons," as adorned, as scented and all more elegant than himself, stood in the embrasure of the handsome window talking together in whispers and eyeing their master.

From the moment of their landing they had seen and fostered the Duke's dislike of the Flemings and his antipathy to William of Orange.

They took as an outrage the limitations imposed on the man who would one day be King of France, they had not come to the Netherlands to be the servants of the States, but to lord it over the inhabitants of the Provinces as they were used to lord it over the French.

The debauched, criminal, and tyrannical Court of the Valois was their model; Roman Catholics, they despised heretics, nobles, they despised the burghers who largely composed the states, worthless, wanton, and always in want of money the wealth and splendour of such a city as Antwerp excited their envy and cupidity.

Such were the men let loose upon the soil of the Netherlands under the pretence of protecting their recently redeemed liberties.

Anjou shared these feelings.

He was not unintelligent and he had quickly seen what position William of Orange expected him to occupy and that Prince's motives in securing for him the sovereignty of the Provinces.

Neither of these was to his liking and he hated the man who, he felt, was merely using him for his own ends.

From the first he had resolved to outwit William; as he had not hesitated to endeavour to overcome the magnificent Leicester in the lists of love, so he did not hesitate to measure himself on the fields of diplomacy with the Prince of Orange.

He had already opened secret and tentative negotiations with Parma and was prepared to deliver to Spain all the liberties which he had so recently sworn to defend if he would find his own advancement in so doing.

But Parma was wary and Philip dangerous; the Duke saw but little to be gained in this direction, at least for the moment.

He began to be discontented with the whole adventure and to feel a deepening spite against the Prince of Orange.

"I will not be another Mathias!" he exclaimed aloud. "No, this Prince mistakes my quality."

"Truly," said one of the young nobles, "I warned Your Grace from the first he was a fellow who spoke always with a double meaning. A man of a serpentine policy."

"Now, however," added another, "he deals with a son of France."

"Not a puppet like Mathias, poor fool."

"But a great Prince."

"He will soon find the difference."

Anjou listened to his flatterers with a satisfied air. He had a higher opinion of his own capabilities than even his courtiers' servility could suggest.

"Seigneurs," he said complacently, "you will see me very easily foil this Prince."

So calmly did the frivolous young adventurer talk of undoing the work at which William of Orange had laboured for twelve years and in which he had spent all his fortunes and energies, so lightly did he consider undermining the liberties which a whole brave people, at the cost of unutterable sacrifices had fought so long to redeem.

"Your Grace must make yourself master of Antwerp and other such cities," said one of the flatterers.

"In this town alone," remarked another, "there are treasures worth the sacking." And his dissipated eyes glittered greedily, for he was encumbered with debts.

"Have you marked the goldsmiths' shops?" cried a third. "I never saw such jewels."

"Nor such stuffs, brocades — cloths of gold, fine tissues."

Anjou smiled as he listened; he intended to make himself absolute master of this wealth that had so dazzled his favourites.

"We shall see," he remarked, "who is lord in the Netherlands — myself or this Prince of Orange."

His valet entered with a glass of orange water in a cutglass flagon on a tray of parcel-gilt.

The Duke ceased to talk of serious things and sat sipping the orange water, dipping therein long sticks of white sugar that were served with it on a little dish of white porcelain.

The "mignons" dispersed about the apartment, admiring themselves in the long mirrors, laughing and whispering together.

The Duke sucked his sugar sticks, sipped his orange water and meditated his plans of thwarting the Prince of Orange and making himself complete master of the Provinces.

His reflections were somewhat suddenly interrupted by the abrupt opening of the door.

St. Aldegonde, pallid and disordered in appearance, stood upon the threshold.

Francis of Anjou, always on the outlook for violence and treachery, clapped his hand to the little Italian dagger he kept concealed in the brocaded folds of his breeches.

"What is this?" he asked.

St. Aldegonde moved his lips but did not answer at once.

The Duke paled.

His suspicious mind scented some disaster, some misfortune which would involve his own person.

"My friend, are you speechless?" he asked, rising.

"The Prince," stammered St. Aldegonde. "His Highness —"

The "mignons" had clustered around the Duke; a gorgeous glittering band they fronted the plain and haggard courtier of William of Orange.

The Duke still had his hand on the dagger, but he had regained his composure and the elegance of his manner.

"What has happened to my cousin the Prince?" he asked with a good show of concern.

"His Highness has been assassinated," returned St. Aldegonde.

Anjou staggered; he felt as if the ground had been cut beneath him.

Instinctively he cowered behind his "mignons," who drew together in a phalanx of glittering jewels and pale satins.

"Assassinated," repeated St. Aldegonde as if he could not believe his own words, "shot through the head by a villain who presented a petition."

A few moments before Anjou was thinking with hatred and impatience of the restraining hand of William of Orange, now that he heard that the man who had placed him where he was had been murdered, he felt a sensation of terror as if he had been abandoned, as if some strength on which he leant had been suddenly withdrawn.

He kept his wits, however, through all his terror, and noticed that St. Aldegonde's distorted face was turned towards him, his bloodshot eyes keenly fixed on him.

240

"They suspect me," thought Anjou faintly and with a lively pang he pre-visioned his probable fate if the Netherlanders held him responsible for the murder of the Prince.

"Has the assassin been caught?" he asked, pressing his perfumed handkerchief to his shaking lips.

"He was stabbed to death instantly by those about the Prince. Count Maurice guards the body."

"A — Spaniard?" queried the Duke.

"Highness, nothing is known yet."

"Certainly it is a Spaniard," said the Duke, taking courage; "these are the first fruits of the Ban."

"Will Your Grace come to the Prince?" he breathed.

"What should I do?" demanded Anjou, trembling.

St. Aldegonde gave a dubious glance at the Duke in whose cause he had been so enthusiastic; he was beginning to doubt the wisdom of the choice of this new protector of the Netherlands.

"Highness," he said sternly, "the Prince's last words, as he fell with his hair alight from the pistol, were: 'Ah, what a servant His Highness loses in me!' — and now the place of Your Grace is by his side."

"What to do!" exclaimed the Duke in agitation, gazing around at his pale and silent courtiers; "how do I know what humour the people are in that I should venture forth?"

"The clean conscience of Your Highness will be your buckler," returned St. Aldegonde who was still by no means certain that Anjou was not implicated in the recent crime.

"I had rather have a hundred armed men," said Anjou. "I do not like your Flemings when they are in an ugly mood."

"All the more reason that Your Grace should show yourself to them. There is a terrible apprehension abroad — Your Highness must face the people."

Anjou and his followers gazed at each other with expressions of undisguised dismay.

"I was abandoned by God the day I left England, where I was both honoured and safe!" exclaimed the Duke.

He stared at St. Aldegonde with an apprehension that was almost ludicrous.

"But I will not go forth," he added defiantly.

St. Aldegonde was spared an answer by the arrival of an officer of the Prince's household with the news that the young Count had found papers on the body of the assassin which proved him to have been inspired by one D'Anastro, a Spanish merchant long since in the pay of the Court of Spain. The crime was entirely the result of the Ban and the French were in no way responsible;

Maurice of Nassau (1567-1625)

Count Maurice had at once communicated this news to the alarmed magistrates of the city, who were thus able to calm the people infuriated by the deed and apprehensive of another Saint Bartholomew.

Anjou gasped with relief at the conclusion of this recital.

"The young Count has shown great wisdom for his years," he remarked graciously. "As for the Prince I would have shed the last drop of my blood sooner than this should have happened. How goes His Highness?"

"He is conscious and he speaks," returned the officer, "but there is little hope of his life." And as he spoke the rough soldier broke into tears.

CHAPTER III

D'ANASTRO'S FAILURE

GASPAR D'ANASTRO, merchant and spy of Spain, had long dallied with the lucrative but dangerous prospect of murdering the Prince of Orange.

It was years since he had been mentioned to Granvelle as a man likely to do the deed.

At last, faced by the prospect of bankruptcy in his own affairs and tempted by the enormous reward offered by the Ban, having made a contract with Philip by which the King promised to award him the Cross of Santiago and eighty thousand pieces of silver for the successful accomplishment of the crime, Gaspar D'Anastro, Venero, his cashier, and Zimmerman, his priest, had combined together to inspire and bribe the poor fanatical fool Jean Jauregay to the execution of the deed for which their own courage failed them.

A vigorous research soon brought these facts to light; Venero and Zimmerman were arrested and wrote a full confession.

D'Anastro himself had contrived to leave the city and was now safe within Parma's lines. But his hireling's shot had failed.

Early in April while the Prince still lay between life and death in his house near the citadel a woman and a child came to Antwerp and lodged in one of the many inns and guest houses for travellers which occupied the great Cathedral Square.

This woman was Rénèe le Meung; she had left Delft for the first time since she had taken up her abode there, seven years before, with the infant daughter of the refugee of Rotterdam.

She had borne with what patience she could the long and terrible suspense that hung over the Netherlands during the illness of the Prince; at last she could no longer endure the waiting and the solitude of Delft, and thus came to Antwerp, feeling very lonely and strange and foolish in this great city so full of movement and commotion, the murmur of great affairs, the splendour of a court and the coming and going of troops of soldiers.

It was so long since Rénèe had had any active part in life, any connection with the world in which she had been once at home, that she felt lost indeed on the tide of momentous events — a middle-aged provincial out of place and out of humour with her surroundings.

She had meant to present herself to the Princess of Orange; but now she lacked the courage to introduce herself once more to Charlotte de Bourbon, whom she had not seen since that interview in Delft, a few days after the wedding — and who would probably not know her now, she told herself.

So she sat day after day in the inn parlour or in her chamber or walked in the busy square and crowded streets, listening to men talking of the Prince, of the Duke — seeing the magistrates, the French and English lords, the burgher guards, the foreign soldiery go by — hearing always this one theme — the Prince, would the Prince recover!

How far she seemed to have travelled since his last illness when she had helped to nurse him in Rotterdam.

Then she had tended him with her own hands — now she must ask news of him in the street, like other humble strangers.

She had not spoken to him since his marriage. Nor, though she lived so near to where he had made his modest home, did she think he had ever seen her.

It had always been her fate to never touch his life deeply enough to be remembered by him, always been that the man who occupied her entire thoughts should never have one thought for her; Rénèe had long since accepted this, a great calm had come to her with the passing of the years and the tending of a little child.

Yet as she sat now, amidst the strangers of an inn, lonely amid the noise and confusion of the magnificent city that was the scene of such vast events, she was astonished at the depth of her own feeling for the Prince, she marvelled herself at this love which had been powerful enough to outlive so much. For she was not thinking now of what the loss of the Prince would mean to the Netherlands or to the Reformed Religion, of his task unfinished or the triumph of Spain — she was thinking of the man himself, sick and in pain, sleepless and weary, consumed by anxiety and helpless.

She had been told that the Duke of Anjou, who was so far proceeding with his administration with tolerable discretion, visited him every day and that the Prince dictated letters from his sick-bed and still was the guiding spirit of the affairs of the Provinces.

"He will kill himself in this service," she had said, and she felt indignant with those who allowed him this labour.

One day she saw the Count Maurice ride past the window, though only fifteen years of age he appeared in every way a man and to Rénèe he seemed his uncle Count Lodewyk thus returned to finish the fight he had left incomplete.

She had often seen him in Delft, but the lad had changed; he seemed to have assumed the mantle of his race, to be now both a prince and a warrior; so firmly and well had he taken his father's place from the very moment that Jauregay's shot was fired.

It was said openly that Anjou was afraid of him and stepped warily for fear of the bright eyes of Maurice.

The day on which she saw the young Count was afterwards remembered as a notable one by Rénèe.

It was cold and stormy and in the afternoon a heavy rain fell.

Two ladies on horseback dismounted and took shelter in the inn parlour where Rénèe sat trying to still her heart by the patient work of lace-making.

She looked at the new comers with interest and they greeted her with ready courtesy.

They were plainly of that world to which she had once belonged, but which she had left so long that she felt abashed before these strangers in their elegance.

Yet it was from their manner only that she judged their quality for their apparel was not rich.

Both wore riding suits of dark cloth that had seen good service and little plain high-crowned hats with heron plumes.

They were both much of an age and both more than ordinarily pleasing and graceful, but one far outshone the other in presence and beauty.

She had fixed Rénèe's attention from the moment of her entrance.

Above the middle height, she had an air of swiftness, of dignity and of tranquillity very charming to behold; she seemed to Rénèe the same type, as she was obviously of the same nationality, as Charlotte de Bourbon; but this lady had greater beauty and a more worldly air than the Princess, was buoyant, and more full of animation.

She attracted Rénèe as Charlotte had never attracted her; she watched with a certain pleasure this graceful creature radiant with youth and health.

The lady smiled at little Wilhelmina, who was seated by the stove before a small pillow of blue linen on which she was carefully pricking out the pattern of a design of lace.

Rénèe drew herself a little further into the corner, she felt a desire to hide herself from the bright presence of the strangers.

But the lady looked at her, smiled, and spoke.

"I have such good news," she said, "that I must share it with all."

"Good news?" faltered Rénèe, she thought at once of the Prince.

It seemed that he was also in the stranger's mind.

"His Highness recovers," she said.

She took off her wet hat and shook out the dripping heron feather; her fair hair, loosened by the wind, hung in full ringlets on to her close lawn ruff.

"Oh, Madam!" cried Rénèe. "Is this true?"

"Certainly. We have just come from His Highness." Rénèe stared at her with wonder and envy; she had not then been mistaken in supposing that these ladies belonged to the great world.

"The blood had begun again to flow from the wound," continued the stranger, "when the Duke of Anjou's body physician thought of this expedient of healing it — one attendant after another to hold their thumb on the place day and night — and today the wound closed."

"And you may see by the look in His Highness' face that he is mending," added the other lady.

"God is merciful," said Rénèe.

"The Prince will not be taken until he has done his work," replied the stranger who had spoken last.

But the other turned to her with great earnestness.

"So you count the powers of darkness so weak?" she asked. "Do we not know of those who were foully murdered before their work was done?"

"Truly I am sorry that the Prince trusts in Valois," returned her companion.

"Uses him, not trusts him, I hope," said the fair lady; "indeed when I met him in the Prince's house today it was difficult for me to pass him in silence."

"You are French and you think of Saint Bartholomew?" asked Rénèe.

"Yes, Madam," answered the fair stranger.

"You are a friend of your countrywoman, the Princess?" added Rénèe, though she did not remember seeing either in Delft.

"No, we are but newly come to the Netherlands. Until now our place of exile has been Switzerland."

"I was for long an exile," said Rénèe, "but now the works of the Prince have secured for us Flemings a place we may call home."

"You live here?"

"No, in Delft."

"Ah, near His Highness."

"Yes," said Rénèe, and then with an effort she added, "I came here because of my great anxiety to hear the truth about the condition of the Prince. There were so many rumours."

"But I doubt if you have come nearer the truth in Antwerp than in Delft," smiled the lady, "therefore I am glad to have met you and to tell you that truly His Highness mends — with my own eyes I saw him this morning. He may not yet speak, but he sits up in bed and writes."

"And the Princess?" asked Rénèe.

"The Princess looked ill. She has hardly left his bedside and seemed worn with fear and hope. She said she had been living in the shadow of death ever since the Ban was published."

"Ah, the Ban," shuddered Rénèe; that too was her constant terror.

"It was the Ban and not some French plot?" she asked.

"Truly I think, though I believe the Valois capable of any baseness. The assassin had nought but Spanish papers and charms in his pocket — a poor fanatical fool driven on by that villain his master — tempted by the rewards offered by Spain."

"And how many others will not that reward tempt?" asked Rénèe.

"We must not think of that," said the stranger.

She replaced her hat with the heron's feather, arranging it before the little tortoiseshell-framed mirror that hung by the stove.

Again Rénèe looked at the Frenchwoman with a certain pleasure, she reminded her of her own lost youth and the rich days in Brussels, so gallant and bright was she in her beauty.

The dark clouds broke behind the tall tower of the cathedral, a pale sun came forth and sparkled in the wet streets.

A long ray came into the dusky inn parlour, fell over the child intent on her pins and cushion and lingered in the light locks of the fair stranger; the two ladies glanced at the weather and took their leave giving a gentle "adieu" to Rénèe.

She went to the window to watch them ride away and her gaze was almost wistful.

"Who are they?" she asked the wife of the host, who entered with her hands full of shining brass platters and dishes. "Do you know them, those two French ladies?"

"It is the widow of Admiral Coligny."

"Coligny's wife?"

"Yes, Madame, and the fair one is his daughter, Madame de Teligny."

"Ah — they have their residence here?"

"For the moment they are in Antwerp — the Princess has received them kindly, being her countrywomen and ladies of such misfortunes. Both widowed by Saint Bartholomew! It is strange that they can live under a Valois!"

"For the moment Anjou is our good friend," said Rénèe, but without much conviction; she had heard nothing but distrust and dislike of the Duke ever since she had been in Antwerp; but she was loyal to the policy of the Prince — she believed there must be some merit in the man whom he protected.

"We need no good friends of that kind," returned the stout Fleming as she arranged her milky, pale-gold brass on the long black shelves. "The Prince is our only friend."

Francis of Anjou (1556-1584)

"But Anjou is now our Duke."

"And a sad thing. Why could not His Highness himself take this charge to rule over us as he has done over Holland and Zeeland, instead of giving us this hunchbacked Frenchman as our master?"

Rénèe smiled; in her heart she agreed with the roughly expressed convictions of the housewife; it seemed to her that

William was indeed the fitting ruler of the country he had himself built up with such immense toil and labour.

But she respected, if she could not altogether understand, William's policy in endeavouring to secure for the Netherlands a royal protector and the friendship of two great nations by his choice of the Duke of Anjou to take the place of Philip as sovereign of the United Provinces; and she knew also, what had been well hinted abroad, the oaths Anjou had had to take prior to his installation as Duke of Brabant, and the way he was bound hand and foot by limitations and restrictions until in reality he had little more power than the unfortunate Archduke Mathias had possessed.

What she did not know was that the Frenchman had been quick to notice that his position was not that of arbitrary kingship which he had hoped for and that he was only waiting his opportunity to assert what he and his followers considered his rights.

The square was now full of sun; a sweet wind blew aside the loose clouds and revealed a vast sweep of sky behind the cathedral; this sky had the blueness of spring.

Rénèe thought of that long dead spring so memorable for her, when she had first seen the Prince at Leipzig; how clearly she could recall his magnificent figure lightly mounting the shadowed stairs to where the poor crooked bride stood shaking in her splendid garments.

Anne of Saxony was dead now; released forever from her prison, from her shame and misery; and her son was almost a man and one who had already shown himself worthy of his father and his grandfather, the great Elector whose name he bore.

Rénèe wondered if the Prince forgave Anne when he looked on her splendid boy.

The sun made jewels of the drops on the windowpane; Rénèe opened the lattice and looked out into the street.

Her mind was still busy with those bitter-sweet memories; she recalled Count Lodewyk — a boy he had seemed then, frivolous and shallow.

When she had found him lolling over the counter of the alchemist's shop her judgment of him had been severe.

Now it was so long since he had gone down in the bloody press of Mookerheyde that men were beginning to forget his name.

Gone too the young son of the Elector, gone Count Adolphus and Count Henry, those youths who had seemed born to ease and pleasure.

How many were left of that brilliant retinue that had accompanied William to Leipzig? Most had met a violent and terrible end in the flower of their days, for this cause which was yet hanging in the balance.

And now he, the leader, the soul of the enterprise, lay brought near to death by that same hand which had beguiled or crushed the others.

It seemed to Rénèe that Philip was as great as he was awful, that the decrees of the Escurial were never in vain.

As the others had gone so, she thought, William would be taken.

This attempt had failed, but the next and the next — if this time a miracle had saved him — there might come a time when the blow would be struck more surely, more skilfully.

Somewhere now, at this moment, the man who was ordained to indeed murder William of Orange might be planning his crime.

And always there were Granvelle and Philip, watching, alert, and implacable.

Rénèe felt that not all the love of the Netherlands could forever shield William from the deep design and long craft of Philip.

She turned again into the room, put on the child's cloak and led her out into the streets now flushed with the full light of the evening sun.

There was an air of joyousness abroad in Antwerp so soon had the news spread that the Prince was mending.

CHAPTER IV

THE VICTIM OF JAUREGAY

RÉNÈE LE MEUNG stayed in Antwerp till after the great thanksgiving service for the recovery of the Prince which was offered in the cathedral amid the profound joy and emotion of the people.

Once more she knelt in church behind William, watching that frail figure on which the strength of the whole nation depended.

When the Prince had risen from his sickness he had been anew implored to accept forever the Countship of Holland and Zeeland, and this time had not been able to resist the outburst of love and enthusiasm evoked by his peril and his recovery.

Rénèe had heard that the Prince was to take the charge of ruling the Northern Provinces, they to thus entirely sever their connection with the Empire and remain a Republic under his Stadtholdership.

Thus, so far, the crime inspired by Philip had but served to closely unite his enemies in his despite and defiance.

The Prince's superb constitution had brought him unscathed through the ordeal he had undergone; he was neither stooping nor feeble as he stood in the great church returning thanks to God for allowing him a few more years of toil.

To Rénèe he seemed little changed save that he was pale from loss of blood and his simple presence seemed the more splendid beside the glittering magnificence of the deformed Anjou.

The new Duke of Brabant was on his right hand and on his left was Count Maurice girt with a sword and wearing the air of a man.

But the Princess was not there.

This surprised Rénèe; she had heard that Charlotte had a light fever but she had not supposed it serious enough to prevent her staying away on this great occasion.

The next day Rénèe was preparing to return to Delft when she received the news, then flying from mouth to mouth, and making a commotion in the city, that the Princess's illness was so suddenly grave that the physician had little hope of saving her life.

The news gave Rénèe a curious shock; the Princess was nothing to her, she told herself, had now indeed become almost a stranger.

But the curious feeling of tenderness that had come over her when she had spoken to Charlotte after her marriage, revived in her now.

No one had thought much about the Princess during the long strain of the Prince's illness. Now that it was over and she was dying, they could see how she had suffered.

Rénèe could imagine what a life of anxiety and tension she had led since the publication of the Ban, she could understand how her strength, already enfeebled by her recent confinement, had been lavishly spent in the service of the Prince; she had done more than she was able and now she paid.

Jauregay had found a victim after all; Philip might now add another to his list, a woman's name, as surely killed by him as had been Egmont or Montigny.

Rénèe recalled the old days at Heidelberg with a strange affection.

She could not grudge Charlotte a happiness which had been so dearly paid for and so short-lived.

Leaving little Wilhelmina in charge of the host's wife Rénèe went to the Prince's house near the citadel and asked if she might wait upon the Princess.

There seemed little hope of this request being granted in such a moment, but Rénèe gave her name to the usher.

Charlotte had always lived in a fashion so modest and simple that there was nothing strange in humble folk (as Rénèe now appeared to be) demanding her presence.

The reception of Anjou in Antwerp was the first time since her own wedding on which the Princess had mingled in any kind of pomp.

Until then she had lived like any burgher's wife in the quiet house in Delft, tending her own children and those of Anne of Saxony with equal devotion and care.

After a little delay Rénèe was admitted to the antechamber.

"The Princess is then not so ill," she thought, "or they would never have brought me here."

A chamber-woman came forward and asked her name: "If you are Rénèe le Meung who was at Heidelberg, Her Highness will see you."

"I am Rénèe le Meung."

"Will you then come to the bed of the Princess, Madam?"

Rénèe passed from the crowded anteroom into the crowded bedroom,

She felt foolishly surprised that Charlotte should have remembered her, yet it would have been strange if the Princess should have forgotten those long first days of her exile when Rénèe was her constant companion.

The bedroom was dark, and furnished by a set of tapestries representing sea pieces, brought by the Princess from Delft.

The bed itself, of huge proportions, was hung with purple satin and covered with a quilt of needlework. Charlotte de Bourbon was sitting up, propped by many pillows.

She was so changed that she seemed only a remembrance of her former self.

Rénèe would hardly have recognized in this ghastly and haggard woman the blooming and neat girl of Heidelberg or the fair matron of Delft.

Death had already embraced Charlotte de Bourbon and the imprint of his cold kiss was on her cheek.

Only the blonde hair remained the same; this, usually so primly concealed under her coif, now hung in loose locks on to her shoulders.

254

She saw Rénèe at once and smiled.

That smile went to Rénèe's heart; the tears filled her eyes as she stood hesitant on the threshold.

The room was full of people — pastors, women, officials, ushers, and children.

The Prince was not there, being engaged in the affairs of the city, but it was the first time that day he had left her and then only on the assurance of the physicians that she was better.

The Princess had indeed shown such an increase of strength that hopes began to be entertained of her recovery.

Even now an earnest young doctor was bending down to assure her that the fever was past and she had only to rest and wait for strength.

Charlotte de Bourbon looked up at him and slightly shook her head.

"I feel the life here," and she laid her hand above her heart, "leaving me." Rénèe had now reached the bedside.

"I am glad you have come," said Charlotte earnestly. "I am glad."

"Highness, I could not hope that you would recall me."

Charlotte smiled away the formal words.

"You always played a part with me Rénèe le Meung. Tell me the truth now, I am surely dying."

Rénèe stood shame-faced with bent head; she was alone with the Princess in the shadow of the bed curtains; the others had withdrawn to the back of the chamber.

"I wished to see Your Highness," said Rénèe at last.

Charlotte lay silent, gazing at her with the long regard of the sick. Her very eyes appeared pallid, and though her figure was supported on so many cushions it seemed to be sinking backwards, so utterly without life were her limbs.

Now that Rénèe's vision became used to the dim shadows of the bed-place she saw that the Princess's right arm was folded around a bundle of fine linen and scarlet brocade.

It reminded Rénèe of that bundle she had taken from the old woman's arms in Rotterdam seven years ago.

"The baby," she said.

"My last baby," answered Charlotte. "They call her Emilia Secunda."

Rénèe bent lower and looked at the exact fair face sleeping so peacefully on the thin breast.

"See what the nuns miss," smiled Charlotte, then she added: "I am sorry to have brought His Highness nothing but girls."

"What should the Prince need with sons?" asked Rénèe.

"True he has his heir, if ever God releases him from Spain. And he has Maurice."

She looked at Rénèe with a certain wistfulness.

"I tried to make Maurice love me. Do you not think him a noble boy?"

"A knight like Count Lodewyk."

"I meant him to redeem it all — the Saxon marriage — his mother's life. And having no sons of my own —"

Her eyes remained opened but their sudden light seemed to fail as if some glory, whose glow they had reflected, had been removed.

"I can hear the shot now," she added. "I have never slept of nights since the Ban. Did you think they would do that — put a price on his head! Even Philip —"

She paused and her head sank a little to one side; Rénèe knelt on the wide bed step to be nearer to her; the purple curtains enclosed them both as if they were in some forest of dark trees.

Rénèe remembered Heidelberg forest and the day when she had surprised the heart of the Princess — the primroses and bluebells would be again out, the trees again fresh with green.

"You live in Delft?" asked the Princess suddenly.

"Your Highness knows that?"

Rénèe flushed hotly; she had imagined she was so safely hidden in the old house in the church square, and all the while the Princess had known of her pitiful concealment.

"I would have had you for my friend," continued Charlotte, "but I saw you did not wish it."

"No, Madam," cried Rénèe. "I have been so humble, so useless, I did think myself forgotten of all. I am the keeper of the church now the old man is dead."

"I know," said Charlotte.

" — and I have a little child I brought up — a refugee's child, Madam."

"I know that, also."

" — and these things made my life. Why should I think of such as Your Highness?"

Charlotte smiled in silence and Rénèe shivered lest her long concealed secret was at last discovered; she dropped her face in her hands and her hands on the edge of the bed, meaning to endure whatever words the Princess might speak.

"The Prince too considered you as his friend and would have been glad to have had you in his house," said Charlotte.

Rénèe looked up; she saw that the Princess did not know.

"But why speak of these things?" continued Charlotte. "These days are over —"

"Oh, Madam, we shall all return to Delft."

"My life is over."

"Your Highness must not think so."

"Rénèe, do not maintain with me the pitiful fiction of the doctor towards his patient. I would I could live since my lord lives. But I feel my strength go from me as water goes from a vessel."

The child stirred in her arm and she was too weak to lift her up.

"Put her on the other side," she said to Rénèe. "So — my little girl — see what fair hair she has. Think — she may live to see the strife over and all these present wounds healed."

"Her life will see the death of Philip," returned Rénèe.

A long shudder shook the Princess.

"Do you think that my lord will escape Philip?" she murmured.

"Has he not just been saved, as by the direct hand of God?"

Charlotte was silent a moment; then she said, under her breath:

"I rejoice that I must die first."

She touched the cold hand Rénèe rested on the edge of the quilt.

"Go to my house in Delft after I am dead and ask for my chamber-woman. I have thought of you and your little child. Stay in Delft, near *him*. He needs all his friends."

"My dwelling will never change."

"And if His Highness marries again, wait on that lady and seek to be a friend to her. Look you, he will marry, he is not one who can live alone."

Her fingers tightened over Rénèe's hand.

"You remember the days in Heidelberg?"

"Yes, Madam!"

"I knew so little — I was half a nun then. I only guessed at life."

Her eyes closed and she seemed to think profoundly. Rénèe waited, listening to the sick woman's difficult breath.

"Was it not strange, my marriage?" said Charlotte at last without opening her eyes.

Rénèe could not answer.

"I have wondered since where I found the courage to do what I did."

Rénèe still was silent; her life had given her no chance for courage or action; but she believed she also could have fulfilled a noble outstanding destiny.

"And now it is all over. And I have been with him such a short while. You remember how we used to speak of him? And of Count Lodewyk? I saw him last night in my dream — I dreamt of Mookerheyde."

"Strange that your Highness should think now of Mookerheyde."

"I did dream of that — I thought the night lamp showing between the curtains was the sun enrobed in clouds — and as the fever overcame me I heard the rush of armies and saw the three young Princes all stained with their own blood and they encouraged me — saying — 'You too, who are only a woman, can die in this quarrel,' and I saw all the marsh, black and wet."

Her head drooped lower and she took her free hand from Rénèe and laid it above her heart.

"I have so little time and I talk so foolishly," she continued with a faint smile. "Lift me up, for I feel as if I fall into the blackness of nothingness."

Rénèe raised her on the deep pillows and gently taking the child from her laid it on the side of the bed.

Charlotte moved a little and seemed to stretch her limbs as with a slight sigh of ease or relief.

"I feel as if I have done nothing," she murmured, "and I meant to do so much."

"Nothing," echoed Rénèe and she thought of her own life.

"It is well," continued the Princess, "that we do not know how short a time we have or we should not have the courage to go on."

She lifted her shadowed eyes and looked up at Rénèe's stooping face.

"You —" she asked with great earnestness, "do you think I have failed?"

"Failed?" Rénèe did not understand.

"We used to speak of these things in Heidelberg — we used to talk of the Prince."

"Yes."

"You must have thought that I had a presumption in marrying His Highness."

Rénèe laughed weakly.

"I brought him nothing. I meant to do so much to help build this nation up. I had dreams of great things. It has just been a round of little cares and one long anxiety."

Her lips trembled and her eyes closed; it seemed to Rénèe that she was very weak; her voice was thin like a flute through which the wind blows feebly.

Rénèe moved back and looked around the heavy curtains to call someone; but Charlotte heard and stretched out her hand.

"Do not go," she said.

Rénèe took the cold searching fingers.

"Goodbye," said Charlotte de Bourbon. "May your life be blessed at last in the name of God and His Reformed religion."

When she had spoken she lay silent, breathing slowly and with difficulty.

Rénèe bent and kissed her hand, then left the deep shadow of the bed.

She saw the silent people moving from the door and the Prince entering.

Without a glance about him, he came to the bedside of his wife and Rénèe shrank into the crowd.

"What a change there is in this life," she thought. "Is this pale gray man in homespun he who danced with Anne of Saxony in the town hall of Leipzig?"

She went her way and that afternoon taught the child a new pattern in lace-making.

Two days later the Princess died and Rénèe was one of the two thousand mourning cloaks that followed her funeral.

CHAPTER V

THE LITTLE CLERK

OF all those who heard the news of the thanksgiving in Antwerp that celebrated the recovery of the Prince of Orange from Jauregay's attempt, none, not even Granvelle or Philip or Parma who found he had paid D'Anastro for nothing, received a keener shock of bitter personal disappointment than a certain little clerk, in the employment of John Duprêle, secretary to Count Mansfield, Governor of the County of Luxembourg.

When this little clerk had heard of the supposed death of William of Orange he had gone on his knees and thanked God.

"Not only for the justice done on a great traitor," he said, "but also because now there is no need for me to put myself in danger."

For this Balthazar Gerard, a humble Burgundian, coming from Vellefaus, had for five years, that is, since he was twenty years old, nourished an idea as deep and intense as it seemed vain and absurd.

It was no less than the assassination of the Prince of Orange.

This fanatical desire had been flamed by the publication of the Ban and motives of cupidity tinged the prompting of religious fervour.

These intermingled feelings returned with renewed strength when he heard of the marvellous recovery of the Prince — and the death of Charlotte de Bourbon.

"She was meant for Jauregay, the Prince for me," he said and braced himself anew for his task.

Those to whom he spoke of his design laughed at him, for he had neither influence nor capacity nor presence nor any appearance of courage or energy. He was also extremely poor, having no means beyond the salary he drew from his modest clerkship.

Nor was he himself at all clear as to the way in which he should endeavour to accomplish the death of the Prince of Orange.

As a preliminary step he resigned his appointment, but, being detained, first by the loss of some money which his sudden departure might have caused him to be accused of taking, and secondly by the illness of his employer, it was some months before he was able to leave Luxembourg, and proceed to Trêves, which city he had selected because it was the seat of a large Jesuit college.

It was the intention of Balthazar Gerard to obtain the advice of these holy fathers before proceeding further on his way.

His journey was considerably lightened by news from the Netherlands.

The Duke of Anjou and his minions had broken loose and set the French soldiery on to Antwerp, pillaging, as far as the news went, that rich and unfortunate city as thoroughly as had the Spaniards during the famous mutiny.

The Prince of Orange, so the report said, had been completely deceived, and had trusted, in common with the magistrates, to the oaths sworn by Anjou as Duke of Brabant and sovereign of the Netherlands.

Therefore, although in the city at the time he found himself without means to make any resistance against the assault of the French troops.

At the same moment a concerted attempt had been made on Dunkirk, Bruges, Vilvorde, and Ghent, the intention of the Duke being to exclusively establish the Romanist religion, make himself absolute master of the Provinces and deprive William of the sovereignty of the Northern States.

Whether this plan had been wholly successful or not did not yet appear, but at least, it was obvious that the Prince of Orange had nourished and cherished with his own hand a creature as dangerous and poisonous as any sent against him by Philip and that the infant commonwealth had found for a protector one who was ready to put his sword to her throat and his hand in her pocket.

Gerard, hearing this good news in the jolting coach that took him to Trêves, rejoiced exceedingly; it seemed to him like a presage of good fortune for himself and his enterprise.

He dined at a humble inn and was further heartened by hearing of the success of the Duke of Parma, who had taken instant advantage of the confusion caused in the Netherlands by the action of Anjou.

"But none of these successes are of any use while Orange lives," said one sitting near to Gerard, and the eyes of the little clerk gleamed as he nodded in silence.

That night before he went to bed he prayed for these three great Princes, the King of Spain, the Duke of Parma, and the Duke of Anjou.

And he added a humble petition that he might be permitted to be the instrument to remove that odious heretic and very cunning villain, William of Orange.

The next morning he presented himself at the college of the Jesuits and, by the use of Count Mansfield's name, obtained an audience of the regent. This personage received him in his study, which was more finely furnished than that of the Governor of Luxembourg and which impressed Gerard accordingly, so that he entered in a very humble manner, bent low and with his hat crushed to his breast.

There were two priests in the room; one sat at a table of ebony and malachite and the other stood behind him, leaning in the angle of the wall.

Gerard soon saw that the seated personage was the regent of the college and made a low obeisance, kissing the smooth white fingers that the priest extended.

"You have important business?" asked the Jesuit with some severity; he was a red-haired man of a graceful figure and a noble pose; he looked with some disapproval at the meagre person of the little clerk. "You have sent me an impression of Count Mansfield's seals," he added and he glanced at the imprint in red wax Gerard had sent in with the name of the Governor of Luxembourg.

"Yes," returned the Burgundian meekly.

"Count Mansfield sent you?"

"No."

"Then?"

"I stole the seals, Reverend Father."

The Jesuit leant back in his chair and looked narrowly at the little man before him.

"You stole the seals?"

"Yes. I was in the employment of the Count's secretary and I took the impress of all the seals — for which sin I need absolution."

The Jesuit did not answer; he continued his scrutiny of the man who stood facing him so meekly yet with such placid dignity.

He saw a young man of a sickly habit of body; narrow-chested, undersized, with a greasy, bilious complexion, muddy eyes and bad teeth; his hair was reddish, fair and scanty, he had an air of timidity and reserve; his whole personality appeared one of utter insignificance; he could not in any crowd, have attracted a second glance.

His clothes were of a piece with his figure, worn and out of fashion, but neat and clean.

The Jesuit looked at him with scant favour, he did not believe that such a one could have anything to say worth hearing; yet he was rather interested in the story of Mansfield's seals.

"Why did you steal these seals?" he asked.

Gerard looked at him with the utmost self-possession and serenity.

"I thought they would be useful in gaining the confidence of the rebels," he replied. "I know the taking of them was a great sin against God and Count Mansfield. And for that I hope to be forgiven."

"Why should you wish to go among the rebels?" demanded the Jesuit.

The little clerk clasped his hands with a gesture of great earnestness.

"Reverend Father," he said, "I hope to kill the Prince of Orange."

Then the priests smiled.

"I have had this design for six years," continued Gerard simply.

"My son," said the regent with more friendliness than he had yet shown, "you show a laudable spirit."

"And now I require the advice of some person learned in affairs as to how I may set about this business."

The two Jesuits exchanged glances.

"Maybe you think that I am presumptuous," added Gerard.

"I certainly think the affair holds many difficulties," returned the priest.

"I am prepared for them — and for the danger," said the little clerk.

The Jesuit played with the impression of Mansfield's seals.

The project broached by Gerard was certainly one which he was bound to encourage; at the same time he knew that ever since the publication of the Ban the Low Countries had swarmed with men eager to take the life of William of Orange, and where all these had failed it was not in the least likely that this obscure little civilian would succeed.

Gerard waited with his eyes fixed hopefully on the downcast face of the priest.

"What grounds have you for hopes in this enterprise?" asked the Jesuit at last. "Any plan, any influence, or opening to the person of the Prince?"

"None."

"And you have heard of the attempts of Salseda and Baza — and, later Pietro Dovdogno?"

"Yes," said Gerard.

The second Jesuit now spoke.

"And of Hanzoon who tried to blow up the church at Flushing when the Prince was at prayers, and the essay of the Marquis de Richebourg who endeavoured to find one to poison him in a dish of eels?"

"All these things I know," returned the little clerk patiently, "and certainly these gentlemen were unfortunate — even the gentle Biscayan who came so near success, and it is for the very reason of the failure of these others that I have resolved to do the deed myself, thereby leaving my employment and my quiet life."

"This is a spirit much to be commended," said the regent of the Jesuits, "and may God bless your holy ardour. Yet I cannot but see danger and trouble in this matter of the forging of Count Mansfield's seals."

"For that I am sorry, as I said," returned Gerard, "and wish your absolution. I thought they would serve as a good passport to approach the Prince, and if I could accomplish this deed maybe the stealing of these seals could be forgiven me. Yet it troubles me."

"Let it not rest on your conscience, my son," answered the priest warmly. "And so surely as you accomplish this plan so you shall not only be forgiven this theft, but be ennobled and rewarded."

"And if I lose my life?" asked Gerard.

"Then you shall be enrolled among the company of saintly martyrs who have suffered for the Holy Faith."

A look of exalted enthusiasm shone in Gerard's pale eyes.

"Will you give me your blessing, Reverend Father?" he asked.

"Assuredly, and all the spiritual comfort that may be."

Here the other priest, thinking his superior was transgressing the limits of prudence so strictly enjoined and observed by their order, touched him lightly on the sleeve and smoothly addressed Gerard.

"We Jesuits deal more in affairs of the other world than in this," he remarked, "and I should advice that this business was laid before His Highness, the Prince of Parma."

Gerard looked disappointed; the Prince of Parma was utterly beyond his reach and he had hoped for more substantial advice from the Jesuits, introductions and perhaps money; he did not need to come to Trêves to be told to put his plan before Philip's general.

But the regent of the Jesuits had taken the cue from his secretary.

"It would be ill accepted by all," he said, "if we were to meddle in politics. And certainly I can give you no better advice than this, to seek an audience of the Prince of Parma."

"I am too insignificant," said Gerard.

Meagre and miserable he looked as he faced the two silently judging him, and little hope had either of the priests that he would ever get as far as the presence of Parma.

"Our blessing and our encouragement," said the red-haired Jesuit, "and if you are determined on this course —"

Gerard drew himself erect; his eyes seemed to suddenly open, disclosing something within from which even the trained hard scrutiny of the Jesuit faltered.

"You think I am too mean to accomplish this thing?" he asked quietly.

Out of his humility, his shabbiness, his commonplace servility and abnegation something seemed to emanate that held silent and almost overwhelmed the two priests who till now had held him hardly worth the time he occupied by his discourse.

Something strange and tremendous and beyond human control and guidance.

"Perhaps you think it is not for me," continued Gerard, "to compass the death of great Princes — but this man must die through the judgment of God."

His pallid eyes shone and with a thin forefinger he tapped his narrow chest.

"That thing was certain even before the publication of the Ban," he said. "As it was certain who would be the instrument. I — Balthazar Gerard. Did you say that Spain has fine captains and cunning agents and that these have failed? I tell you that was bound to be, for I am he who is to do this task."

"He who is so convinced of the success of his mission is well armed," returned the Jesuit. "Get you to Father Gery, the

Franciscan at Tournay, and he will give you letters to someone about Parma's person."

"I will go to Tournay tomorrow," said Gerard resolutely.

The priest opened a box of filigree silver that stood among his books and took out a gold piece which he handed to the little clerk.

"This will help you on your way, my son," he said; "for the enterprise itself you will need money and this His Highness will supply you if he thinks well of your story."

Gerard put the money carefully away in a purse of perished leather.

"Whether the Prince of Parma is willing or no to pay my expenses I will carry this thing through — if I get to Delft in rags and footsore or well clad and in a coach."

His air of sad humility had again dropped like a veil over his face; he looked once more so insignificant and useless that the Jesuit thought he must have mistaken that sudden flash of superhuman energy and almost regretted the gold piece.

However, he gave Gerard his blessing and instructions where to find Father Gery at Tournay and the Burgundian left the college and returned to his close and dirty chamber under the leads of the town's worst inn.

Besides the Jesuit's charity all that he possessed in the world were a few white bits and the residue of the miserable savings with which he had left Luxembourg — a hoard he wished to leave untouched. This, however, did not in the least dishearten him, he did not doubt that his further needs would be supplied as had been his present ones.

He was sorry not to have received more direct and definite assistance, but rested on the interview with Father Gery.

He was at the same time doubtful whether he would bring either the Franciscan or the Prince of Parma to finance his scheme, for he knew his own lack of eloquence and humble appearance and birth were much against him, and he was quite friendless and without influence of any kind.

After a long prayer and telling his beads he crept downstairs to the tavern kitchen, from where issued a rich smell of cooking that had roused his appetite.

Shivering in among the bolder and more prosperous folk who were crowding around the table, or the fire, with their plates and dishes, Balthazar Gerard ordered a frugal cut of meat and bread and listened eagerly to the political gossip that was passing from one greasy mouth to another.

The news from the Netherlands was not so triumphant as had at first seemed; the burghers of Antwerp had flown to arms, twisting even the buttons off their doublets and the silver ducats out of their tills into bullets and had driven out the treacherous French with great loss; Anjou himself had been forced to flee leaving behind him even his personal effects and the city remained in the hands of the Prince of Orange.

The similar attempt on the other cities of the Netherlands had likewise failed.

The little clerk was vexed but he did not lose heart.

"All these troubles will be ended when I have dispatched the Prince of Orange," he thought as he munched his supper and this reflection comforted him marvellously as did that other, that when he had earned the reward promised by the Ban he would no longer need to eat in a tavern kitchen.

CHAPTER VI

IN DELFT

"WHAT have I accomplished," said William of Orange, "after so much danger, so many losses, and confronting such perilous enmities? — Nothing, nothing."

He quietly folded up and sealed the packet of papers that he had been reading; papers that showed what base treachery, what low motives and ignoble cunning were undermining the fabric of the new republic he was so labouriously erecting amid the stormy politics of Europe.

Among these documents that he put by was a letter from Catherine de Medici left behind in her son's lodging on his flight from Antwerp, which urged him to re-establish the Roman Catholic Religion in the Netherlands and promised him the hand of the Infanta of Spain as a reward.

The other papers proved the fact that Anjou was holding secret meetings with the agents of Parma and that the extent of his demands was the only reason why the bargain had not yet been concluded by which he was to sell himself to Spain.

The powerful Prince who was to protect the provinces had proved a mere rogue, an impudent adventurer, empty alike of shame or noble thought and capable only of mean attempts at his own aggrandisement, regardless alike of honour, policy, or prudence.

Parma dealt with him simply because there was only one sickly life between him and the throne of France, and for the same reason William had to disguise his wrath and contempt; France must not be offended, nor Elizabeth of England, who also had her word to say for this miserable Anjou.

"Such instruments!" said William, "such instruments!"

He locked his desk and went into the outer room that looked on the courtyard; he was expecting his brother John and Marnix of St. Aldegonde, but the brass clock told him that it yet lacked half an hour to the time of their appointment.

It was strange to find himself alone; he was so used to business occupying every minute of his time that he felt himself at a loss in these few moments of leisure; and there was no woman now to come and distract his thoughts with sweet and intelligent companionship; his children had been moved into his sister's household and he lived alone.

His right arm and hand ached with his endless labour of the pen; he seated himself in the great black chair by the fireplace where a few logs were burning, and his mind, tired and ill at ease, reviewed the result of his long labours — a position perilous and doubtful, a task but half achieved.

He had founded a republic in the Northern States, but he had not yet accomplished that union of the Provinces which he had striven for from the first moment of his defiance of Philip, and the treachery of Anjou rendered this object yet more difficult of attainment.

The Prince of Orange in his barge

He had been betrayed by one in whom he had believed, fooled by one whom he had trusted, deceived and smitten by one whom he had placed in a position of all trust and honour. The defection of the Duke of Anjou, his attempt to seize by force the Netherland cities entrusted to his protection, his secret plots with Parma had rendered the position of the Prince of Orange even more delicate and perilous than it had been before.

It was impossible for him to openly break with the French and found a Union of the States independent of all outside assistance as was his darling inmost wish, for he knew well that the Provinces were still too weak to stand alone.

Even such as Anjou must be tolerated rather than range against them such powerful enemies as France and England — for they had no other friends. The Empire was cold and Germany almost openly hostile.

And in Alexander Farnese, the Prince had an opponent, and Philip a captain, beside whom Don John, Resquesens, and even Alva had been as nothing.

Brilliant, cool, subtle, unscrupulous, wary and patient, equally an adept at the game of war and the game of politics and the yet more difficult game of underhand plot and tortuous intrigue, Alexander Farnese, Prince of Parma, was an enemy to be feared.

And William did fear him, as much as it was in his nature to fear anyone.

He had been the equal of Alva, more than the equal of Don John and Resquesens, but in Parma he was matched with a man who called forth his utmost skill and daring.

In the first intercepted correspondence he had noted with what art Parma played Anjou, how he had read that rogue, smiled at him and yet was using him — and at Spain's own price.

These four years of Parma's administration had been more difficult for the Prince than any previous; Philip's fifth Governor seemed to be able to accomplish, as far as the impossible was capable of accomplishment, the almost superhuman task of ruling that confusion to which tyranny and bigotry had reduced the Spanish administration in the Low Countries.

William felt neither baffled nor daunted by the Italian Prince, but to a certain extent he felt himself held in check by him and saw himself as considerably weakened as the enemy was considerably strengthened by the betrayal of Anjou.

A great weariness came over him as he surveyed the vast field of the endless struggle, a certain deep sadness as he compared himself with his rival. Parma was young, not much older than he himself had been when he had first thrown down the gage to Philip.

Now, he was past the turn of life; though he knew himself full of health and vigour, still his growth and his best years were behind him.

"And what have I accomplished?" he asked himself again. "If one of Spain's hired rogues was to get his knife into my heart tomorrow would this work I have done endure?"

A melancholy touched him at the thought; it seemed to him that nothing was yet on a sure basis, that the defences of his infant country were not yet secure against the powerful foes who menaced her, that all his infinite labour and sacrifice had not yet achieved anything solid and enduring, that with his death the provinces would fly asunder as had the Empire of Alexander of Macedonia and be parcelled out likewise among sects and factions.

There was Maurice! He had great hopes of Maurice — but he might be taken before his son was a man.

And his heir, the Count of Buren, remained in the hands of Philip and William's precious wish of redeeming him remained as far from realization as ever.

He had lately been told that he had gained enough honour and renown to satisfy any man; this did not move him in the least; he had never been ambitious of fame.

All that personally he cared for in life he had resigned when he had first entered on this quarrel, his lands, his dignities, his wealth, his easy, pleasant life. And in return for this — what?

Under his own scrutiny his life work seemed little and incomplete, like a piece of tapestry once full of fair figures and bright colours torn rudely across so that the original design was no longer discernible.

But the future — that was still his, brave days and years still stretched ahead of him to use as he would, mistakes might be redeemed, successes consolidated, all in the untarnished future.

Though he might envy Parma his youth, he knew that in capacity, energy and strength he was himself still young.

Much might be accomplished, much should be accomplished if —

If Philip's assassins did not succeed in adding his name to that long list in the drawer of the King's private bureau in the Escurial.

A sad smile touched William's lips as he reflected how completely it was in the power of any mean ruffian to end and therefore largely destroy his work.

He was without vanity, but he knew that his death would mean more to the Spanish cause than the taking of many towns and that it would probably render forever an idle dream the union of the seventeen Provinces that was his dearest desire.

It was because of this uncertainty of his own life and the constant danger that encompassed him that he had so persistently refused and still continued to reject the offer of that sovereignty which Anjou had so betrayed.

He wished the states bound together by a stronger union than the common rule of one man who might at any moment leave them masterless, united under the leadership of one whose position and whose life was more secure.

He sat silent, busy with these thoughts, gazing into the fire, leaning forward slightly, his fine hands on his knees.

His face was thin now, lined and sunken in the cheeks, the hair worn from the temples by the pressing of the helmet, the dark eyes shadowed and faded by much work and thought, but there remained the old charm and elegance, the graceful turn of the small head, the exact chiselling of the classic features, the poise of perfect self-control and perfect calm.

Neither the long years of labour, constant disappointment, the goad of failure or the excitement of success, neither cruel losses, deep bereavement nor the constant apprehensiveness of assassination had undermined the courage of William of Orange.

His nerves were as splendidly balanced, his temper as equable, his humour under as absolute command as when he had been a careless grandee with all the world paying court to him.

No disaster had evoked from him an expression of passion or despair, no one had had to bear the brunt of private ill tempers, or secret sullenness, a constant courtesy, a constant good temper, the calm mind in the healthy body, had sweetened his life.

Even now, bitterly as he had been disappointed in Anjou, he lost little time in reviling that Prince, but began at once to consider how he might best repair the damage caused by his treachery and still make use of this son of France.

His brother and St. Aldegonde came upon him while he was thus deep in reflection.

They reproached him with the ease with which they had been able to enter his presence — there was not even a sentry at the gate.

"No, there should have been," smiled William. "I must keep more state."

Count John looked at him lovingly.

"You make a jest of it," he said, "but others cannot forget the Ban."

The Prince looked at the only brother this quarrel had left him.

"Do you think I can evade the Ban by a sentry at the door?" he asked.

"You can take precautions," replied St. Aldegonde anxiously.

The Prince smiled again, not in bravado but in resignation.

"To take precautions is to die a thousand times," he answered, "to suspect all who come near me, to doubt the bread I eat, the water I drink — and I have lived too long in this easy fashion. I cannot now adopt a close suspicious habit."

"Yet it were well Your Grace did," said Count John gravely, "for the spies of Spain are in every part."

"And therefore it is useless to avoid them," laughed the Prince, taking his brother's arm and rising; "remember I am a Calvinist. What God ordains man cannot avoid."

"Amen," said St. Aldegonde. "Yet Your Highness might have a sentry at the gate."

"You shall be satisfied," said the Prince, still smiling, then, as he looked from one loving face to another — his two faithful lieutenants, the only two left of those who had started with him in the morning of this enterprise, the sudden tears smote his eyes.

Behind the gray head of Count John he seemed to see the three young heads of Adolphus, Lodewyk, and Henry who were dead in this quarrel and almost forgotten.

"Come," he said with an effort, "let us get to our politics."

With a charming, half-deprecating gesture he laid his hand on his brother's shoulder.

"I fear I shall displease you," he said, almost wistfully.

"Your Highness is ever doing that," returned the Count, with a certain grimness, for he guessed what the Prince was going to say.

"Yes," added St. Aldegonde, "we have had some inkling of Your Highness's intentions from your letters."

"And what has brought me to Delft but the hope to dissuade you," said Count John, "since I have long ago left all active part in the governing of these Provinces of yours — but I do suppose it is useless to argue with you."

"Quite useless," answered the Prince quietly.

"Then," said the Count bluntly, "I am to believe that you refuse the sovereignty of these Provinces, so often urged, still pressed?"

"I do refuse any honour but that I have as the chief magistrate of these Northern States."

"And instead offer the country to that thrice false rogue, Anjou?"

"Brother," said William gravely, "we cannot, we must not, offend France."

"As soon Spain as France — if there must be a tyrant why not keep the old one?" asked the Count with some bitterness.

St. Aldegonde was silent; though he heartily approved of what the Count said he did not feel at much liberty to endorse him, as he had been one of those most completely deceived in Anjou, one of those who had most urged him on William.

"I cannot enter now," said the Prince, "into all those fine arguments and devious reasonings which have made me so hold my mind, even after this rude treachery which shows how poor a creature is this French Duke. But this I know and do maintain that without some powerful foreign Prince to set against Philip we are no better than lost. And at this moment no one offers but this Anjou."

"A vermin," said Count John.

"A son of France," answered William drily, "and the friend of England. Parma cannot offend him, do you think we dare to?"

"Better offend him than give him our throats to cut," returned his brother.

"He did not succeed before in his attempt on our liberties, and this time shall be so hedged about he will be powerless — believe me, I have played better men than Anjou to my own ends."

St. Aldegonde answered —

"That is where we are sore, Highness. Why should you play other men! Why do you not take besides the actual power you have also the semblance of the power. This is your work — take the reward of it!"

William knew that in these blunt, almost rough words of his old friend, was expressed the sentiment of the whole people whom by God's grace he had liberated and championed, but he was not moved.

"I am a landless man with a price on my head." he answered simply, "and such is not the man the Provinces need."

There was nothing to be said in answer to the bold truth of the first statement, but Count John replied stoutly to the second.

"You and you only are the man this nation needs, no great Prince could mean to the Netherlands what you mean."

William shook his head.

"You will not persuade me," he answered. "If my first reason was not strong enough I have yet another."

"What other can there be?" asked St. Aldegonde, "since it is impossible that Your Highness is afraid of the dangers of the post."

"No," replied William simply. "I had not thought of that, and as for dangers I do believe I am already involved up to the neck in them and have nothing more to lose but my life, and that is worth but a poor price."

"What other consideration then can move you?" demanded Count John.

William looked straightly at him as he answered —

"I have lost everything — and without regret, I have endured much and shall not lament, there is one thing I will do for my own sake, one course I will take to please myself — I will not make it possible for men to say I have done what I have done for ambition. I will not be open to the charge that in this struggle I have found my advantage."

They spoke to him no more about his acceptance of these honours, but in their hearts they were not convinced.

When he was alone again William went to the window and looked out into the cold twilight. The quiet night seemed full of figures, advancing, menacing, encouraging, pressing onwards to new events, new struggles, new victories.

Warriors and statesmen there, as the Prince saw them, the dead and the yet unborn mingling together to weave the warp and woof of fate.

Philip was there and Parma — but William did not see a third — the shabby figure of a little clerk walking the dusty road from Trêves to Tournay to save the coach fare.

CHAPTER VII

THE PRINCE OF PARMA

BALTHAZAR GERARD had his interview with Father Gery at Tournay and received much encouragement and solace from that learned Franciscan whereby he was considerably heartened and strengthened in his project.

But this priest had the same delicacy as the Jesuits of Trêves in mingling with affairs politic and could give Gerard no practical assistance beyond repeating the advice to lay the matter before the Prince of Parma.

He supplied some money for the present meagre needs of the little clerk and urged him to put his case without delay before the Governor of the Netherlands.

Balthazar Gerard, inspired by the approval of so learned and holy a man, indeed desired nothing better than to at once attempt his scheme.

But he was still baffled by his insignificance and his poverty.

His few miserable savings he had until now kept untouched, for he was haunted by the fear that he might be baulked in his design by actual lack of pence.

The months went by and he still hung about Tournay, hungry, alone, earning a little money by clerk's work of the lower kind, brooding ever on the same idea.

He had frequent recourse to Father Gery and was an enthusiastic attendant at the Franciscan church.

At last in the spring, and, as he realized with impatience, nearly two years since Jauregay's attempt, he resolved to wait no longer for some outside assistance which seemed as if it was indeed never forthcoming, but to follow the advice of Father Gery and seek out the Prince of Parma.

Accordingly he packed his poor belongings into a wallet that he strapped on to his back and proceeded, largely on foot, to near Oudenarde, where the Governor then held his court and camp, having profited by the treachery of Anjou to advance into the enemy's country and cast his eye on Bruges and Ghent.

Before he had left Tournay Gerard had written, with much sincerity and earnestness, a letter in which he set forth what he proposed to do and his reasons for doing it; one copy of this letter he left in the hands of the principal of the Franciscan college, the other he kept inside his shabby doublet for presentation to Parma.

At Oudenarde, then but recently captured from the rebels, he again put himself in touch with the priests, quoting Father Gery, and by this means obtained an introduction to one of the councillors of the Prince, a certain D'Assonleville, to whom he delivered the letter he had written for Parma.

While he was waiting for a response to this epistle he heard the news that the fourth marriage of the Prince of Orange, that with Louise de Coligny, which had until then pleased no one, had been rendered popular by the birth of a son.

Gerard heard this news with a yet grimmer determination to remove one who had still further added to his manifold offences by this blasphemous marriage with the daughter of that arch-heretic, Coligny.

A few days after the delivery of his letter, he was summoned into the presence of the Prince of Parma, who had but recently returned from a successful attack on Ypres and Bruges — which two cities he looked to see soon fall into his hands through the treachery of the Prince of Chimay, the Governor of Flanders, who was engaged in a plot with Granvelle's brother, Champagny, and Imbige, to deliver that province back into the hands of the King.

Parma had not been particularly impressed by the letter Gerard had written with so much pains and enthusiasm, and he was cynical of anyone succeeding in taking the life of the Prince of Orange, so many had tried and failed, so many had taken payment and not even tried, and William was now established and guarded in the city of Delft among his own people and it was by no means easy for any foreigner to gain access to the city.

Therefore, though Parma had long been looking for someone to rid him of the man who was effectually preventing him from reducing the chronic rebellion of the Netherlands, he would not have accorded an interview to the runaway civilian if Gerard in his letter had not spoken of a new plan by which to reach the person of the Prince — "a trap to bait the fox."

These words interested Parma, for until then all attempts on William had been direct — to get him by guile was a new scheme and one that recommended itself to the cold heart and subtle head of Alexander Farnese.

He received Gerard in the plain room of the modest house he occupied when in Oudenarde; a widower Prince, not fond of women, of wholly martial tastes and not given to any frivolity or display though his life was full of a sombre magnificence, he held no court in the proper sense of the word and fixed his residence where he pitched his camp during a vice-royalty that was one long campaign. D'Assonleville conducted Gerard into the presence of the Prince, who was alone with Haultfenne, another of his councillors.

The only splendour in the apartment gathered in the person of Parma, whose bronze satins were closely worked with pearl and gold, whose triple ruff was of the finest lace, and whose sword and baldrick shone with jewels.

He stood in the embrasure of the latticed window and faced Gerard directly on his entrance.

His was a figure calculated to inspire awe and even terror in the hearts of his inferiors and those, and they were many, whom he despised or disliked.

Tall, with the powerful and graceful figure of an athlete and the carriage of an accomplished swordsman, his features were of a serene and regular beauty, his complexion pale and dark, his hair close and black, his expression at once cold and haughty. His face was marred by the eyes which, instead of being full of fire and passion as befitted their size and brilliancy, were hard and steady in their gaze and had something both narrow and menacing in their look.

Such was the person who directed his searching and contemptuous glance at Balthazar Gerard; a glance before which many a more exalted individual had quailed.

But the little clerk returned his scrutiny with the same modest self-possession and absolute calm with which he had fronted the priests at Trêves and Tournay.

He was not abashed either by Alexander's splendid presence nor by Alexander's discouraging frown, but stepped into the centre of the room and made his reverence.

The Prince came to the point.

"You have a project to remove William of Nassau?" he asked.

"Your Highness," said Gerard, "I have had this project for seven years."

"And it was quickened by the publication of the Ban, eh?" demanded Parma cynically.

Gerard eyed him without flinching.

"For the matter of my reward I will trust to the liberality of His Majesty. I do not do this for money — but because of *the unalterable determination I have to kill the Prince of Orange.*"

"And from where comes this determination" asked Alexander.

"The reasons are set forth in my letter," answered Balthazar meekly.

Parma replied haughtily and briefly —

"I do not recall your letter. Your reasons?"

The little clerk was not abashed.

"Is it not enough," he asked with some dignity, "that I am a faithful Roman Catholic and loyal subject of His Majesty and that this Prince is a wretch who has brought much evil on my religion and my King?"

Alexander regarded him closely; he saw only an undersized sickly shabby little civilian and he was not prepossessed in Gerard's favour.

"Do you not know," he asked with a cold smile, "that every day men come to me on this errand? Men of all nationalities and breeds? Are you aware that I have listened to French, Scotch,

English, Italian, Irish, Germans, all coming with tales like yours, all promising me to kill the Prince of Orange?"

"I know," answered the little clerk quietly, "that many have come forward — but I am he who was ordained to do this deed."

"Are you so sure?"

" I am very sure." The two regarded each other for a moment in silence.

Parma was still not greatly impressed by the shabby little stranger; he could not believe him capable of a deed of daring and of bloodshed.

"Do you have the courage for this enterprise?" he asked, without attempting to disguise his disdain.

"Yes," replied Gerard, almost as if he answered a question of little importance.

Parma glanced at Haultfenne, the councillor who stood beside him in the window space.

"I think that this fellow does not know what he talks of," he remarked.

"I should advise Your Grace to listen to him," returned the other. "It seems to me that he is very much in earnest."

Parma lifted his dark brows and again fixed his peculiar hard cold glance on Gerard.

"Disclose to me your plan for approaching the person of the Prince of Orange," he demanded.

Gerard who had maintained the same attitude of reverent humility, yet complete composure, answered at once.

"I have the idea of going to Delft and applying to some friend of the Prince, as some heretic councillor or priest, and representing myself as a heretic, a Calvinist ruined for his faith and wishing for some employment — I will show Mansfield's seals as a guarantee of my truth and I will complain of the cruelties I have undergone, saying that my father was executed for his religion, and I shall explain the great use that may be made of the Count's seals in forging seals for spies, and with such feints and frivolities I shall gain the confidence of those about Nassau and sooner or later shall surely obtain access to his person."

Alexander Farnese (1547-1592) the Duke of Parma

"And then?" asked Parma drily.

"Then," answered Gerard quietly, "I shall kill him with any weapon I may have in my hand."

Parma smiled.

The Burgundian lifted his head.

"Does Your Grace think I shall fail like Jauregay did?" he asked. "My hand will not tremble nor my wit fail."

"And are you not aware how slight are your chances of escape and how horrid is the death these rebels will give you?"

asked Parma, not because he in the least cared what would become of Gerard; he would have thought the death of the Prince of Orange cheap at the cost of the lives of a thousand such — he wished to test the nerve of the little clerk.

"If I die, I die a martyr," quietly replied Gerard. "The holy fathers have assured me that. And I shall have rendered a great service to His Majesty, who I hope will not forget, in his great generosity, my poor family."

"Certainly," said Parma, "if you do this thing you lose your life, and the reward shall be paid to your family, if you escape, to you."

"Then I am happy indeed!" exclaimed Gerard with enthusiasm.

"But I tell you this," added Alexander, "there are at present four men in Delft, all unknown to the other and of different nationalities all seeking to encompass the death of the Nassau."

"If they succeed I am relieved from my task," said Gerard meekly, "but I do not think they will succeed since I am the man ordained to do this thing."

Parma again glanced at Haultfenne and very slightly lifted his shoulders.

"Go your way," he said, "only do not ask me for a white piece in advance, I have paid too many and to no purpose."

Gerard was considerably disappointed at this statement; he saw the old lack of money which had meant such a long delay in the execution of his task again rising up to hamper and perhaps defeat him.

Parma saw how his face fell and this competed his bad opinion of the man; he thought he was, after all, but after the money, like so many other of these adventurers who had come to him with the same scheme. Therefore he said brusquely:

"I need to make economies, my friend. If you are in earnest, you will accomplish this design without my bounty."

"This will I do," said Gerard, "and in a short while you shall hear from me."

Parma waved his hand to D'Assonleville to take away the little clerk.

Gerard followed the councillor out into the street, where the sun shone with a pale clear light.

D'Assonleville turned to his companion with some curiosity.

"And what will you do now, my son?" he asked kindly.

"I shall go to Delft — the Governor has encouraged me, has he not?"

"Certainly he has encouraged you."

"Then I shall continue on my way," replied Gerard, with a look full of joy and enthusiasm.

"But remember you must not involve the Prince of Parma," said D'Assonleville, leading him gently by the arm, "you must not say, even under torture, that he encouraged you and thereby expose him to the vengeance of frantic rebels."

"I shall not," replied Gerard solemnly, "*even under torture*."

"God give you courage and fortitude," said the councillor.

"I hope I have pardon for the stealing of the seals?" asked Gerard anxiously.

"I can assure you forgiveness for that — since the deed was done with this great end in view," replied D'Assonleville gravely.

Still Gerard was not wholly satisfied.

"If you could be my mediator with His Highness to obtain an absolution from the Pope for this deed, I should be easier, especially as I have to further stain my soul by mixing with heretics and in some sort conforming to their ways."

"I will speak of it to the Governor," replied the councillor.

They had now reached the door of Gerard's lodging near the gate.

The little clerk hesitated on the step.

"If you could get His Highness to advance me fifty crowns," he began timidly, stroking his thin beard.

But D'Assonleville was firm on that point.

"It is useless. His Highness has paid too often for nothing."

"But this time it will not be for nothing," replied Gerard simply.

The councillor lifted his shoulders.

"The Prince is a hard man. Especially in the matter of money."

Gerard sighed.

"I have no hope at all," said D'Assonleville, to close the subject.

"You yourself, Seigneur," asked Gerard, "you could give me these fifty crowns to be repaid with interest when I obtain the reward?"

D'Assonleville shook his head.

"I have not a spare stiver," he said conclusively. Gerard sighed again.

"Well," he answered, "I will pay my own expenses, and, as I told His Highness, you shall hear of me — and in a short while."

"All the world will hear of you," returned the councillor warmly.

Gerard's eyes sparkled.

"You will earn the gratitude of Spain and gain for yourself an immortal name," added D'Assonleville.

So saying, he patted him encouragingly on the back and smiled with benevolent friendliness into the eager face of the little clerk.

"Go quickly to Delft," he concluded, "lest someone gets there before you in this glorious deed."

"You shall hear of me," repeated Gerard with trembling lips, "you shall hear of me."

He hastened upstairs to his attic room and pulled out the pitiful hoard that was his last resource.

With the strictest economy and most painful self-denial it would be enough to take him to Delft.

A sigh escaped him at the thought of Parma's parsimony; he needed new shoes, his suit was miserable and by instinct he was neat and liked to go decently. But, after all, what did this matter if he could achieve his grand, his supreme object?

With a rush of enthusiasm he went on his knees and thanked God for the possession of the few coins that rendered the journey to Delft possible.

CHAPTER VIII

LOUISE OF ORANGE

RÉNÈE LE MEUNG was present at the baptism of the Prince's infant son in the church of which she was now the sole guardian, and Wilhelmina, in a long gown of lavender-blue silk and a lace cap of her own making, was allowed for a moment to hold the baby, who was named Frederick Henry after his two royal sponsors.

The new Princess of Orange had seen Rénèe in Delft and was not to be denied her acquaintanceship.

Louise de Coligny was of a nature different from Charlotte de Bourbon, neither so shy nor so placid, and she had not listened to Rénèe's protested desire for quiet and humble retirement nor found it ridiculous that the wife of William of Orange should be friends with such as Rénèe le Meung.

"I knew we would like each other when I saw you in the inn at Antwerp," she had said and Rénèe could not resist her; she thought too of the child, she was now a middle-aged woman, and the little girl who was to her as her own flesh would soon need more than she could do for her; so Rénèe, after all these years, became intimate in the house opposite the old Kirk where she had gone to watch the light in the Prince's windows when she first came to Delft.

William received her as an old friend, even with a certain tenderness. Probably, thought Rénèe, he recalled Heidelberg and Charlotte de Bourbon.

Nothing seemed strange to her now, not even the sight of this foreigner as mistress of the Prince's house.

Jealousy was dead in Rénèe; Louise did not trouble her as Charlotte had troubled her; she felt a kindness that was almost maternal for the beautiful high-spirited generous and intelligent
288

young woman who had known suffering and poverty, for William, for the second time, had married a penniless exile and found happiness with a woman whom none had approved of as his wife.

The position of the Princess, as had been at first that of her predecessor, was sufficiently isolated and even lonely, and she chose to make a companion of Rénèe, who submitted, though with a sense of irony, to this friendship which formed another link in the chain which bound her life to that of William of Orange.

The spring of the birth of the Prince's third son was a time of anxiety and trial for the Netherlanders; the defection of the Prince of Chimay, and of William's brother-in-law, the Count van der Berg, had involved the Provinces in the loss of several important cities, including Bruges, and Parma was known to be straining every nerve to crush the patriots.

William was pushing negotiations with Anjou, who had retired to Cambrai, and endeavouring to persuade him to come to terms for the resumption of the government of the Netherlands; meanwhile preparations were being made for the formal and ceremonious installation of the Prince as Stadtholder of the Northern Provinces, a position he had finally definitely accepted and the authority of which he already exercised; whether or no he ever achieved his cherished ambition of uniting the entire seventeen provinces under one ruler, here at least in that corner of earth where he had sworn to maintain himself or find his grave, he had established liberty and independence and the Reformed religion on a basis that the rudest shocks of tyranny were not likely to disturb.

And despite the general perils, alarms, and anxieties that beset the little Republic, from the Prince down to his humblest soldier, there reigned in this spring of 1584 a feeling of hopefulness, of enthusiasm, of confidence, almost of joyousness.

All seemed to feel that their most cruel trials were over, their darkest days past, their bitterest suffering completed.

And men even forgot the Ban.

In May Rénèe was walking with the Princess of Orange along the smooth brick path beside the quay.

It was a year of sunshine corresponding to the feeling in people's hearts.

The lime trees were already far advanced in leaf and cast a pale shadow on the waters of the canal that sparkled with light.

The Prince was absent and the Princess had begged Rénèe's company.

"I hope to be trusted and loved in this country where I have made my home," she had said simply, "but, at present, I am only a foreigner."

"You have your son, Madam," Rénèe had answered, "all love you because of him."

They walked now quietly side by side in a musing humour, Rénèe in her severe gray gown of a Dutch matron, the beautiful hair, now threaded with gray, bound back beneath a linen cap, the still beautiful face framed by a stiff ruff of pleated lawn.

The French Princess was simple also in her attire, but she always went more splendidly than her royal predecessor.

Her blonde locks were unconfined by net or cap, her falling collar was open at the rounded throat, her dress of citron-coloured cloth trimmed at hem and sleeve with silver embroidery.

She walked too with an air which, while wholly unconscious, was considered too sumptuous for a Calvinist Court.

"Tell me," she said, "looking back over your life, does it not seem strange?"

"Strange?" echoed Rénèe. "No, Madam, nothing is strange to me now."

"To me my life seems curious beyond any tale."

"But you are young."

"And you are not old."

"Old enough," smiled Rénèe, "to have passed the strangeness of things."

"But to see this revolt — this new nation formed," persisted the Princess, "to have watched His Highness as you have watched him engaged in this long struggle, to see him change as you must have seen him change —"

Rénèe interrupted.

"I have changed too," she said.

"Ah, yes, and so we do not notice the change about us — but, it is curious —"

She paused, gazing at the bright waters of the canal.

"Yes, Madam?" asked Rénèe gently, still with that little smile.

"What things we live through," said the Princess; she was thinking of Saint Bartholomew when her young husband had been murdered so soon after the wedding, when she, but a child in years, had been turned from her home, an exile.

"What things we forget," she added.

"No," said Rénèe, "what has once entered our hearts never leaves it, Madam — but our hearts close sometimes and we lose the key — but forget, no, no."

Louise looked curiously at this woman whom she had taken into her confidence, but of whom she knew so little, and she wondered what Rénèe's memories were and what was the secret of her loneliness and her calm.

"Here comes Monsieur de Villars," said Rénèe, "and he has a stranger with him."

The Princess glanced along the quay and saw Mynheer de Villars, a pastor and confidential friend of the Prince, approaching, accompanied by a young man in a shabby suit.

"A Frenchman?" said the Princess, "a refugee?"

The couple approached and the clergyman dismissed the young man, who with a humble reverence turned away down a side street.

Louise was sorry for him because he was so plain and sad and humble looking, but she did not like his face, which appeared to her to be singularly unprepossessing.

"Who is your friend?" she asked Monsieur de Villars.

"A poor refugee."

"I thought so — your charity shelters a number of such!" smiled Louise.

"His father was an executed Calvinist, he himself has long secretly professed the faith and has brought here copies of Count Mansfield's seals, which may be useful."

"What does he want?"

"Employment, Highness."

"Have you spoken to the Prince?" asked Louise, her pity struggling with her repulsion.

"Yes, and His Grace told me to send him to Biron, at Cambrai. He thought he might find these seals of some account."

"I am glad he is leaving Delft," said the Princess impulsively. "I think he has a villainous face."

Louise de Coligny (1555-1620)

The pastor smiled.

"Poor Gaion! He is an honest soul, Madam, and most religious."

The Princess was as quick to withdraw her opinion as she had been to voice it.

"You must not listen to me, Mynheer de Villars — a woman's foolish judgment of a face!"

The pastor was still eager to defend one whom he had taken under his protection.

"Since he has been at Delft, Madam, he has never missed a church service and I have not seen him without a Bible under his arm."

"I withdraw," smiled Louise, "I withdraw, Mynheer."

"No," returned the pastor, "I admit that Your Highness is right in as much as the fellow has an insignificant aspect — a poor mien, but I have conversed with him, and observed him, and found him honest and sincere."

"Then I am glad you have found him employment," said the Princess. "Was he not pleased to go to France?"

"No, Madam, he seemed strangely disappointed from the first, he expressed a most earnest desire to be near the Prince, for whom he has a great devotion."

Rénèe had listened with little interest to this conversation; the young man had not attracted her attention as he had attracted that of the Princess.

She was wondering if the Prince would return that night to Delft, she was speculating on how his affairs went with the Duke of Anjou; her thoughts were never long from William and his business.

Monsieur de Villars dismissed, the two women turned to the Prince's house.

The courtyard was full of sunlight, and pigeons blue and lavender and bronze flew over the roof of the house, across the canal opposite, to their nests in the niches of the ancient church whose massive shape rose above the shadowed water.

There were one or two soldiers at the gate, for the rest the place was like the house of any burgher or merchant.

Rénèe would have gone home but the Princess pressed her to enter and the two went up to Louise's chamber where the infant Count Frederick Henry lay in his cradle and the Prince's sister, Catherine, sat at a frame, embroidering a wreath of crimson roses.

Louise seated herself with a little sigh, the languor of the spring was in the air and the day seemed long; she did not yet fit as perfectly into her place as had Charlotte de Bourbon, she was still a stranger among strangers and the household missed the exact, careful, and placid rule of its former mistress.

But when the step and voice of the Prince were heard below she rose at once, alert and animated; with him she was never at a loss, never at fault; in intelligence, in sympathy she was Charlotte's equal.

Rénèe remained sitting between the cradle and the embroidery frame, listening to the chatter of the nurses and watching the calm countenance of the Prince's sister.

It seemed to her, in that moment, as if her life was over and she watched the lives of others with a vision absolutely detached and disinterested.

She soon rose to take her leave; Wilhelmina had a maid now, but Rénèe did not leave her long alone.

As she descended the curved dark stairs the Prince came from the dining-room and, turning, stood across her path.

Even he, she saw with a clearness and a coldness as if he had been a stranger.

He was then fifty-one years of age and though spare and haggard retained a look of youth and an expression of unconquerable energy; he still wore his broad-leaved hat and his doublet and travelling cloak of gray frieze; his dark complexion looked pale above the plain linen falling collar and his eyes were very tired.

Rénèe wondered if he thought of the Brussels days as he looked at her; she knew that she too had changed — she knew that if she meant anything to him, she must mean strange memories.

"Your Grace is thoughtful," she said, for he continued to look at her without speaking.

"I am wondering about this work of mine, these poor people," he answered simply. "Daily the difficulties increase — I know not how I do even what I do."

"By the grace of God," said Rénèe.

"By the grace of God," repeated the Prince reverently. "In His hands, yes." He sighed, like a man over-fatigued.

"I always think of you as one who knew Count Lodewyk," he added irrelevantly. "I dreamt of him the other night. Very clearly."

He ascended the stairs and Rénèe, to allow him to pass, stepped into a little archway that was sunk into the wall. With extraordinary vividness there came before her eyes the picture of her first meeting with him, when he had mounted the stairs of Leipzig Town Hall in all his magnificence . . . She seemed to feel the heat, to smell the perfume, to see beside her the deformed figure of Anne of Saxony . . .

The Prince saluted her kindly and passed up the stairs.

Rénèe went her way.

CHAPTER IX

THE PROGRESS OF THE LITTLE CLERK

IN the July of that year Francis Gaion, the young Calvinist who had claimed the protection of Monsieur de Villars and of the Prince, returned to Delft, carrying important dispatches.

On a Sunday morning he sat, breathless, dusty, and shabby in the hall of the Prince's house; William was still in bed and the dispatches had been taken up to his chamber.

The messenger stared through the open door at the early sunshine lying on the cobbles of the courtyard, at the figure of the sentry leaning in the gateway and the flock of pigeons hurrying after the yellow grain scattered for them.

This was a moment of triumph for Balthazar Gerard, calling himself Francis Gaion, for not only had he returned to Delft, but he was actually in the house of the Prince; he could not doubt that his long patient waiting would be at length rewarded and that he would finally find himself in the presence of William of Nassau.

He had been meek and patient and humble, he had gone to France, though greatly against his wish, and he had waited till the chance had come for his return; his good conduct and his piety had earned him the confidence of Marshal Biron, and finally he had been chosen as the messenger to send to Delft.

He was tired and ill-fed and poor; his services had been paid with a sum sufficient only for his bare living, but the calm and desperate character hidden under his miserable exterior never faltered in the fixed idea of the one terrible design.

He felt content now, like a man who has reached his goal and needs but to put out his hand to take the prize which is the reward of his toils and labours.

He was in Delft, he had the confidence of the rebels, it was but a question of patience.

And Balthazar Gerard was well schooled in patience, it was now some years since he had stuck his dagger into a doorpost, vowing that so some day he would reach the heart of Orange.

As he sat there, staring out at the sunshine and turning over in his mind under what excuse he might introduce himself into the presence of William, he was touched on the shoulder by the Prince's secretary and told that His Highness wished to see him immediately.

Gerard rose; his countenance was so agitated that the secretary thought that he was overwhelmed at the honour suddenly granted him and encouraged him kindly.

The messenger followed up the dark stairway to the private apartments of the Prince.

He was ushered directly into William's bedchamber; the secretary left him alone with the man whom he hated with a hatred almost superhuman and by whose death he meant to satisfy his conscience, obtain worldly honours, and heavenly glory.

The Prince was in bed, unarmed, only the linen of the bed-gown protected that heart Gerard had vowed to God to quiet forever.

The Burgundian's emotion was so considerable that he could not speak. He stood within the door; a shambling meagre figure, staring at the man sitting up in bed; William, too, was troubled.

For the dispatches of Biron contained the news of the death of the Duke of Anjou.

The Valois had succumbed to a ghastly and rapid illness of the same nature as that which had proved mortal in his brother, King Charles, and William must now choose another figure-head for his scheme of consolidation of the Netherlands.

The death of this worthless young man had upset schemes long pondered and deeply cherished. The loss of Anjou might mean the loss of the friendship of England and France.

William lifted his eyes from the documents scattered over the bed coverlet and looked at the messenger.

"You are Gaion, who was recommended to me by Monsieur de Villars?" he asked.

"I am he, Highness," said Gerard, who could scarcely articulate the words. "In the service of Monsieur de Schoneval."

But William did not notice the messenger's agitation; his thoughts were entirely absorbed by the news which he had just received.

He saw in the persecuted Calvinist whom the pastor had recommended to him, a puny young man of an insignificant aspect and thought no more of him.

"You were at Cambrai on the occasion of the death of the Duke?" he asked.

"Yes, Monseigneur."

"Then you can give me more details than are contained in these dispatches."

Gerard could hardly answer; his mind was concentrated on the one thing; that here was his enemy, his predestined victim, the heretic rebel, the cause of so much woe to His Majesty and to the Holy Church, lying alone before him, unarmed and helpless.

The great opportunity so long prayed for and toiled for had at last arrived; and it had found him unprepared.

For he was without weapons; had he possessed even a two-inch dagger he would have used it; he even thought of his bare hands, but one glance at the Prince showed him that William was by far the stronger man and could easily have defended himself.

The Prince waited for a reply. He thought the fellow stupid or embarrassed.

"What name did they give this illness of the Duke?" he asked again.

"Poison, Monseigneur," stammered Gerard. "Some said poison."

"Was it so sudden?"

"Very sudden, Monseigneur. He was taken with great pains so that his cries could be heard all over the castle. Great torments, they said. And he sweated blood, like his brother, His Majesty King Charles."

William turned over the papers thoughtfully; he remembered Saint Bartholomew; he believed his wife would say the horrible deaths of the Valois Princes were well deserved.

"And there is nothing known, nothing suspected?"

"Nothing," replied Gerard. "His Grace was not much lamented."

"Why, no," said William drily, "he had done little to be loved."

"And his death was a just punishment for his crimes," said Gerard, who had hated Anjou for allowing himself to be used by William against Philip.

The Prince thought that the messenger, as a Calvinist, referred to Anjou's attempt on the liberties of the States.

"Ah, my friend," he answered "this young man was a Prince of France and as such useful to the poor provinces."

"Nevertheless he perished as a reward of his crimes," said Gerard stubbornly. "And so will all perish who follow his example."

William noticed the curious emphasis of these words and smiled.

"You have but little charity, Francis Gaion."

"Towards the enemies of the faith I have neither charity nor pity, Monseigneur."

The Prince sighed.

"Intolerance is a hideous thing," he said, "but how uselessly do I make war on it! We who abhor the Romanists, must we imitate them in that? Do you know any other particulars concerning the death of His Grace?"

Gerard controlled himself to answer calmly.

"It was all terror and confusion, Monseigneur — some said the Duke had been poisoned by a candle, some the dessert —"

"But what was the motive, and who the murderer?" asked William, who was thinking of Spain.

"They talked of a woman, Monseigneur."

"A woman?"

"You are surprised, Monseigneur?"

"Surprised, no — but I had not thought of it," replied the Prince.

"Your Highness thought of politics?"

"I thought of Parma — or of Granvelle," said William.

Gerard started; his limbs were so shaking with excitement that he had to lean against the bedpost to support himself.

"Of Parma?" he cried.

"Parma has his murderers," answered William, "and Granvelle his agents."

Gerard controlled himself; he put his hand to his trembling mouth.

"There was no talk of Parma," he said in a dull voice.

"No, he may be clear of this — Spain could have bought Anjou as all the world knows, but Parma is thrifty and might have found this the cheaper way."

"Yes, Parma is thrifty," thought Gerard, "or I should not be standing here weaponless!"

And he felt bitter against D'Assonleville who had refused to advance him the money with which he could have bought a good dagger to carry always about his person.

As it was this golden opportunity was lost — lost, and he could only stare at the Prince and bite his finger with vexation.

"That is all," said William, dismissing him.

"A passport — a passport," stammered Gerard, clutching at any excuse to return into the presence of the Prince.

"A passport?" William looked up from the papers which he was re-reading.

"I have to return to Cambrai, Monseigneur. I am attached to the service of Monsieur de Schoneval," returned Gerard, clutching his hat to his breast.

"I will see later about the passport — you will stay a few days in Delft?"

"Yes, Monseigneur," said Gerard, and in his heart he added, "I shall not leave Delft while you, Monster, are alive."

There was now nothing for him to do but to take his leave.

He slowly descended the stairs and noticed the shallow arch near the vestibule.

As well as he was able he observed the plan of the building, which was old and rambling, having in former times been the residence of the priors attached to the church opposite.

Both cloister and church had been horribly profaned in Gerard's eyes; he furtively crossed himself and muttered a prayer for the soul of the last prior who had been hanged by the heretics.

He noticed that the dining-room was to the right of the vestibule, and that to reach the Prince's apartments above, the dark bend of stairs containing the arch had to be passed.

He went to further inspect the building, but was interrupted by a young man of about eighteen, fair and martial in appearance, who entered suddenly from the courtyard.

Gerard knew him for Count Maurice.

He passed without a glance at the Burgundian, who bowed humbly to his face and lifted his lip at his back.

Gerard would have liked to spit at him as Catherine de Medici had spat at the mangled body of Coligny.

Slowly and shambling a little he crossed the courtyard and lingered about the house to observe the outside; in making the plan for his escape he would need to know the arrangements of the building.

He had already marked that the left wall formed one side of a narrow lane which ran alongside the Prince's stables to the city ramparts.

Now he was noticing with a keen eye where the sentry was posted, the position of the gate, and the height of the walls.

The people began to enter the church opposite for the morning service.

Gerard approached the gate and watched them, an orderly procession crossing the little bridge over the canal, passing under the shade of the full-leaved limes and entering the wide porch of the church.

The sentry, who had long been aware of the solitary little stranger hesitating around the courtyard, now came from his place and spoke to him.

"Do you have any further business with the Prince?" he asked pleasantly.

Gerard glanced up at the good-natured Netherlander; he saw here an opportunity to further his supreme purpose, which now, as ever, put on hold for a lack of means.

"I am one of Monsieur de Schoneval's gentlemen," he said, "and have come with a message from Cambrai. And truly I would like to join those pious people opposite, but in such attire how can I enter the church? I was ashamed to approach His Highness in these weeds!"

And he pointed to his broken shoes, threadbare hose, and shabby garment.

"Is it the lack of means that prevents you, my friend?" asked the sentry.

"Even that," replied Gerard. "I am a poor Calvinist of Bescanon who lost all because of my faith."

At this moment a young officer entered from the street and the sentry approached him, telling him of Gerard's plight.

"And I think he lacks a good meal as much as a pair of shoes, Mynheer," added the halberdier.

"I will speak to the Prince," replied the officer, after a glance at Gerard. "It is the little clerk who was recommended by Monsieur de Villars."

"The same," said the soldier, "a poor little fellow, always starving."

The other went towards the house and the sentry returned to Gerard.

"The captain is speaking to the Prince about your needs," he said,

"The Prince?" Gerard lowered his eyes. "I am sorry to disturb His Highness for such as I."

"His Highness never sends anyone away," returned the soldier. "You should have told him your situation before."

"I was ashamed," murmured Gerard.

"Oh," said the halberdier, "as for that, His Highness has himself starved and gone in broken shoes." Gerard glancing sideways under his lids, saw the officer returning and his heart gave a great leap; was he at last to obtain the money with which to carry out his purpose?

The young captain approached him smiling.

"His Highness at once sends you this for your immediate wants, and he says he will speak to Monsieur de Villars about you and tell him to see that you are supplied for your return journey."

As he spoke he put into Gerard's hand three gold pieces.

At finding himself at last in possession of the means to accomplish his design such a deep exultation shook the soul of Balthazar Gerard that the light leapt to his eyes and such a hideous smile parted his thin lips that the officer felt a sudden touch of horror as if he looked at something extremely powerful and extremely evil.

The next instant the little clerk was humble and downcast and profuse in his gratitude and the soldier could not credit his senses for that swift impression of horror.

Afterwards he remembered it.

The people had all passed into the church now and the great doors were shut.

Gerard hurried along the harbour with William's bounty clasped tightly in his hot hand.

"I will repay your heirs out of King Philip's reward," he said, and laughed aloud, for the joke pleased him; he was indeed supremely happy.

The money was sufficient to buy a weapon and to leave enough for his journey from Delft, if, indeed, it was God's will that he should escape.

It would also procure him the pair of shoes and hose he must have to avoid comment on his return to the Prince's house.

He now turned to the outskirts of the town towards the Rotterdam canal where no one who had noticed him that morning would be likely to see him. Here he found a modest tavern of the sort usually favoured by him, and entering ordered a meagre meal, the cost of which was covered by the few pence of his own he had left. William's charity was left untouched for William's murder. Frugality was a choice and a habit with Gerard, he did not notice the scantiness of his meal; the three gold coins laid carefully in the rusty pouch, from which he never took his hands, afforded him such infinite satisfaction, that, rather than disturb them, he would have gone without food at all though he had not eaten since yesterday.

It gave him a pleasant sensation also to look around the tavern at these jolly fresh-faced heretics and rebels, so comfortable and secure in their eating and drinking and to think that he, the little insignificance they did not even notice, would shortly throw them into terror and confusion and despair.

He exulted in the thought that he was alone against all these, that he alone in this city stood for the true faith and the true King, and his hatred of the man whom he had come to kill, and of the people by whom he was surrounded led him with strength like wine.

He had laid his plans of escape, but he knew that they were not likely to succeed; this, however, did not trouble him in the least, for Balthazar Gerard was absolutely without fear.

When he had finished his meal he approached a soldier who was drinking beer by the door and asked him if he knew of a shop where he could buy a good pistol.

"I know of many such," replied the soldier briskly, "but you must pay a high price these days." He glanced at Gerard and added, with the patronage of the soldier towards the civilian, "Do you know a good pistol, Mynheer?"

Gerard was at once deprecating.

"No, I cannot pretend to much knowledge of these things — but the truth is, I have a long journey to undertake to Cambrai. I have come unarmed and will not so return. The roads are dangerous for one alone."

The Netherlander agreed.

"As long as those dogs of Spaniards pollute the land."

Gerard shivered with an exquisite sensation of rage; his light eyes flickered.

"So if you know where I could get a weapon," he repeated meekly.

"As for that, as I said, it is a question of price — if you like to pay —"

"I cannot afford much," said Gerard quickly. "And I need bullets, there is a kind of chopped slugs I have a fancy for."

"Well," answered the soldier reflectively, "I have such a weapon myself I would sell you for a reasonable sum."

He went and fetched a pair of small pistols from a pile of his possessions he had heaped on the floor in the corner.

Gerard looked at them keenly; they were in good condition, which was all that he required for his purpose. After a long chaffering over the price, he secured the weapons for a moderate sum, together with a supply of bullets.

Balthazar Gerard (1562?-1584)

CHAPTER X

MAURICE OF NASSAU

THE next day Balthazar Gerard employed in purchasing his shoes and hose and a pair of bladders which he meant to blow up and fasten to his person when he should cross the city moat; for his desperate plan of escape was this: to run down the lane at the side of the Prince's house, scale the ramparts, and drop into the moat; once he could pass the water unobserved he had every hope of gaining Parma's lines.

But be remembered the fate of Jean Jauregay and knew that this might very likely be his — or a worse if he was captured alive by the infuriated Netherlanders, this thought did not, even now, on the eve of his attempt cause him to hesitate or even a shudder to shake his puny body; his courage was as complete as his resolution.

When in Cambrai he had managed to purchase from one of the roguish attendants of the Duke's physician a small quantity of a virulent poison which he had declared he wanted for a cat which annoyed him by continually penetrating into his chamber. With this he now thoroughly saturated three of the bullets he had purchased with the gun and then carefully loaded the weapon.

After which he said his prayers, begging especially to be excused the stealing of Mansfield's seals, and imploring a blessing on his great enterprise.

He prayed for his own soul (it was a matter of regret to him that he had not been able to confess and obtain absolution since he had left Cambrai, where he had secretly visited one of the Duke's priests), for the Duke of Parma and the King of Spain, for Cardinal Granvelle and the holy Spanish Inquisition.

The next morning, after a night of sound sleep, he left his room (it was a humble chamber in a street off the market-place), and, armed with his pistols, his charms, his money, and his bladders inside the pocket of his doublet, he started for the Prince's house.

As he crossed the wide square he saw a woman and a child coming towards him.

He had trained himself not to forget faces and he remembered that this was the lady whom he had seen walking with Louise de Coligny along the canal the day that Monsieur de Villars had sent him to France in the suite of Monsieur de Schoneval.

It occurred to him, that, as she was a friend of the Princess she might be useful in obtaining an entrance for him into the Prince's house. Therefore he approached and saluted her.

Rénèe did not remember him, but seeing him so humble and inoffensive she smiled.

"I am the poor Gaion, Madam," said Gerard, "who was with Monsieur de Villars one day when he met you walking with Her Highness."

Rénèe recalled him.

"Ah, you have returned to Delft — for long?"

"No, Madam, I must return to France, even today — I go now to see if I may obtain a passport — you see I am armed for the journey," he added with a smile, for he had seen Rénèe glance at the pistols.

"The roads are dangerous?"

"For a civilian travelling alone, yes."

He walked beside Rénèe across the square; she did not notice the repulsiveness in his appearance that had impressed the Princess; to her he was a poor little refugee, one of the drift and wreckage left from the bloody sea of Spanish cruelty, and she was sorry for him.

And the fierce and implacable spirit that was hidden in the miserable exterior of the man who walked beside her was hating her bitterly as a type of the rebel heretic to him utterly abominable.

He hated her grave fair face, her plain attire, her precise white linen of cap and kerchief, he hated the serious blonde-haired child in the long gray kirtle and modest hood.

"It is your daughter?" he asked.

"The child of a refugee like yourself," replied Rénèe. "Her father went down at Mookerheyde with Count Lodewyk — how long ago it seems!"

306

"Long enough for Count Lodewyk to be forgotten," replied Gerard.

"No, he will never be forgotten while the House of Nassau is remembered, and that will be to the end of time," replied Rénèe proudly.

"The Prince at least will be remembered," said Gerard.

"Among the greatest of men."

"And I," said Gerard quietly, "I also hope to make a name — even one that may be written alongside that of the Prince."

Rénèe glanced at him curiously; she had not credited him with being either crazy or ambitious.

"Well, you are still young," she answered, humouring him.

He lifted his shoulders and suddenly laughed.

They were admitted without difficulty into the Prince's house.

Rénèe went upstairs to the apartments of the Princess to present to her a deep border of her exquisite lace that she had just finished.

Gerard loitered around the entrance-hall until one of the Prince's secretaries spoke to him, when he asked for a passport.

He was told that one would be given him; that it was, in fact, ready and only required the Prince's signature.

At this moment and before Gerard could well realize it, the Prince turned the corner of the stairs and crossed the vestibule to go to the dining-room.

The Princess was beside him, leaning on his arm, her blue gown laced with silver contrasted with his sombre gray frieze and leather, as her youth and her vivacity contrasted with his dignity and stateliness; but he as ever was lighthearted; he was laughing over his shoulder at those who followed him; Gerard saw the silver of the famous medal gleam beneath the high white ruff.

He pressed forward and Louise saw him and knew him instantly.

Her former impression of him was revived so vividly that she could not forbear an exclamation. "What is that fellow doing here?"

The Prince turned.

"A passport," muttered Gerard.

"See that the passport is made out," said William and went on.

"It is a villainous face." murmured Louise.

But the Prince reassured her, saying it was only the messenger from Cambrai come for his papers, and so they passed into the dining-room.

The secretary asked Gerard to come into his chamber, but the Burgundian excused himself, saying he had a headache and desired the fresh air; indeed he looked so pale that his words were easily believed.

"Besides," he added, "it is a fine sight to see the Prince and his family. I would like to behold them pass again. You do not know, Monsieur, what it means to me to look upon William of Nassau."

So he was allowed to remain in the courtyard, where for two hours he wandered up and down, none among those who came and went taking any notice of his insignificance.

Rénèe from an upper window, where she stayed with the Princess's women, observed him and was sorry for him, he looked so shrunken and puny and drew aside so humbly from every passerby.

Presently Gerard stepped out of the sunshine into the darkness of the vestibule.

There was no one about, but he could hear sounds from the dining-room and the voice of the Prince, cheerful, animated.

Gerard turned and stepped into the arch he had noticed on descending from the Prince's chamber two days before.

Though the stairs were lighted by the large window half-way up, the vestibule was in darkness and the arch which concealed Gerard was in the complete shadow of the door.

At the back of it a narrow entrance opened on to the lane which led to the ramparts; it was by this that Gerard intended to make his escape.

The Prince appeared in the door leading from the diningroom; he was talking to the Burgomaster of Leeuwarden, his guest, and said something about the future of Friesland.

"No future for you," whispered Gerard, "here ends the history of William of Orange."

He fixed his eyes with an intensity of hatred on the noble figure of the Prince as he leisurely crossed the narrow vestibule,

"No future for you," whispered Gerard,
"here ends the history of
William of Orange."

as if he wished to imprint on his memory the last look and gesture of his victim.

William was smiling; he put his foot on the lower stair and turned his head to speak to the burgomaster.

Gerard stepped from the arch; he was but two paces from William and he discharged the three poisoned balls full at the Prince's body.

"Now the King's vengeance is completed!" cried Gerard, and dashed out of the door beside his hiding place.

A little shriek rose from the women; William fell backwards into the arms of the master of his house.

"God have mercy on my soul!" he exclaimed. "God have mercy on this poor people!"

His hat fell off, revealing his face already distorted with the terrible expression of the final agony; he sank on to the stairs.

"He is fainting," said the Princess.

"He is dying," said Count Maurice, and, lifting up his father in his strong young arms, he conveyed him, with the assistance of the burgomaster and the master of the house back into the diningroom.

They laid him on a couch; the meal from which he had just risen was still on the table; no one could believe what had happened; Louise fell on her knees and tried to loosen his ruff and doublet but her fingers laboured uselessly at the fastenings.

"Do you commend your soul to Christ?" asked Catherine of Schwartzburg.

"Yes," said William, and on the word the last breath passed his lips.

"Dead," said Maurice, bending over him, "Dead — oh, my father."

The room was full of the frightened household; Rénèe was in the crowd, catching the ghastly truth as it passed from one trembling lip to another.

She saw the murderer dragged in through the side door from which he had made his escape covered with the filth

Death of William the Silent

into which he had fallen, bleeding from rough usage, but calm and triumphant.

"I would come a thousand miles to do this deed again," he said.

She was pushed along in the press, the little girl clinging to her hand. One word was on everyone's tongue, it beat in her brain as the sound of the sea beats in the brain of the watcher at the window nearby — this one word — "dead, dead, dead."

It seemed to her that all life had ceased everywhere, and that these were but ghosts that ran and cried and commanded and lamented.

Thrust against a corner of the dining-table she saw, through the moving press of figures, a glimpse of that still form on the couch, not the face, but the shapely body and one fine hand with the fingers curled inwards slackly. The burden of the murmur about her forced itself on her stunned consciousness.

"Dead — dead," she said aloud.

A young man passing turned at these words.

"The Prince is dead," he answered, "but the Netherlands live."

"How do they live — now?" cried Rénèe.

"In such as these," he pointed to the child, "and in me, Maurice of Nassau."

Surely, if God had willed it,
When that fierce tempest blew,
My power would have stilled it,
Or turned its blast from you.
But He Who dwells in Heaven,
Whence all our blessings flow,
For which aye praise be given,
Did not desire it so.

Unto God and His power
I do confession make
That ne'er at any hour
Ill of the king I spake.
But to the Lord, the greatest
Of majesties, I owe
Obedience first and latest,
For Justice wills it so.

Monumental Tomb of William of Orange in the Nieuwe Kerk, Delft

Doctor Adrian by Deborah Alcock
A Story of Old Holland

Doctor Adrian was a scholar living in quiet seclusion in Antwerp, the Netherlands, until a fugitive Protestant preacher and his daughter Rose sought sanctuary in his rooms. Before he knew it, he became involved with the Protestant cause, and eventually embraced it in theory. When the persecution of the Reformed was stepped up, Doctor Adrian made the dangerous journey to Leyden with his family. They survived the siege of Leyden, along with Adrian's sister Marie. When the siege was lifted by the fleets of William of Orange, they moved to Utrecht. Doctor Adrian's faith in the Reformed religion died when he experienced the loss of some of his loved ones, but a new faith in the Author of that religion took its place.

This is a tale of a doctor and his contact with William, Prince of Orange, and of his spiritual journey.

Time: 1560-1584	Age: 12-99
ISBN 1-894666-05-4	Can.$15.95 U.S.$13.90

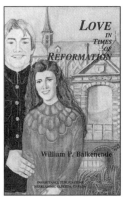

Love in Times of Reformation
by William P. Balkenende

N.N. in *The Trumpet*: This historical novel plays in The Netherlands during the rise of the protestant Churches, under the persecution of Spain, in the latter half of the sixteenth century. Breaking with the Roman Catholic Church in favor of the new faith is for many an intense struggle. Anthony Tharret, the baker's apprentice, faces his choice before the R.C. Church's influenced Baker's Guild. His love for Jeanne la Solitude, the French Huguenot refugee, gives a fresh dimension to the story. Recommended! Especially for young people.

Time: 1560-1585	Age: 14-99
ISBN 0-921100-32-9	Can.$8.95 U.S.$7.90

The TowerClock Stopped by J. DeHaan
A story during the time of the Reformation

An amazingly true story about a surprise attack by the Spanish army on Sluis, a small city in a southern coastal province of The Low Countries, now known as The Netherlands. The Dutch fought for their freedom from Spain in an eighty-year war, from 1568 to 1648. The surprise attack on Sluis is part of that war.

"As soon as I finished reading this book, I had to check Motley's *United Netherlands* to see if these amazing facts really happened! Yes, the Towerclock truly stopped!" — Roelof A. Janssen

Time: 1606	Age: 8-99
IP0000008516	Can.$9.95 U.S.$8.90

Coronation of Glory by Deborah Meroff

The true story of seventeen-year-old Lady Jane Grey, Queen of England for nine days.

"Miss Meroff . . . has fictionalized the story of Lady Jane Grey in a thoroughly absorbing manner . . . she has succeeded in making me believe this is what really happened. I kept wanting to read on — the book is full of action and interest."

— Elisabeth Elliot

Time: 1537-1554	Age: 14-99
ISBN 0-921100-78-7	Can.$14.95 U.S.$12.90

William of Orange - The Silent Prince
by W.G. Van de Hulst

Whether you are old or young you will enjoy this biography on the life of William of Orange. Read it and give it as a birthday present to your children or grandchildren. A fascinating true story about one of the greatest princes who ever lived and already by his contemporaries justly compared to King David.

Time: 1533-1584   Age: 7-99
ISBN 0-921100-15-9   Can.$11.95 U.S.$9.90

It Began With a Parachute
by William R. Rang

Fay S. Lapka in *Christian Week*: [It] . . . is a well-told tale set in Holland near the end of the Second World War. . . The story, although chock-full of details about life in war-inflicted Holland, remains uncluttered, warm, and compelling.

Time: 1940-1945   Age: 9-99
ISBN 0-921100-38-8   Can.$8.95 U.S.$7.90

Augustine,
The Farmer's Boy of Tagaste
by P. De Zeeuw

C. MacDonald in *The Banner of Truth*: Augustine was one of the great teachers of the Christian Church, defending it against many heretics. This interesting publication should stimulate and motivate all readers to extend their knowledge of Augustine and his works. J. Sawyer in *Trowel & Sword*: . . . It is informative, accurate historically and theologically, and very readable. My daughter loved it (and I enjoyed it myself). An excellent choice for home and church libraries.

Time: A.D. 354-430   Age: 9-99
ISBN 0-921100-05-1   Can.$7.95 U.S.$6.90

Martin Shows the Way
by Cor Van Rijswijk

It was cold and dark outside. Yet there were some boys walking in the streets.

They were going from one house to an other. Do you know what they were doing? Listen! They were singing. Suddenly a door was opened. A kind woman gave the boys something to eat. How happy they were.

Time: 1483-1546   Age: 4-9
ISBN 1-894666-80-1
                           Can.$9.95 U.S.$8.90

John is Not Afraid
by Cor Van Rijswijk

John Knox was smart. He could study very well and learn quickly. Father and Mother really liked that. One day, John was called to go to his father. "John," he said, "you are a big boy now. You must either work, or keep going to school."

Time: 1513?-1572   Age: 4-9
ISBN 1-894666-81-X   Can.$9.95 U.S.$8.90

Salt in His Blood — The Life of Michael De Ruyter
by William R. Rang

Liz Buist in *Reformed Perspective*: This book is a fictional account of the life of Michael de Ruyter, who as a schoolboy already preferred life at sea to being at school. De Ruyter is known as the greatest Dutch admiral, who, in spite of his successful career as a sailor captain and pirate hunter, remained humble and faithful to his God who had called him to serve his country. The author brings to life many adventures at sea that keep the reader spellbound, eager to know what the next chapter will bring. . . This book is highly recommended as a novel way to acquiring knowledge of a segment of Dutch history, for avid young readers and adults alike.

Time: 1607-1676   Age: 10-99
ISBN 0-921100-59-0   Can.$10.95 U.S.$9.90

The Shadow Series
by Piet Prins

One of the most exciting series of a master story teller about the German occupation of The Netherlands during the emotional time of the Second World War (1940-1945).

K. Bruning in *Una Sancta* about Vol.4 - The Partisans, and Vol. 5 - Sabotage: . . . the country was occupied by the German military forces. The nation's freedom was destroyed by the foreign men in power. Violence, persecutions and executions were the order of the day, and the main target of the enemy was the destruction of the christian way of life. In that time the resistance movement of underground fighters became very active. People from all ages and levels joined in and tried to defend the Dutch Christian heritage as much as possible. The above mentioned books show us how older and younger people were involved in that dangerous struggle. It often was a life and death battle. Every page of these books is full of tension. The stories give an accurate and very vivid impression of that difficult and painful time. These books should also be in the hands of our young people. They are excellent instruments to understand the history of their own country and to learn the practical value of their own confession and Reformed way of life. What about as presents on birthdays?

Time: 1944-1945   Age: 10-99

Vol. 1 The Lonely Sentinel	ISBN 1-894666-72-0	Can.$9.95 U.S.$8.90
Vol. 2 Hideout in the Swamp	ISBN 1-894666-73-9	Can.$9.95 U.S.$8.90
Vol. 3 The Grim Reaper	ISBN 1-894666-74-7	Can.$9.95 U.S.$8.90
Vol. 4 The Partisans	ISBN 0-921100-07-8	Can.$9.95 U.S.$8.90
Vol. 5 Sabotage	ISBN 0-921100-08-6	Can.$9.95 U.S.$8.90

William III and the Revolution of 1688
and *Gustavus Adolphus II*
2 Historical Essays by Marjorie Bowen

F.G. Oosterhoff in *Reformed Perspective*: I recommend this book without any hesitation. The two biographies make excellent reading, and the times the essays describe are of considerable interest and importance in the history of our civilization. Moreover, although Bowen obviously is not one in faith with Gustavus Adolphus and William of Orange, her essays relate incidents that are testimonials to God's mercies in preserving His Church. Remembering these mercies, we may take courage for the present and for the future.

Time: 1630-1689   Age: 14-99
ISBN 0-921100-06-X   Can.$9.95 U.S.$7.95

The Huguenot Inheritance Series

The Escape by A. Van der Jagt
The Adventures of Three Huguenot Children
Fleeing Persecution
Huguenot Inheritance Series #1

F. Pronk in *The Messenger*: This book . . . will hold its readers spellbound from beginning to end. The setting is late seventeenth century France. Early in the story the mother dies and the father is banished to be a galley slave for life on a war ship. Yet in spite of threats and punishment, sixteen-year-old John and his ten-year-old sister Manette, refuse to give up the faith they have been taught.

Time: 1685-1695   Age: 12-99
ISBN 0-921100-04-3   Can.$11.95 U.S.$9.95

The Secret Mission
by A. Van der Jagt
A Huguenot's Dangerous Adventures
in the Land of Persecution
Huguenot Inheritance Series #2

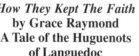

In the sequel to our best-seller, *The Escape,* John returns to France with a secret mission of the Dutch Government. At the same time he attempts to find his father.

Time: 1702-1712   Age: 12-99
ISBN 0-921100-18-3   Can.$14.95 U.S.$12.95

How They Kept The Faith
by Grace Raymond
A Tale of the Huguenots
of Languedoc
Huguenot Inheritance Series #3

Christine Farenhorst in *Christian Renewal*: Presenting a moving account of the weals and woes of two Huguenot families during the heavy waves of persecution in seventeenth century France, this book, although its onset is a bit slow, is fascinating and moving reading. Covering all aspects of Huguenot life during this difficult time period, this goodsized paperback volume is a well-spring of encouragement for Christians today and highly recommended as reading for all those age twelve and over.

Time: 1676-1686   Age: 13-99
ISBN 0-921100-64-7   Can.$14.95 U.S.$12.90

The Young Huguenots by Edith S. Floyer
Huguenot Inheritance Series #4

It was a happy life at the pretty chateau. Even after that dreadful Sunday evening, when strange men came down and shut the people out of the church, not much changed for the four children. Until the soldiers came . . .

Time: 1686-1687   **Age: 11-99**
ISBN 0-921100-65-5   Can.$11.95 U.S.$9.90

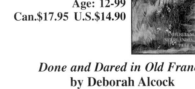

Driven into Exile
by Charlotte Maria Tucker
A Story of the Huguenots
Huguenot Inheritance Series #5

Christine Farenhorst in *Christian Renewal*: "Set in the days following the Revocation of the Edict of Nantes, (an edict in effect from 1598-1685 providing religious freedom for the French Protestants), this story follows the lives of two Huguenot families. Losing all to remain constant, the La Force family flees to Britain, while the Duval family remains in France. Suspenseful, the unfolding panorama of persecution and intrigue is well-suited for twenty-first century church goers who take freedom of religion for granted."

Time: 1685-1695   **Age: 13-99**
ISBN 0-921100-66-3   Can.$9.95 U.S.$8.90

The Refugees by A. Conan Doyle
A Tale of Two Continents
Huguenot Inheritance Series #6

The Refugees is a fast-paced exciting historical novel filled with daring and adventure. It depicts the escape of Louis De Catinat and his cousin from France after the revocation of the Edict of Nantes in 1685. Fleeing aboard a merchant vessel they attempt to reach America but find themselves stranded on an iceberg. The result is a hazardous trek through Canadian forests, avoiding both Roman Catholic Frenchmen and savage Indians.

Follow the adventures of well to do people, bereft of all convenience and fleeing for their lives to seek refuge in a country where freedom of religion returns stability to their lives.

Time: 1685-1686   **Age: 12-99**
ISBN 0-921100-67-1   Can.$17.95 U.S.$14.90

Done and Dared in Old France
by Deborah Alcock
Huguenot Inheritance Series #7

Christine Farenhorst wrote in *Christian Renewal*: Ten-year-old Gaspard, accidentally separated from his parents, is raised by a group of outlaw salt runners who fear neither God nor man. . . . Through the providence of God, Gaspard's heart turns to Him in faith and after a series of adventures is able to flee France to the safer Protestant shores of England. Fine and absorbing reading. Deborah Alcock has wonderful vocabulary, is a marvelous storyteller, and brings out the amazing hand of God's almighty power in every chapter. Highly recommended.

Time: 1685-1697   **Age: 11-99**
ISBN 1-894666-03-8   Can.$14.95 U.S.$12.90

With Wolfe in Canada:
or, The Winning of a Continent by G.A. Henty

Through misadventure the hero of the story, James Walsham, becomes involved in the historic struggle between Britain and France for supremacy on the North American continent. The issue of this war determined not only the destinies of North America, but to a large extent those of the mother countries themselves. *With Wolfe in Canada* will take the reader through many battles of this conflict. Meet a young George Washington and General Braddock as they fight the French and Indians, join up with Rogers' Rangers, and learn of the legendary generals Wolfe and Montcalm. *With Wolfe in Canada* is a model of what a children's book should be with its moving tale of military exploit and thrilling adventure. This classic provides a lesson in history instructively and graphically, whilst infusing into the dead facts of history new life. Mr. Henty's classic *With Wolfe in Canada* is a useful aid to study as well as amusement.

Time: 1755-1760   **Age: 14-99**

Cloth ISBN 0-921100-86-8	**Can.\$17.95 U.S.\$17.95**
Paperback ISBN 0-921100-87-6	**Can.\$14.95 U.S.\$14.95**

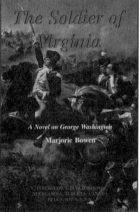

The Soldier of Virginia - A Novel on George *Washington* by Marjorie Bowen

"Mr. Washington — and who is Mr. Washington?"
"It is the Governor of Virginia's envoy, Monsieur — bearing a letter from his Excellency."
St. Pierre gave his inferior officer a quick glance; two things occurred to him: the first was that Dinwiddie must be serious if he had sent a messenger in such weather; the second was that it would have been more courteous if the envoy had been a man of some rank; he remarked on neither of these things, but quietly requested that Mr. Washington should be brought into his presence. The scene was St. Pierre's room in the newly erected Fort le Bœuf; December cold filled the apartment despite the huge fire of logs that roared on the hearth; and the view from the window was of a frozen lake, great trees against a drab sky, and the steady falling of snowflakes.

Originally published in 1912, this is a fictionalized biography on America's first President by one of the best authors of historical fiction.

Time: 1755-1775   **Age: 14-99**

                    ISBN 0-921100-99-X   **Can.\$14.95 U.S.\$12.90**

ALL FOUR IN ONE

Journey Through the Night by Anne De Vries

After the Second World War, Anne De Vries, one of the most popular novelists in The Netherlands, was commissioned to capture in literary form the spirit and agony of those five harrowing years of Nazi occupation. The result was *Journey Through the Night*, a four volume bestseller that has gone through more than thirty printings in The Netherlands.

"An Old Testament Professor of mine who bought the books could not put them down — nor could I."
— Dr. Edwin H. Palmer

"This is more than just a war-time adventure. The characters have vitality, depth and great humanity."
— *The Ottawa Citizen*

Time: 1940-1945   **Age: 10-99**
ISBN 0-921100-25-6   **Can.\$19.95 U.S.\$16.90**

The Seventh Earl by Grace Irwin

A dramatized biography on Anthony Ashley Cooper, the Seventh Earl of Shaftesbury, who is most widely remembered as a 19th-century British philanthropist and factory reformer. "This is Grace Irwin's strongest and most poignant book . . . I have been moved and enriched by my hours with *The Seventh Earl*," wrote V.R. Mollenkott.

Time: 1801-1885   Age: 14-99
ISBN 0-8028-6059-1   Can.$11.95 U.S.$9.95

A Stranger in a Strange Land by Leonora Scholte

John E. Marshall in *The Banner of Truth*: This is a delightful book. It tells the story of H.P. Scholte, a preacher in The Netherlands, who being persecuted for his faith in his own country, emigrated to the U.S.A., and there established a settlement in Pella, Iowa, in the midst of the vast undeveloped prairie. . . The greater part of the book is taken up in telling the stories of the immense hardships known after emigration. Interwoven with this story is an account of Scholte's marriage and family life. . . It is a most heartwarming and instructive story.

Time: 1825-1880   Age: 14-99
ISBN 0-921100-01-9   Can.$7.95 U.S.$6.90

Captain My Captain by **Deborah Meroff** author of *Coronation of Glory*

Willy-Jane VanDyken in *The Trumpet*: This romantic novel is so filled with excitement and drama, it is difficult to put it down once one has begun it. Its pages reflect the struggle between choosing Satan's ways or God's ways. Mary's struggles with materialism, being a submissive wife, coping with the criticism of others, learning how to deal with sickness and death of loved ones, trusting in God and overcoming the fear of death forces the reader to reflect on his own struggles in life.

This story of Mary Ann Patten (remembered for being the first woman to take full command of a merchant sailing ship) is one that any teen or adult reader will enjoy. It will perhaps cause you to shed a few tears but it is bound to touch your heart and encourage you in your faith.

Time: 1837-1861   Age: 14-99
ISBN 0-921100-79-5   Can.$14.95 U.S.$12.90

By Far Euphrates by **Deborah Alcock**
A Tale on Armenia in the 19th century

Alcock has provided sufficient graphics describing the atrocities committed against the Armenian Christians to make the reader emotionally moved by the intense suffering these Christians endured at the hands of Muslim Turks and Kurds. At the same time, the author herself has confessed to not wanting to provide full detail, which would take away from the focus on how those facing death did so with peace, being confident they would go to see their LORD, and so enjoy eternal peace. **As such it is not only an enjoyable novel, but also encouraging reading.** These Christians were determined to remain faithful to their God, regardless of the consequences.

Time: 1887-1895   Age: 11-99
ISBN 1-894666-00-3   Can.$14.95 U.S.$12.90

Andy Man by Amy Le Feuvre
Golden Inheritance Series # 10

Andy, the orphaned son of a London policeman at the beginning of the twentieth century, becomes John's handy man out in the country. But honest head-strong Andy finds himself in some troubling situations. Will he be allowed to remain with John? And what about the mysterious visitor?

Subject: Fiction   Age: 9-99
ISBN 978-0-921100-95-9   Can.$ 8.95 U.S.$ 8.95

Other volumes of the popular Golden Inheritance Series:

1 Jessica's First Prayer & Jessica's Mother by Hesba Stretton
2 Probable Sons by Amy Le Feuvre
3 Pilgrim Street by Hesba Stretton
4 Legend Led by Amy Le Feuvre
5 Little Meg's Children by Hesba Stretton
6 Teddy's Button by Amy Le Feuvre
7 Lost Gip by Hesba Stretton
8 Harebell's Friend by Amy Le Feuvre
9 Cassy by Hesba Stretton
10 Andy Man by Amy Le Feuvre

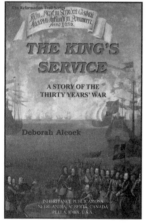

The King's Service by Deborah Alcock
A Story of the Thirty Years' War

Once again Deborah Alcock has delicately woven together an accurate historical novel. This book gives wonderful insights into some of the events surrounding the thirty-years-war in which Gustavus Adolphus of Sweden gives his life for the Protestant cause. But even amidst the ravages of war life continues to weave its story of intrigue, romance, loyalty, and treason. Two motherless children, Jeanie and Hugh, have been in the care of their Uncle Charlie ever since their father left about eight years earlier to fight for the Protestant cause. Uncle Charlie, a restless bachelor, subsequently leaves the bulk of Jeanie and Hugh's upbringing to the Presbyterian minister. He faithfully teaches these orphaned children the beautiful tenets of the Reformed faith. But when Uncle Charlie decides to leave his beloved Scotland to join the army of Gustavus Adolphus in Germany, Hugh wants to go along. Jeanie will go along as companion to Captain Stuart's wife and meets Fraulein Gertrud von Savelburg in Germany. Sifting through the reports and rumours of the times she comes to some disturbing and perplexing conclusions. What has made Uncle Charlie so sad, and why does a Roman Catholic priest regularly visit Hugh?

Time: 1630-1632   Age: 12-99
ISBN 978-1-894666-06-0   Can.$11.95 U.S.$11.95

Struggle for Freedom Series
by Piet Prins

David Engelsma in the *Standard Bearer*: This is reading for Reformed children, young people, and (if I am any indication) their parents. It is the story of 12-year-old Martin Meulenberg and his family during the Roman Catholic persecution of the Reformed Christians in The Netherlands about the year 1600. A peddlar, secretly distributing Reformed books from village to village, drops a copy of Guido de Brès' *True Christian Confession* — a booklet forbidden by the Roman Catholic authorities. An evil neighbor sees the book and informs . . .

Time: 1568-1572   Age: 10-99

Vol. 1 - *When The Morning Came*   ISBN 0-921100-12-4   Can.$11.95 U.S.$9.90
Vol. 2 - *Dispelling the Tyranny*   ISBN 0-921100-40-X   Can.$11.95 U.S.$9.90
Vol. 3 - *The Beggars' Victory*   ISBN 0-921100-53-1   Can.$11.95 U.S.$9.90
Vol. 4 -*For the Heart of Holland* ISBN 978-1-894666-20-6 Can.$12.95 U.S.$12.95

In This Hour
by Rudolf Van Reest
A Story of World War II and the Floods of 1953

"That's a rather rough expression, brother Melse — 'traitor.' How could you call someone a traitor if he's simply obeying the government? I would rather not hear such language from the mouth of an elder."

"I maintain that such work as building bunkers is treason against our land," repeated David Melse. "The bunkers have a definite purpose: when armies come to liberate us from the power of the Germans, the bunkers are supposed to hold them back. Each bunker could help sink one of the naval vessels approaching our coast. And on those vessels are our friends — perhaps even our own soldiers. Reverend, you should think carefully what those bunkers represent."

Rev. Verhulst shook his head. "You people have completely the wrong idea about those bunkers. Do you really believe that Germany will one day sink to its knees before England? If you do, you're completely mistaken, brother Melse. Germany will take control of all of Europe and will never let itself be overthrown. Germany is much too powerful to be defeated. Moreover, if you had listened carefully to last Sunday's sermon, you would know full well how I think about these matters. The apostate covenant people spent seventy years in the grip of Babylon, and I'm sure that our time under foreign domination will not be any less.

Time: 1942-1953   **Age: 15-99**
ISBN 0-894666-68-2   **Can.$15.95 U.S.$13.90**

How Sleep the Brave by James H. Hunter
A Novel of 17th Century Scotland

> *"Hush ye, hush ye, little pet ye,*
> *Hush ye, hush ye, do not fret ye,*
> *The Black Avenger shall not get ye."*

Even though the Scottish covenanters endured harsh persecutions by the King's Inquisition the mysterious name of the Black Avenger sent thrills of hope and courage to many a tormented soul. Yet the captains and dragoons feared this elusive figure while at the same time determining to place his head on the Netherbow. Many faithful Presbyterians were murdered on the spot or threatened with a touch of the thumbscrew or a place on the rack if they did not disclose the hiding place of some sought-out Covenanters.

Lady Marion Kennedy, the beautiful daughter of the Lord of Culzean Castle, was also threatened with similar reprisals if she refused to marry Luis Salvador de Ferrari, the usurper of Fenwick Ha', and supporter of the Inquisition. Yet her heart longed for Duncan Fenwick, the rightful lord of Fenwick Ha'.

An exciting, fast-paced historical novel regarding the events of Scottish history in 1688.

Time: 1685-1688   **Age: 12-99**
ISBN 978-1-894666-41-1   **Can.$15.95 U.S.$15.95**

A Loyal Huguenot Maid
by Margaret S. Comrie
Huguenot Inheritance Series #8

Azerole, a young fugitive, was serving at Castle Brianza at Piedmont as governess to Madame de Rohan's crippled and plaintive foster son Christophe. But Azerole was a Huguenot maid, and Castle Brianza was ardently Roman Catholic. Madame's son Gaston, who was serving in the French army, was said to be a fiery Roman Catholic and tolerated no Protestants. What would happen to Azerole when he came home?

Azerole and her brother Léon struggle amid many troubles to keep their faith alive. When Michel unexpectedly comes on the scene a new unforseen danger lurks in the shadows. Would these two young Huguenots remain safe under the roof and shadow of Castle Brianza?

Time: 1686-1690   **Age: 12-99**
ISBN 978-0-921100-68-3   Can.$15.95 U.S.$15.95

Roger the Ranger by Eliza F. Pollard
A Story of Border Life Among the Indians

Indians, Frenchmen, Englishmen, wars, strained friendships, and romance are all interwoven in Eliza Pollard's fast paced historical novel.

When Charles Langlade deserted his birth place in upper Canada to marry an Indian squaw and then to fight with his Indian tribe for the French against the English, he also lost his best friend, Roger Boscowen, who

led his rangers for the English against the French. Meanwhile the historically famous General Louis de Montcalm entered Canada on behalf of the French and things took a turn in favour for the French due to the help of Langlade. But would the jealous government of French Canada succeed in using De Montcalm's daughter Mercedes — who had come with her father from France with the intention to enter a Canadian convent — to destroy Montcalm's fame?

And would Charles and Roger indeed fight each other? Would their friendship ever be restored?

Time: 1754-1760   **Age: 12-99**
ISBN 978-1-894666-31-2   Can.$14.95 U.S.$14.95

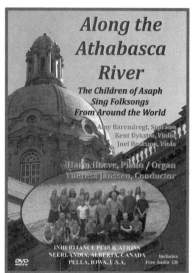

DVD
(with FREE AUDIO CD)
Along the Athabasca River
The Children of Asaph Sing Folksongs
From Around the World
Amy Barendregt, Soprano
Kent Dykstra, Violin
Joel Bootsma, Viola
Harm Hoeve, Organ
Theresa Janssen, Conductor
1. Sing Along; 2. Something to Sing About
3. Hedge Rose; 4. a) Christopher Columbus;
b) The Prairie Schooner; c) In the Ropery;
5. My Heart Ever Faithful (Soprano Solo);
6. Along the Athabasca River; 7. The Canadian; 8. Bugle Note; 9. The Spider
and the Fly; 10. The Blue Bells of Scotland; 11. The Good Comrade; 12. a)
Maple Trees; b) Paul and the Fox; 13. The Londonderry Air (Piano & Violin);
14. The Ashgrove; 15. Ducks on a Pond; 16. Bells; 17. Swing High; 18. This
Land is Your Land; 19. William of Nassau; 20. Our Gracious God.

IPDVD 114-9 (includes free CD) $29.95

DVD (with FREE AUDIO CD)

With Joyful Psalm and Song
The Children of Asaph
Sing Anglo-Genevan Psalms
Amy Barendregt, Soprano
Peter De Boer, Baritone
Kent Dykstra, Violin
Joel Bootsma, Viola
Vanessa Smeding, Cello
Harm Hoeve, Organ
Theresa Janssen, Conductor
Psalms 76:1, 3, & 5; 93:1-4; 85:1 & 2;
114:1-4; 35:1 & 2; 6:1 & 2 (Soprano
Solo); 47:1-3; The Song of Mary; Psalms
33 (Organ Solo); 79:1, 3, & 5; 89:1-3;
119:1, 4, 13, & 40; 24:1, 2, & 5; 144:2
(Strings & Baritone); 84:1-3; 55:1, 2,
& 9; 71:1 & 8; 138:1-4.
IPDVD 113-9 (includes free CD) $29.95

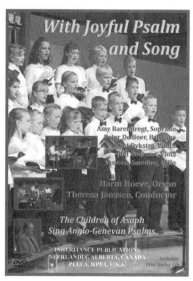

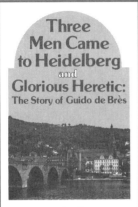

Thea B. Van Halsema

Three Men Came to Heidelberg & Glorious Heretic: the Story of Guido de Brès
by Thea Van Halsema

From the sixteenth-century Protestant Reformation came two outstanding statements of faith: The Heidelberg Catechism (1563) and the Belgic Confession (1561). The stories behind these two historic documents are in this small book.

Frederick, a German prince, asked a preacher and a professor to meet at Heidelberg to write a statement of faith that would help teach his people the truths of the Bible. The result was the Heidelberg Catechism. The writer of the Belgic Confession was a hunted man most of his life. Originally he wrote the confession as an appeal to the King of Spain to have mercy on the Protestants he was persecuting in the Lowlands. Not only was the request denied, but for his efforts the brilliant heretic de Brès was imprisoned and hanged by the Spanish invaders.

Time: 1556-1587   Age: 12-99
ISBN 978-1-894666-89-3   Can.$9.95 U.S.$9.95

Mrs. Van Halsema served for many years as professor of social work and dean of students at Kuyper College, formerly Reformed Bible College, in Grand Rapids, Michigan, U.S.A. She has retired from her ministry of speaking, teaching, counseling, and serving with her husband who led orientation programs in Mexico and the Middle East. She is the author also of I Will Build My Church, With All My Heart, *and* Safari for Seven.

This Was John Calvin
by Thea Van Halsema

Roger Nicole: "The most lively and readable biography of Calvin available in English."

J.H. Kromminga: "Though it reads as smoothly as a well written novel, it is crammed with important facts. It is scholarly and popular at the same time. The book will hold the interest of the young but will also bring new information to the well informed. . . . This book recognizes the true greatness of the man without falling into distortions of the truth to protect that greatness."

John Calvin comes alive as the author brings imagination as well as research to bear upon her subject. Her portrayal of the Genevan reformer is both appealing and honest.

From this account, Calvin no longer is seen merely as "carved like a monument in the panorama of human history," but has become vivid, lifelike, and real. This is biography at its best.

This Was John Calvin has been translated into Spanish, Portuguese, Korean, Chinese, Indonesian, and Japanese. This is its fifth printing in English.

Time: 1509-1564   Age: 12-99
ISBN 978-1-894666-90-9   Can.$11.95 U.S.$11.95

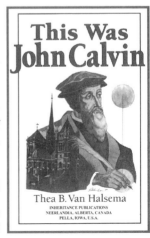

Thea B. Van Halsema
INHERITANCE PUBLICATIONS
NEERLANDIA, ALBERTA, CANADA
PELLA, IOWA, U.S.A.

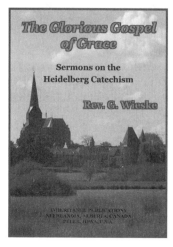

The Glorious Gospel of Grace
Sermons on the Heidelberg Catechism
by Rev. G. Wieske

. . . our great and gracious God will reward the faithfulness of His children. Not because He has to, but because He wants to. He is like a father who promises his children to reward them for the work he gives them to do. Because He loves His children, He wants to encourage and inspire them . . . Who performs the good works believers do? Who is the source that allows them to produce fruits of thankfulness? Who else but God? Who else but the Spirit of Jesus Christ? . . . All thoughts of merit disappear in the light of the gospel of the crucified Christ . . . What an incredible display of divine mercy! The only answer to it is a life of love for the mercies of our God. Merit implies calculation. Earning credit points does not demand love. But true believers don't keep a record of their good works. They are overwhelmed by the gospel of grace. Their fruits of faith well up from hearts that stammer: "What shall I render to my Saviour now, for all the riches of his consolation?"   — From the sermon on Lord's Day 24

Subject: Heidelberg Catechism   Age: 14-99
ISBN 978-0-921100-71-3   Can.$39.95 U.S.$39.95

Dort Study Bible V
2 Chronicles - Job
The number one choice for personal Bible Study and for group Bible Study!

"The importance is that we see how ecclesiastical awareness runs throughout Scripture, and that we use this to teach us what church consciousness really is. The men who gave us the *Staten Bijbel* (the Dutch title of *The Dort Study Bible*) had an eye for that. This is clear from the annotations which are still worth while to consider."

—Rev. H.H.J. Feenstra (in *Was Abraham Reformed?*)

Subject: 2 Chronicles - Job   Age: 14-99
ISBN 978-1-894666-55-8   Can.$24.95 U.S.$24.95

Other volumes also available:

Vol. 1 Genesis and Exodus	ISBN 1-894666-51-8	Can.$24.95 U.S.$21.90
Vol. 2 Leviticus - Deuteronomy	ISBN 1-894666-52-6	Can.$24.95 U.S.$21.90
Vol. 3 Joshua - 2 Samuel	ISBN 1-894666-53-4	Can.$24.95 U.S.$21.90
Vol. 4 1 Kings-1 Chronicles	ISBN 978-1-894666-54-1	Can.$24.95 U.S.$24.95

". . . was sorting through old pictures today and found this one. It was taken eleven years ago . . . on my son's birthday party. See all those party boys listening to a beautifully told Bible story by Anne DeVries! We have read these books over and over and they are now falling apart. I would love to buy a big stack to equip my

grown up children (we have nine — all busy growing) [with] these two bible story books so they can read them to their children. They are written precisely to Scripture, by a man who clearly understood God's redemption plan and portrays it in a faith-building way. I have bought and read other Bible stories but none so able to build a child's faith. My Mom read these books to me and my siblings in Dutch and how I loved them. So I am pleading with you to republish them." — MvV at Q, BC

Story Bible for Older Children
by Anne De Vries

This story Bible is a classic in which Anne DeVries touches on the episodes recorded in Scripture one by one, bringing them to life for children through dramatic dialogue, imaginative description, and careful attention to narrative structure. The exquisitely detailed and unique illustrations by Cornelis Jetses reinforce the story of God's dealings with His people in a beautiful way.

For Age: 7-12

Old Testament	ISBN 978-0921100-96-6	Can.$29.95 U.S.$29.95
New Testament	ISBN 978-0921100-97-3	Can.$29.95 U.S.$29.95
SET OF OLD & NEW TESTAMENT	0921100-96-6/97-3	Can.$55.95 U.S.$55.95

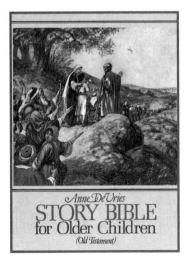

Anne DeVries
STORY BIBLE
for Older Children
(Old Testament)

Anne DeVries
STORY BIBLE
for Older Children
(New Testament)

Prince and Heretic
by Marjorie Bowen
A Novel on William the Silent vol. 1

"The mind and the soul are not in the keeping of king nor priest — no man has a lordship over another man's conscience. All history has proved that." — William of Orange

Here is a fascinating historical novel for teenagers and adults about one of the greatest heroes of all time. William of Orange, considered today the father of Europe (and who can also fittingly be called the step-father of North America and the whole free western world) sets the stage as stadtholder of the Roman Catholic King of Spain, Philip II. William, though a nominal Roman Catholic at the time, determines to help the persecuted Protestants and in the process marries the Protestant Princess Anne of Saxony. But will Anne truly be a helpmeet for her husband? When he is pressed to take up the sword against King Philip he does not hesitate. In his struggles, William not only finds the God of his mother but grows in courage and the conviction that God has chosen him to be a faithful instrument to gain freedom for Christ's Church. William sacrifices all his possessions to pay the hired soldiers, but is it of any use? His brothers, Lodewyk, John, Adolphus, and Henry, also give all they have for the cause of freedom of a country which can hardly be called their own. Behind these heroes, a faithful praying mother, Juliana of Stolberg, waits for news at the German castle of Dillenburg.

Time: 1560-1568
ISBN 978-0-921100-56-0

Age: 13-99
Can.$17.95 U.S.$17.95

Proceedings of the International Council of Reformed Churches, 2009 - New Zealand

Including the following papers on
The Vitality of the Reformed Faith:

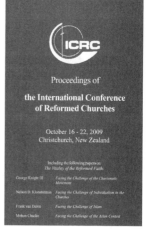

George Knight III: Facing the Challenge of the Charismatic Movement
Nelson D. Kloosterman: Facing the Challenge of Individualism in the Churches
Frank van Dalen :Facing the Challenge of Islam
Mohan Chacko: Facing the Challenge of the Asian Context

Subject: Theology / Ethics
ISBN 978-0-921100-70-6

Age: 12-99
Can.$12.95 U.S.$12.95

Bobby's Friends
by Phia van den Berg

The publisher's most favourite juvenile story

"Lights!" Jessie announced loudly.

Suddenly everyone was awake. Karachi appeared beneath them on the lefthand side. At first they saw only a narrow strip of tiny lights, but soon it broadened. The plane swung sideways as it turned, gliding above the sea of city lights. The children hadn't paid much attention to the other landings during the trip, but this one became very exciting!

Pakistan! Every year a part of Western Pakistan underwent a drastic flood, washing away all the gardens and homes of the inhabitants. Father Falois, agriculturist, was asked by the government to try to control the floods. But life in Pakistan was so different for Bobby and his siblings. The worst part was understanding the people, that breach between the rich Muslims and the poor Christians. How would Bobby find friends? Would the screaming, proud, millionaire's son, Sadiq, be a friend, or would Jahja, the very poorest of all? Who would be faithful when danger came?

Subject: Fiction   Age: 9-99
ISBN 9780921100515   Can.$9.95 U.S.$9.95

The Baron of Salgas
A True Huguenot Story by Sabine Malplach
and
The Cross and the Crown
& The Carpenter of Nîmes
Two Huguenot Stories by Deborah Alcock

The Cross and the Crown tells about a man by the name of Gabriel Vaur. After the Revocation of the Edict of Nantes (1685), life once again became very dangerous for the Huguenots in France. When the Dragonnades came, Gabriel tried to get help, leaving his father, sister, and brother behind. Would he ever see them again? Would he ever be able to flee France and reach England?

The Baron of Salgas is the true story of the Baron and Baroness de Salgas. Even though her husband forbids her to be an open Huguenot, the Baroness knows that her Saviour had said that whoever would deny Him would be denied by Him. So one night she made her escape to Geneva. Would her husband follow? Would he recant? What would happen to their sons who were taken to the convents?

The Carpenter of Nîmes goes back more than a century to the year 1569 and tells about a man named Jacques Maderon. When the pastor tells him that Christ had said, "Son, go work today in My vineyard," he knows it is time to do something. Then the father of his friend was imprisoned. Would he succeed to cut the bars of the gate and so make way for the Huguenots to enter the city and deliver it?

Time: 1568-1715   Age: 13-99
ISBN 978-0-921100-69-0   Can.$14.95 U.S.$14.95

The Lion of Modderspruit
by Lawrence Penning
The Louis Wessels Commando #1

A wonderful historical novel in which Penning has interwoven love, pathos, and loyalty. The conflict the Boers endure with England involves not only a fight to maintain their independence (to which the British agreed in 1881) but also a deep religious significance. Louis Wessels, eldest son of a well-established Transvaal Boer family, is betrothed to Truida, a Boer maiden living in the British colony of Natal, and educated in British-governed schools. When England sends over thousands of troops to invade the independent Boer colony of the Orange Free State, causing the Boers of the Transvaal Colony to prepare to invade Natal, the two lovers are confronted by more than a political conflict — two loyal hearts separated by loyalty to conflicting causes. The horrors of the war drag both Louis and Truida through heights of joy and depths of despair. How can these two hearts, beating strongly for each other but also strongly for their separate causes, ever be reconciled? On which side is justice to be found?

Time: 1899   **Age:11-99**
ISBN 1-894666-91-7   **Can.$10.95 U.S.$9.90**

The Hero of Spionkop
by Lawrence Penning
The Louis Wessels Commando #2

A company of twenty-five horsemen with an officer in command galloped into the yard. They jumped down, fastened their horses to the young fig trees which bordered the broad driveway, and in silence awaited orders from their commanding officer.

He carefully scrutinized the terrain and set out five soldiers as watchmen. Five others were ordered to make a thorough search of the barn. Ten were posted at the various exits from the house and with the remaining five the officer entered the livingroom . . . "Do you have a Boer from the Transvaal hiding here?" asked the officer.

Time: 1900   **Age:11-99**
ISBN 1-894666-92-5   **Can.$10.95 U.S.$9.90**

The Scout of Christiaan de Wet by Lawrence Penning
The Louis Wessels Commando # 3

It is the year 1900 and the Boer War continues to ravage the South African Free State and Transvaal. The English are relentless in their attacks and pernicious in seeking to achieve political power. But the Afrikaners refuse to submit and continue the struggle to maintain their freedom.

Louis Wessels, the young hunter, and the Dutchman Jan Tromp, despite skirting danger, falling into traps, confronting traitors, hiding and escaping, slowly achieve their mission as they transverse the Transvaal as scouts for General Christiaan de Wet. Yet when they are finally trapped with no seeming escape, they meet an old acquaintance.

Even though these dedicated Afrikaners are surrounded by the horrors and ravages of war there is time for laughter at Blikoortje's exploits, and time to receive encouragement from loved ones.

Time: 1900   **Age: 11-99**
ISBN 978-1-894666-93-0   **Can.$11.95 U.S.$11.95**

The Victor of Nooitgedacht by Lawrence Penning
The Louis Wessels Commando # 4

The commando of Louis Wessels continues to roam the South African countryside, joining whichever division needs them most. But defeat and loss, ruin and devastation seem to be the order of the day. Blikoortje and Jan Potgieter are captured, Wonderfontein is pillaged and ruined, and the church is desecrated. The ravages of this ghastly war are pressing in on all sides and the reality of total defeat looms large in all its starkness. The English Minister Brodrick had declared in the British parliament that "never — but never — had a more civilised war been waged!" Yet all the evidence showed the English army to be full of wantonness, lustful pillaging, savagery, destructiveness, and pitiless cruelty towards women, children, and the defenceless.

Lawrence Penning gives a close up account of some of the events and issues surrounding the Boer War. The English declared they wanted the gold South Africa offered, but was there more at stake? This book, along with the others in the series, are great aids in coming to grips with the South African conflict in a fascinating manner.

Time: 1900   **Age: 11-99**
ISBN 978-1-894666-94-7   **Can.$11.95 U.S.$11.95**

The Colonist of Southwest Africa by Lawrence Penning
The Louis Wessels Commando # 5

After three years of fighting, the Boer War was nearing its bitter end. Even though the Boer armies seemed defeated by the superior British armed forces, many Boer commandoes refused to give up and continued to strike at the English military. The enemy's retaliation was horrible. Systematically the Rednecks combed out the country: farms were burned and the women and children were taken to concentration camps. Malnourished, neglected, and ravaged by Typhus fever, thousands died in those camps.

Under the leadership of Louis Wessels, a commando planned a rescue, but with difficulties and traitors abounding, failure and capture were imminent realities. Was escape still possible? Could comfort be found in the words of the field preacher who not only condemned England's insults and scorn heaped on the Boer entreaties for help, but also entreated his fellow Christians to throw dust and ashes on their heads "for we and our fathers — we have sinned grievously! We have erred. We have served alien gods, and now the Lord is visiting us with His scourge." Addressing the Boers, and also the British doctor, the field preacher concluded, "Brothers, let us be silent in this oppression. Let us confess our sins and lift our penitent hearts in prayer to the hills from whence our salvation will come."

This last volume of the Louis Wessels Commando series brings the dark reality of the Boer War into stark focus. May the words of the field preacher never need to be addressed to us.

Time: 1901-1904   **Age: 11-99**
ISBN 978-1-894666-95-4   **Can.$11.95 U.S.$10.90**

Special Price for set of all 5 books
Can.$49.75 U.S.$45.75

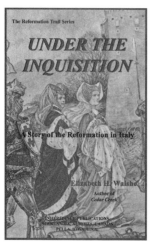

Under the Inquisition
by Elizabeth H. Walshe
The Reformation Trail Series
A Story of the Reformation in Italy

"You have forgotten that you should confess Christ's Name; and do you not remember, O deluded people, that whoever confesses not Christ upon earth, shall be denied by Him before His Father and the holy angels? Certainly you are not alone in this backsliding. There may be some in our valleys of the Alps who carry with them certificates that they are genuine papists, and have their children baptized by priests with all the mummeries of superstition, yes, and go to the so-called sacrifice of the mass, openly bowing the knee to Baal, that they may be seen of men; and they excuse themselves — verily a fancied excuse! — by saying secretly when they enter the mass house, 'Cave of robbers, may God confound you!' I have heard that similar practices extend even here. My brothers, such duplicity is intolerable to the righteous Lord. Do you think that He will not protect the men who range themselves under His banner against Antichrist, in the face of all the world? I tell you, that if all the devils on earth and in hell were leagued to destroy you, mightier is He that is for you than all that can be against you! Your Father can sheath the sword and quench the faggot of the persecutor, if it is His will; and if it is not His will — O servants of Christ! Will there not be a quicker entrance into the joy of your Lord, and a more dazzling crown of glory!"

Sobs and moans came from that excitable southern audience; glowing eyes, betokening glowing hearts, met the youthful preacher's every look.

. . . Thus Paschali enunciated the principles which were to guide his ministry.

Time 1554-1563   Age: 14-99
ISBN 978-1-894666-30-5   Can.$17.95 U.S.$15.90

Calvin's Doctrine of the Word and Sacrament
by Ronald S. Wallace

This is a careful and fresh study of Calvin's Commentaries, Institutes, Sermons, and Tracts designed to meet the practical needs of those who wish clarification of the doctrines which lie behind traditional Reformed church practice. The book is also valuable for the insight it gives into Calvin's method of interpreting Scripture, especially the Old Testament.

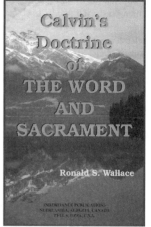

In the preface the following two sentences aptly sum up the content and purpose of the work: "What is most important in the study of Calvin today is to reveal what the Reformer himself actually said, in order that misconceptions about his teaching may be cleared away. Therefore this work is not a critical study of Calvin but an attempt to express his teaching as copiously, fairly, and sympathetically as possible."

Subject: Bible and Sacraments   Age: 16-99
ISBN 978-1-894666-50-3   Can.$17.95 U.S.$16.90

THE CZAR by Deborah Alcock
A Tale of the Time of the First Napoleon

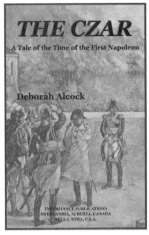

As, with a hand still trembling, Clémence poured out the tea, she remembered the stories she had heard of such evening visits made by the Czar, "to talk at his ease," and recalled the words of De Maistre when someone criticised this habit in his presence: "It is a touching thing to me to see the ruler of a great empire, in the age of all the passions, find his recreation in taking a cup of tea with an honest man and his wife."

Ivan Ivanovitch Pojarsky, an orphaned Russian Prince, adopted by loyal people in the village of Nicolofsky meets the great Czar Alexander of Russia while the Czar does his best to bring back to life a seemingly dead carpenter. This historical fact, and many others related in this captivating story, gives a very accurate picture of the life in Russia during the time of Napoleon.

Time: 1795-1825   Age: 14-99
ISBN 978-1-894666-11-4   Can.$19.95 U.S.$17.90

Life in the Eagle's Nest
by Charlotte Maria Tucker (A.L.O.E.)
A Tale of Afghanistan

Afghanistan! To many an uncivilized land of terror and hatred. To others a land of intrigue and adventure. A land where few dare to tread. Go with Walter Gurney, the seventeen-year-old orphan son of a British missionary in India, who, after meeting handsome, boastful Dermot Denis, joined him on a trip into Afghanistan. Negating the danger of such a perilous trip, Walter eased his conscience with the thought of evangelizing. Infected with the exultation of his companion, nothing for the time seemed more enjoyable than this wild foray into a dangerous land.

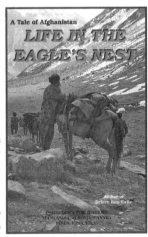

Yet within a few days they were surprised by a brutal group of Pathan Afghans. Despite his companion's ridicule and the danger lurking in his path Walter knew that nothing could separate him from the love of Christ. God's will always comes to pass and as God's child he was safe in the arms of his Saviour. Will Walter be able to hold on to this faith when pressed by a Moslem Holy man? Will Sultána, the daughter of the chief, be able to help him and her people in the Eagle's Nest? Witness with Walter the blessings of God in bringing His Gospel to hungry hearts in ways unimaginable by men.

Subject: Mission / Fiction   Age: 11-99
ISBN 978-1-894666-29-9   Can.$11.95 U.S.$10.90

Crushed Yet Conquering
by Deborah Alcock

A gripping story filled with accurate historical facts about John Huss and the Hussite wars. **Hardly any historical novel can be more captivating and edifying than this book.** Even if Deborah Alcock was not the greatest of nineteenth century authors, certainly she is our most favourite.
— Roelof & Theresa Janssen

Time: 1414-1436   Age: 11-99
ISBN 1-894666-01-1   Can.$19.95 U.S.$16.90

Hubert Ellerdale by W. Oak Rhind
A Tale of the Days of Wycliffe

Christine Farenhorst in *Christian Renewal*: Christians often tend to look on the Reformation as the pivotal turning point in history during which the Protestants took off the chains of Rome. This small work of fiction draws back the curtains of history a bit further than Luther's theses. Wycliffe was the morning star of the Reformation and his band of Lollards a band of faithful men who were persecuted because they spoke out against salvation by works. Hubert Ellerdale was such a man and his life (youth, marriage, and death), albeit fiction, is set parallel to Wycliffe's and Purvey's.

Rhind writes with pathos and the reader can readily identify with his lead characters. This novel deserves a well-dusted place in a home, school, or church library.

Time: 1380-1420   Age: 13-99
ISBN 0-921100-09-4   Can.$12.95 U.S.$10.90

Luther the Leader by Virgil Robinson

Martin Luther's life is truly an inspiration to every Christian boy and girl. He was a pioneer among the Christians in his age and remains a leader of Christians in our age. Luther stands out among men in history as one who would not compromise his conscience.

Time: 1483-1546   Age: 9-99
ISBN 1-881545-78-4   Can.$8.99 U.S.$5.95

The Romance of Protestantism by Deborah Alcock

A wonderfully warm and loving book about the beauty of Protestantism. This topic, too often neglected and forgotten, has been revived by the author in a delightful way. Glimpses of our Protestant history are strewn in our path like jewels, whetting our appetite to read on and discover the depth of our history. Too often our role models tend to be found outside of our Christian heritage "to the neglect of the great cloud of witnesses, the magnificent roll of saints, heroes, and martyrs that belong to us as Protestants." This book is not only for adults. Young people and even older children will find riches in its depth which will encourage and build up to carry on the work of God in our own day and age.
— Theresa E. Janssen, home educating mother

Time: 1300-1700   Age: 12-99
ISBN 0-921100-88-4   Can.$11.95 U.S.$9.90

Under Calvin's Spell by Deborah Alcock
A Tale of theHeroic Times in Old Geneva

They had now reached the Forte Neuve, by which they entered the town, with many others who were returning from the Plain-palais. As they walked along the Corratorie they met Berthelier and Gabrielle, taking the air, as the afternoon was very fine for the season of the year. Both the lads saluted; De Marsac with a flush and a beaming smile.

"I did not know you knew them," said Norbert.

"Oh yes; did I not tell you I was going to see them? Master Berthelier's sister, Damoiselle Claudine, and I are fast friends. Some years ago when I came here first, a mere child, I was one day in the market, looking about me and buying cherries or the like, when I saw this poor damoiselle being frightened half out of her senses by a group of angry, scolding fish-women. That was before such good order was put in the market, and in all the town, thanks to Master Calvin. She had told them, quite truly, that they were trying to cheat her. I fought her battle with all my might, which in truth was not great, and at last brought her home in triumph. She was much more grateful than the occasion required, and has been my very good friend ever since. I — they — they are all good to me, though lately, being much occupied with my studies, I have seen them but seldom."

"Do you not think the young damoiselle very pretty?" asked Norbert. "I do."

"She is beautiful," Louis answered quietly; and the subject dropped.

Time: 1542-1564	**Age:14-99**
ISBN 1-894666-04-6	**Can.$14.95 U.S.$12.90**

John Calvin: Genius of Geneva by Lawrence Penning
A Popular Account of the Life and Times of John Calvin

The publishing of this book is a direct fruit of the reading and publishing of *Under Calvin's Spell* by Deborah Alcock which is a great novel and gives a very good description of life in and around Geneva. However it tells little about Calvin himself. As a result I read Penning's book and was quickly convinced that both books should be published as companion editions, Alcock's book being the introduction and Penning's book the "full" story. Also today the world needs to know it's most important historical facts and since upon the mouth of two witnesses the truth of a matter is to be established we send out in these two books the true story of John Calvin.

Calvin is perhaps the most important person who lived after Biblical times (seconded by Martin Luther, William of Orange, Michael de Ruyter, and William III of Orange). To know and understand how the Lord has used these people in the history of His Church and world will stir in any reader the desire to follow them in their footsteps.   — Roelof A. Janssen

Time: 1509-1564	**Age:15-99**
ISBN 1-894666-77-1	**Can.$19.95 U.S.$16.90**

The Spanish Brothers by Deborah Alcock
A Tale of the Sixteenth Century

"He could not die thus for his faith. On the contrary, it cost him but little to conceal it. What, then, had they which he had not? Something that enabled even poor, wild, passionate Gonsalvo to forgive and pray for the murderers of the woman he loved. What was it?"

Time: 1550-1565	**Age: 14-99**
ISBN 1-894666-02-x	**Can.$14.95 U.S.$12.90**

The Governor of England by Marjorie Bowen
A Novel on Oliver Cromwell

An historical novel in which the whole story of Cromwell's dealings with Parliament and the King is played out. It is written with dignity and conviction, and with the author's characteristic power of grasping the essential details needed to supply colour and atmosphere for the reader of the standard histories.

Time: 1645-1660   Age: 14-99
ISBN 0-921100-58-2   Can.$17.95 U.S.$15.90

The William & Mary Trilogy
by Marjorie Bowen

The life of William III, Prince of Orange, Stadtholder of the United Netherlands, and King of England (with Queen Mary II) is one of the most fascinating in all of history. Both the author and the publisher of these books have been interested in this subject for many years. Although the stories as told in these books are partly fictional, all the main events are faithful to history.

F. Pronk wrote in *The Messenger* about Volume 1: The author is well-known for her well-researched fiction based on the lives of famous historical characters. The religious convictions of the main characters are portrayed with authenticity and integrity. This book is sure to enrich one's understanding of Protestant Holland and will hold the reader spell-bound.

D.J. Engelsma wrote in *The Standard Bearer* about Volume 1: This is great reading for all ages, high school and older. *I Will Maintain* is well written historical fiction with a solid, significant, moving historical base . . . No small part of the appeal and worth of the book is the lively account of the important history of one of the world's greatest nations, the Dutch. This history was bound up with the Reformed faith and had implications for the exercise of Protestantism throughout Europe. Christian high schools could profitably assign the book, indeed, the whole trilogy, for history or literature classes.

C. Farenhorst wrote in *Christian Renewal* about Volume 1: An excellent tool for assimilating historical knowledge without being pained in the process, *I Will Maintain* is a very good read. Take it along on your holidays. Its sequel *Defender of the Faith*, is much looked forward to.

Time: 1670-1702   Age: 14-99

Volume 1 - *I Will Maintain*	ISBN 0-921100-42-6	Can.$17.95 U.S.$15.90
Volume 2 - *Defender of the Faith*	ISBN 0-921100-43-4	Can.$15.95 U.S.$13.90
Volume 3 - *For God and the King*	ISBN 0-921100-44-2	Can.$17.95 U.S.$15.90